The Ration Card

www.TheRationCard.com

The Ration Card

A novel

by

Eric K. Augspurger

Copyright 2015 by Eric K. Augspurger

All rights reserved. No part of this publication may be reproduced or transmitted without written permission from the publisher. Posting, distributing, or otherwise transmitting or displaying this publication in whole or in part via any form of the Internet, including personal, commercial, or any other type of website or e-mail, is expressly forbidden. Requests for permission to make copies of any part of the work should be e-mailed to: Permissions@TinWhiskersBooks.com.

The Ration Card is a work of fiction. Names, characters, places, and incidents are exclusively creative inventions of the author. Historical figures and events are represented accurately except in instances where creative license has been applied and, therefore, should not be taken as claims of fact.

The fictional newspaper The Blooming Grove Review contained within this work presents information as it was reported on the date indicated. The information is factual as it was reported, but in certain instances may be incorrect according to the current historical record.

Cover and interior design:
♣ Dog's Paw Studio

www.TinWhiskersBooks.com

ISBN10: 0-9962829-0-4
ISBN13: 978-0-9962829-0-1

15–19 18 17 16 15–10 9 8 7 6 5 4 3 2 1

Cover photographs used under license from Shutterstock.com.
Salome Hoogendijk/Shutterstock.com; Tom Plesnik/Shutterstockcom
Printed in PRC.

Acknowledgement

TD, without your extensive assistance, this novel would not exist.

The Ration Card

www.TheRationCard.com

VOL. XXXII—N° 343　　　Monday, December 8, 1941　　　Three Cents

EXTRA EDITION! WAR DECLARED!

Pearl Harbor Bombed! Empire of Japan Attacks with Great Loss to Our Military

HONOLULU, H.I.—U.S. Pacific Fleet is attacked by the Empire of Japan. Shortly before 8 a.m. local time on December 7, carrier-based warplanes of the Imperial Japanese Navy bombed Pearl Harbor Naval Base, Hickam Field, Wheeler Field, and other military installations in the Hawaiian Islands. Reports state over fifteen hundred killed; that number likely to increase. The Japanese also carried out attacks on American, British, and other Allied outposts across the Pacific, including the Philippine Islands.

President Roosevelt, addressing Congress at 12:30 Washington, D.C., time today, declared December 7th as "...a date which will live in infamy..." and asked for a declaration of war, which Congress granted within an hour of the president's address.

WEST COAST PREPARES FOR RAIDS
Southern California Filled with Prime Targets

LOS ANGELES, Calif.—Measures to detect air raids have been employed at defense factories across Southern California. The commander of the Fourth Interceptor Command, Brigadier General William O. Ryan, issued the order "...activate your observation posts immediately." Around one thousand of the California State Guard were mobilized. In the Los Angeles area, they are policing oil fields and refineries. A blockade has been set up around Los Angeles' Terminal Island by army troops and federal agents. The harbor has been closed by the government. San Francisco is also on alert. Mayor Angelo J. Rossi declared a state of emergency last night. The police department there installed a heavy presence in the Japanese-American neighborhood.

ATTACKS THROUGHOUT PACIFIC
Guam, Phillipenes, Wake Targets

WASHINGTON, D.C.—After the attack on Pearl Harbor, Hawaii, Japanese forces conducted other attacks across the Pacific. The White House has announced that on Guam the American navel base has been attacked by Japanese planes. Reports of an attack on Manila in the Philippine Islands have come in, but have not been confirmed. Also unconfirmed are reports of attacks against the British in Singapore and the Malaysian peninsular. Tokio radio is reporting "Japanese naval and land forces are in a state of war with American and British forces in the West Pacific." Reports from London indicate the British government will declare war against Japan "...within the hour..." of an American declaration of war against Japan. Wake and Midway Islands have also been attacked, with Wake captured. British Hong Kong has been bombed. Thailand (Siam) has been invaded and Bangkok bombed. The Empire of Japan has made great gains across the Pacific.

The Blooming Grove Review

VOL. XXXIII—N⁰ 312   Sunday, November 8, 1942   Three Cents

OPERATION TORCH
Allies Land in North Africa

MOROCCO, N. Africa—While America slept Saturday night, American forces saw their first action in the European Theater of Operations (ETO). Under the command of General Dwight D. Eisenhower, Operation Torch commenced before daybreak local time. American forces landed at three points in this North African nation defended by French troops serving the Vichy government. French forces inflicted heavy losses, but American and British forces have established beachheads in Morocco and Algiers and are progressing inland. Vichy France has severed diplomatic relations with the Allied countries.

ALLIES NEAR JAPANESE BASE
New Guinea Advance Approaches Buna

MELBOURNE, Australia—Headquarters of General Douglas MacArthur's announced today Allied forces have advanced on the Japanese base at Buna, New Guinea. The Allies now hold all of the Paupan peninsula except for local areas around Buna and Gona. Australian forces have been advancing through the mountainous central area of New Guinea for the past five weeks. They are engaged in fighting in the foothills in the north. American troops in support of the Australians have been flown in over the past few weeks, and now have advanced to Buna. Allied air forces have been brought to bear, forcing the Japanese to endure nearly constant strafing.

GASOLINE RATIONING NEARING IN MIDWEST
Registration Begins this Week

CHICAGO, Ill.—Gasoline rationing will descend on the Midwest starting November 22 of this year. This Thursday, Friday, and Saturday, motorist will register for the upcoming rationing.

Passenger cars will be issued A stickers, which will provide the driver with four gallons of gasoline a week. If a motorist can demonstrate an occupational need for extra gasoline, he may apply for a B sticker after registering for an A sticker. The Office of Price Administration (OPA) states that rationing of gasoline is needed to conserve the rubber in tires. Each automobile owner is allowed five tires, but any additional tires must be turned over to the government no matter their condition. The tires a motorist intends to keep must be registered with the OPA by each tire's serial number.

WOMEN WAR WORKERS FLOCK TO THE WOWS
Organization Is Barely a Month Old

CHICAGO, Ill.—The WOWs, which is the acronym for the Woman Ordnance Workers organization, was formed with the belief that munitions are not the only important aspect of wartime, but morale is equally important. The stated purpose of the organization is to "...maintain health, promote friendship, co-operation, and fun." The organization was formed just a few weeks ago by women workers at the Hurley Machine company. Miss Helen Janata is secretary of post No. 1, and she states each day "scores of letters" are received from women war workers and war plant managers inquiring into the WOWs. Between 50 and 75 posts have already been established.

№ 1

"Tomorrow…"

There was a bit of nervousness and apprehension in Josephine Troyer's voice. From the radio in the background, the refrain of Martha Tilton singing *I'll Walk Alone* drifted to the dinner table. Gerald Troyer sat across the table from Josephine. He was slightly turned with the newspaper held up in front of him, catching up on recent events around the world. Boldface type on the front page announced that the Allies had landed in North Africa in Operation Torch. It was Sunday, November 8, 1942, and the Troyers were just sitting down to supper.

"…I'm gonna go down to the thresher plant and apply."

Pearl Troyer was bringing supper in from the kitchen. She was in her mid fifties, like Gerald, with graying hair that she almost always had neatly tucked up in a bun. She wore round, wireframe glasses, which, on occasion, one would find her peering over the top of when she was scolding with her eyes.

The grandfather clock in the front room chimed once to indicate half past the hour. At six-thirty, the night sky had

already settled in. Gerald folded the newspaper, smoothed the few remaining strands of hair over the top of his head, and squared himself up to the table. Pearl set down a serving bowl of soup in front of him. Living with wartime rationing required simple meals, and the soup was no exception, made with potatoes and dried, rolled beef. As the steam from the soup drifted upward, the sharp smell of garlic and onions subtly permeated the dining room.

"What on Earth for?" Pearl asked, smoothing her apron with both hands. She continued, chiding Jo over the top of her glasses. "That plant is no place for a lady. The air down there is thick with soot, so thick that everybody working there is covered head-to-toe in it. Foul, it is. And the men there have foul mouths. They could cuss out the devil to make him blush. A young lady like yourself should be looking for a proper job...*if* she feels the need to work."

The factories in Blooming Grove, like so many others across America, had switched production to war matériel. Blooming Grove was located near the end of the first third of Route 66, south of an S curve winding between two moraines. As the road weaved through this natural chicane, it descended slightly into the small depression where the town lay, straddling a river that provided the town with its birthplace.

"I hear they are really shorthanded. Besides, with the rationing and all I figure if I got a job, I could use the money to at least help out around here. Maybe buy some chickens and keep them in the backyard for eggs, something like that."

Blooming Grove was typically Midwestern, its size determined by who described it. For those who lived on the surrounding farms, Blooming Grove was the end-all, be-all of hustle and bustle. In the early days of the 1940s, dozens of boys from these farms would stream into town weekly, and nearly as quickly stream out of town, making the Blooming Grove train station or bus depot the last sight of home as they headed first for boot camp, then to Europe or the South Pacific.

On the other hand, people from the large cities, such as Chicago or Saint Louis, would think the town to be a deprived collection of houses, not worthy of consideration of any sort. For

most of those living in Blooming Grove—those not teenagers—it was the perfect size, a grand town nestled between what once were the great forests of the east and the vast prairie to the west, a town of self-reliance and self-sufficiency. The bounty of American grit and determination flowed in from the nearby farms, the mines and mills to the east, and the forests of the north and flowed out as goods and nourishment for a nation.

"After you and Alfred got married, we asked you to move in here when he shipped out—and of course you graduated and couldn't live out in the state building anymore." There was a sternness to Pearl's voice as she continued. "You're kin now, and we certainly aren't going to ask you for money."

Like so many thousands of other young boys and girls, Josephine Hatcher and Alfred Troyer got married in those few short days between high school graduation and the beginning of boot camp. June of 1942 was a busy time for churches, synagogues, chapels, and justices of the peace.

"I know that," Jo replied. "I didn't mean it that way. I just…well…I'm feeling a bit lost, like I need to do something. To help out, I mean."

Jo tipped her head a bit, knowing she had offended the Troyers, and unconsciously rubbed the divoted scar above her right eyebrow. She looked down at the table, slowly turning her soup spoon over and over on the cloth napkin next to her bowl.

"You know, I've never really had any family, and I want to help out somehow."

"Hon, you do a real good job helping me around the house." Pearl offered Jo the ladle for the soup. "Think of it as practice for when Alfred gets back from the war. Not many girls your age get the opportunity to practice, you know."

"I think I could be doing more, something for the war, if I worked at the plant." Her words were as firm as she was on doing this. She had grown up having to look out for herself, and this was about what *she* wanted. "Besides, Al's in the Pacific, and rumor is, most of that stuff the plant makes ends up there. It'd be like I was helping Al."

"What would you do?" Pearl's voice teemed with distaste, as if biting on a tart cranberry, for the thought of Jo working in a factory. "They don't have any secretarial staff to speak of, 'cept that Rose Ellington, and you don't know how to do any of the work the menfolk do. Besides, it's so filthy, you'd never be able to get your clothes clean. Just thinking about it I can smell the odors from those factories hanging over the river down there. Putrid stench it is. The smell'd get all in your clothes and hair. And your hair...Lord, what a mess you'd have with that."

Pearl worked hard keeping a good house and raising her son. In return, she expected her husband to provide for her. It's what she expected of Jo, too. A job of any kind, let alone working in a factory, would not allow Jo to keep a good house, even if she didn't have her husband around at the moment.

"I'm sure I could learn. I'm sure most of those men didn't know what they were doing when they started, either." Jo's voice raised and quickened a little, her excitement starting to bubble up. "Plus, the plant is hiring women. I see them going to and from every day."

Pearl thought about how to make her point stronger. War or no war, a daughter of hers should not be traipsing around a factory with strange men and women of questionable behavior. Jo was an adult, yet still showed an adolescent self-interest and lack of concern for the world around her. Pearl would have to put her foot down. But she was not Jo's mother; was it her place to grant or deny Jo permission?

"Well, if you think you must, I guess."

Pearl looked down at the table as she replied. Jo had seen the same telltale sign of disapproval in Al. Jo again unconsciously rubbed the scar on her forehead throughout the uncomfortable pause that followed. She was going to apply at the plant whether or not Pearl approved, but having her approval—tacit as it may be—helped tame her apprehension.

"Just don't tell Alfred," Pearl continued. "He has enough to worry over without thinking about you running around in a factory, with all those men and *those* ladies...running around in slacks...closer to men's trousers than a proper woman's clothes. Frightful."

The emphasis Pearl added confirmed to Jo that she shared the same view of women who chose to work in industry as so many others did. They felt it was okay—usually—for a woman to hold down a job as a secretary or teacher or, if she wanted to be in the medical profession, a nurse. But it was a completely different story if a woman wanted to work in industry, especially if she was viewed as taking a man's job.

However, war production needed workers, and the war needed men. This meant women were needed in war production. So the following day, Jo would take the same first step that tens of thousands of other women across the country were taking. She would apply for a factory job as a war worker. It would be a life-changing step—Jo knew that—but neither Jo, nor Pearl, nor Al had any idea how much her life was about to change.

The Blooming Grove Review

VOL. XXXIII—№ 313   Monday, November 9, 1942   Three Cents

NO MORE CARS!
Industry Continues Retooling for Bombers and Tanks

DETROIT, Mich.—The auto industry continues to ramp up output as it switches from making cars to war production. Ford's new Willow Run plant turned out its first B-24 bomber just over a month ago on October 1. By the end of this year—barely one year after Pearl Harbor—automakers will have produced forty-seven thousand planes for the year. Working with the War Production Board (WPB), the Automotive Council for War Production, which was formed at the end of last year, continues to promote and coordinate efforts between automakers to switch to war production. As of February of this year, automobile production has been completely suspended until further notice.

PRICE CONTROLS ARE LAW
OPA Issues Stern Warnings to Retailers

WASHINGTON, D.C.—The Office of Price Administration (OPA) on Saturday issued a warning to in excess of 4,000 retailers in its strongest and most encompassing enforcement of price controls to date. Retailers were warned that they will lose their rights to sell with continued violation of the maximum price regulation. Leon Henderson, chief of the OPA, admonished other retailers "...more drastic action..." is held for retailers guilty of more grievous actions, including decreasing per-package quantities, selling of inferior-quality product, and "plain overcharging."

ENEMY LOSSES MOUNTING IN SOLOMON ISLANDS
Total of 5,188 Reported Dead in Action

WASHINGTON, D.C.—The Navy announced Saturday in communiqué No. 185 that since August 7, when the Guadalcanal-Tulagi campaign began in the Solomon Islands in the Southwest Pacific, at least 5,188 Japanese troops have been killed. The total does not include enemy killed as the result of aerial action or in action in remote areas. Secretary of the Navy Frank Knox stated "enemy casualties were more than five times as great" as American losses. The Navy also reported 369 enemy planes have been destroyed in the South Pacific in October, and 529 since the beginning of the Solomon Island campaign. On Sunday, November 8, American planes attacked ground installations on Guadalcanal. West of the current American position, six landing boats were destroyed and, at Rekata Bay on nearby Santa Isabel Island, three float-type biplanes. East of Koli point on Guadalcanal, American destroyers shelled enemy positions, the Navy reported. Advances have also been made to the east of the vital airfield Henderson field.

FIRST LADY IN BRITAIN
Mrs. Roosevelt Visits British War Industries

LONDON, England—First Lady Eleanor Roosevelt spent the past two days touring British war industries. She reports that in one airplane factory she toured, twenty-three per cent of the workers are women. In another factory, a full eighty per cent of the workers are women. Mrs. Roosevelt reflected, it "...seemed to me in many ways very like our factories at home where the women are gradually taking over in a great variety of departments."

№ 2

Jo paused at the front door, straightened her dress, and then stepped out onto the porch. She descended the three steps to the concrete path leading to the sidewalk.

That Monday morning was typical of early November in the upper Midwest. A white frost covered the grass, which was still clinging to the last traces of green for the season. The trees lining both sides of the street stretched fifty or sixty feet in the air and spread a continuous umbrella of orange and red and yellow. The street and sidewalk were dotted with piles of brown leaves, in corners and under bushes where the wind had randomly packed them. The crisp air chilled Jo's nose, numbing any scents in the air, and her breath was just visible when she exhaled. The bright morning sun filtered through the low-hanging haze, making the ground-level clouds look as if they possessed an ethereal self-illumination. She pulled her coat closed over her chest.

Jo figured it would take her about forty minutes to get to the plant—down Mill Road where she lived with the Troyers, left on Staton for about a dozen blocks and over the river, and then right on River Run for another eight or so blocks. She could

make it in less time if she were wearing flats, but she had decided to dress up and wear her pumps. The black leather shoes complemented her dark blue dress, but made walking any distance troublesome. About halfway down Staton, Jo's feet started giving out. She could feel at least two blisters forming on her instep and the balls of her feet were sore. She then wished she had worn different shoes, but would later realize how silly it had been for her to wear her best outfit to apply for a factory job.

Staton cut through downtown Blooming Grove and formed the northern edge of the square. To the north of downtown were the schools, and not far from there was the state-run orphanage where Jo had grown up—the *state building* as the locals called it. She had been given up at birth, the product of bootleg liquor and teenage hormones.

The downtown, wrapped around the square, was filled with all sorts of businesses, from the department store and hardware store, to the butcher and grocer; it was where almost all shopping was done and was a gathering point for many varied social events. East of downtown was the main residential area, although houses and a few small apartment buildings—relatively new sights in town—were sprinkled throughout the town.

The Sugar River used to be the lifeline for the town, flowing alongside downtown just to the west of the square. Since the turn of the twentieth century, the town's lifeline was the railroad running through the west side of town, roughly parallel to the river. The west side of the river was the industrial section and where the two grain elevators stood. Most Midwestern towns of any size greater than a few houses could be identified from a distance by their church spires and grain elevators rising from the flatness of the prairie.

The soul of the city was found in the locomotive repair shops lining a railroad spur into the industrial section. The entire industrial section—simply called either *the factories* or *the yards* by the locals—radiated out from the repair shops. Sprinkled around the railyards were a few factories, some supporting the repair shops, some industries themselves. The late 1940s would be remembered as the sunset of steam locomotives, and as that age ended, so too would Blooming Grove's railyards. By the end

of the twentieth century, the town would have transformed itself into a mix of white collar and blue collar industries.

The thresher plant was just across the river on the east side of River Run Road, between the road and the river. In years past, the plant received raw materials from barges on the river and sent completed threshers out the same way. Now, a rail spur ran into the plant, and the river had become scenery. As Jo walked along River Run, a steam locomotive was gasping and puffing alongside her as it picked up speed. The smoke and steam pulsating from the locomotive briefly billowed skyward before an atmospheric inversion forced it downward and spread the vapory mixture across the road in great tendrils. Jo wiggled her nose back and forth for a second as she adjusted to the acrid air.

As she continued walking toward the plant, Jo looked at the long line of flatbed railroad cars the locomotive was pulling, each carrying one tracked vehicle painted a matte sea-gray blue. What once were threshers destined for the world's breadbasket had turned into tracked amphibious landing craft for the military machine. In military jargon, these vehicles were *landing vehicle tracked*, or *LVT*, but Jo would soon find out they were commonly called *amtracs*. Once a month a train would pull out of the plant carrying twenty or so amtracs. Jo wondered if Al would be or had ever been in one of the amtracs built in his hometown.

Across the top of the brick factory building was painted *Farm Thresher Industries*. The name had not been repainted in several years and was starting to peel and fade. At the plant entrance, a large, freshly painted wooden sign read simply *FTI*, and an American flag was painted below that along with a slogan extolling workers to do their part in winning the war. A newly constructed wooden guardhouse stood at the plant entrance, and a boom gate was lowered over the drive. On the street side of the guardhouse, visible to everyone who walked past or through the gate, a large placard scolded workers not to discuss war work with anybody, because the enemy had spies everywhere.

Jo stopped for a moment. She took in the sounds and smells of the plant. A sooty, smoky odor hung in the air, as if a campfire had just been doused with cold water. Jo glanced up to the plant's chimney and for a second watched the coal-black smoke

bubble up and then dribble downward, settling above the river before being gently nudged upward by the gray-white wisps of water vapor rising from the warmer water into the chilly air above it. Inside the fenced-in factory yard, Jo could see men scurrying about in tractors and forktrucks, moving pipes and beams and sheets of metal and bundles of wire. It all seemed so random and chaotic to her.

After absorbing the scene for a while, Jo started examining the workers to see if she could see any women. Disappointed she could not, Jo decided the women workers must be inside; she *had* seen women coming and going on the half-dozen days she had walked there to contemplate her decision before announcing it to the Troyers.

Jo noticed the guard by the gate was eyeing her. Perhaps he thought she had a camera concealed in her handbag and she was recording the chaos in the yard. A bit of an internal wall flashed around her as, briefly, the guard was replaced in her mind with a state administrator from the orphanage—one authority figure taking the place of another. She smoothed her dress and brushed her coat sleeves straight, stepped through the internal wall, and walked up to the guardhouse.

"I'm here to apply for a job," she announced to the guard, who had stepped out to meet her. He held a clipboard prominently in front of him as if to validate his authority in some way, certain nobody would think someone manning a guardhouse *and* carrying a clipboard was unimportant.

"Do you have an appointment?"

He still cast a suspicious eye on her, and his voice had an almost accusatory tone to it. He ran his finger down the clipboard even before Jo responded, anticipating she would answer in the affirmative and give him her name. On her doing so, he would dutifully verify her name on the list, next to which he would record the official time of entry.

"No, I don't, but I heard they are hiring."

He looked up from the clipboard through the tops of his eyes. He locked eyes with Jo for a moment that to her stretched into five minutes. Then he let out a little sigh and his shoulders slumped a bit; he would not be making an official check mark on his clipboard or writing down an official time of entry. Jo wondered if he was bothered by the fact he would have to do *more* than make an official check mark and write down an official time of entry.

"Just a minute," and he stepped back into the guardhouse.

Jo could hear him talking on the phone, using words and phrases that made him sound very official, like *unannounced personnel* and *inquiring regarding employment*. She shifted her weight from foot to foot. Now that she had stopped walking, her feet were on fire. She took a lace-trimmed handkerchief from her purse and padded along her brow. The crispness of the morning air had faded, and the walk had made her forehead just a bit moist and her coat almost unnecessary. Then, the guard stepped from the guardhouse.

"Ma'am, somebody will be here in a minute to take you inside. Wait here."

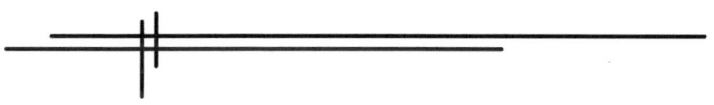

The harsh din from the plant was muffled quite a bit in Mr. Jensen's office, but a rhythmic pulsing could be felt moving low across the floor. Mr. Jensen was the owner of FTI. He was a barrel-chested man with close-cropped white hair. He had briefly shown Jo around the plant and described the various tasks workers were performing. Then, after she had filled out an application, he had brought her to his office and asked her several questions. After she answered his last question, he scrunched up his face and sighed a bit; he had made his decision.

"I gotta be honest here, Josephine."

"Jo," she interrupted with a smile, trying to sound more personable, hoping in some small way that would make Mr. Jensen more likely to hire her. A great wave of nervousness splashed over her, as if a prospective father was making a decision whether or not she was the one to adopt.

"Jo...I don't think we can use you."

Her heart sank. She tried to keep her smile and not to show her disappointment, wishing her pleasantness would somehow convince Mr. Jensen she was worth having around. She could be a good child and help out around the house...but she was not a child, and she would not be helping out around the house. She was a woman, Jo told herself, and she wanted a job.

"We *are* a bit shorthanded, but, I mean, you just don't have any skills. Almost all of the women we do have here either came from another plant in Chicago or Davenport or somewhere or from the farm and are handy. I guess what I'm saying is, they knew something about industry or equipment coming in. You don't."

"Mr. Jensen, I know I don't have any training, but I'm a real fast learner. I know I can help out here." A bit defiantly, she pointed out, "You hire men right out of high school. They don't have any training."

"That's a bit different. Most of those guys have had shop in school, plus I can look at them and tell if they've got the back for work that doesn't require know-how. You sure don't look like you can slug steel around at all, let alone for an eight- or ten-hour shift."

He looked Jo up and down as she sat in the chair in front of his desk. It made her uncomfortable, thinking he was looking at her as a man looks at a woman. She pressed her knees together even tighter than they had been before. Mr. Jensen was actually looking for muscle size and definition or some other indication that Jo could do physical work. All he saw was a slender frame with none of the bulk where he needed it.

"That means I gotta put you someplace that requires *some* sort of skill. And you don't have any."

"Look, Mr. Jensen, I want to do something to help out with the war effort."

Her smile faded, and her face took on a seriousness. It was her last chance to convince him to take her. She leaned forward, brushed the curls from her forehead, and absentmindedly rubbed the scar above her eye for a half second.

"I *need* to help out. Al—my husband—is gone serving in the marines, and I have nothing to do all day but sit around and think about what may be happening to him. And besides, rumor has it a lot of this equipment made here ends up in the Pacific, where he is, so I'd feel like I was helping him directly, not just helping the war effort in general."

Mr. Jensen again scrunched up his face. He stared at his desk and aimlessly pushed around a paperclip. At first Jo thought the nudges and flicks were in time with the pulsations coming up from the floor, but there was no order to his fidgeting. After a few seconds, some of the longest seconds of Jo's life, he looked up. His face had relaxed a bit.

"We've got a few ladies with husbands overseas, and a couple of our boys have left, too."

Mr. Jensen leaned back in his chair and pointed to the wall. The wooden chair creaked, and the metal springs squeaked as he moved. On the wall was tacked a large world map. Pushpins dotted it.

"Red ones are battles," Mr. Jensen said, referring to the pushpins. "White ones are for somebody who worked here or a relative of somebody who works here. At least where they were last we knew. I update the map first thing every Monday morning. Was actually doing that when the guard called about you."

Jo looked at the map. There were at least a dozen white pins. She glanced briefly at the cluster of white pins in North Africa, but quickly focused on the pins spread out across the Pacific. She wondered where Al was. It would be night there now. Was he asleep in a bed or curled up on the ground beneath some jungle tree? She squinted trying to read the names of the islands, then realized Mr. Jensen had continued talking and quickly returned her focus to the conversation.

"I still think of this as a business…and it is…but I also tend to forget we got people here who are sacrificing a lot. I guess I'll give you a shot, guess I owe you that much since you're so keen on helping out with the war effort, and your husband, he being overseas and all."

"Thank you, Mr. Jensen!"

Jo jumped up from the chair and reached her hand across the desk with the enthusiasm of a high school pep clubber. She grabbed his hand and shook it vigorously. Her smile had returned and was bigger than before. She didn't even feel the power of his grip squeezing her hand. Her entire face was aglow with elation; she had been chosen!

"I'll make sure you don't regret this," she said, her excitement bumping each word into the next, making the sentence sound like a single word.

"But," his voice tensed a bit, and he pointed at her with his free hand, "if you screw up, I'll have to cut you loose."

"I understand. I won't, but I understand," she reassured him, her shoulders flitting from side to side as she talked.

She finally let go of his hand. It was only then she felt a small amount of pain from Mr. Jensen's crushing grip. She tried to surreptitiously splay her fingers to push away the discomfort.

"Okay. I'll put you on first shift. They start at eight, work 'til six. We're only running one shift now, but we sometimes have to run doubles. Be here tomorrow around seven-thirty, and tell the guard out there you're to report to Fred Thompson. Fred'll get you all set up." He pointed to the map. "I'll also get your husband up here on the board."

"Thank you, Mr. Jensen."

Jo couldn't stop smiling. Her first job! She bounced a little at the knees.

"Rose?" Mr. Jensen leaned down into the intercom on his desk.

"Yes."

"Take Mrs. Troyer here, get her a set of coveralls, and then show her out. Oh, and type up the certificate and bring it in."

"Yes, sir."

"The first set's on me," he looked Jo up and down, but this time it didn't make her feel uncomfortable. "After that, you'll need to buy your own. Get some boots, too. Steel-toed."

"Yes sir, thank you, sir."

The office door opened; Rose Ellington walked in and handed Mr. Jensen a paper, which he signed and handed back to Rose. She then led Jo into the hallway. At the end of the hall, Rose stepped inside a large supply closet for a second and then reappeared. She handed Jo a set of new coveralls.

"We only got three sizes: big, medium, and little. I gave you little, but you might still need to tuck them up a bit. And you'd best find some slacks to wear here. That dress won't cut it. Don't wear nothing nice, 'cause you're gonna get dirty, and it'll just be ruin'd."

"Mr. Jensen said I should get some boots. Any idea where I can go to get some? I've never bought but ladies shoes before."

Rose disappeared into the closet.

"I think we might have Lester Collins' old boots in here. He shipped out a few months ago and left his stuff. He's a small guy. Think he ended up on a submarine, or some damn thing. Yeah, here we go."

Rose reappeared from the closet, this time carrying a pair of well-worn boots. She held them down near Jo's feet.

"Might have to stuff newspaper in the toes, but they should hold you until your first paycheck, or longer if you can't find boots anywhere. I know boots are getting' hard to come by with rationing."

"Oh, thank you. These will be fine."

The boots certainly lacked any shred of feminine sensibility; basic leather construction with hard soles. Work boots. Not pretty, not flattering, but they weren't supposed to be either. Work boots; that's all they were. But they were *her* work boots. Her *work* boots. The thought made Jo smile and bounce at the knees again. She clutched the coveralls and boots to her chest.

"Once you get started here, ask around to some of the other ladies. They should be able to help you out with where to get boots. C'mon. I'll show you out. Oh, and bring a headscarf with you. You'll need to tie up that hair when you're working."

As Rose led Jo through the plant and over to the security checkpoint at the building's exit, she pointed out various details—areas to be extra careful in, where the lunchroom was, where the ladies' changing room was. The inside of the plant still held the persistent odor of machine oil Jo had noticed earlier on the first walkthrough, not the doused-campfire smell of outside. She was sure she could feel her face getting oily just walking through the plant. Once or twice she even quickly drew a finger across her cheek to see, but her skin was no more oily than it had been. It was just the pungent smell tricking her brain. At the security checkpoint, the guard searched Jo's purse and then waved her on. Rose opened the door to the yard and pointed to the gate on the other side.

"Guardhouse is over there. You'll need to check in there, then come through this checkpoint here. You have to go through this checkpoint each time you come or go, but you don't have to check in with the guardhouse when you leave, just when you get here."

Jo nodded, still smiling, and clutching the coveralls to her chest.

"Just watch for trucks as you're walking in the yard. Oh, and here. If they end up extending gas rationing beyond those eastern states, like they're sayin', take this to the rationing board. You'll need it to get your B sticker."

"B sticker?"

Jo looked down at the paper Rose had given her. It said *Certification of Employment* across the top. Jo's name and address were typed on it, and Mr. Jensen had signed down near the bottom. She furrowed her brow.

"Yeah, you're a war worker now. That means you'll get extra gas each week under rationing instead of the standard."

"Oh...but I don't have a car."

Her expression changed from confused to puzzled as she looked up from the paper and at Rose.

"Maybe you'll get one. Welcome aboard," Rose smiled at Jo before closing the door.

Jo walked across the yard to the guardhouse. Behind her, the noises of equipment and machinery began to fade, and the machine-oil smell was quickly replaced by chimney smoke. At the gate, the guard nodded to her. She waved, turned right, and started walking down River Run Road on her way back to the Troyers'.

This time, her feet didn't hurt quite as bad. Yet they still hurt; if she had a car, she wouldn't be walking. *A car? Of my own?* The thought had never even occurred to her before Rose brought it up. Al had always driven everywhere. Then, after he left for boot camp, Gerald or, infrequently, Pearl had driven whenever it was too far to walk or she was shopping. Al had started sending part of his military pay home. *Maybe between that and what I earn I could buy a car*, she thought, *if I can find one.*

VOL. XXXIII—N⁰ 313   Monday, November 9, 1942   Three Cents

GAS RATIONING NATIONWIDE
Rationing No Longer Limited to Eastern States?

WASHINGTON, D.C.—Seventeen eastern states have been under gasoline rationing since May 11 of this year. Due to Japanese seizure of natural rubber supplies in the South Pacific, gasoline rationing is required in those densely populated states to limit driving and preserve tires. Most citizens receive A stickers and have to make do on three gallons a week. War workers receive B stickers and are allotted five gallons a week. There is talk the Petroleum Administration for War (PAW) will extend the mandatory rationing to all states by the end of the year. Weekly allotments may be higher outside of the eastern states. Midwesterners and Westerners, get ready to make the Basic Mileage Coupon book your friend just as Easterners have for the past six months.

HITLER BOASTS ATTACK COMING IN AFRICA
Fears Spread of Attacks Against American Forces

LONDON, England—The German people were promised last night by Adolph Hitler that he would in "due time" strike a counterblow against the American forces in North Africa. He stated, "Wherever the fronts may be, again and again Germany will parry and go over to the attack." While mention of American landings in Algeria and Morocco were brief, he went on to say the "last and decisive word will not be spoken by Mr. Roosevelt." The statements were made in a speech in Munich, where the Reichsfuehrer was addressing some of his oldest comrades as Nazis marked the anniversary of the 1923 Munich Putsch. Hitler went on to dismiss British gains in Egypt as "advances of a few kilometers" when in fact the German army there had been defeated.

ENEMY LOSING GROUND IN NEW GUINEA
Steadily Pushed from Port Moresby

SYDNEY, Australia—Only six weeks ago, Japanese forces were within thirty-two miles of the Allied base at Port Moresby, New Guinea. Today, they have been cleared from all positions in central New Guinea, and the enemy continues to lose ground here to Allied forces. Allied forces also hold the northeastern shore of Papua, New Guinea, and it is from this point that air strikes may be launched to intercept enemy shipping headed southward destined for support of Japanese forces opposing the Allied campaign in the Solomon Islands. That campaign includes the action still underway on Guadalcanal. Many observers here were surprised by the recent gains in New Guinea.

WAR MARRIAGES
Two Sides of the Fence

NEW YORK, N.Y.—Much has been written regarding young men and women who marry before he ships out for war, most of it admonishing patience until after the war. However, Dr. Guilelma F. Alsop, co-author of a book on marriage and a physician at Barnard College, the women's college here in New York, today had this advice to give, "once assured in your own mind, marry him…before he goes to war." Dr. Alsop goes on to say "a lot of nonsense is being written and said about marriages."

She is clear, however, she does not advocate the so-called weekend wedding: meet on Saturday, marry on Sunday, and part on Monday.

N° 3

As Jo walked down the block toward the Troyers' house, her pace quickened until she slipped off her shoes, ran past the last two houses, and sprinted up the path to the porch. She pulled open the screen door so quickly that it flew back and hit the house. She let out a little gasp, holding her hand over her mouth. She giggled and pushed the front door open, gingerly pulling the screen door closed behind her and then gently closed the front door. Jo turned from the door and stood for a moment. Then she bounced up and down and called out.

"Pearl?...Pearl!"

"In here."

Still wearing her coat, Jo ran to the kitchen. She giggled the entire way, which made Pearl stop what she was doing and start out of the kitchen to see what was happening. The two nearly collided in the kitchen doorway.

"What has gotten into you, Josephine?"

"I got hired! Pearl, I got a job!"

Jo nearly screamed the last sentence. She could barely control her voice, and definitely couldn't control her energy as she continued to bounce up and down.

"Hon, slow down, you're going to break a blood vessel with all that excitement."

"I can't help it. I'm just so happy. I'm going to be working!"

"Here, sit down at the table, and I'll make you some cocoa. And for land's sake, take off your coat."

Jo dutifully removed her coat and draped it over the back of the chair next to her. Pearl moved a pan to the stove and set about making hot cocoa. Jo fidgeted in her chair, just like a little girl impatiently waiting for a treat, until her excitement bubbled over again.

"And look, they gave this certificate to take down to the ration board to get a B sticker...for my car...I don't even have a car! Maybe I should get one! You know, so I have a place to put my sticker."

Pearl rolled her eyes a bit, hoping Jo was joking, but also knowing the idea of getting a car was now in her head.

"A red one maybe. Or blue. Some pretty color. But, it'd have to be shiny, too."

"Well, when you get enough saved up, I think Gerald has a friend with an old car he's looking to sell. I think it may be his son's, who's overseas."

"Oh, that would be wonderful. How much does a car cost?"

"I don't know. When Gerald gets home from work, you can ask him."

Jo leaned back in her chair and looked up at some distant spot on the ceiling. This was her first moment without movement since she got home. Images of her in a car of her own filled her head. For a few minutes, she imagined driving around town where everyone could see her, then flying down country roads outside of town, the windows rolled down and her hair blowing in the breeze. Just her and her car, driving the miles away.

Then it dawned on her; she was alone in the car. Al was not on the seat next to her. It struck her as quite odd that her imaginary world of freedom didn't have Al in it. Pearl's voice brought Jo back to the kitchen.

"Well, Josephine, I certainly hope it makes you happy working. Still don't think that plant is any place for a lady, but if *you're* happy..."

"I'm sure it will, at least I hope it will. If nothing else, it gets me out of the house. When Al and I got married right out of school, and he shipped out right away after that, it kind of left me with nothing to do. Guess we didn't think that out too well, did we?"

Jo snickered on the realization. But her energy had faded a bit, too, with the thought of Al not being in the car with her on her imaginary drive. She did not have the exuberance of before; now a bit of confusion and slight sadness had replaced it. Why could she—why *did* she—imagine a future where Al was not in it?

"Perhaps you could have waited a bit, but then again, why? You and Alfred were such good friends in school. It only made sense."

"Yeah. Al was the first person to treat me as that, a person, and not as somebody who grew up in an orphanage. In fact, for a long time I started thinking he didn't even know."

"That's my Alfred. Not a mean bone in his body."

"Yeah...he's a really good guy, Pearl. He treats me very well."

"Well, if he ever doesn't, you tell me straightaway, and I'll turn him over my knee. I told him when he shipped out that just because he's a marine didn't mean he wasn't too big to turn over my knee and paddle if he gets into trouble."

The two laughed at the thought of Pearl trying to spank Al all dressed up in his marine uniform. A recruiting poster that image would not make.

"Pearl, you're a stitch."

"Oh, hon, you gotta laugh. Especially in these times. But, seriously, I do try to look out for you. You know that."

"I do."

"I get concerned at times, like you running off to work in that old factory. You probably don't know, but I feel like you are my daughter."

"I sort of knew. And it was easy for me to look at you as a mother, not only because I never had one, but also because you are such a good mother to Al."

"Stop, Josephine. You're going to make me blush."

Eric K. Augspurger

The Blooming Grove Review

VOL. XXXIII—N° 314   Tuesday, November 10, 1942   Three Cents

SECURITY FOR WAR PRODUCTION FACILITIES
Army Oversees Security for War Plants

SAN FRANCISCO, Calif.—One recalls the posters from the Office of War Information (OWI) admonishing, the enemy is everywhere. In June of this year, Nazi sabotage teams landed on Long Island and in Florida; they were quickly captured. In February of this year, a Japanese submarine shelled an oil refinery in Goleta, California, and just two months ago, on September 9, a submarine-based Japanese plane bombed the Oregon coast. Officials remind everyone, especially war-production workers, of the seriousness of security. Security in war production facilities must conform to the recommendations of the Plant Protection Office of the army, which is based here at the Presidio.

MARINE CORPS CELEBRATES BIRTHDAY
Action in Pacific Another Chapter in the Story

WASHINGTON, D.C.—On this day one hundred and sixty-seven years ago, the Continental Congress authorized the creation of what would become the United States Marine Corps, the first military branch of our great nation. Since then, marines have engaged in over two hundred actions, including actions currently underway throughout the world, the largest of which is in the Solomon Islands in the South Pacific. As marines bravely take the fight to the enemy on Guadalcanal and elsewhere, they pause today to honor the leathernecks who came before them with the reading of the traditional birthday proclamation.

WOMEN WAR WORKERS
Ladies Answer Call by the Millions

WASHINGTON, D.C.—The Social Security Administration (SSA), in its bulletin Vol. 5, No. 7 released in July of this year, reports it estimates that by the end of 1942, "...about 4.5 million women will be directly engaged in war work." Among the details presented in the report, it has been found that women workers require less supervision than men, and once trained and as experienced as a man—even on difficult machining operations—a woman can transfer to other jobs as readily as a man. The SSA report goes on to state that "...some means will have to be found to relieve women homemakers of part of their family obligations before they can assume work outside the home."

PRESIDENT PROCLAIMS ARMISTICE DAY
Speech Planned in Arlington National Cemetery

WASHINGTON, D.C.—Today, President Roosevelt proclaimed Armistice Day should be observed tomorrow as it is normal to do despite the world once more being embroiled in global conflict. His proclamation stated, "Faith can be kept with those of the first world war, only by prosecuting to final victory the great war in which we are now engaged, and by crowning that victory with peace which shall safeguard and extend these essential freedoms." The freedoms he referred to are those championed by the United Nations of freedom of speech, freedom of religion, and freedom from want and fear. Mr. Roosevelt has a speech planned for tomorrow, November 11, at the amphitheater in Arlington National Cemetery.

Nº 4

The guard led Jo into a room at the back of the guardhouse to get her photo taken for her identification card. He told her to stand in front of a wallboard with *FTI* painted in one corner and a military seal painted in another. She looked at the black ink on her fingers from the fingerprinting he had just done and wondered what to do about it. On the other side of the room, the guard stepped behind a camera on a tripod and, with no warning, snapped a photo. The flash of the bulb startled Jo, who had anticipated at least a *say cheese* beforehand. She had not been at all ready for the photo and dreaded seeing what it looked like.

She thought about asking if he could take another after she removed the bandana and fixed her hair, but the guard abruptly informed her to stop by on her way out after her shift to pick up the finished identification card. He very sternly informed her that if she failed to pick it up on the way out, she wouldn't be admitted the following day; then he whisked her out of the guardhouse and pointed toward the main building. The whole process was over in less than three minutes, and Jo found herself walking across the yard with the other workers, wondering if it had actually happened or if she had imagined it.

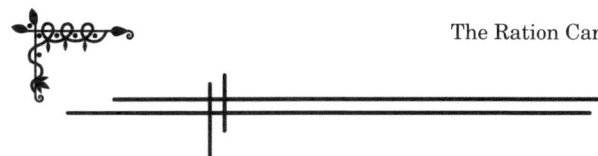

As Jo entered the FTI building, she was greeted with the same machine-oil smell as the day before. She curled up her nose for a second, hoping it wouldn't take too many days for her to get used to the distinctive odor. The plant was more serene than her last time in it. The machines lay silent—dutifully waiting to be cranked up for another day's production—and the most noticeable noise was a nondescript drone of the workers chatting as they waited in line at the security checkpoint, then ambled to their stations.

Jo's eyes nervously zipped around the plant, desperately in search of somebody she knew, perhaps from school, someone she could latch on to and sit with at lunch. Try as she did to hold them at bay, flashes of her first day in high school whirled through her head. She clutched her purse and lunch pail tightly to her chest, as if they were school books in danger of being knocked from her arms by some mean boy. As the line moved forward, she craned her neck, looking for other women, and noticed that several of the men who had already clocked in were motioning and looking at her. She dropped her head a bit and scratched the scar on her forehead, trying to blot out the onlookers with her hand.

Fred Thompson was waiting for Jo at the security checkpoint. He was the factory foreman and waved her over after she cleared the checkpoint. He explained she would have to clear the checkpoint every day when she arrived—the same thing Rose had told her—then go over to the time clock and punch in. He started pointing to various parts of the plant. He explained in detail what each area did; she felt a bit of mundane repetition as she had been through this before with both Mr. Jensen and Rose. Fred was going into more detail, so Jo tried hard to remember what he said, but there was so much, and she didn't understand most of it.

This pointing and explaining took about fifteen minutes, during which he called Rose and asked her to give Jo a locker in the ladies' changing room so she could stow her purse and lunch pail, then he started walking Jo to a small room in the middle of the plant with walls made of what Jo thought to be very thick chicken wire. Fred called it the *tool crib* and told Jo she would have to check out and in any tools she needed. *Tool crib*, she thought, *so it isn't far off from chicken wire. Maybe they should call it a tool coop instead.*

Fred said something to the man in the tool crib, but Jo was lost in the joke she had just told herself and didn't catch what was said. The man quickly handed Fred three items; Jo recognized gloves and something that looked like eyeglasses, but the third thing she'd never seen before. To her, it just looked like one side of a large bottle with some sort of hat on top of it. Fred explained that she would have to wear gloves, safety glasses, and a face shield at her station. The gloves were so large and heavy that Jo thought they looked more like shoes for the hands than gloves. She had been sort of right about the one thing being glasses, and she deduced the large half-bottle to be the face shield. She couldn't imagine for the life of her what she would be doing that required her to wear safety glasses *and* a face shield.

Fred kept talking as they walked away from the tool crib. Jo tried to pay attention, but she had long since given up on trying to understand all of the things he was saying. As they walked, she took stock of what she had to wear.

She had huge, clunky boots on her feet. She wore coveralls buttoned up the front. Inside the coveralls, she wore the least-nice shirt she or Pearl had and slacks, the latter giving her a feeling that made her more than a bit fidgety. Between the slacks and the coveralls, she kept feeling like something was moving up her inner thighs, like a man getting too fresh on a date. Every once in a while, she would surreptitiously try to shake one leg or the other to get the fabric back in order.

Her shirt was heavy cotton, and on her hands she had to wear these gloves; the shoe-gloves. On her head, she wore a bandana—as Rose had instructed—and now she had on the safety glasses. Fred had showed her how to put on the face shield and how to flip it up and down as she worked. As they walked across the plant, she kept the shield up. Occasionally, not conscious of the extra height the up position of the shield gave her, Jo bumped it on a cable or machine and she flinched.

By now, all of the workers were busy, and mechanical sounds filled the plant. The rhythmic thumping and all of the noise she had experienced the day before were back in force. Fred walked Jo over to the time clock and pointed out where her timecard would be, telling her to grab it, align the day with the pointer, and press down on the bar. Jo removed her gloves and did as she was told. When she pressed down on the bar, the clock snapped a loud clunk, which vibrated in her fingers. She jumped, let out a little squeak, and lost her grip on the card. It floated to the floor, but she quickly snatched it up and held it in her trembling hands. Fred said nothing, rather simply showed her where to put the card on the "in" side of the board, first initialing it to indicate she had actually arrived on time instead of late as the timestamp showed.

Jo caught a slight reflection of herself in the glass on the front of the time clock. She thought at first somebody was standing behind her, even turning to see who, but realized it was herself. As quickly as she could, she tried to straighten her bandana and pulled three blonde curls from under it into coiffure on her forehead. It was a losing task trying to look pretty in all of the gear suited for a man, but she didn't want to *look* like a man if she could in any way help it.

As Fred walked Jo across the plant, she continued trying to adjust the bandana and her hair. Her steps were clump-clumping because of the too-big boots, and she felt as if she had to pick her feet up higher than normal with each step, sort of like walking in deep snow, so she wouldn't trip over her own feet. Jo was sure she looked like some ungainly adolescent moose trying to adjust to its growing legs. She began to notice other women at their stations in the plant. They were all dressed like her, which eased Jo's apprehension at her appearance.

"This is your station," Fred said, waving his arm at what looked to Jo to be a jumble of metal and motors. "After you punch in every day, you can come right here and get to work. Since you've never worked in a plant before, we'll start you off small."

Jo nervously glanced around. The workers were a mix of men and women, but mostly men. Everybody seemed to be looking at her, like they knew she had no idea what she was doing. Every once in a while, she caught the glance of a woman who gave her a nod. That made her feel better, a bit less overwhelmed. Jo didn't realize it, but almost all of the woman had, at some point, started working in a factory someplace with as little idea what she was doing as Jo.

"Now, this line here," Fred pointed toward the conveyor belt running past the station, "comes from the foundry back yonder."

He tipped his head toward the other side of the plant, which was bathed in a dull orange glow. Jo nodded so he would know she wasn't lost, at least not just yet.

"Between you and her," Fred pointed to the woman on the opposite side of the conveyor belt, "you have to grab each one of these parts. Those ladies down there are all doing the next step, and the next, and so on. At the end of the line, these parts are finished and ready to send over to where they are assembling the undercarriages."

Jo had no idea what an undercarriage was, just guessed it went under something. She figured one of these days somebody would tell her under what. Fred motioned down the line. Jo could see a half dozen more workstations, some with drill presses, some with arbor presses, and some with measuring devices. She didn't yet know that they were called such, but she eventually would learn.

Each station was being worked by a woman. They were busy taking parts from the conveyor belt, dipping them into the grinders, drilling holes, pressing in bearings, or performing a quality check. The screech of metal against the grinding wheels and the rumble of drill bits cutting holes, along with all of the other sounds coming from around the factory floor, were continuous.

The women Jo saw in the plant were of all ages, from young to old. Most were a bit larger than Jo, spreading in the hips, as Pearl would say. A couple of the younger women were of what Jo considered a more-normal size; in other words, closer to her size. A few of the women were quite mannish, and Jo had to consider them for a second to be sure they were indeed women. One or two of the women Jo thought were quite attractive, or would be if not dressed in coveralls and man-boots. What they wore

underneath the coveralls was as varied as the women themselves. Most wore their hair under a bandana, as Jo did following instructions, but a few chose to wear a flowery hat or other dainty head covering. Jo snickered when she saw the hats, thinking how out of place a ladies' hat seemed in a gritty factory.

"What is this part?" Jo asked. "It kind of looks like a blob of metal that has fallen into a bucket of sand."

Jo was very curious. But little did she know how close she was in her description. The roughness she saw on the metal was indeed caused by sand. Fred explained that the foundry molds were made by packing sand into a box around a master part, called a core. When the sand was packed tightly, the core was removed and molten metal was poured into the void. After the metal cooled, the sand was cleaned away and the part was sent on down the line for finishing. That was where Jo and the other women on her line came into play.

"You'll get different types of parts, depending on what the foundry is making that day. These here parts are the drive gears for the tracks. They're pretty important. If they don't work, our boys could be stuck on a beach and sitting ducks, so if you see any that are cracked or damaged, be sure to pull them and throw 'em in the scrap bin."

"I understand," Jo said.

She nodded to be sure Fred could tell she knew the importance, then looked closely at the part. It was big, about a foot and a half in diameter and about an inch thick. It looked like a wheel with spikes on it, and after Fred described how the part functioned on the amtrac, Jo realized more or less what it was. The spikes fit into the tracks, and as the wheel rotated, the tracks moved the vehicle forward.

"The parts need to be cleaned up a bit before they go any further. You grab a part from the line." He reached over and plucked a casting from the conveyor belt. "See this here? This is called flashing."

He traced his finger along a rough ridge of metal running along the part. Then, he flipped the power switch on the grinder at Jo's station.

"You need to grind this off...like so."

As he held the casting on the grinding wheel, orange specks showered the table and floor, bouncing once or twice in a form of controlled chaos before fading to dark bits. The screech of grinding metal made Jo think the part was sort of screaming in pain—not receiving a nice manicure, but having a fingernail ripped to the nail bed. Fred handed her the part and motioned to the grinder. She reached out with both hands and took the part, but was still surprised by its weight and almost dropped it.

"Flip that lid down or you'll get a face full of sparks."

Fred tapped the face shield that was still standing straight up above Jo's head. Seeing the shower of sparks, she now understood why she needed it. Jo snapped her head to flip down the face shield just as Fred had showed her, stepped forward, and placed the part on the grinding wheel.

The wheel promptly grabbed the part and threw it across the shop floor, catching Jo's inner forearm in the process. The part clanged two or three times on the floor before it skidded to a halt. Jo jumped and let out a squeal. The men in the shop cheered and started clapping. She felt the heat rise in her cheeks, and she was sure her face was as red as a ripe tomato.

"Ya' gotta hold on to it, missy. Until you get used to it, set the part on the tool rest," he pointed to a flat strip of metal just in front of the grinding wheel, "and gradually move the part into the wheel."

He grabbed another part from the conveyor belt, handed it to her, and again motioned toward the grinder. She straightened her face shield, took the part, and tried again. This time, she held the part so tightly she thought it would break. It wasn't the easiest thing to grip with her hands in the heavy shoe-gloves and because of its size, but there was no way she was letting that piece of metal get the better of her. Mr. Jensen had picked her, and she wasn't going to let him think he had made a mistake. As the sparks flew from the grinding wheel, the flashing on the part slowly disappeared.

"Just enough to remove that ridge," Fred said, moving his finger along the part in the spark shower.

Jo gradually moved the casting back and forth across the wheel. The orange shower danced across her feet. She could feel the part heat up, even through her leather gauntlets. Jo held up the part for Fred to see, and he nodded his approval.

"There you go. That's it."

Jo smiled. She felt a calming sense of satisfaction set in. The heat in her cheeks disappeared, and she felt a bit more at ease.

"Now, put it back on the belt and send it down to the next station," he motioned to the moving belt, "and then grab another one. You have to make sure each part that gets past you has this flashing ground off."

He was again running his finger along the flashing on a raw casting. Jo nodded to indicate she understood. He offered her the casting. She wiggled her fingers in the gauntlets to readjust them on her hands and then took the part, her lips pursed in determination.

"Alright, have at it. If you have any questions, just ask one of the ladies here, like Roz." He pointed to the woman at the station next to her. "Welcome aboard," Fred said, and then he walked away.

"It's okay, Hon," Roz leaned over from her drill press, "you'll pick up lickity-split."

Roz ran the back of her glove over her brow, brushing a shock of straight, jet-black hair from her eyes. The rest of her hair was tied up in a bandanna, just as Jo had done with her own hair, except Roz's bandanna was red, not blue like Jo's. Roz smiled and offered Jo her hand.

"Rosalind. Rosalind Abe, but everybody calls me Roz."

"Josephine...Jo," and she shook Roz's hand.

Jo noticed Roz's delicate beauty behind the factory grime on her face. With most of her hair tucked under a bandana, her Asian features were apparent, even though her eyes were partially obscured by safety glasses. Jo correctly guessed Roz was in her early thirties.

While she was never one to judge people, the irony was not lost on Jo that the woman working at the next station very well could be Japanese while her husband was in the Pacific *fighting* the Japanese. In fact, Roz was a third-generation American of Japanese descent—a *Sansei*. Her grandparents had immigrated in the early 1890s.

"And don't let those men get to you," Roz jerked her head in the direction of the male workers. "They jus' bein' on'ry."

Roz spoke with a gritty vocabulary, full of factory smoke and city grunge. It wasn't simple and country like most people around the area, nor was there the smallest hint of her Asian lineage. It was the accent you would hear in a taxi or behind the counter at a neighborhood deli in Chicago, which is where Roz had grown up.

"Okay," Jo nodded and then glanced back at the men, scowling a bit at them. They were still mingling before Fred chased them back to work.

"Most'a the older men don't care so much for the women working, but they don't hassle too much. The younger ones, they give you a hard time, but mostly they is just worried they be called up soon. One more woman in the plant means one less man…and probably one more man gone off to fight."

Jo understood.

"Best get to work, now." Roz pointed to the conveyor belt rolling by the stations. "You'll do fine. On your first day, everybody is a little lost…even them men."

Roz smiled at Jo and jerked her head toward the couple of men who were still standing around and staring. She had the speech and mannerisms of an American—but then of course she was. Only her softly flattened eyes and black hair betrayed her Japanese bloodline. Jo smiled back, glanced at the men, and then turned to her station.

The Blooming Grove Review

VOL. XXXIII—N⁰ 314   Tuesday, November 10, 1942   Three Cents

HEALTH HAZARDS FOR WOMEN WAR WORKERS
Many Women Unaccustomed to Industrial Conditions

WASHINGTON, D.C.—The Women's Bureau of the United States Department of Labor has just released Special Bulletin No. 7, Hazards to Women Employed in War Plants on Abrasive-Wheel Jobs. This bulletin outlines the effects of grinding, buffing, and polishing operations on women's health compared to men's health. Dust, especially metallic dust, is a chief problem. Another common problem is dermatitis, which is an acne-form eruption of the exposed skin. Bits of metallic grinding debris may wound the skin, which becomes infected. Hair follicles may also become plugged and infected. The bulletin states, "...some authorities say that women are especially susceptible to such infection because their skin is tender." Dermatitis among women is being studied by The Women's Bureau.

NORTH AFRICA FIRST
Europe in Four Months

WAHSINGTON, D.C.—Predictions from some diplomatic sources in Washington are of an invasion of Europe within four months. The invasion of North Africa and securing the region are seen as the first steps to an invasion of Western Europe. The optimistic diplomats see winter as possible for an invasion of Europe citing the foggy winter nights along the coast during December, January, and February as ideal for covering the movement of the large body of ships and men necessary for action across the English Channel into Western Europe.

NAVAL ACTION IN SOLOMON ISLANDS
Two Enemy Vessels Reported Sunk

WASHINTON, D.C.—The Navy announced yesterday the probable sinking of two Japanese vessels on Saturday in the Solomon Islands area. North of American positions on Guadalcanal in the Solomons, motor torpedo boats attacked two enemy destroyers in the morning local time, and one of the vessels is believed to have been sunk. After noon the same day, American aircraft engaged Japanese ships approximately one hundred and fifty miles north of Guadalcanal. One cruiser and one destroyer were damaged. Nine other destroyers were undamaged. The cruiser is believed to have been sunk. Twelve enemy aircraft were destroyed in the attack. Four American aircraft did not return from the action. The same naval communiqué said the marines continue to make progress against the enemy in the Solomon Islands. Marines pushing eastward on Guadalcanal have yet to contact the main body of Japanese in the area.

RIDE-SHARING TO WIN THE WAR
Local Workers Step Up to Save Rubber

BLOOMING GROVE, Ill.—All around Blooming Grove one can see our patriotic citizens heeding the calls of the Office of Price Administration (OPA) to share rides in an effort to conserve tires. As one of the OPA posters that can be seen around Blooming Grove admonishes, "When you ride alone, you ride with Hitler." Ride-sharing helps reduce the amount of rubber we consume. The supply of natural rubber is primarily from the Far East, most of which has been under Japanese occupation since early this year. Since December 27 of last year, rubber rationing has been in effect.

Nº 5

As Jo's first day at the plant passed, the repetitiveness of the work began to set in: take a part from the belt, grind the flashing, put the part on the belt. It numbed Jo's mind. A couple of times throughout the day, Roz would lean over and point out when Jo had done a good job and sprinkled in a few "you need to do this area better" comments along the way. Each time Roz said something, she smiled at Jo. Roz sure was friendly, and that was just what Jo needed on her first day.

When the shift was over, the factory whistle blew and the conveyor belt shuddered to a stop. Roz removed her safety glasses and wiped the perspiration from her forehead with the back of her glove. Jo was still intently grinding the flashing from a part.

"Hey. Jo! Day's over."

Jo looked up at Roz, then switched off the grinder and flipped up her face shield. The three curls that normally bounced down over her forehead were now matted blonde scrolls plastered to her skin. Her face felt gritty; black streaks ran into each nostril from the grinding debris she had been inhaling all day. Her

sinuses felt swollen. Yet, when she looked at Roz, Jo smiled with a satisfaction she had never felt before.

"One day down. My first day!"

"You did good. You'll pick up in no time. C'mon. Let's hit the road."

Jo followed Roz across the plant floor to the locker room. A rudimentary wall had been erected to divide the room into men's and woman's sides; before the war, all of the workers on the factory floor had been men. The sounds of chatter, clinking lunch pails, and the opening and closing of locker doors combined into dull white noise. At their lockers, Jo and Roz used towels to wipe the grime from their faces and arms as best they could.

There were some showers, but mostly the men only used them if they were headed someplace after work. On Fridays or Saturdays, the men could, and did, head straight from work to a bar. None of the women ever dared use a shower, lest face the danger of an "accidental" run-in with one of the male workers. And, besides, a woman could not go straight from work to a night out on the town. She had to go home first, regardless, to get appropriately cleaned up, dressed up, and made up. Even though the women had gotten used to wearing slacks to work instead of skirts—Jo was sure hoping she would eventually get used to wearing them—no woman would dare head out on the town in slacks. A man didn't respect a woman who didn't wear a skirt or dress; or worse, expected a certain ease of conquest if she was wearing slacks.

Most people just used a towel and one of the round, concrete washing stations, taking advantage of the company soap to remove sufficient grime so as not to soil anything they touched until they could get home and change out of their work clothes. After cleaning their hands and arms and necks and faces as much as possible to be reasonably presentable in public—or so Jo convinced herself—Roz and Jo headed for the exit and got into line with everybody else at the security checkpoint.

At the checkpoint, lunchboxes were searched, as were bags and purses, for anything that could be used to disrupt the war production or stolen items being taken home. Jo wasn't sure just exactly what they were looking for, but she dutifully allowed her lunch pail and purse to be searched just like everybody else. It made her a bit uncomfortable having some strange man looking through her purse, but the other women didn't seem to mind, so Jo figured she'd get used to it pretty quickly. The guard at the building checkpoint was pleasant—unlike the guard at the gate—and he didn't needlessly poke around in her purse, which eased Jo's discomfort a bit. After clearing security, Jo and Roz walked out of the building and into the yard. Roz started toward the parking lot, but Jo stopped her.

"Thanks, Roz."

"For what?"

"For being nice to me." Jo had a bit of a sheepish look on her face. Had she found a friend on her first day?

"Oh, come now, I didn't do nuthin'."

"You did more than you think. I'll see you tomorrow, okay?"

Jo turned and started walking toward the main gate. She was worn out from the day's work. She felt like her feet were dragging on the ground behind her as she walked. Her muscles were already starting to stiffen and ache, yet she had a spring in her step, at least morally if not physically. The satisfaction of completing a day of work—on her own—made Jo forget about how tired she was. She wasn't even thinking about the long walk home, just about how she couldn't wait to tell the Troyers about her first day at work. Passing the guardhouse, Jo waved to the guard. He stared at her as she walked by, his clipboard in hand ready to record anything official he could. As Jo turned and started walking down the road, a car slowed next to her.

"Hey!" It was Roz. "You not walking home, are you? You shouldn't be walking in the dark like this."

"Yeah, I don't have a car," Jo raised her voice a bit to be heard over the engine and the noise of traffic pouring out of the parking lot and down the road. "I think I'm going to try catching a bus in downtown, though. I'm pretty beat."

"Naw. C'mon, I'll give you a ride. It'll be a bit tight, but we can squeeze you in."

"Okay, if you're sure it's no problem."

Jo opened the door and squeezed into the back seat with three other woman. Up front, two men sat next to Roz. Seven people in the car was indeed a bit tight, just a little on the wrong side of uncomfortable. As Roz began the rounds of dropping off the other workers, everybody chatted.

Once the men were dropped off, the chatter took a decidedly feminine turn. Even though each of the women wore a fine coat of grime, the conversation easily slipped into discussions on shoes, dresses, and hairdos. Since one couldn't buy silk stockings anymore, a good hairdo and manicure were sure ways to brighten a lady's mood, one of the women pointed out. Jo even learned that once you wore a hole in the sole of a good pair of shoes, you could take a stiff piece of thin cardboard, cut it to the shape of the sole, and put it inside the shoe. With rubber rationing, it was nearly impossible to get a pair of shoes resoled.

One of the women asked Jo how her first day in a man's world went. Jo said it was fine, and that she was exhausted. She mentioned how repetitive the work was and hoped it would get better. The women reassured her it most certainly would *not*, but one of them said she had read in a ladies' magazine to use the repetitive movement as exercise to tone up the muscles. Moving heavy parts around all day was a good way to firm up the arms, and if you had to squat to pick up something, the legs and tummy would be slimmed.

Jo soaked up the information, along with the female companionship. She had never really had only female friends. Growing up, the kids from the orphanage always stuck together, boys and girls. Then there was Al, and she always seemed to be around him. After Al shipped out, there was Gerald and Pearl. Now, for the first time, Jo found herself in a group of women with whom she shared at least a small something: a job. For Jo, it was an automatic bonding, and she reveled in it.

Roz dropped off Jo last. As she eased the car to the curb in front of the Troyers', she reached over and gently bumped Jo's shoulder a couple of times with her fist.

"You did good today, I mean it."

Her tough, city-way of speech was, in some way, reassuring to Jo. Her words felt to Jo like Roz had accepted her into some unspoken group, sort of a *here, kid, follow me and I'll get you through...anybody gives you problems, you see me.* It was a role reversal for Jo because she had been the one at the orphanage to take the younger kids under her wing. Jo was warmed by the thought, and it took a lot of the weight off of her shoulders. She didn't feel quite as overwhelmed as she had earlier, and she began to think that perhaps she would, indeed, make it through another day at the plant.

"Thanks, Roz. I really didn't know what I was doing. I hope I pick up everything soon."

"You will. You need a ride in the mornin'?"

"No, that's okay. The car was kind of crowded. I'll manage."

"Okay, suit yourself. I see you at the plant t'morrow then."

Jo got out of the car and shut the door. She waved to Roz as the car pulled away from the curb.

The house was dark. Just a thin halo of light escaped around the edges of the blackout sheets Gerald had hung shortly after the attack on Pearl Harbor. All up and down the street the houses were dark, save the random halos of faint light around the windows. The neighborhood was having another blackout drill. It was a bit of being caught up in the hysteria sweeping the nation at that time. It wasn't too likely an air raid would happen this deep in the Midwest, but everybody felt it a duty to hang the blackout sheets and participate in the drills. Then there was the story the local paper, The Blooming Grove Review, ran showing how Nazi-occupied Norway was actually closer to Chicago than it was to New York City. That didn't at all help to quench the hysteria.

Jo climbed the steps onto the front porch and went inside.

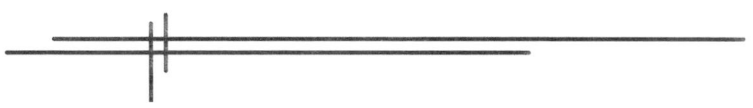

In the upstairs bathroom across from her bedroom, Jo removed the tan slacks and medium-blue long-sleeve shirt she had worn to work. At least those were the colors they started the day as, but both were mottled with dirt and grinding dust, with the occasional dab of machine oil or grease. *All of that in one day*, she thought. And the distinctive machine-oil smell of the plant had trailed the clothes home.

Stripped down to her undergarments, Jo looked at herself in the mirror hanging above the sink, really *looked* at her face. Even after cleaning up at work, she still appeared more like a waif chimney sweep than a lady, a point Pearl had made when Jo entered the house. Each nostril was rimmed in black from inhaling grinding dust, a fact to which her sore lungs could attest. Various streaks of black crisscrossed her face as if somebody had pushed her head down into the coal bin next to the furnace in the basement. Jo wondered for a minute how she could have gotten these streaks with a shield in front of her face all day, then realized she must have been rubbing her eyes or nose with her gloves.

Jo pulled the knotted bandanna from her hair. There was a distinct dividing line of color; the curls that had been hanging down from beneath the bandanna were strawlike in color and texture, while the hair protected by the bandanna remained brightly yellow and supple.

"Uhg," Jo grunted, leaning in toward the mirror and pulling at the soiled hair.

She pushed the stopper into the drain and filled the sink with hot water. Taking a washcloth from the towel rack and a bar of soap, she worked up a lather on the cloth. Then, she wiped and wiped on her face, pushing just a bit harder with each swipe in an attempt to get every last bit of grime removed. The washcloth developed a progressively darker and darker gray color, but in the end she decided no more grime would come off and she was merely pushing around the remaining grit. After rubbing the cloth along the inside of each nostril—and withdrawing something she was sure was the color of death, not life—Jo declared to herself a surrender in the washcloth battle.

Jo turned from the mirror, stoppered the tub, and began drawing a bath. She removed her brassiere; no small feat considering neither arm wanted to twist around behind her. At the bequest of her aching arms, she decided she could slip each arm through the shoulder straps, twist the brassiere around so the back was forward, and then unclasp the hooks.

"Uh, good Lord," she said in disgust, seeing the vee of grime between her breasts.

She daintily wiped one fingertip from her diaphragm to her neck, twice. The irony of the daintiness hit her, and she conscripted the washcloth for one last duty.

The bathwater at the proper level, Jo shut off the water, then removed her panties. As she did, she saw a dark ring around her waist, ending precisely where the elastic had been. She grunted in disgust, brushed off the looser grinding dust, and then stepped gingerly into the bathwater.

Slowly submersing her body into the hot water had the intended result. Jo felt progressively greater waves of relaxation flow through her body. Her muscles began to loosen, and she could move with a little less resistance.

She sat in the water for a couple of minutes, then grabbed a bar of soap and began a full-body scrubdown. Once, twice; but still some of the factory grime refused to release itself, especially from her forearms and hands. Paying extra attention to the dirt embedded under her fingernails, Jo for the first time noticed she had broken one nail completely back to the fingertip. This caused her much concern, for she had yet to learn that having pretty nails while working in a factory was an impossibility.

After declaring the grime battle over for the day—more of an armistice than a victory—Jo leaned back and slid down into the water until her chin just touched its surface. She sat and soaked for several minutes. As her body adjusted her bloodflow outward to compensate for the increase in body temperature, she noticed bright red speckles around each wrist.

She held her wrist close to her eyes, examining the small, pimple-like bumps. Some were festered up, but others were just

red spots. She squeezed one of the festered bumps—one with a dark spot in the center—until it popped. Clear fluid oozed from the bump, along with a fragment of metal, smaller than a grain of sand. Jo quickly realized that the pimple-like condition was due to the shower of sparks from the grinder assaulting her wrists when her sleeves rode up higher than where her gloves protected.

Done fighting the battle for cleanliness for the day, she simply dropped her arms to the side of the tub and soaked until the water cooled.

Eric K. Augspurger

VOL. XXXIII—N⁰ 314 Tuesday, November 10, 1942 **Three Cents**

TIRES FOR ALL CARS
OPA Plan to Keep Nation's Autos Moving

WASHINGTON, D.C.—A new plan from the Office of Price Administration (OPA) intends to keep cars and trucks on the road by authorizing tire replacement with recaps, used tires, or new tires of various grades. The plan announced tonight is the first official statement that the government will attempt to provide tires to all vehicles. OPA head Leon Henderson stated that in all cases, replacement will be of the "...minimum grade of tire that will serve the mileage granted in the gasoline rationing book." However, OPA officials point out that the plan does not promise tires for everyone, rather "...that's what we hope to do." The five-point plan is as follows. "1. Rationing of used tires and recaps, and new tires now in stock to provide as far as possible the minimum essential mileage to each of the nation's passenger cars. 2. Actual control of each car mileage through the rationing of gasoline (scheduled to begin November 22) to prevent unnecessary driving as far as possible, and to hold the national average down to 5,000 miles per car per year. 3. Compulsory periodic inspection of all tires to guard against abuse and to prevent wear beyond the point where they can be repaired. 4. Denial of gasoline and tire replacements to cars whose drivers persistently violate the national 35-mile-per-hour speed limit for rubber conservation. 5. Capacity use, through car-sharing, of every car on every trip so far as possible."

BATTLE FOR GUADALCANAL RAGES ON
Offensive Continues after Henderson Field Victory

SYDNEY, Australia—Allied forces engaged the Japanese 4th Infantry Regiment on November 1 in the Point Cruz area of Guadalcanal. By November 3, the Japanese forces were destroyed. With victory in sight, our forces were surprised by Japanese forces landed by the Tokyo Express—the nighttime Japanese naval actions—near Koli Point on the Lunga River perimeter. Col. Chesty Puller and his marine battalion along with two battalions of the 164th infantry attacked the Japanese at Koli Point. On November 8, Allied forces began an encirclement of the Japanese forces at Gavaga Creek near Koli Point; this action is still underway.

RENEWED ATTACKS IN SOLOMON ISLANDS CAMPAIGN
Marines Stop Japanese From Landing Reinforcements; Fighting Continues

WASHINGTON, D.C.—Commandant of the Marine Corps Lt. General Thomas Holcomb said today that it is increasingly more difficult for Japanese forces on Guadalcanal to be reinforced. As Holcomb put it, "...things are shaping up..." to stop Japanese reinforcements from reaching Guadalcanal. Despite this, the Navy announced today in communiqué No. 146 that "During the night of October 7–8, the enemy continued to reinforce his force on Guadalcanal." American and Allied troops appear to hold the advantage on Guadalcanal after three months since the beginning of the first American offensive of the war. A push by the Americans at Koli point on the island is intended to encircle the enemy in that area.

N⁰ 6

That night around seven-thirty, Jo sat down for a late dinner with the Troyers. She was exhausted and very hungry after her first day on the job, a day that seemed longer than most. Yet it was satisfying; she had worked her first day.

Pearl had made a special meal of roasted chicken, and the tantalizing aroma drifted around the house. Jo ravenously scooped forkfuls of mashed potatoes and chicken gravy into her mouth, any precept of ladylike etiquette losing out to her depleted body's call for food. After dinner, with her eyelids dropping lower and lower, Jo excused herself, deciding to go to bed early.

"Oh, I forgot!" Pearl exclaimed, as Jo pushed back her chair. "How could I forget! You received a letter from Alfred today." Pearl nearly ran to the counter where the letter lay.

"Al! Really?"

Jo's eyes snapped open. She hadn't received mail from Al in many weeks. She slipped a fingernail under the flap and drew it across the envelope, breaking the tape that said *Opened by*

Censor. As she scanned the letter, the parts that hadn't been cut out by the military's cullers of information, she knew why she hadn't heard from him in so long. Al had seen his first combat about three months earlier—in August—in an amphibious assault.

> *Dearest Josephine*
>
> *My first exposure to combat has been on an island called Guadalcanal. We just call it "the 'canal." By the time you read this, I am sure you will have heard about the battle on the radio or in the paper. I was going to write you before we disembarked (that's what the Corps calls "leaving the ship"), but I was too worked up to do anything but pace. I had the pucker bad. That's when you're so scared your rear pulls up inside you.*
>
> *I went with the rest of the guys over to the service the chaplain was having. Seemed like it couldn't hurt. Frankie...you know that guy I told you about from boot camp, Frankie Noylan? Who'd practice quick-draws on sentry? Anyway, he says nothing sets a man to his faith like a beach assault. Turns out the beach wasn't the hard part.*

Frankie Noylan was from Harlan County, Kentucky. Al asked him one night when they both pulled sentry duty why he practiced his quick-draws. Frankie said, in that heavy hillfolk drawl of his, it was because in Harlan you had to know how to handle a gun "real quick-like." He had told Al that living in Harlan County was a bit like living with 1840s frontier rules in the middle of 1940s America. Jo continued reading the letter.

> *There are about _____ of us Marines here and some Army and Navy boys, too. We took them by surprise when we landed, but they have been fighting back hard. My unit has lost _____ in the first few weeks. The _____ landed on the _____ to reinforce us. I think we got them on the run now, though. Every day, we go out and _____ and that usually works to flush them out. Tomorrow, we're going out on patrol along the _____ with the _____ and the _____. We think there is the _____ unit out there, along with a*

_____ of the _____. If we find them, we're gonna hit 'em hard.

As she read the letter, Jo found herself stumbling on the names of places and islands that Al described; that is, those the censors had left in. Names with, for Jo or any American, unusual combinations of vowels and consonants: Tulagi, Gavutu, Tanambogo, Lunga, Koli, Matanikau, Taivu, Tenaru, Rabaul. Jo couldn't pronounce them when she had read them the first time in the newspaper, and she still couldn't. Al could have been randomly stringing together letters, as far as she could tell. But she made an extra effort to sound out the names because she now felt a personal connection to those places. Aloud, she slowly pronounced each letter of the names, guessing at how some letter combinations should be pronounced.

Jo noticed the censors had been gentler on the more-personal areas of the letter. In a way she was thankful for the kindness, but at the same time it made her realize somebody else had read these personal thoughts. She felt a bit of a chill, but it passed quickly as she finished reading.

Things are not what I expected out here at all. Not sure what I was expecting, but not this. Mostly, it's just a lot of boredom interrupted by bouts of sheer terror. Don't believe most of that stuff you hear about this being a paradise out here in the South Pacific. Sure, it doesn't snow, but it gets hot, damn hot. "Not hot" here means it only gets to 90 during the day. And damn bugs everywhere. Flying sickness, they are. Most of the guys have gotten a least a mild case of malaria. I got a touch once. In a way, parts of it weren't so bad. After the hot flashes, I'd get the chills. It was kind of nice to be wrapped up in a blanket in 100 degree heat and still be kind of cold. And if all that weren't enough, when it finally does start raining, it rains for weeks, and that turns everything into a big mud puddle, sometimes as deep as your knee...sticky red-brown goo that will pull a boot right off your foot. I saw a jeep disappear into a big mud puddle. No foolin'.

In history class, Mr. Sharff talked of war being part of the human condition, but he didn't say how war

conditions the human being. I don't know that anybody who has not been in a war, I mean really in war, can say how. I've only been in combat a short time, especially compared to a few of these guys, but I can see I've changed already. Death, it's all around you on the battlefield. The first time I saw a dead body, I froze. Let me tell you, that's not something you want to do in the middle of a battle. Now I can walk right past a body without even thinking about it, unless it is somebody I knew. That still tears me up, when somebody I know gets killed, especially if they're all ripped open.

Jo held one hand under her nose and unconsciously pressed her fingers hard against her lips as she read about the terribleness Al had already experienced. Inside, she was recoiling in horror at the conditions Al described. Fright and terror gripped her for a moment—the first moment the war became very real for her.

Well, I suppose war is war, and change is inevitable. Could you send me a toothbrush? I haven't seen hide nor hair of one in weeks. Been using a twig. Anyway, best to all. And tell everybody we're kicking the hell out of those Japs.

Your husband,

Al

Jo visibly winced at the last sentence. She had heard the term many times since Pearl Harbor; it was everywhere. But this time when Al said it, the derogatoriness of *Jap* really jumped out and hit her. Maybe she was just more sensitive to it because Roz had been so friendly and she was Japanese, at least Jo was pretty sure she was, but Jo had never really known Al to judge people. That was one of the qualities she had been drawn to when they met in high school. She tried to shrug it off, telling herself it is different when somebody is shooting at you. Still, Al's use of the word just didn't sit well with her.

Truth be told, even though Al had developed a hatred of the men trying to kill him, the word had just become commonplace for him. It certainly was an obtuse assault on race, but it also had become simply part of his daily lexicon, its usage no less a common occurrence than a visit to the slit trench used as a latrine. Al could utter the word as casually as *hello* or *nice day*, as could every other marine in his unit, with no prescience toward racism; Jo did not and could not know that. But, there were also times when the word passed his lips with deliberate and poignant purpose; this is only what Jo felt as she read his use of the word.

In the schizophrenic life on the front lines of war, where in an instant a South Pacific paradise could be turned into a hell of flying metal, splattered blood, and disemboweled young men, Al could not have known how he would have felt toward Jo's emerging friendship with Roz. But Jo would not burden him with this. She would later dutifully write to her husband, the young war bride playing the same supportive role thousands of other war brides would, and tell him of her new friend, but she would not tell Al that Roz was Japanese. She decided it would only be after he returned home that Al could learn of Roz's bloodline.

VOL. XXXIII—N⁰ 315 Wednesday, November 11, 1942 Three Cents

DISNEY JOINS THE WAR EFFORT
Winning the War with Food

BURBANK, Calif.—Walt Disney Studios has released several animated short films to inform the American public about the importance of conserving food. The film Food Will Win the War, produced for the U.S. Department of Agriculture, stresses the importance of high output from our nation's farms.

In another film, Out of the Frying Pan and into the Firing Line, which was created for the War Production Board (WPB), Minnie Mouse saves bacon fat to be made into munitions, much to the disappointment of Pluto the dog. We all must make sacrifices, even Pluto.

OLD CARS FALL UNDER OPA AUSPICOUSES
Intent is to Prevent Sale of Cars with Bootleg Tires

WASHINGTON, D.C.—The Office of Price Administration (OPA) today received the power to ration the supply of used automobiles. At the same time, the OPA stated it had at present no aim to use the new authority. The basic intent of the new power is to allow the OPA to block the sale of any used automobile that may be found shod with bootleg tires. Also announced today by the OPA, it has extended rationing allowance of new automobiles to taxicab companies that rent or lease cabs to their drivers, which were not previously covered under rationing of new automobiles. A certificate of war necessity from the Department of Defense Transportation is required for a taxicab company to be allotted a new automobile.

AMERICANS GAIN STEADILY IN SOLOMONS
Heroic Acts in No Short Supply

SYDNEY, Australia—Lt. General Thomas Holcomb, Commandant of the Marine Corps, stated yesterday after returning to Washington, D.C., that the battle for the Solomon Islands is "...shaping up rapidly in our favor." American forces are reported to outnumber enemy forces on Guadalcanal. The Marine First Division, the first unit in action on the island, is still on the front lines. In reports of action in the Solomons, there is no shortage of stories commenting on the bravery and heroic

DAY OF REMEBERANCE
Armistice Day This Year About Troops Overseas

WASHINGTON, D.C.—Twenty-four years ago today, hostilities in World War I formally ended. This Armistice Day, we remember the soldiers and sailors who served in the Great War, but it is also a time to remember those who are now serving our country overseas in another great conflict from Europe and North Africa to the South Pacific and Asia. Speaking in Arlington National Cemetery in Virginia, President Roosevelt spoke of "...the future which we begin to see opening before us—a picture illumined by a new light of hope." All hope that next Armistice Day we will be celebrating the defeat of the Axis powers.

actions. Take for example the case of Private Thomas Cook and two comrades, who fought of wave after wave of Japanese attackers, perhaps numbering as many as one hundred and fifty enemy, for over seven and one-half hours on Sunday morning, October 25, before making their way back to American lines. The Americans had been caught as the Japanese line advanced in attacks on that day.

No 7

The next morning, as Jo rolled over to turn off the alarm clock, she realized her entire body was stiff and sore. Her muscles ached, almost as if she had the flu, but it was from the stress of manual labor. Roz had warned her she would be sore in the morning, but Jo had no idea just *how* sore. She struggled to slip on her housecoat, but finally managed.

As she staggered through the bedroom door, Jo bumped her left forearm against the door frame. A pain shot up her arm, through her shoulder, and into the base of her neck. She winced and stopped dead in her tracks. Pulling up the sleeve of her housecoat revealed a large bruise, about the size of a man's hand. When that first part got away from her at the grinder the day before, it slammed into her arm before shooting across the floor. Now, a dark-purple mark, nearly black in the center, showed her exactly where the part made contact. It also gave her a pretty good indication of the shape of the part, with three triangular points on one side of the bruise indicating where the teeth on the part had hit. She snickered to herself and wondered if the guard at the gate would accuse her of smuggling a blueprint out of the plant.

Jo shuffled down the hallway toward the kitchen. Her legs were not in bad shape. Her feet did hurt from standing all day, but it was her upper body that protested every movement she tried to make. Jo began to regret turning down Roz's offer of a ride to work. It would be a very long walk; perhaps the bus was in order today.

In the kitchen, Jo set about making her lunch for work. She took a slice of bread and placed it in a bread slice-a-slicer. Pulling a knife through the device, one slice became two. Using these two thin slices of bread, she quickly assembled a simple sandwich of a little leftover chicken and a couple of thin onion slices. Then she made some coffee; it would be weak as the grounds were already twice-used. As the coffee brewed and its thinned aroma drifted around the kitchen, she cooked and ate some oatmeal.

After breakfast, Jo finished getting ready and then headed to work. The more she moved, the more the pain in her muscles relaxed. She hoped the walk to work would further loosen them up. It was very important to her to do a good job. She didn't want to disappoint Mr. Jensen. More so, though, she didn't want to disappoint herself.

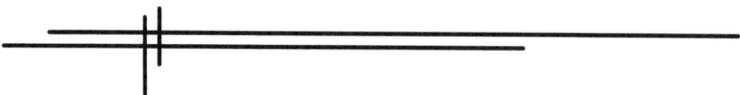

"Mr. Jensen?"

"Yeah? Jo, come on in. How was your first day?"

"I think I'm catching on."

She was still moving a little slow, but her muscles had loosed up quite a bit during the walk to work.

"Listen, I got a letter from Al...my husband...yesterday, and he was in Guadalcanal. I was wondering if we could put a pin up there on the wall for him."

"Sure. Absolutely. I've already got a red pin there for the battle." He reached into a desk drawer, pulled out a push pin, and walked over to the map. "There we go. One white pin on Guadalcanal for Al Troyer."

"Thank you, Mr. Jensen."

Jo had followed him over to the map. She stood there silent for a moment, just staring at the pin he had stuck in the map. For the first time, it really hit her how far away Al was. She reached out and touched the pin, then slowly ran her fingers all the way across the map to Blooming Grove. She moved her fingers back to the white pin on Guadalcanal and held them there for a second. She wondered if he was still there or if he had been shipped to some other jungle on some other island.

Jo realized she had been standing there silent for a few minutes. She looked at Mr. Jensen. He had a kind look on his face, and he reached out to place his hand on her shoulder.

"Sorry," Jo said, dropping her head slightly. "I should get to work."

"It's okay, hon. Take your time. I'm gonna run down to the floor. Got a couple of things to do."

His words rang a bit hollow, as if he had just said that to get out of the office so Jo could have a couple of minutes alone. She stood in front of the map...looking at the white pin for Al...looking at Blooming Grove...looking at the red pin on Hawaii where it all started. For the first time since Al had shipped out, she felt alone, like the little orphan girl stuck in the state building her entire childhood because nobody wanted her.

Yet at that same moment, she felt a certain inner voice telling her to get to work. She figured it was just her mind telling her she couldn't do anything about Al being away, so she might as well keep herself busy and distracted. But it was something else, a drive, an ambition, a desire to prove herself as something more than just another war bride defined by where her husband was fighting. She didn't want to be introduced as, "Josephine Troyer, her husband is on Guadalcanal." She wanted to be introduced as, "Jo, she works down at the thresher plant." She turned from the map and headed down to the plant floor.

VOL. XXXIV—N? 182　　Thursdsay, July 1, 1943　　Four Cents

WAR INDUSTRIES WORKING HARD
Workers Sacrifice with Long Hours

WASHINGTON, D.C.—In 1940, the average weekly hours of a worker across all industries was 38.1. That changed for war workers on February 9 of this year when President Roosevelt ordered a minimum 48-hour week for all war industries. However, many war industries were already running double shifts to meet quotas. Orders for equipment and matériel have steadily increased as the Allies prepare to take back Europe and the Pacific. As men leave industry for overseas duty, women have continued to entered the workforce to take their places. That brings to mind the iconic Norman Rockwell image entitle Rosie the Riveter, which appeared on the cover of the May 29 issue of The Saturday Evening Post.

NEW OFFENSIVE IN SOLOMON ISLANDS
Move Is Against Munda and Its Bases

WASHINGTON, D.C.— American forces landed yesterday morning in a combined navy and army operation on the island of Rendova in the New Georgia group in the Solomon Islands. The operation is under the command of General MacArthur. Secretary of the Navy Frank Knox said this is "...an offensive against the Japanese base of Munda and its surrounding bases." Specific details of the attack have not been released. From Rendova, American forces can stage for attacks on Munda approximately five miles to the north. Munda is the main Japanese stronghold in the area. Once taken, American forces can launch from Munda to Bougainville at the north of the Solomons chain and Rabaul on New Britain. Rabaul is one of the main Japanese bases in the Pacific Theater and a key link between the Solomon Islands and northern New Guinea. This new offensive represents the strongest threat to the Japanese position in the Solomon Islands to date and to the enemy's defensive line from the Solomons extending two thousand miles to Singapore. Rendova is approximately one hundred and seventy miles from Guadalcanal, site of the first American offensive of the war.

KNOX DECLARES MIRACULOUS PROGRESS
Word of Island Invasions Flashes Just Before Speech

HOLLYWOOD, Calif.— Secretary of the Navy Frank Knox opened a speech to an audience of twenty thousand last night at the Hollywood Bowl by stating Japan no longer dictates the war: "The war lords of Tokyo know not where or when the next blow will fall." After the opening statement, he paused and smiled before declaring, "Just before I took the rostrum, I was informed that other enemy-held islands have been occupied by the navy and marines." The secretary was referring to news that had just been flashed of invasion by forces under General MacArthur of the Trobriand, Woodlark, Rendova, and New Georgia island groups. He went on to tell the audience that over the eighteen months since the nation entered the war "...we have wrought a miracle." Secretary Knox was speaking at the Hollywood Bowl in support of the opening of a new bond campaign to finance a new cruiser named the U.S.S. *Los Angeles*.

N⁰ 8

"Okay, men..." Mr. Jensen paused for a second, realizing over a third of his workers, all gathered before him, were no longer men, "and ladies." He cleared his throat and sheepishly glanced down at his clipboard before continuing. "Now, this Sunday's the fourth, as you all know. Take time to celebrate the birth of our nation, but also make sure you take time to remember our boys who aren't here. They've been off fighting now for quite a while, some of them for a full year and a half. But make sure you enjoy your weekend. Because..." his voice hung in the air, suspending the word in time, "on Monday morning, six a.m., we start double shifts, eight hours each."

There was a barely audible, collective murmur. The idea of putting in sixteen-hour days was not something to look forward to, even for those who fully supported doing more for the war effort. Fred Thompson, standing next to Mr. Jensen, made downward motions with his outstretched arms to quiet the grumbling.

"I know, six to ten is a lot of hours, and we're gonna have to run a single shift on Saturdays, too," Fred started explaining.

"But we start switching over to a new model on Monday—they're called LVT2s—and we got a big order. We got ten weeks to get one hun'ert of these new models done and shipped out...without fail. This is A—S—A—P stuff, people."

A dead silence settled over the group. Nobody said anything...because they all knew what the big order and tight deadline meant, even if they didn't know the specifics. Not a single person asked why, nor would anybody talk about it. Each would go home to his or her family, tell them double shifts started Monday, and that would be the end of it. No questions would ever be asked, no comments ever made, and not a word of detail would be spoken outside of the plant. That was part of the life of a worker in a war industry.

But the point of the double shifts would never fade from anybody's mind, either. Each person standing on the factory floor that day knew deep in his—or her—heart the reason production was being ramped up. In a few short months, men would be dying on a beach somewhere. Jo felt a small burning in her stomach, like a gulp of too-hot coffee. Echoing in her ears were the words she had first heard many weeks ago: *Hon, ain't too many beach assaults in Europe.*

Jo didn't remember who said it, or even if it had been a man or a woman. She just remembered the words and how they had almost knocked her flat on the floor. That had been the moment it had fully hit her, that what she was doing, the parts she was making, all ended up in the Pacific with the marines. An order this large meant a major amphibious assault; Jo and everybody else in the plant knew it. A flash of Al standing on a beach with bullets and shrapnel whizzing all around him made her stomach convulse for a second before she could shake it away.

"Okay, your crew chiefs will give you more info next week," Mr. Jensen continued. "For now, get back at it. Except crew chiefs, you stay, and..." he pointed at Jo, "Troyer, you stay, too. And remember...everything we do here helps out our boys."

The workers started making their way back to their stations. The crew chiefs gathered in the front of the break room next to Mr. Jensen and Fred Thompson. Jo looked at Roz, who gave her a crooked stare and then smiled.

"Think you might be movin' up in the world." She patted Jo on the shoulder. "Good luck."

Jo nervously smiled at Roz, then apprehensively walked against the flow of workers returning to the shop and made her way to the group of crew chiefs. Mr. Jensen waved his arm at her, motioning her to hurry up. She trotted the last few feet to join the group. Her steps were no longer awkward and clumping in the boots as they were a half year ago. She moved as easily in the boots as if she was barefoot.

"The rest of today and tomorrow, you guys need to look over the plans and figure out what needs to be changed first thing Monday—which lines need to stop and which ones can keep going. The new model shares a lot with the current one, so most of production can continue. After that, you need to get the new parts up and running aye-sap. We don't have much time, and we have a lot of work to do. This order is over double our normal output."

He handed each crew chief a folder. When he got to Jo, he paused a half second, then gave her a folder as well.

"Jo, I'm going to have you crew your line. That line hasn't had a chief since George shipped out a couple months back, and I think you can do it…me *and* Roz. I was going to give it to her, but she told me to give it to you, said you're better suited for it with your smarts. I have to admit, I didn't think you'd last a week when I hired you, but you've become quite an accomplished worker."

He extended his hand and she shook it. His grip was strong, and six months ago it hurt her hand, but wrestling with metal parts every day had made her hands tough and sturdy.

Jo beamed as she took the folder with her left hand. She had proved herself; Mr. Jensen had picked her and she proved he made a good choice. She was no longer *one of the women workers*, or *one of the gals*; she was not even a new employee anymore, man or woman. She had a father-boss and she had sibling-coworkers—she had a family. And she was a crew chief. Now when men outside the plant called her a skirt, she could just

smile and let it go, knowing full-well she was respected by her factory family for her work. The greatest retort was the one unsaid.

The other crew chiefs clapped a couple of times; those standing closest to her patted Jo on the back. Jensen nodded to her and then turned to face all of the crew chiefs.

"Of course you know this, but mum's the word on any details about the new model outside the plant…I know your crews understand that, too, but just make sure. Go to it."

He waved his hand toward the shop floor. The chiefs made their way into the shop and back to their respective areas.

The Blooming Grove Review

VOL. XXXIV—N° 204   Friday, July 23, 1943   Four Cents

PRESIDENT AVOIDS VACATION QUESTION
Bypasses Gas Ration Issue from OPA Ruling

WASHINTON, D.C.— Paul Leach, Washington correspondent for the Chicago Daily News, today questioned President Roosevelt at a press-radio conference why, due to a ruling by the Office of Price Administration (OPA), an Easterner holding an A gasoline ration card could take a vacation amounting to several hundred miles of driving while another person holding an A card is prohibited from driving a mile and a half to the golf course. The president side-stepped the question, but quipped, "Won't Frank let you take a vacation?" The Frank in question is Secretary of the Navy Frank Knox, who is the publisher of the Chicago Daily News and, therefore, Leach's boss. The president's quip drew laughter from those gathered for the conference.

WOMEN RAPIDLY REPLACING MEN IN WAR WORK
Number of Women Machinists Increasing

WASHINGTON, D.C.— The Women's Bureau of the United States Department of Labor just last month released Special Bulletin No. 197, Women Workers in Some Expanding Wartime Industries. This bulletin details the results of a survey conducted in the summer of last year with respect to the status of women employed in war production. The survey found that nearly three in ten workers are women, one in seven of whom hold jobs that would normally be occupied by men. The bulletin reports that "In machine and machine-tool production, ...women were half of the personnel in factory jobs...". The bulletin goes on to state, "Women appear to be replacing men more rapidly at machines than in any other type of work."

PACIFIC WAR LASTING INTO 1949?
Admiral's Statement Shocks the Nation

WASHINGTON, D.C— The Navy is planning for the Pacific war to last into 1949, Vice Chief of Naval Operations Vice Admiral Frederic Horne said on Wednesday, informing that the Navy has plans to wage war until then. His statement shocked the country. Secretary of the Navy Frank Knox reinforced the vice chief by warning against "...an almost criminally careless belief that the war has already been won...", but stressed "...we can win before that time." When asked about the admiral's statement, Director of War Mobilization James F. Byrnes did not contradict the admiral, but said, "If anyone else is planning on that basis, I do not know that they are."

HEAVIEST RAID YET POUNDS NEW GEORGIA
Defenders Counterattack Allied Ground Forces

SYDNEY, Australia—In the heaviest air raid to date in the southwest Pacific, one hundred and fifty American bombers dropped one hundred and thirty-three tons of bombs on the Bairoko harbor in a day-long raid. The harbor is one of the last two Japanese bases remaining on New Georgia island. On the ground, marines and soldiers moved closer to the base, while Japanese forces from a larger garrison to the south counterattacked marines closing in on the Mundo air base. The counterattack was repulsed with heavy losses, according to a communiqué from General MacArthur's headquarters.

No 9

The plant was especially hot in late July. Mr. Jensen had begun to start shifts a bit earlier in the morning, allow two hours for lunch, and then run shifts a bit later at night. This helped a little, but even with the ventilation fans running full speed, by the end of the second shift, Jo was nearly spent each day. The cumulative effect of the heat drained just about every ounce of energy from her body. The adjustment in hours also meant she had to get up for work at five a.m. and wouldn't be home until a half hour or so before midnight. The barely five hours of sleep a night and the exhaustive heat were taking a toll on her.

As Jo walked to work that day, moonbeams dropping from the predawn sky made the grass glisten with dew. The heavy dew meant the day would be very humid, and she was not looking forward to it. The humidity would make the normal factory odors, which Jo now usually failed to notice, fester into an almost unbearable stench. She took a couple of deep breaths as she walked, conscious of the clean air and savoring it. As she crossed the river and turned down River Run Road, the sun started to bleed over the eastern horizon in a luminescent sweep of bright magenta, and she was sure the air felt warmer already.

Once at work, Jo headed to the changing room, slipped into her coveralls, and stowed her purse and lunch pail in her locker. Then, after a quick cup of company coffee with Roz in the break room, she headed to the time clock to punch in before the shift whistle blew. Jo snorted derisively when she realized the classroom bell she had timed her life by a baker's dozen of months ago had been replaced by a factory whistle. Her life was still timed, just the sound of the metronome had changed. At the time clock, Mr. Jensen was there to greet her.

"Jo, I like the way you jumped in last week when the line was behind and really got things back on track," he said.

"Thank you," she replied.

She hadn't taken the initiative to get noticed; it was something that simply needed to be done. After all, she was a crew chief. It was up to her to make sure her line met its schedule.

"Fred told me you've been doing real good running your line. You've shown a lot of dedication and smarts, like taking on the quality-control role for the line."

"I'm just trying to keep up."

Jo found herself shrinking from the attention. She nervously glanced left and right to see if their conversation was drawing eyes. The most productive machine in the plant was the rumor mill, and she wanted no part of it. She imagined a myriad of "boss's pet" yarns being woven throughout the plant. She didn't like how people already talked about her behind her back because of her past; she didn't need another annoying buzz orbiting her.

"No, Fred told me about that batch of drive gears you caught, the ones that were all cracked. We had to change our molding process in the foundry, but if it weren't for you taking the responsibility of stopping them and tracking down the problem, those parts may have gotten all the way to the field and failed there. Could have cost some of our boys dearly. You showed real intelligence and initiative."

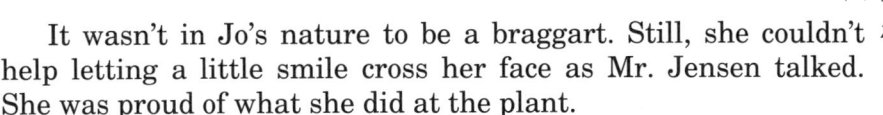

It wasn't in Jo's nature to be a braggart. Still, she couldn't help letting a little smile cross her face as Mr. Jensen talked. She was proud of what she did at the plant.

"Fred and I were talking, and we'd like to move you to a different area...see if you can handle it there."

Almost imperceptibly, Jo's eyebrows lifted and her eyes opened a little wider. "Really?"

"Yeah, like to put you on one of the mills over in the machine shop. It's gonna require a lot more skill being a machinist, so don't feel bad if we end up moving you back to where you are."

"Oh, no, I'll do my best. I'm sure I can pick it up."

"I am, too. Jo, you're a smart gal. I think you'll do us better in a skill position."

Her posture straightened as she stood there, her shoulders a bit more square and her chin a little higher. For perhaps the first time in her life, she looked a person of authority in the eye. She had the sense she was being judged by what she was capable of doing, not by her gender or the man whose ring she was wearing. She was now Jo, machinist in a war industry, not Josephine, wife of Al Troyer. The little orphan girl was fading quickly in the rear view mirror.

"Thank you, Mr. Jensen. When do you want me to start over there?"

"Tomorrow. We'll give Roz the lead on your line."

"She'll do a wonderful job. Look what she did for me!"

Jo dipped a little in a slight curtsy and held out her arms at her side; the little girl inside her was trying to tug at the coveralls. Jo quickly slapped her away and showed Mr. Jensen a more serious side, one apt for a worker who had again moved up the company ladder.

"Sure did." Mr. Jensen agreed. "Oh, and as a machinist, you'll get another twenty cents an hour."

"I figured those guys made more, but I didn't know it was *that* much more."

This time, her eyebrows raised to the point of creasing her forehead—the increase in pay was a third of her current wage. She quickly tempered her surprise to show the maturity required of her new position of great responsibility.

"It's not as much as you'd make as a machinist in one of the aircraft plants out west, mind you, but it's the best we can do. Out there they pay ninety-five cents, maybe even as much as a dollar ten an hour. Us little guys just can't compete with the big boys when it comes to pay. In fact, that's why the job is open. One of my guys picked up and moved to Long Beach to work at Douglas Aviation. Don't you go running off on me."

"No, sir, I won't."

The gears in her mind started spinning as she walked back to the plant floor. What would she do with the extra money? It was a lot; could she buy some new shoes? She had the ration coupons to buy shoes, but would she even be able to *find* shoes? Maybe a dress? But then, she often found herself wearing slacks even for leisure activities these days, not that she had encountered any leisure time for the past few weeks. The sensible thing would be to save the money. That would give her and Al a head start when he got home. Still, she was pretty sure she'd be getting something for herself, at least with the first larger paycheck.

The Blooming Grove Review

VOL. XXXIV—N° 212 Saturday, July 31, 1943 Four Cents

RUBBER REMAINS RATIONED
Tires Among the Rationed Items

WASHINGTON, D.C.— The Office of Price Administration (OPA) reminds citizens that its Tire Ration Order 1A, implemented on December 30, 1941, is still in effect. The Rubber Bureau of the War Production Board (WPB) is the agency responsible for determining which types of tires are rationed in what quantities. Citizens must apply for purchase of a new tire by completing OPA Form R-1 at their local rationing board. If the purchase is authorized, and if sufficient quota exists, a ration certificate R-2B will be issued, which must be turned in at the tire dealer in order to receive the new tire. Dealers are not allowed to sell tires to anyone lacking a ration certificate.

GASOLINE RATIONED TO SAVE RUBBER
Sticker Needed to Purchase Gasoline

WASHINGTON, D.C.— William Jeffers, Rubber Director of the War Production Board, quoted from the September 1942 Baruch Rubber Report submitted to President Roosevelt when he said, "Gas rationing is the only way to save rubber." Nationwide gasoline rationing has been in effect since December 1 of last year. The Office of Price Administration (OPA) reminds citizens that in addition to the required gasoline ration coupons, an appropriate mileage ration sticker must be affixed to a vehicle's windshield in order to purchase gasoline. To receive a mileage ration sticker, one must appear before his local War Price and Rationing board and certify both a need for a gasoline ration and ownership of no more than five tires.

MUNDA DEFENDERS BEING SQUEEZED
Flamethrowers Used for First Time in Pacific

SYDNEY, Australia— American forces advanced through the Lambetti Plantation east of the Japanese airbase at Munda, New Georgia, General MacArthur announced today. A spokesman said American forces are now within nineteen hundred yards of the airbase. This is a gain of about two hundred yards since Tuesday. In the island war in the Pacific against a tenacious defender, this is considered a substantial advance. In the action at Munda, flamethrowers were used for the first time in Pacific island operations to dislodge defenders from pillboxes made of logs and coral.

BLACK GAS HARMS WAR EFFORT
Chiseling and Coupon Abuse Are Problems

WASHINGTON, D.C.—In February of last year, the Petroleum Administration for War (PAW) issued recommendations that service stations remain open no more than twelve hours a day and no more than seventy-two hours per week. The Office of Price Administration (OPA) warns that use of black market gasoline, so-called black gas, harms the war effort. Chiseling—the practice of dealers selling gas to those without appropriate ration coupons—and selling of coupons are not only illegal, but also undermine the war effort. The PAW states that black markets "...drain millions of gallons of sorely needed gasoline from legitimate users."

№ 10

Jo set out down the sidewalk, off to see a friend of Gerald's about a car. She had two envelopes tucked away in her purse, one with money she had saved for buying a car and another containing money from Al's military pay that he had sent home. Jo thought about writing to Al and telling him she didn't need him to send money, that she was doing okay on her own, but she didn't know how he would feel about his wife working. Even though she'd had a job for almost a year, she hadn't yet told him about it.

In fact, with the large increase in pay from her recent promotion, she was doing more than okay. She had even considered finding a small apartment of her own—maybe with Roz—and getting out of the Troyers' house. In the end, every time she thought about it, she imagined the conversation with Pearl and Gerald and convinced herself otherwise. Even with her factory family, the strings to her home family—Al's family—were still wound around her. She contented herself being an independent woman who could earn her own money and letting the little orphan girl hide in the shadows of the Troyers' house.

Jo arrived at her destination, a clean and well-kept bungalow-style house on Schroeder Drive. The walk in the July heat had made her forehead quite moist, and she patted a bandanna on her brow. Her dress clung just slightly to her body. She pulled the chest panel in and out, blowing air over her skin to cool it. After a couple of seconds ventilating, she knocked on the front door. A tall, thin man answered the knock.

"Hi. I'm Josephine. Gerald Troyer—my father-in-law—told me you have a car you might sell me."

Jo extended her hand. John Fitzgibbon reached out and shook it. He was probably about Mr. Troyer's age, she figured. His clothes were neat and stylish. He seemed to be a person who made a comfortable living.

"Yeah, it's around the side here."

John motioned with his arm as he turned and walked across the yard and toward the side of the house. Jo noticed the yard was very well kept. Rounding the corner, a vast mat of iris with full blooms spanning the color spectrum cast an intoxicating fragrance into the air. John spoke as they walked, using very short, simple sentences.

"It's a '28. Ford. Black. Pretty plain. Not much to look at."

Jo followed him along the side of the house. Two strips of concrete set apart as far as the wheels on a car led to the back of the house and to the garage. The car was off on the grass to the side of the garage. It was a sedan, not a coupe; the back was squared off. Its two headlights were large and attached to a bar that transversed the radiator. The car had thinner fenders than what had become standard in the late '30s. Running boards connected the front fenders to the rear fenders. Inside, four could sit comfortably. If you could squeeze a third person in the backseat, it could carry five. And, save for a limited number of chrome trim pieces, the car was all black.

"Wife's got a victory garden back over there."

He pointed to the other side of the backyard. There, his wife was kneeling and cultivating the garden, throwing weeds into a pile at the edge. She was wearing a large round sun hat. She looked up from her weeding and waved to Jo, who returned the greeting. Jo thought Mrs. Fitzgibbon looked very content and wondered if she, too, would get as much enjoyment if she were to plant a victory garden.

"Keeps her busy. Plus with the rationing and all." He motioned to the car. "There she is."

"This is my first car," Jo said with a big smile. "I don't know much about cars. Al taught me how to drive…'course, nobody at the state home had a car."

"Gerald already looked at it," he smiled back. "He said it'll do fine for ya'."

"Oh good. The Troyers are always looking out for me." She leaned closer and almost under her breath said, "They're very good that way."

"It's my boy's. He's over in Europe. Wrote me a while back. Told me to get what I could for it. Guess 'bout hundred fifty'd be fair."

Jo stopped for a second. Even with overtime, that was more than a month's pay. She had only brought one hundred, plus the twenty-five Al had just sent home. If she used the money from Al it would mean she didn't do this all on her own, that she needed help from somebody. But even with the money from Al, she didn't have enough.

"I…I don't have, I mean, I didn't bring that much."

"Said that'd be fair, not what it'll cost ya'," John smiled. "If ya' got a hundred, car's yours."

"I do." The smile returned to her face, wider than before. "Thank you. Oh, I'm so excited!"

Jo skipped over to the driver's door and got in the car. She sat there with her hands on the wheel and a big smile on her face. For a few moments, she stared straight ahead through the windshield. She imagined what everyone would think, their reactions, when she showed up at the plant in her new car.

That'll put those men in their place, she thought. And now, she and Roz could take turns driving the group of coworkers who shared a ride.

"Tires oughta last you a while. They're in good shape. No spare, though. Had to give that up to the scrap drive a while back. They wanted to take the whole damn car, but I talked them out of it. Figure next time they come I won't have a choice. Rather see you have it."

"No, they can't have *my* car."

Jo beamed from the driver's seat, her hands firmly planted on the steering wheel.

"There's a bit of gas in it. I started it the other day when Gerald was here. If you don't drive but around town, you probably got about two days of gas. You'll need to get your ration sticker pretty quick, though."

"I'm going to the rationing board from here. They told me at the plant that I get a B sticker."

"Gerald mentioned you're working over at Thresher. It's good you're pitchin' in to help out the boys. I know some folk don't take too kindly to women working in a man's job, but I say it sure helps our boys overseas."

John swung the driver's door shut and touched one finger to his eyebrow in mock salute.

"Hope the car suits you."

"I'm sure it will...very much so."

The smile still stretched across Jo's face. She reached into her purse, pulled out an envelope, and handed it to John.

"There's a hundred in there. You can count it."

"No need," he replied as he took the envelope.

John tapped on the roof of the car to signal the deal was done. Jo started the engine, put the car in gear, and slowly eased it off of the grass and down the driveway.

Jo pulled into downtown and found a parking space just off the square. After a quick stop to register her car, she walked across the square to the local rationing board. The Office of Price Administration, which most people called the OPA, directed all rationing across the country. It had been set up to control prices on certain key products and to manage the fifty-five hundred rationing boards nationwide.

The OPA was one of many so-called alphabet agencies—because of the jumble of acronyms resulting from the names of the agencies—that had sprung up during the dawn of war. Acronyms weren't limited to just governmental agencies. The plant where Jo worked was now an acronym, too—FTI instead of Farm Thresher Industries.

When Jo arrived at the storefront where the rationing board had set up shop, she pushed the door open and stepped inside. A bell on the door tinkled to announce her arrival. After a moment, a short, pudgy man stepped out of the office in back and walked up to the counter. His suspenders struggled to keep the waistband on his pants close to the proper height.

"What can I do for you, ma'am?"

There was a genuine pleasantness to his voice, far from what Jo had expected from a governmental worker. His thick glasses enlarged his eyes, giving him a bit of a horsey look, and the afternoon heat made beads of sweat form on top of his balding head.

"I need to get a gasoline ration sticker. Here's my certificate from Thresher saying I'm a war worker."

Even though the name of the plant had changed to FTI, everybody still just called it Thresher. Blooming Grove was a town of familiarity set in its ways.

The man nodded, then reached into a cubbyhole behind the counter and withdrew a form. He quickly filled out the date, checked a few boxes, and placed a few X's on the form, then handed it to Jo. She filled in her personal information dictated by the X's and handed the form back.

"Okay. How many tires do you have? You don't have more than five, do you?"

"Um...no...four. The car...has...four wheels."

Jo scrunched up her face as she tried to figure out why he had asked the question. Was he playing a joke on her, maybe because she was a woman? He was busy filling in information on the form, so he did not see her expression.

"I...I don't understand."

Finally, he realized Jo didn't grasp the reasoning behind his question. He looked up and smiled; a pleasant smile, not a sarcastic one. His glasses rode up a bit on his ruddy cheeks. Jo thought maybe this is what Santa Claus would look like if he had shaved and taken a governmental job during the summers.

"No, hon, see, you can have five tires...one spare, you know...but no more than five. If you have only the four, you're fine. *If* you find another tire, you're allowed to have it—with the appropriate OPA paperwork, of course—but good luck finding one. I'd take good care of the ones you have."

"Oh...okay."

The administrator recorded the last of Jo's information onto a folder. Then he handed her a book of coupons. He also handed her a B sticker.

"Here's your Basic Mileage Ration book. In there you'll find your coupons. Write your license number on each coupon before turning it in. The station attendant will take the appropriate coupons when you get gas. And put the sticker on your windshield. That gets you eight gallons per week. The OPA allots us Midwesterners a bit more than Easterners. If you don't have your coupons and that sticker in your window, you won't be able to get any gas. Questions?"

"No. Thank you so much."

He nodded, smiled, and turned back toward his office. As Jo pulled open the door to leave, the bell tinkled again. She stepped out and then walked back across the square to her car.

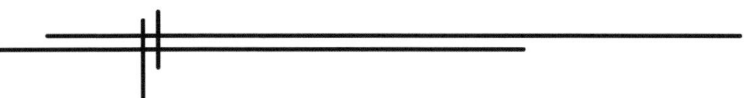

The ding-ding emanating from the service bay announced Jo's arrival as she nosed her car next to the gas pump. Two uniformed attendants trotted out from the bay, wiping their hands on shop towels. One grabbed a squeegee from a bucket between the two pumps and started cleaning the windshield. The other approached the driver's window and tipped his hat.

"Ma'am. What'll it be?"

He smelled of grease and motor oil. The creases in his hands were black, creating a patchwork of skin. Under his fingernails was what seemed like a lifetime of grime. His uniform was in similar state. Jo briefly wondered if that was how other people saw her after a day at the plant. He finished wiping his hands, as if they were now clean, and stuffed one corner of the shop towel in his back pocket, leaving most of the towel hanging out like an off-center tail.

"Eight gallons, please."

The attendant glanced at the windshield and noted the B ration sticker. Jo couldn't conceal a slight smile; he knew she was a war worker.

"Right away, ma'am."

He started the pump chugging away, its ding-ding-ding counting gallons. The smell of raw fuel drifted over the car. The other attendant finished with the windows and then opened the hood. Jo could see his hands running about all over the engine, unscrewing a cap and screwing it back on; pulling out a dipstick, wiping it off, and sticking it back in only to pull it out again; tugging on the engine belts. All that done, he closed the hood and made eye contact with Jo through the windshield.

"All good under there, ma'am."

Jo nodded, and he tipped his hat. Then he walked back into the service bay and continued his work in there. She heard the other attendant pulling the nozzle from the car and hanging it back up on the gas pump. He walked up to the driver's window.

"One dollar sixty-eight...and I need your ration book. Is that on an account?"

"No, I have my own money."

Jo again smiled with satisfaction as she handed him one dollar bill and three quarters. "Thanks so much...keep it."

She snapped her coin purse shut, folded the billfold closed, and put it back into her purse. The attendant checked the license number on the car against the coupons, then removed the appropriate coupon from Jo's Mileage Ration Book and gave the book back to her.

"Thank you, ma'am. Come see us again whenever you need gas or service."

He tipped his hat and Jo nodded. The attendant then returned to the service bay. Jo put the car in gear and eased out onto Staton Road. The warm breeze blew in the open windows; it felt good blowing across her skin, and she became very relaxed driving down the street. A bliss settled over her as she drove *her* car.

Eric K. Augspurger

VOL. XXXIV—N⁰ 219   Saturday, August 7, 1943   Four Cents

FALL OF MUNDA ANNOUNCED BY GENERAL VANDERGRIFT
General Hints at New Offensive in South Pacific by Amphibious Assault

SYDNEY, Australia—Lieutenant General Alexander A. Vandergrift announced the fall of the Japanese base at Munda, New Georgia and at the same time suggested a new offensive is impending. Speaking yesterday to correspondents at an advanced Allied base in the South Pacific, he stated, "An amphibious corps is ready for action." In a bulletin released by General MacArthur's headquarters it was stated one thousand six hundred and seventy-one enemy dead had already been counted at Munda. The airfield at Munda was one of the key Japanese bases in the South Pacific. Now that it is in American hands, it allows fighter escorts on bombing missions throughout the Solomon Islands and New Britain. General Vandergrift had just returned from the United States where he was awarded the Congressional Medal of Honor and promoted to lieutenant general. It was one year ago today that the general led troops ashore at Guadalcanal. Also reported yesterday in Washington by Colonel Royal L. Gervais was that the Japanese lost forty thousand five hundred on Guadalcanal, either killed or captured, out of the total of forty-two thousand Japanese forces present on the island.

SILK STOCKINGS GO TO WAR
Powder Bags Made From Only Silk

BOSTON, Mass.—Ladies stockings have fallen victim to the war effort; all silk is destined for military use. The gunpowder bags used to charge large guns must be constructed of silk, as it leaves no residue inside the barrel when the gun is discharged. The synthetic fibers nylon and rayon could be alternatives to silk for stockings, but these resources are needed for parachutes, tents, ropes, tires, and other military applications. As a result, many ladies have turned to leg makeup to fool the eyes. Products such as Leg Silque Liquid Stockings, made by the Langlors Company here in Boston, can make the legs appear to be sheathed in stockings. Leg makeup is commonly known as bottled stockings, cosmetic stockings, liquid stockings, and phantom hosiery.

VICTORY SPEED FOR SAFETY
Penalty Is Loss of Ration Coupons

BALTIMORE, Md.—One report from the National Safety Council stated in part "...forty-six per cent of cars driven by war workers had at least one tire with the tread worn smooth, twenty-three per cent with at least two tires worn smooth, and eleven per cent with at least three." Due to the extreme shortage of rubber, the national wartime speed limit of thirty-five miles per hour was enacted on October 28 of last year, enforcement of which began on November 10. Drivers are reminded that the so-called Victory Speed is law. As an example, the Baltimore Afro-American reported in the August 3 edition that three individuals were arrested for speeding and their gasoline ration coupons revoked by the Office of Price Administration (OPA).

Nº 11

The factory horn sounded as the clock ticked to seven o'clock and the day ended. The plant was still running double shifts, but on Saturdays it only ran one twelve-hour shift. Jo finished up the part she was milling and tossed it into the bin next to her machine. She then swept the metal shavings into the scrap bucket. She took pride in not only the parts she made, but also in keeping her station in the machine shop clean. Once her station was shut down, Jo headed for the locker room. On the other side of the plant, Roz straightened up her workstation before making her way toward the locker room as well.

Since Jo had been promoted to machinist, she and Roz didn't work in the same area, so they barely saw each other at work. They'd get a quick cup of coffee before work and sit together at lunch. Of course, there was the ride shared with other coworkers. Roz had started picking Jo up first and dropping her off last, and when it was Jo's turn to drive, she would do the same with Roz.

The few minutes together before the car filled up and after it emptied out was their time to talk hair, nails, shoes...which

guys at work they thought were cute. With their time in private limited, Roz often found herself shutting off the engine and sitting talking with Jo in the evening. In the darkness it was easy to lose track of the time they spent parked on the curb in front of the Troyers' house, sometimes talking away the better part of the night—and dragging through the following day at work.

When Jo got to the locker room, Roz was already there. Roz was wiping her face and neck with a towel, trying to rid herself of the day's grime. Jo plopped down next to her on the bench and took the spare towel Roz offered her.

"I'm headin' to Tanner's to meet a couple girlfriends for a few drinks." Roz had to elevate her voice a bit above the din of the locker room. "Why don'chew come along?"

"Oh, I don't know. I don't think so. I wouldn't know anybody."

Jo concentrated on wiping her hands with the towel. Her eyes flitted toward Roz a couple of times through the curls dangling down in front of her face.

"You'd know me."

"I meant, I wouldn't know anybody else."

She looked at Roz through the tops of her eyes. If she wore glasses, she might have looked like Pearl scolding someone.

"C'mon. You need to get out. You been working here for months now and you ain't never talked 'bout going out nowhere." Roz's city dialect was especially heavy when she was excited. "C'mon, it's Saturday night. We been working double shifts for weeks. You owes it to yourself to have some fun!"

"I don't..." Jo hesitated, realizing this would be the first time she was around people outside of work whom she knew nothing about—and Al wouldn't be there as a pillar behind which she could hide. The thought dried her mouth a bit and made her hands quiver just so slightly. She would be around strangers in public—people she didn't know and a place she'd never been. For a split second, she thought about jumping into bed and pulling the covers over her head; the creaking of the springs in her bed at the orphanage resonated in her ears.

"Look, it's just 'bout three or four of us girls. We jus' getting' some food and a few drinks. Ain't nothing more."

"I shouldn't..." she stared at her feet and scratched the floor with the toe of her work boot. "You know, with Al out in some jungle, I'm not sure it would be right."

Even to Jo the statement sounded like an afterthought. She looked up, and Roz's expression confirmed it. With a sheepish smile, she acquiesced.

"Well..."

"Good, it's settled. Now, grab your lunch pail, close that locker, and let's get outta here."

Jo looked at herself in the small mirror stashed inside her locker. She bounced the three blonde curls that hung down her forehead and looked at her eyes. No eyeliner or mascara, at least not the kind bought in a store. The eyeliner she wore now was the residue of endless grit floating around in the factory air. She picked up the damp towel from the bench and mopped her face as best she could until only the faint, young lines in her face held trace amounts of grit.

"Oh, I'm such a mess."

It wasn't vanity that drove the statement, rather the innate desire every woman had to look good. Jo wanted to look nice especially if she was going to meet new people. She looked down at the slacks she wore, and Pearl's voice echoed in the distance chiding her appearance until Roz's voice drowned it out.

"You're fine." Roz hooked her arm in Jo's. "We'll stop by my place on the way over, get freshened up. 'Sides, it ain't that kinda bar. You'll fit right in."

Jo grabbed her handbag and closed her locker. The churning in her stomach changed from sour to sweet, and it briefly transported her to being a child on Christmas evening. She would lie in her bed all afternoon, not waiting for the thumping of hooves on the roof, rather the squeaking of tires in the snow. She knew every year several of the orphanage workers would return in the evening with gifts for the children and for a special

dinner. And as she lay there, her stomach would spin until it was twisted into a knot. Christmas evening was as close as she ever got to having a family as a child, and Christmas dinner had come to be a very special time for her each year. Now, headed to a bar of all places, that same excitement was suddenly twisting her stomach, and briefly—oh so briefly—the tantalizing smell of roasted turkey tickled her nose.

Jo and Roz walked from the plant out to Roz's car, a '36 Buick. It was a little newer, a little nicer, and a little fancier than Jo's, but Jo still liked her own car better. Her *own* car...she bought with her *own* money...and it gave her as much freedom as she could coax from eight gallons of gas a week.

As they drove through town, the two workers sharing the ride made small talk with Roz and Jo until first one and then the other was dropped off. Then Roz looked at Jo, nodded, and gunned the engine, shooting the car down the street. The thinning tread on the tires refused to grab the road, and the car fishtailed as the rubber squealed. The two woman laughed, the anticipation of a night of fun building within them. After a block, Roz let off the accelerator. Even that brief thrill of pseudo speed—and especially the rubber-wasting tire spinning—would draw frowns. Along every road were signs urging, *Victory Speed 35 M.P.H.* Roz guided the car the rest of the way through town at a much more patriotic pace.

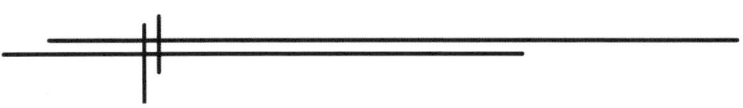

"Everybody's still at work," Roz said as she turned the key in the lock and pushed open the front door. "C'mon, my room's upstairs."

Roz shared the house with her parents and brother. The house was nicely decorated. There was a subtle Japanese flavor to it, but you had to look to see it. The house itself was very similar in construction to the Troyers' house, a standard four-square commonly built around the turn of the century in this part of the country. It had a kitchen, front room, dining room, and parlor on the first floor. The second floor had three bedrooms and a bathroom. Out behind the house was a single-car garage, which opened into an alley running through the middle of the block.

Jo followed Roz up the stairs. In her bedroom, Roz flicked on the light and pulled the shades. Her family, too, had installed blackout curtains, and even though there was not a drill under way, it had become habit for most people to draw the blackout curtains at night. Roz walked over to the closet.

"Here, you can wear this dress. Ge'choo outta those slacks." Roz pulled a light blue dress from the closet. "I know, it's a little plain, but it's brand new. They've really cut back on things to save material. For the war I guess, but I can't see how nice French cuffs are going to lose us the war." Roz also held out a pair of shoes that worked well with the dress.

It was a nice dress. The light blue cotton fabric had small white flowers printed on it. The collar was white to match the lapels, but both collar and lapels were thinner than they would have been in years past. The buttons were simple and made from wood instead of being of fancy metal construction. The short sleeves were appropriate for the August heat, which was wandering through the bedroom window with a sultry breeze carrying scents from the large magnolia tree across the yard.

Jo slipped out of the slacks and shirt she wore to work and wriggled into the dress. She was slightly taller than Roz, but both women had a similar slender build, so the dress didn't fit too poorly. It was just a bit shorter than perhaps Jo was entirely comfortable with. The neckline was cut a bit lower than necklines used to be, and the hem now was to be at least one inch above the knee. The hemline was a requirement of the Office of Price Administration in an effort to save fabric, but on Jo's taller frame, the blue dress more than met the one-inch requirement.

In the meantime, Roz had pulled a yellow dress out of the closet and slipped it on. Jo looked at herself in the full-length mirror. She turned sideways, smoothed the dress over her stomach, and nodded her head approvingly. Roz stood behind her and pricked at the fabric on the shoulders until it fit Jo's frame, then ran her hand across the top of Jo's back to smooth the dress.

"I think this looks good on you."

"Me, too."

"Here, sit down. Let me get some makeup on you."

Jo obeyed and sat on the edge of the bed as Roz grabbed a tin of Max Factor Pan-Cake from the dresser. Roz began to apply the darker-than-skin foundation to Jo's cheeks, chin, nose, and forehead. Jo winced and pulled back as Roz brushed the makeup across Jo's forehead. Jo drew the hair back across the divoted scar above her right eyebrow to cover it.

"Sorry. I just…my scar."

Jo shook her head just briefly, as if to chase away something buzzing around her, then lifted her chin and presented her face to Roz. Roz resumed applying the foundation, this time gently nudging the curls away from the scar as she worked. After a couple of seconds of silence, Roz spoke.

"Nothing wrong with a little scar."

"No, I know. It's just…well…I've had it most of my life."

Roz finished with the foundation and picked up a tin of fuchsia rouge. She took a puff and began dabbing the powder onto Jo's cheeks to add a triangular patch of color to each.

"Everybody got scars. Can't barely see it."

Both women let the white lie pass untouched. Unless Jo kept her hair draped over the scar, the divot was distinct. As Roz kept applying the rouge, Jo squirmed on the inside. She had never told even Al how she came to have the scar, and Roz wasn't asking, but the story was now bubbling up inside her. The void in the conversation became too much for Jo to stand.

"I got it when I was eight—at school."

"Jo, you don't—"

"No…a boy was teasing me for being an orphan, being very mean, and threw part of a brick at me. I know it's stupid, but I always feel everybody sees it as an orphan mark. A brand."

Roz finished with the rouge and set down the tin. She gently brushed the curls from the scar, then whisked them back into place and smiled.

"You know, men find scars sexy."

"What? No they don't!"

Still smiling, Roz twisted the end on a tube of bright red lipstick. She drew the color onto Jo's lips, exaggerating the upper lip to make it look fuller.

"Yeah, lot'em do."

Jo scowled, unable to speak least she make Roz smear lipstick all over her face.

"Here, blot. Then we'll make them shiny."

Roz handed Jo a tissue. Closing her lips on the tissue, Jo blotted the lipstick as Roz spun the lid off of a jar of petroleum jelly. Freed to speak for a second, Jo protested.

"Even if that were true—and I don't believe you—I'm married. I don't need to have men think I'm sexy."

"Don't mean you can't show all those other men what they lost out on." Roz smiled, then dipped her finger into the translucent gel and wiped a glaze over Jo's lips. "Okay, let's do something about those legs."

A bit startled, Jo looked down at her bare legs. Roz walked over to the dresser, opened a drawer, and pulled out a bottle.

"This'll do the trick."

"What is that?" Jo asked, bewildered.

"Bottled stockings."

"What!" Jo had never heard of such a thing.

"You know how you can't find silk stockings anymore, or even nylon?"

"Yeah?" Jo's reply was more of a question than an answer.

"Bottled stockings," Roz shook the bottle in her hand to emphasize the point. "Here, stand up. We just gotta paint this on up to above your hemline."

The two woman hitched up the bottom of their dresses, folding the fabric inward so it would stay up. Roz then proceeded to show Jo how to apply the makeup to her legs. As Jo watched, slowly Roz's legs took on the appearance of having some sort of stocking on them. She began to do the same to her own legs. Once all four legs were covered, the women sat on the edge of the bed for a minute to let the dye dry. Then they stood up and walked over to the mirror.

"That's amazing," Jo exclaimed. "You really can't hardly tell!"

"Yeah, now come here. Turn around."

"Why?"

"We need to give you a seam."

Roz grabbed an eyebrow pencil and kneeled behind Jo. Skillfully, she moved the pencil down the back of Jo's legs with a very light pressure, first one leg, then the other. Almost magically, the stockings had a seam, or at least that was the appearance.

"See what I did?"

"Roz, that's incredible!"

"Yeah, now give me a seam."

Jo repeated the same process on Roz's legs. Then the two stood in front of the mirror, smoothed and adjusted each other's dress, and nodded approval in unison.

"All set, just a puff or two of perfume and let's get going."

"Yay!"

It was all Jo could muster at that point. She was surprised by how much excitement had built within her. The half hour of preening with Roz, transforming from a grimy working man into a fresh lady—wearing "stockings," no less—only increased the excitement. Roz had helped Jo push the little orphan girl far into the past, and Jo just now realized it. With a job and paycheck—and a woman who had turned into her best friend—Jo knew the little orphan girl wouldn't come back, but as she contemplated that, she found herself agitating the scar above her eye. She quickly pulled the curls over it; after a moment, she slightly brushed the curls to one side, just revealing the scar. No, she was definitely a woman, and the woman was here to stay. The two women left the house and began their drive to the bar.

VOL. XXXIV—N° 219 Saturday, August 7, 1943 Four Cents

HALSEY PROMISES RETURN TO TOKYO
Says More Trouble Coming for Japanese

SYDNEY, Australia—The American commander in the South Pacific, Admiral William F. Halsey, said today, "We have a little engagement to return Tokyo to ashes and dust to dust." The admiral was speaking today at a press conference on the anniversary of the opening offensive in the Pacific one year ago on Guadalcanal. Halsey said the United States enters the second year of the war "...with every confidence in ultimate victory." He also stated, "We shall push forward until the battle of the South Pacific becomes the battle of Japan." The admiral's statements were issued after the capture of Munda by American forces. Navy Seabees and Army engineers are expediently engaged in repairing of the captured airfield so it may be used in operations throughout the Solomon Islands and against the main Japanese base at Rabaul, New Britain. The next action for American forces is expected to be the capture of Vila airfield on the island of Kolombangara, which is approximately nine miles north of Munda.

MORE GASOLINE PREDICTED FOR EASTERNERS
Transportation Problem Said To Be Whipped

CHICAGO, Ill.—Speaking here two days ago at a public hearing on his equalization plan for rationing of gasoline, Secretary of the Interior Harold C. Ickes, also the head of the Petroleum Administration for War (PAW), stated "...the oil transportation problem has been about whipped." The fixing of the transportation problem will allow more gasoline to be transported to the eastern states. Ickes was speaking to fifty-eight Senators and Representatives from thirty-two Midwestern states and told them that to be fair would mean "...to take more of the petroleum products out of the Middle West and Southwest instead of continuing to take a disproportionate share out of the East." Chairman of the Eastern gasoline committee of representatives in Congress, Fred A. Hartley, Jr., stated that based on his conversations with Office of Price Administration head Prentiss M. Brown and officials in the Petroleum Administration there are definite assurances of Easterners getting more gasoline. The amount of additional gasoline that will become available to Easterners was not indicated.

CONSUMER WHISKEY SOURS
Military Production Drinks Up Distilled Spirits

WASHINGTON, D.C.—The War Production Board (WPB) issued an order on October 18 of last year that required all distillery production to be for military uses. Alcohol is used in the production of smokeless powder and synthetic rubber. The powder for a sixteen-inch gun blast may contain as much as sixty gallons of alcohol. Production of one hundred and ninety proof alcohol is up to two hundred and fifty million gallons this year. Much of this output is due to the absence of whiskey and other distilled spirits from the consumer marketplace. The warehouse stock of distilled spirits for consumer consumption is dwindling, down eighteen per cent in the eleven months since the WPB order. Traditional brand-name spirits have all but disappeared from store shelves, replaced by alternatives made from scrap products such as potatoes.

№ 12

Roz eased the car into the parking lot of Tanner's. It was a standalone building about two miles outside of town on a curve where the road wrapped around a moraine. There were no fancy signs or decorations, just a basic entrance with a Coca-Cola machine next to the door. A simple sign running the length of the roof peak displayed the bar's name. Several single-bulb lights extended out from the roofline to give some light to the outside. At the edge of the road was a single light pole that illuminated the curve in the road and showed where to turn into the parking lot.

Inside, it was surprisingly well-lighted. A warm orange glow permeated everything. The distinct smell of fermented grain hung thick in the air, almost completely overpowering the scent of the charcoal grill in the kitchen. There was a large crowd, maybe fifty or sixty people. Some were standing at the bar, some were gathered around the two dozen tables spread throughout the room, and some were dancing the jitterbug to the jukebox music. Jo smiled, thinking Pearl was certainly one of those who felt this suggestive dance was thinly veiled foreplay. First a job, then wearing slacks, and now at a bar where they danced the

jitterbug; she would definitely not be telling Pearl about the events of the night.

"They over th'air," Roz pointed to the far corner of the room near the bar, her voice raised so Jo could hear her above the noise and music.

Jo saw four women waving to them and motioning them over. Roz grabbed Jo's arm, and the two navigated through the crowd. Various musks and perfumes danced around Jo's nose as she and Roz weaved through the gathered mass. On the other side, they made their way to the table where the four women were sitting, pulled two chairs from an empty table nearby, and sat down.

"This is Jo, I work with her at the plant," Roz said as they sat down. "That's Janey, Sarah, Margaret, and Mary." Roz pointed to each woman as she introduced them from left to right. Each smiled and indicated they were happy to meet Jo.

"Oh, I'm so excited," Jo said, looking around the room.

Her eyes hadn't stopped moving since they got there, save for the introductions. This was so new and unknown to her, so many people all at once, each laughing or dancing or chatting…having a good time. She half expected to see chaperones standing in a corner, waiting to scold people when they got out of line. But no, nobody to oversee the good times, nobody to shepherd everyone off at a prescribed hour. It was completely up to her when she would leave.

"All right, let's get some drinks," Roz raised her voice over the din as she got up and walked over to the bar. She soon returned with a serving tray filled with shots and beers. "Ladies," she said as she doled out the drinks. "Sorry, they outta real whiskey again, so we gotta settle for that Olde Spud."

Jo shot a questioning glance at Janey sitting next to her, who explained that Olde Spud was, as the name implied, a whiskey made from waste potatoes. After the first two or three shots, nobody seemed to complain much, but some lamented the loss of real whiskey to the war effort.

Roz raised her shot glass to the center of the table. The other four women followed suit, clinking glasses. Jo was a half step behind the others, but she quickly caught on and clinked her glass as well. Then the other women put their glasses to their lips, tipped their heads back, and threw the alcohol down their throats.

Jo held her glass to her lips and watched, studying how it was done. Then she threw her head back and tossed the whiskey down her throat. Slamming her glass onto the table just as the other women had, she began coughing and wheezing, something the other women had *not* done. The table erupted with laughter. Holding her hand tight to her chest, Jo turned to Roz with a bit of a hurt look on her face.

"Hon, we not makin' fun'a you," Roz said with a big smile. "Just, you should'a seen the look on your face!"

"That tastes like gasoline!" Jo exclaimed, now smiling. Not that Jo knew what gasoline tasted like, but then again she didn't know what whiskey tasted like either, real or fake.

"Yeah, it's pretty nasty. Here, wash it down with some beer." Roz pushed a mug in front of Jo. "That goes down easier."

"I sure hope so," was all Jo said as she reached for the beer. It wasn't the first time she had beer, so the taste was expected.

"I've got a treat for us," Roz said with a big smile, pulling her handbag up to her lap.

"Peaches!" The women squealed in almost perfect unison as Roz pulled a fruit from her handbag.

"Where did you get fresh peaches?" Janey asked.

"One of my dad's suppliers brought them in yesterday."

"I thought all fresh fruit was going over to the cannery in Morton for military supply," Margaret said.

"Usually does, but the ration board allowed some of it to be released to the public. I guess there was a surplus in this year's crop or something. Dad set some aside, and I bring them to *you*." Roz's last word was an exclamation point on the sentence as she placed the last peach in front of Jo.

"How did your dad get these exactly?" Jo asked.

The Ration Card

"I told you, one'a his suppliers."

"I'm confused, what does your dad do?"

"Oh, she never told you?" Mary spoke up from across the table, her worlds slurped through a mouthful of the sweet fruit gifted to her.

"Her dad runs Abe's Grocery Store," Sarah said.

"Your dad is Abe?" Jo asked. "We shop there all the time."

"Yeah. That's actually our last name...and it's pronounced *ah-beh*, not *ayb*."

"Wow, I never made the connection. Now that I think about it, I guess I never even knew how to spell your last name!"

"What, you thought they'z *two* Japanese families in town?" Sarcasm cut through Roz's voice. She and her friends laughed.

"Well, no, I just didn't...I don't..." Jo's voice faded to an almost inaudible level, "think that way."

The sound of a chair settling in between Jo and Roz made them both turn. A man had pulled a chair over to their table, turned it around backward, and sat down straddling the seat with his arms folded on the chair back. Jo instantly noticed the power in his forearms. Not an ounce of fat hid the striations of muscle extending from his rolled-up sleeves to his hands. Several large veins criss-crossed his arms. With every slight movement of his hands or fingers, ripples flowed across his forearms.

"Ladies," he said, flashing a devilish smile. His voice twanged with just a hint of what big-city folk would mistake for a Southern drawl, but it was rooted in the fields and pastures of Midwestern farms.

"Oh, God," Roz exclaimed, rolling her eyes. "Just what we needed."

Jo looked at Roz, then at the man, then back at Roz. The quizzical look on her face showed she wasn't quite sure what to make of this intrusion, and she wasn't sure she was happy about it, either.

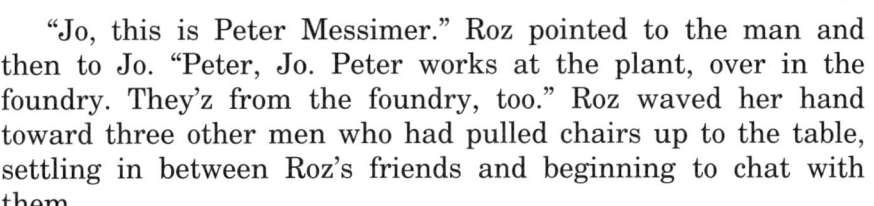

"Jo, this is Peter Messimer." Roz pointed to the man and then to Jo. "Peter, Jo. Peter works at the plant, over in the foundry. They'z from the foundry, too." Roz waved her hand toward three other men who had pulled chairs up to the table, settling in between Roz's friends and beginning to chat with them.

"Oh, very nice to meet you," Jo said, offering her hand to Peter. In an instant, he went from interloper to just another coworker hanging out with the group.

"Pleasure's all mine." Peter shook her hand, still brandishing that devilish smile.

"She's married, Peter," Roz said sternly.

"All right, okay." Peter held up his hands as he leaned back slightly. Jo laughed.

"You get used to him," Roz quipped, turning to Jo. "He grows on you, kinda like'a mold."

"What say I buy you ladies a round. Payday, yesterday. I got this ten dollar bill, and we're not leaving here tonight until it's spent." He pulled the bill out of his shirt pocket and snapped it to emphasize his point.

"Peter! What on Earth you doin' walking 'round with a ten dollar bill," Roz said in a tone both of questioning and accusation. "More importantly, if you plan on drinking all that, I hope you don't have anything going on t'morrow."

"Work, Monday morning, is my next plan," he said with a smile. He got up, walked over to the bar, and ordered a round for the table.

Peter was a strapping man, and Jo sized him up as he stood. He was a bit older than Roz. He wore his brown hair short, so it was easy to see his hairline was receding and he was thinning a bit on top. She guessed maybe he was in his mid thirties, but thought he could be a bit younger or older. It was hard for her to be sure. He was a little above average height, maybe, but no more than six feet tall. He had the build of a man who had spent years slinging steel. He wore a loose cotton shirt, but as his arms moved, his biceps bound up in the sleeves. He was not overtly

muscular, just a powerful man. His chest was broad and thick. He was as slender as his muscular frame would allow, with only a bit of softness in front just above the belt.

Jo imagined him spending eight hours with a sledgehammer pounding away at some large, fiery-hot piece of steel. Suddenly, she realized the heat was not imagined, it was in her cheeks. She turned away, back to the table, and sipped her beer. She glanced at the other women over the top of her mug, but none had noticed her blushing. Why had she just done that? Peter returned to the table with the round of drinks and sat down with his chair facing the proper direction. Jo quickly spoke up to get her mind on something else.

"Mr. Messimer, what do you do in the foundry?" Having just met him and he being several years older than herself, Jo was not comfortable with using his first name.

"Please." Peter rolled his eyes just slightly. "Mr. Messimer is my father."

"He chases all the women around," Roz teased. She had known Peter for a few years. She liked him; he was easy to get along with and always having a good time.

"No, seriously, what do you do?"

"I'm the lead over there. What do you do?"

"I used to work next to Roz, on the grinders, but now I'm in the machine shop."

"Wait…" Peter paused, sort of squinting and cocking his head back and forth, trying to coax a spark of recognition or recall from his mind. "…Jo…you're the one who caught the casting flaws last week."

"Yeah, that was me."

Jo could feel her shoulders square up with pride, and she smiled. Then it dawned on her that the foundry may have gotten in trouble for the flaws, and her smile faded.

"Boy, you sure saved our hides in the foundry." Peter reassured her it was a good thing. "Would've caught hell if those parts had gotten any further along. Plus, could you imagine if those parts had actually made it onto a rig in the field? That was a great catch."

"Thank you."

Jo blushed a bit again, but this time it was over pride for her work, not embarrassment over imagined physical exertion by Peter. Even though she had become used to receiving compliments for her work, she didn't know Peter and his compliment made her a bit shyer. She shifted the topic.

"How long have you been there, Mr. Messimer?" Jo asked.

"'Bout, mm, ten, no, fifteen years," Peter replied. "And stop callin' me Mr. Messimer. It's Peter!"

"Sorry. Pete. Do anything before that?"

His smile showed he was not upset. Everybody called him Peter, not Pete, but he did not say anything about it.

"Little of this, little of that."

"He don't like talking 'bout it," Roz interjected, "but he played baseball before the plant."

"Seriously?"

Jo was genuinely surprised. It was not every day you get the chance to meet a professional ballplayer. She was also surprised by how she seemed a bit awestruck, which made her turn away from Peter and bury her face in her glass of beer, afraid she may blush again.

"Minor league," Peter tried to downplay the experience. "Not major league."

"That's still pretty impressive."

Jo's eyes seemed frozen on him as she sipped her beer. At first, she was almost talking into the glass, but with each sip, the glass ended up farther from her face until she rested it on the table between sips.

"Not really, but it was a lot of fun. I spent a lot of time in the southern league, a lot of winter ball type of stuff."

"Why'd you stop?" Jo asked.

"Realized I wasn't moving up to the bigs and was getting older and injuries were startin' to become a problem. Kind of missed home, too, I suppose. So I came back here and started working at the plant. Been there ever since."

"You must have some great stories."

Jo's normally reserved demeanor melted away as the night disappeared and the alcohol numbed any inhibitions. With each passing moment, Jo became enveloped in the pocket that she, Peter, Roz, and the others had carved out within the crowd. It was almost as if everything else going on at the bar was just a movie playing in the background as they sat alone in a room. Jo realized she was very comfortable, and a pleasing sense of relaxation flowed through her body, partly from the alcohol, but there was something more. Maybe when she sobered up the next day she would ponder what, but right then she was living in the moment.

"Oh, yeah, I got stories. Can't tell most of 'em to a lady, though." Peter turned to Roz. "I can tell you, of course."

Roz smacked Peter on the arm. She leaned across Peter's chest to get closer to Jo.

"Peter don't talk 'bout his baseball days. N'fact, he don't talk much about hisself at all." She leaned back. "He's just that way."

"C'mon!"

Jo looked into Peter's eyes, transfixed by the streaks of tan radiating outward from his pupils and across his dark-brown irises, like sunbursts of earth tones. She could tell Peter wanted to talk about his baseball days. She knew in that way a woman knows, even if she herself had yet to learn it was that way only a woman knows. What she didn't see was that Roz was being truthful—he didn't talk much about himself. Jo wouldn't understand for some time to come how uncharacteristically part of a pack Peter was being that night.

"Tell me a story."

"Naw, it'd just bore you."

Peter had leaned back and was balancing the chair on its two back legs.

"Tell me a story! A *baseball* story!"

Jo suddenly realized just how open she was being that night, and she felt this new openness suited her. *God, how Al would be shocked*, she thought.

"Well, okay then."

In one quick, fluid motion, Peter jumped up, spun the chair around backward again, and sat back down, leaning forward onto the chair back. His hands hovered over the table, fingers sketching out action on an imaginary baseball field as he talked.

"We were down around Mobile…this would have been '23, '24…score was tied, bottom of the ninth inning. There were two outs and the home team had a runner on second base. All of the sudden, the sky turned dark…I mean pitch-black dark…and the wind started blowin' crazy…I mean howling like four she-wolves in heat. Turns out this hurricane was pushing inland down the coast and we were getting the fringe thunderstorms. Well, the umpire, a home umpire mind you…"

Peter continued with the story. When that one was done, Jo coaxed him into another story and then another. With each story, Peter's passion for the game surfaced. He began to describe his involvement with the game almost as if it were a woman with whom he was deeply, madly in love. At various points, salt shakers, napkins, shot glasses, and beer mugs were used to construct a diamond and players to illustrate the narrative. As he told these stories, Jo looked deep into his eyes with each new passage, transfixed by his raging passion for the game. It was something she'd never seen before, that kind of passion for something, as if life itself would cease to exist without that one thing, that source of the passion.

Jo wondered if Peter had ever looked at a woman that way. Had *any* man ever looked at a woman that way? Al looked at her with caring, but she had never seen a passion in his eyes like she saw in Peter's that night.

As the night continued, so did the stories. Some were surely tall tales, boastful bravado, but the passion was there in Peter's

eyes for each and every one. Jo wondered if she would ever have that type of passion for something.

One by one, the others at the table left as the drinks slowed and the night passed. Finally, it was down to Roz, Jo, and Peter.

"Jo," Roz almost yelled over the dwindling crowd. "Stop lookin'at'da clock."

"I'm sorry," Jo responded, a bit sheepishly. "I think this is the first time I have been anywhere when I didn't have to be back someplace by some time."

"Nobody gonna come drag you outta here. You a grown woman. You can take care of yourself. Well, mostly. And what you can't, I'z here ta' take care of."

With that last statement, Roz leaned over and bumped shoulders with Jo. As the two women roared with laughter, Peter shook his head, stood up, and walked a more-or-less straight line toward the bar for another round. Jo and Roz watched him walk away, their heads touching, and with every slight waver in his path, they would point and giggle.

The three of them—Jo, Roz, and Peter—laughed the remaining night away, along with every penny from Peter's ten dollar bill, until the bar closed down. They stepped out into the hot summer night and made their way across the parking lot, laughing and giggling the entire way as only alcohol-saturated fun could allow. Even well past the witching hour, the air hung hot and heavy. Jo's dress clung to her body, and she could feel beads of sweat run down between her breasts and dampen the bottom of the cups in her brassier.

Across the parking lot, Peter turned serious for a second, making sure Roz was in good enough shape to drive. That made an impression on Jo, though she wasn't sure she'd remember it in the morning. Nonetheless, she thought it was very nice that Peter showed the concern; he didn't just ask, he stood there as she and Roz got in the car and watched as Roz drove away.

As Roz aimed the car down the road, Jo turned around for sort of one last look at the place where she had such a good time that night. She saw Peter still standing there, watching the car disappear. Her smile softened, not enough that anybody would notice, but a little, and her face took on an expression of caring. *He's really a good guy*, she thought. *He and Roz get along really well. I wonder if they've ever dated? Maybe they should.*

Peter saw Jo turn around and raised his hand in a muted wave. She raised her hand in return. Satisfied Roz would get them home safely, Peter turned and headed across the parking lot to his truck. If he remembered on Monday, he'd make a point of finding Jo and Roz in the plant. *What am I thinking, of course I'll remember. I sure had a helluva good time with Roz and her friends tonight.* For a man who could feel alone in a crowd, for the first time in years he had felt...well, connected. That was probably the best way to put it.

The Blooming Grove Review

VOL. XXXIV—N⁰ 232 Friday, August 20, 1943 Four Cents

LADIES TAKE TO THE DIAMOND
Cubs' Owner Lets Girls Play Baseball

CHICAGO, Ill.—Phillip Wrigley, owner of the Chicago Cubs major league baseball team, has spearheaded an effort to create a professional baseball league composed of all women players. Wrigley is determined to fill the stands with spectators at the professional level by fielding teams that play quality baseball. Launched this spring, the All-American Girls Softball League recently changed its name to the All-American Girls Baseball League. Four teams have been established within driving distance of Chicago. League play began on May 30 of this year and ends one hundred and eight games later in early September. Fear not, though, these ladies are still ladies. They must adhere to a strict code of conduct—wearing of pants is expressly forbidden.

NEGRO LEAGUE BASEBALL THRIVING
Northern War Industries Supply Fans

CHICAGO, Ill.—Negro families have moved north by the tens of thousands to work in war industries. With their pockets full of war-worker money and gas rationing preventing motor trips, fans pack the grandstands at Negro League games. Business is so good that a new minor league has been started, the Negro Midwest League. Furthermore, the Negro League World Series was revived last year, which had been on hiatus since 1927; game one this year is scheduled for September 21. Many of the teams continue the practice first started in the 1930s by the independent team the Indianapolis Clowns, a pantomime game used to warm up before the competition begins that has come to be known as shadow ball.

WAR HELPS ORPHANS
War Industry Wages Allow More Adoptions

NORMAL, Ill.—The Illinois Soldiers' and Sailors' Children's School (ISSCS) reports that in 1942 its population decreased to the lowest level since 1924. The decrease in population at orphanages can generally be attributed to an increasing number of families who can now afford to adopt children or care for their own children—decreasing the numbers entering orphanages—thanks to the jobs and high wages these families have found in war industries. Approximately three hundred and fifty of the school's former residents are serving overseas; several have been killed in action.

WAR A BOON FOR MARRIAGE
Rise in Marriage Signaling Future Problems?

WASHINGTON, D.C.—The U.S. Census Bureau reports that 1.7 million couples went to the altar in 1941, and slightly more made the trip down the aisle in 1942. While brides had to find alternatives to silk dresses, the most common attire for bridegrooms in 1942 was a military uniform. Does this foretell problems? In her syndicated editorial on November 30 of last year, entitled Marriage as an Institution Taking a Pounding in War, Dorothy Dix wrote "…statisticians report that divorces are increasing to an unheard of degree…". She ponders what will happen after the war when "…the war bridal couples take a second look at each other and see what they have gotten."

№ 13

"Hey, Mr. Messimer...I mean Pete...Roz and I, we're heading to the Maidens' game tomorrow," Jo said as she and Peter left the plant's locker room area. It had taken a couple of weeks, but she was almost comfortable using his first name, though slipped every once in a while. "You wanna come?"

"*Girl's* baseball? I don't know..."

The Maidens was one of the teams in the All-American Girls Baseball League. Blooming Grove was the team's home.

"Oh, shut up."

Jo reached out and smacked Peter on the arm. He recoiled in fake pain. It was a playful incident a little out of character for the difference in their ages. It was something more suited for friends, and they were indeed becoming good friends. And it was the feistiness of the strong women he liked, the same feistiness Roz had always shown toward him.

"You know you want to go," Jo continued. "'Sides, you have better plans for a hot Saturday afternoon?"

The thought of spending some time with Jo outside of work drew Peter in. He found it very difficult to remember that Jo was almost young enough to be his daughter, if he were to have had kids. He found it much easier to see her as a peer, a friend.

Since that night in the bar a couple of weeks earlier, he found Jo creeping into his mind when he least expected. While Peter always seemed to be around people, he was, in reality, mostly a loner. But he enjoyed being around Jo. She certainly wasn't hard to look at, either, but it wasn't just him being attracted to a pretty, young woman. He found her smart, witty, and fun.

"Yeah, alright…but only to celebrate Roz being moved up to machinist's helper. Bet you're glad she's working in the same area as you again."

"Yeah, I am," Jo said. "Okay. Roz and I will meet you there."

The plant was still running double shifts during the week, but had canceled the Saturday shifts since work on the big order was a little ahead of schedule. The air hung heavy in the bright sun as the fans filed into the grandstand. Jo and Roz had arrived at the park just after noon and were sitting in the stands watching everybody, fanning themselves with programs. Even in the shade of the grandstand, the humidity was stifling. Jo was glad she wasn't stuck inside the oven of a factory that day.

It was a rather small crowd of maybe two hundred. The heat most likely kept some fans away, but also women's baseball had not quite caught on yet. Peter arrived just a few minutes before first pitch. He quickly located Jo and Roz and sat in the spot next to Jo.

"Don't worry, ladies. They wouldn't start without me."

"I've heard different," Roz quipped. "N'fact, I've heard they finish without you, too."

She and Jo laughed, but Jo wasn't exactly sure what the

humor was. She glanced at Roz who gave her a look that said *I'll tell you later*, and Jo knew it was something dirty.

"Moving on," Peter quickly changed subjects, "get your scorecards ready. We gonna play some baseball."

"Scorecard?" Jo said quizzically.

"Yeah. Scorecard. You know. So you can keep score."

"Isn't that what the scoreboard is for?" Her words were sheepish.

"That only shows you the score...wait here, I'll go get you one."

"Oh, we're not going anywhere," Jo replied sarcastically as Peter got up and walked down the bleachers, trying to deflect her ignorance of scorecards.

"And get us some beers," Roz shouted after him. He waved without turning around, acknowledging his additional task.

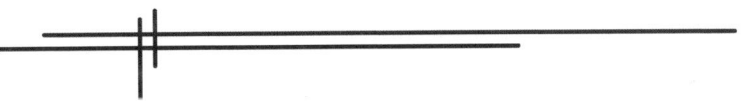

"Look there," Peter jabbed his outstretched finger toward the infield. "Keep your eye on the ball!"

Jo leaned forward on the slab of pine that served as benches for the grandstand. She watched as the players warmed up on the field before the game. On the diamond, the pitcher wound up and appeared to throw a pitch. The batter swung and ran to first base, rounded it, and headed toward second. As she neared second base, the infielder crouched and swung her glove across the base path. The runner slid in toward the bag, trying to get in under the tag. The second base umpire, also participating in the warm-up, emphatically jerked his arm up with a clenched fist, bellowing, "OUT!" The infielders appeared to fire the ball around the horn, from position to position, ending up back at the pitcher. Then, the whole process started over again. Jo leaned forward a bit more and squinted intently.

"I...I can't see the ball. They're throwing it too fast!"

"Ain't no ball," Peter was grinning ear to ear as he saw Jo's confusion. "That's called shadow ball. I seen it first when I was playing ball down south. That's how the Negro League teams warm up. Guess the girls picked up on it. Sure is fun to watch."

"Really?"

It looked so real, Jo couldn't believe she just wasn't seeing the ball. The pantomime, all impromptu with no choreographing, was indeed convincing. The players reacted on cue as if a ball had been thrown or the batter had made contact. But there was no ball. It was all an act to wow the crowd.

"Yeah, see, they make a big deal about the show in the Negro League. These girls are pretty good, but they're better at it down in the Negro League."

"Wow, 'cause they're pretty good at it here, too."

Jo leaned forward again and watched the warm-ups. She was impressed with the talent the women showed. They clearly had developed skills a girl couldn't learn in high school. She reflected on her own skills she had developed at the plant, skills a boy might have learned in high school shop, but not anything *she* could have learned in school.

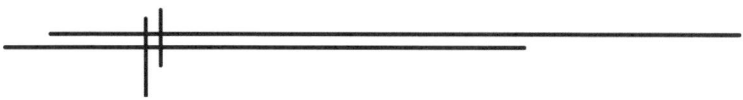

"Oh, she got that one!" Peter exclaimed.

He jumped up just a half second before the rest of the crowd; his finely tuned baseball sense gave him a head start. The ball carried into right field toward the homerun fence, then settled in short of it in the right fielder's mitt.

"Aw, see, it's the damn balls." Peter's disgust was genuine, and it was clear in his voice. "She would've taken that one over the fence if they didn't have to use golf ball centers. Damn war."

"The baseballs have golf balls in them?" Jo asked. Roz was also looking at Peter for an explanation.

"Yeah, sort of. Before the war, they had centers of cork and rubber, see. Now, 'cause for some reason cork and rubber are needed for the war, the balls have some center that is the same as the center in golf balls. It's made the balls dead. Did you see how it just died out there? She shoulda had a homer." Peter looked down at Jo's scorecard, his tone quickly changed from disgust to curiosity. "Did you score that one?"

"Oh, yes," she said as she made the notation on the card. "F9." She turned the card slightly so Peter could see.

"You remember what I told you 'bout why the ball went to right field?"

Jo paused, then answered. "Because she's a lefty and lefties pull to right, while righties pull to left."

"Yup, you got it."

Peter had shown her how to fill in the scorecard and she had picked up right away. As she learned more about the intricacies of the game from Peter, she became more fascinated. What to her had seemed like a bunch of guys—girls, in this case—playing catch now took on a life for her. With each explanation, Jo could see the passion rise in Peter's eyes, just as it had that night at the bar. She would watch his eyes as he explained every last detail to her. But somehow, Jo thought she saw something different this time. She still saw Peter's passion for the game, but there was some added element, a fleeting glint in his eye when he looked at her. She just couldn't quite figure out what it was.

At one point, she lost herself in his eyes, trying to see into his soul, and completely tuned out what he was telling her. Realizing this, she quickly nodded and looked away, hoping her flushed cheeks were not too noticeable. She could tell the man everybody knew was not the real person, that there was some sort of wall he built at some point in his life to keep others at a distance. Roz had even mentioned to Jo while Peter was making a beer run that she had not seen this side of him before, and she had worked with Peter for over five years.

On the field, the pitcher wound up and delivered the ball. The crowd let out a collective *oo* as the ball came inside and the batter jerked her whole body back, falling on the ground to avoid being hit.

"That's the high heat, there," Peter said, nudging Jo's arm with his.

"High heat?" she asked.

"Yeah, high heat. You know, the heater…high and inside."

Jo looked at Peter blankly.

"The pitch. It was high, out of the strike zone, see, right under her chin. And the heat, that's the fast ball. Ya' throw the high heat inside whenever ya' feel like the batter is crowdin' the plate."

Peter went on to explain the various pitches—heater, curve, slider, knuckleball—and locations. He told Jo when you'd throw inside and high, and when you'd throw outside and low. He explained that sometimes a batter moves close to the plate, trying to force the pitcher to throw the ball where he—or she—could best hit it. And, he said, that's maybe when you just have to come inside with the high heat to knock them down and make them take notice of you, make them respect what you're bringing to the plate.

After the third out in the top of the seventh inning, the crowd all stood and joined in a singing of Take Me Out to the Ballgame. Roz took the opportunity to head to the concessions stand. As the crowd settled back down into their seats, Roz returned with another round of beer.

"See, this is the secret to baseball," Peter said, leaning in toward Jo. "The seventh inning stretch."

"Oh, how is that?" Jo asked, her voice dripping with skepticism.

"It's the point where things start getting interesting, 'cept for those games that're over almost before they began."

"So the first six innings mean nothing?" Jo said, her voice carrying a certain aloofness masking her puzzlement.

"No, no, they mean something. It's just after the seventh inning stretch, everything gets serious. The game is about two-thirds the way over. The number of at-bats is dwindling and every move, every play takes on more importance. You can't waste a move after the seventh inning stretch."

"I guess that makes sense," Jo contemplated Peter's explanation.

"Everything is that way. Life, for example. About two-thirds the way through it, things usually start loosening up and getting interesting. That midlife crisis thing, that's life's seventh inning stretch."

"Hm…okay. I guess I can see that," Jo nodded agreement to Peter's take on things.

"Yeah, see, all the stuff you do before that means something, but it is really sort of the groundwork for the good stuff to come later. Everything is that way. Relationships, even."

"How so?" Jo's voice rang with inquisitiveness.

"See, if there's this girl you like, you go through all that initial stuff, you see if you like her, and you have fun doing it. Hopefully, that is. But it comes down to the seventh inning stretch of dating. That's the point where you both know something is happening, something good, something that will last. From then on, the relationship is more interesting because you've gotten all that part out of the way where you're trying not to scare the other person off. After the relationship's seventh inning stretch, you can be yourself because you know what you have."

"Hm, okay." Jo rolled her eyes a bit so Peter wouldn't know she was buying into his philosophy.

"Peter," Roz chimed in. "Have another beer."

The two women laughed, leaning into each other's shoulder. Peter smiled, shook his head, muttered something about women under his breath, and took the beer Roz offered him.

The Ration Card

As the game headed into the late innings, the sun started casting long shadows on the infield. Jo realized just how much fun she'd had that day. For the first time in weeks—the first time since she and Roz had gone to Tanner's—she'd had a day filled with nonstop enjoyment. From laughing with Roz to watching Peter's eyes as he told his baseball stories, she was very content and at peace. Roz got up and headed to the concessions stand for more beer. Peter held up a dollar as she walked by, telling her the round was on him.

"So, how come you've never asked me?" Jo asked Peter after Roz had walked away. Her voice had that girlish, inquisitive tone, just three steps to the left of flirtatious.

"Ask you what?" Peter knew exactly the reference Jo was making.

"How I grew up. You *do* know, don't you? It's pretty much the first thing people say about me behind my back when they get to know me."

"Yeah...I know." Embarrassment at playing dumb resonated in his voice. "And yeah, it is."

"It's not a big deal, least not what people make it out to be. It's part of me, who I am. Not something I can forget."

"Everybody's got secrets, or perhaps things they don't want to talk about. Figured you're no different. If you wanted to tell me, you would."

Peter had two fingers stuck in the bag of peanuts he was holding, fishing around for the right one. His head down, he stared at the bag as he shook it and dug around in it. Jo had held a fixed gaze on Peter's face since she'd asked the question, but he had not stopped looking down at the peanuts. She suddenly realized it was not embarrassment he was feeling, but guilt over concealing his own secrets.

"Pete?"

She only called him Pete, never Peter. Nobody called him that. With everybody else, it was always Peter. It felt good to him that she called him Pete.

"Yeah."

"Look at me." She reached over and, with one finger softly placed under his chin, raised his head until their eyes met. "Really, it's not a big deal. Don't be embarrassed you never brought it up."

"Yeah, no, I know. Just some things people keep quiet about. Figured this was yours."

Jo smiled and then looked to the action on the field. She reached down, picked up her bottle of beer, and took a swig before continuing.

"People think I have this stain, a tarnish, because of my mother. Truth is, I never knew her…ever. Don't know much about her, really, just that she was young—fourteen or fifteen—and got pregnant. Some say she went out drinking with boys and it happened, some say she was just *one of those girls*. 'Course, they don't say it *to* me, but I hear. No matter, either way, I came along and she gave me up."

Jo looked back at Peter. Her eyes darted back and forth, from one of Peter's eyes to the other. There was something there, just behind the surface of those eyes. She couldn't quite put her finger on it, but it was something. She *thought* she had seen it earlier, but convinced herself otherwise. Now, however, she *knew* she saw something. It was a bit like the passion that rose in his eyes as he talked about baseball, but somehow different. She just couldn't quite bring it into focus.

"That's gotta be rough, not growing up with parents." Peter showed genuine empathy.

"Can't miss something you never had." The slight bitterness in her tone surprised Jo. "No, the bad part was just how people treat you. I don't think most people even realize it, but as soon as they find out you grew up in an orphanage, they just look at you different."

"I've tried not to."

Peter wondered if that's what the whole question was about, pointing out that he looked at her differently from how he looked at other women. He didn't think he did, but if indeed it was true,

it was not because of her childhood as a ward of the state. When he looked at her, she stirred something in him.

"I know…and you don't," Jo smiled reassuringly.

Peter smiled, then stared down at the peanuts in his hand, not sure exactly what she meant. "Good." He cracked open a peanut and tossed it in his mouth. "I'd feel bad if I was like all those others."

"Ha! You like *any* other? Not likely."

Jo laughed, and the mood lightened. Peter responded by throwing a peanut at her. She promptly threw it back at him.

"Anyway…" Her voice held a tone of temptation, of revelation. There was the pause of something trying to burst out from inside her, yet being held back.

"Jo, you don't have to tell me anything."

"No, I want to. I can talk to you. Most people I can't…about this, I mean. Not Al. Not even Roz." Jo was momentarily distracted by how she placed Roz higher than Al. "Don't get me wrong, the Troyers never treated me as tarnished or broken because I grew up in an orphanage. In fact, they were the first I can remember who *didn't* treat me that way. I think that's why I got close to Al. He treated me like just one more person. I care about him a lot for that."

Jo's choice of words was not lost on Peter. She could have said she *loved* Al for that, but she didn't. Then again, maybe he was reading too much into it. He knew something was stirring inside him, but he also knew she was married. Married to a man off fighting a war. And she was much younger than he. He had to be, once again, just misreading a woman's friendship, figuring there was no way she would be interested in him in that way.

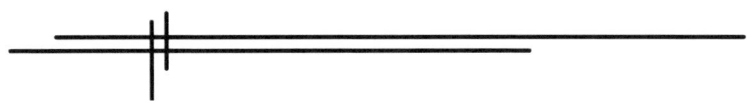

After the last out in the ninth inning, the crowd started filtering out of the stadium. Jo chatted with Roz and Peter as they flowed through the crowd. Peter was walking behind the women, and Jo could feel his hand gently touch her back, guiding her through the crowd. Each time he did so, a small pang hit her stomach. She wasn't sure what was happening. She glanced down to see if he was doing the same to Roz; he was, being a gentleman. Every once in a while, the crowd would unexpectedly slow and the momentum forced Peter to bump into Jo. Somehow, even though several people were pressed against her, Jo only felt Peter. It didn't feel strange to her, which in and of itself made her feel strange. Once outside the stadium, the three stopped and chatted for a bit.

"Stay here," Roz said to Jo. "I'll go get the car," and she turned and walked away.

"I'm over here under that shade tree," Peter pointed to his truck in the corner of the lot.

"Roz," Jo yelled and pointed. "Pick me up at Pete's truck."

Roz wave an acknowledgement and continued on to the parking lot. Jo and Peter continued walking rather slowly toward his truck. When they got closer, Jo saw a dog pop its head up from the bed and stick its nose over the side.

"Oh, you have a dog," she said and then trotted the rest of the way to the truck. Peter was just a few steps behind her.

"This is Barney, Barney the bloodhound."

Peter held his hand up to the dog and leaned against the truck. The dog sniffed Peter's hand, up his arm, and to his face. Then, he began licking Peter's face furiously. Jo laughed and the dog suddenly stopped. He looked in the direction of Jo and began feverously sniffing the air. Peter dropped the tailgate and Barney jumped to the ground, turned to his right and bumped his head into the truck. Peter gently moved his head back the other way.

"This way, buddy." The dog quickly turned and pressed his nose against Jo's leg. "Barney's mostly blind. He kind of bumps into things a lot. Can't barely see a thing."

Jo reached out her hand. The dog sniffed two or three times, then took two big, deep sniffs.

"He's trying to remember you," Peter said.

"Oh, that's so sad he can't see."

"Naw, he's got a good life. Lays around mostly, waiting for me to feed him."

"Ohhh." She kneeled so the dog could lick her face. "He's such a lover!"

The dog was wiggling as he sniffed Jo, then turned to Peter and sniffed to make sure he was still there before sniffing his way toward the grass next to the truck, tail wagging the entire time.

"See, he gets around alright, mostly, but I do have to keep an eye on him. He can manage in the house because he has everything memorized. He still gets around there okay, and I take him wherever I can."

"How come he can't see?"

"Partly age, partly because of a fight he had with a 'possum couple years ago."

"You're so sweet, Pete, taking care of him."

"Yeah, he's a good dog. He's my best bud. He can't do much by himself outside the house. Lot of people tell me I need to put him down, but I just can't do that. How're you supposed to put down your best friend? I'll do whatever to make him comfortable. 'Sides, he keeps me company."

Jo was startled by this side of Peter, seeing through the veil of deprecation of Peter's last quip. She wasn't sure exactly why, but it surprised her that he had such a soft side. From the time they had first met at the bar, she had known Peter as nothing more than a happy-go-lucky kind of guy. He never talked about anything other than what was happening right then at that moment, and he never seemed to be in anything but a happy mood.

Barney had worked his way back to Jo, who squatted to pet him. Jo looked at Peter as she pressed Barney's face to hers. This time, she knew exactly what she was seeing in Peter's eyes, the welling of tears. The passion he had showed for baseball had impressed Jo, but now she was seeing a truly caring man. She wondered what it would take to get inside his thick armor, but was certain that anyone who did get inside would find a wonderful heart. She kneeled there scratching the dog and looking into Peter's eyes.

"What?" Peter was surprised by Jo's look.

"Nothing." She turned and looked face-to-face with Barney. "You surprise me." She looked back to Peter. "You're not the man people make you out to be…that you make yourself out to be," she said in a caring voice.

"Hey, don't start spreading stuff around." Peter waved his hands at Jo in a hush-hush motion. "Don't want people to start getting all mushy on me."

Jo looked into his eyes, smiled, and nodded as she stood up. "Don't worry, nobody'd believe me even if I did tell them."

The sound of a car pulling up behind them broke the mood. Roz wheeled the car next to Peter's truck. Leaning across the seat, she yelled through the passenger's window.

"You two done yet?"

"Done what?" Jo asked with marked curiosity.

"Uh-huh…c'mon, get in."

"You'd better go before she beats me up," Peter laughed.

Jo got in the car, and Peter shut the door behind her. Jo looked up at him for a second, smiled, then looked at Roz and laughed. It seemed like there was a whole conversation going on between Peter and Roz that she couldn't hear. Peter shook his head and tapped on the car roof.

"Go on, get." Then, he looked at Jo and said, "I had a pretty good time watching *girls* baseball. Maybe again sometime."

"Yeah, I had fun, too." Roz began to pull away, then Jo exclaimed, "Wait!"

Jo leaned out of the car window, and Roz pumped the brakes, sending Jo into the window frame with a jolt. Jo was waving at Peter.

"Here," Jo said, extending her hand. In it was the scorecard she had filled out. "Something to remember me by."

"You sure you don't want it? It's your first."

"No, I want you to have it. You're the one with the passion for the game."

"What? No. I haven't played for fifteen years. That fizzled out long ago."

"Yeah, you can say that, but I see it in your eyes." She now wore the devilish smile Peter claimed as his own. "Thanks for teaching me baseball. I had a wonderful time. Maybe see you Monday?"

Peter took the card and slid it into his shirt pocket. "Thanks. I'll be sure to keep the dog away from it."

Jo sat back down on the car seat, still laughing, and leaned into Roz's shoulder. Roz gave Jo a slight glare, then shook her head. She pushed Jo back to her side of the car, waved to Peter, and nosed the car into the traffic leaving the ballpark.

"Scratch Barney's ears for me," Jo yelled back at Peter, her head sticking out of the window.

Peter patted the score card in his pocket and waved as the car pulled away. He took the card from his pocket, whisked the dust from it, and looked at the marks Jo had made. She had followed his instructions to a tee. All of the boxes were filled in correctly and completely.

Peter leaned against the truck and watched the car drive away, just as he had watched Jo and Roz drive off from the bar weeks early. Barney was in the bed of the truck slurping from a bucket of water, then he leaned over the bed and rested his head on Peter's shoulder. It was almost as if he knew Peter was watching Jo and Roz driving away. Peter reached up and scratched the dog's free ear. Barney then commenced licking Peter's ear. After six licks, Peter said, "I know, boy, I know," climbed in the truck, and drove home.

Eric K. Augspurger

The Blooming Grove Review

VOL. XXXIV—N° 237   Wednesday, August 25, 1943   Four Cents

TERRAIN MORE FOE THAN JAPANESE
Returning Officers Tell of Situation

HONOLULU, H.I.—Veterans of the jungle war in the South Pacific, several returning officers talked Thursday of the situation there. The officers faced the enemy on Guadalcanal and New Georgia. Colonel Douglas H. Gillette of Texas said, "Terrain is really our main difficulties in the Solomons." Gillette had spent nearly nine months on New Georgia and Guadalcanal. The officers also reported much of the fanaticism attributed to the Nipponese warrior is a myth. Speaking to the spirit of the enemy, Major Harry A. Dosch of Maryland said, "The Japanese don't want to die for their emperor. They are as scared as anyone." Major Robert W. Kenny of Washington disputed reports that the Japanese fight to the last bullet. "I saw one...with his toe in the trigger guard and a bullet hole through his head. He had committed suicide with thirty or forty rounds of ammunition left. That's not saving the last bullet for yourself. That's enough ammunition for a day or more if you aim carefully." Lieutenant Colonel George G. Freer of Ohio related a story of fifteen minutes in Japanese-controlled Bairoko harbor. "The coxswain was so excited he got in the wrong harbor. It was pretty dark, so keeping quiet we were able to get out."

OCCUPATION DETERMINES DEFERMENT
Family Status No Longer Basis for Draft Deferment

WASHINGTON, D.C.—New regulations issued just two weeks ago by the War Manpower Commission (WMC) have shifted the focus of draft deferment from a man's family status to his occupation. Starting on October 1, the question becomes one of whether a man aged eighteen to thirty-eight can better serve his country in the armed forces or in war production. According to WMC chairman Paul V. McNutt, the goal is to "hold essential workers on war-useful jobs, to assure transfer of workers to jobs aiding the war effort, and to supply men needed for the armed forces without cutting war production." Lawrence A. Appley, executive director of the WMC, also stated he hoped the new regulations would "...make an outright labor draft unnecessary."

SHIFT OF 2,600,000 WORKERS NEEDED
WMC Head Says By July 1

WASHINGTON, D.C.—War Manpower Commission (WMC) chairman Paul V. McNutt said on Monday that 2,600,000 workers will need to make the shift from non-essential jobs to "war-useful" jobs by July 1 of next year. Most of that number, 2,100,000, must make the shift by the beginning of the new year. Workers are urged to consult their local United States Employment Services offices if they are in doubt of the war usefulness of their current jobs. Citing the military's plan to increase by two million from July previous to July next, McNutt stated, "It is easy to see why such a large-scale transfer must take place...These men and women will be drawn from war-useful jobs as well as from other occupations." McNutt emphasized workers should only shift from one war-useful job to another if it results in a better use of their talents. He went on to insist this is a voluntary manpower program despite indirect pressure put on workers to serve in war-useful jobs. When asked if a labor draft would be requested when Congress returns on September 14, McNutt said, "Let's wait till they get back."

N⁰ 14

The air was thick and heavy; the sun beat down bright and hot. Jo leaned back against the trunk of an especially large maple tree that stood in a grassy area between the plant building and the river. Many of the employees took their lunches outside in good weather or, in the case of the summer heat, to get out of the plant. She tore a bite off of her sandwich with her fingers and poked it into her mouth.

Jo looked toward the plant and saw Peter step outside from the break room and look around. Shielding his eyes from the late-August sun, he scanned back and forth until he saw Jo. She smiled as she tore another bite from her sandwich and slowly chewed it, keeping her gaze on Peter as he walked toward her. It made her happy that Peter sought her out to spend time. He could eat lunch with any number of people at the plant—men or women—but it was her with whom he chose to spend his lunch time.

Truth be told, she had really begun to expect him to be around. He made her feel wanted in a way Al never did. He just made her *feel* like Al never did. Whenever she realized she was thinking that way, guilt set in, like somehow she was betraying

Al, but she reminded herself it was only spending time with Peter, nothing else. She always decided she couldn't change the fact that she had made some sort of connection with Peter.

"Man, I'm beat an' it's only noon," Peter said as he approached Jo. "No Roz today?"

She nodded her head and pointed back to the plant, meaning Roz was working through lunch. Peter let out a sigh as he backed into the tree and slid down its trunk to sit next to Jo. His face and arms were covered in black foundry grime, and his musk was especially strong. A dark vee of sweat stained the chest and back of his shirt, under his arms were dark circles, and his hair was matted in thick, wet strands. He pulled a red handkerchief from his pocket and wiped his neck and forehead, but the salty beads immediately popped again and ran down the sides of his face. Jo tore off another bite of her sandwich and offered it to Peter.

"Naw, thanks. I got leftover meatloaf from the diner in here in a sandwich." He tapped his lunchbox before opening it and removing the sandwich. Jo could smell the onions as he unwrapped the sandwich and sunk his teeth into a corner.

"How old're you, Pete?"

He stopped mid-bite and looked at Jo through the tops of his eyes. Finishing the bite, he shifted the food to his cheek, like a chipmunk, and replied.

"Didn't your momma tell you about polite questions?"

"She did, well, the house mother did. Yeah…how old're you?"

"Forty-one. Born in '02. Why?"

He was a bit older than she had guessed. Not that it mattered, it just surprised her a bit. The years of hard manual labor had not torn him down as it does so many men. In fact, it looked to Jo like Peter's body had taken the labor and used it to sculpt his figure.

"Just wondering why you're not in the war." Jo stared at her sandwich as she tore off another bite.

"War worker. And four F anyway…medically unfit. Shredded my ankle playing ball. Besides, they don't want old guys like me. Least not yet. There's a whole bunch of eighteen-year olds who'd—"

His voice didn't trail off, it just stopped. It was as if somebody had instantaneously shut off the air flowing through his throat. He didn't breath, he didn't move, he just froze. After what seemed to him like eternity, Peter snapped his head toward Jo.

"Jo, I am *so* sorry. I really—"

"Don't." Jo stopped him and shook her head just briefly. "It's okay. It's easy to forget. Most people do, caught up in their everyday life. I even forget sometimes that Al is in the South Pacific. I feel bad when I do, but that's the way it is."

"Still, I should have thought before I spoke."

"Why should we break all that tradition?"

She smiled at him, that infectious smile she could flash at anybody. But, when she aimed it toward Peter, he seemed to see something just below the surface, something he thought only he could see, even if he hadn't figured out *what* he was seeing. Nonetheless, he was glad she lightened the moment and gave him an out for his foot-in-mouth moment.

"You're right. I've gotten along so far without thinking. Why ruin a good plan that's working." Peter smiled back. They looked at each other for a long two seconds, smiling, basking in a warmth that each thought only he or she felt.

"Was your dad in the Great War?" Jo asked, turning the conversation back to her original point.

"Oh, Christ, no. *He's* the old man in the family. He was fifty when I was born. Ninety-one now. Doesn't get around like he used to, but he still manages. Mom's seventy-three, so they get by good enough. Why all these war questions?"

"I don't know, I've been thinking a lot lately…'bout things…'bout Al." She turned to Peter. "We were *so* young when we got married. It's only been a year, but it seems like so long

ago, and that I'm so much older now. Sometimes I wonder if we met today if we'd just be strangers." She turned away from Peter and looked down at her sandwich. "Everybody said don't do it, don't become a war bride—the radio, Reverend Turner, all the ladies' magazines. They all said to wait, that your man may come back injured or just different, *if* he comes back. That you'll spend all your time worrying. I do worry about him, but somehow it seems different than I think it should, almost like...I don't...I'm just talking crazy here."

She shook her head, tore another piece from her sandwich, and placed it in her mouth. The sharp bite of mustard pinched her tongue as she pondered what she hadn't said.

"Jo, I've never really told anybody this before, but I had a brother."

She snapped her head up, stopped chewing, and looked at Peter. He had never said anything that would have led her to believe he had any siblings. Roz hadn't either, nor anybody else at the plant.

"Some people know, those who go back some time here, but most don't really know nuthin' 'bout me," Peter continued. "Most think I'm just this goof who goes chasing all the skirts. Well, I guess that's not all wrong, but honestly, a lot of that is just an act."

Jo finished chewing and swallowed hard. There was a look on her face that Peter recognized right away. Somehow, a softness had set over her features. More than just her normal aesthetically pleasing lines and curves, it was one of genuine interest, of caring to hear what he had to say. It was as if she was saying to him, *I am here, not because I want to know, but because I want you to know I am here*. He felt as if her dark brown eyes were gently caressing his face, not just scanning it in the normal course of a conversation.

"Had?" Jo's voice raised in a little squeak, even though she had tried to be nonchalant.

"Yeah, twin brother. We were crazy close. You might expect, being twins and all. When the war broke out in Europe in '14, that's all he talked about. He just wanted to go *over there*. Me, I

figured it was mostly the same thing again, the same way they'd been fighting for centuries, and none of my business. But he insisted it was the right thing to do."

"Al talked that way after Pearl Harbor. It was all he thought about…signing up so he could go fight. I swear, he thought about that more than he thought about anything, even me. Certainly thought more about that than school."

"It's like a fever, I think," Peter continued. "Anyway, one night in the summer of '17, he just never came home…he'd run off and joined the marines."

"Al joined the marines." Jo's voice was soft and she dropped her head to her chest. The last of the sandwich lay on her lap.

"Lied 'bout his age," Peter continued. "Long story short, he never came back. Some place called Belleau Wood. That was in '18."

Jo looked up at Peter. He was staring at some nonexistent spot in the sky. She could feel a pain inside him, the kind of pain a man hides deep down. When it rises in a man, he either withdraws or seeks a heart. Which was it with Peter?

When he continued, Jo knew he wasn't withdrawing.

"I guess my point is, things change. When he left, I worried about him, of course, but it was just different. I never really got close to anybody after that." He turned to face Jo. "It's okay if it's different. It's nothing wrong."

She looked deep into his eyes and nodded. Their eyes locked in an embrace for several seconds. Jo saw that fleeting element—thought? emotion?—just below the surface. *Damn it, what is that?* She had seen it in Peter many times before. Each time, it fluttered away before she could get it into focus. She strained hard to see it—emotion?—and then it would move. Thought? And it moved again, finally fluttering away as it always had. *Is it there or am I imagining it?* She was struck by how important this had become to her. *It is there, it can't be just me.*

Behind them, the shift whistle blew to indicate the lunch hour was over. Peter stood up and dusted off the seat of his pants. He offered his hand to help Jo up; she accepted. He pulled her to her feet, and she could feel the grit on his hands rubbing her skin as she moved. His skin was hot and moist, and he had to squeeze tightly to keep her hand from sliding out of his grasp. She looked at his face as she allowed her hand to linger in his, trying to coax that fleeting sense out, but it had definitely gone back to its hiding place.

It took a concerted effort on Peter's part to keep the emotion hidden. She was a married woman and half his age. He told himself, once again, he was misreading a woman's friendship for the something more that he wanted. Something he was fairly certain he would never find. He was sure he was just one of those guys destined to be the friend, and he pulled his hand from Jo's.

"Anyway, I finally decided it was selfish on his part, running off like that. 'Course, I felt bad about that after I found out he'd been killed, but he made his choices. C'mon, let's get back at it." And the shell had returned to surround Peter.

Jo smiled at him, and the two walked out from under the shade tree and back to the plant. She realized Peter had just given a piece of himself to her, before the wall went back up. In a way, she felt he had taken a part of her in return. That thought made her heart jump a beat and then another before settling back into its normal rhythm. For half a moment, she pondered why that had happened.

"And that stuff 'bout my brother…don't tell nobody. Thems that know, know, thems that don't got no business knowin'."

"I know."

She bumped her shoulder into his as they walked and smiled at him. She let the double meaning of her statement hang in the air, waiting for Peter to grab it. He looked at her, their eyes fixed for a long second. Then he smiled, chuckled, and sarcastically shook his head.

"C'mon, you. Get me in trouble making me late for my shift." Suddenly, Peter started giggling and took off in a slow run to the building. He wasn't forty-one any more, he was nineteen...nineteen with a few snaps and pops and a couple of squeaky joints.

"Hey! Oh!" and Jo took off after him.

They arrived at the plant door, grabbing the handle at the same time. Laughing, Jo pulled the door open and squeezed past Peter to be the first inside, wiggling her body between him and the doorframe. Inside, they went their separate ways, but the smiles remained as each walked to their station.

Off and on throughout the day, Roz would catch Jo smiling for no apparent reason. She'd simply roll her eyes and waggle a scolding finger at Jo, as if to say, *You gettin' ideas in that head.* Roz already knew what Peter and Jo had yet to find out themselves. She liked both Peter and Jo and could see the good when they were together. She also knew the barriers that were in place. Roz wouldn't push, wouldn't meddle. She just hoped in the end, no matter what the end was, that Peter and Jo would be around each other somehow. She could clearly see it was a good thing for both of them.

The Blooming Grove Review

VOL. XXXIV—N° 240　　Saturday, August 28, 1943　　Four Cents

MRS. FDR SURPRISE VISIT
New Zealanders Welcome First Lady

AUCKLAND, New Zealand—First Lady Eleanor Roosevelt made a surprise visit yesterday to army hospitals and camps in New Zealand. Her welcoming committee consisted of Governor General Air Marshall Sir Cyril Newall, Prime Minister Peter Fraiser, Minister to Washington Walter Nash, and others. Speaking to the gathered officials, she said, "Long ago you were kind enough to ask me to see the work the women in New Zealand are doing…Last autumn, I saw the work of the British women and am pleased now to see your accomplishments." She went on to say that she would take those experiences home to the United States and share them with the women workers there. This is Mrs. Roosevelt's first trip outside of continental North America since her visit last November to England, where she spent nearly a month touring British war industries and military camps. It was only twelve days ago that she and the president were hosting British Prime Minister Winston Churchill and his daughter Mary at their Hyde Park home in New York. The method of transport for Mrs. Roosevelt was not disclosed, and recently her specific location has been officially blacked out.

V-MAIL WILL HELP WIN THE WAR
Use of Victory Mail Urged to Free Cargo Space

WASHINGTON, D.C.—To carry one hundred and fifty thousand one-page letters overseas, it requires thirty-seven mail sacks weighing nearly twenty-six hundred pounds. The solution is V-mail, or Victory mail. Writing a loved one a letter on theses specially formatted, combination letter sheet and envelope—available at all post offices—allows the letter to be microfilmed for shipment overseas. Those same one hundred and fifty thousand one-page letters in V-mail require only a single mail sack that weighs forty-five pounds, a savings of ninety-eight per cent. The government states that if all overseas correspondence were to be sent by V-mail, twenty-five Liberty ships would be freed for carrying war matériel. Despite this, most people are not using V-mail; the government urges you to do so.

BLACK MARKET COMBAT GEARS UP
Home-front Army of Millions Signs Pledges

WASHINGTON, D.C.—The Office of Price Administration (OPA) announced last Tuesday that a home-front army of over one million has been enlisted to fight black markets in a community-by-community campaign across the nation. Currently active in twenty-five states, volunteer civic committees are working with housewives and merchants to sign pledges against black markets. In addition to obtaining pledges, the home-front army seeks to educate housewives to pay no more than top legal prices and to accept rationed goods only after surrendering the appropriate ration stamps. Many merchants are also signing a similar pledge not to charge more than top legal prices or to sell rationed goods without collecting ration stamps. Those who sign pledges receive red, white, and blue window stickers to display in recognition of signing. The nation-wide drive by the home-front army started August 2 in Columbus, Georgia. By mid-September of this year, the reach is expected to be into nearly every part of the country.

№ 15

Jo and Pearl walked down the sidewalk in the downtown area. While Blooming Grove had gotten bigger over the years, it had not outgrown its sense of small-town community. The downtown stores were packed in, one wall forming the side of the store next door. Large plate glass windows in the front allowed shopkeepers to showcase their best wares.

Some stores had ornate stonework on the front, often with a small canopy over the doorway. Other storefronts were adorned with rich, dark wood, the doorframes and stoops slowly carved over the years by hundreds of hands and feet rubbing them as people passed through. Every shop had a bell that rang on opening the door to announce a customer, and each store had its own unique aroma. The grocery store smelled of spices and fresh fruit, while the hardware store was rich with the smell of wood and lubricating oil.

Abe's grocery was located on one corner of the square. The entrance was angled so it was open to two streets, yet faced neither squarely. Over the door hung a small sign that simply stated *Abe's*. Everybody in town knew that was the grocery store.

The Ration Card

It had been the grocery store for decades before the Abes took it over, and they had been running it for several years.

Above the sign hung a large American flag. In the windows were placards urging the purchase of war bonds and posters exhorting victory and quips about the work needed to accomplish that. Patriotism was rampant across America, but some had to voice it more overtly than others.

"Hi, Mr. Abe," Jo said.

The bell clanged twice as the door swung closed behind her and Pearl. The man behind the counter was very short in stature by American standards. His black hair was graying, giving a dusty look to his Asian features. To Jo, Mr. Abe looked to be about sixty, so she figured he must have been in his late twenties or maybe even his early thirties when Roz was born.

"Hello. You pronounced my name correctly," Mr. Abe said.

There was much surprise in his voice. Where Roz had a city accent—at times heavy—picked up when the family lived in Chicago, Mr. Abe had a slight Japanese accent, a remnant of growing up with parents who had moved from Japan to America. Mr. Abe was *Nisei*—a second-generation Japanese-American, born in America. His accent was just below the surface, but there nonetheless. He was well-spoken; he certainly did not speak in pidgin.

"Yeah, I work with Roz at the plant. I'm Jo."

She extended her hand. Mr. Abe shook it and bowed ever so slightly, almost unnoticeably. Jo wasn't sure if that was due to the Japanese tradition or if it was simply because he was a nice man, or both. She couldn't have known that he had been trying very hard to keep any signs of his heritage suppressed since the Pearl Harbor attack, at least in public view, or that he found some traits were harder than others to hide. After dipping his head slightly, he nervously glanced around and then at Jo, but there was no one else to see what he had done, and neither Jo nor Pearl made any acknowledgement of the action.

"So, you work with my Rosalind," there was almost a sigh of relief behind his words. "I'm sure she has mentioned you. Welcome to my store. What may I help you with today?"

"We need a couple of things," Pearl said, handing Mr. Abe a list.

"Certainly, I'll be right back."

Mr. Abe disappeared into the back room for a moment before reappearing with a wooden box. He then set about checking items on the Pearl's list, collecting the can or box from the shelf, and carefully placing it in the wooden box. Jo and Pearl fidgeted around the front of the store, passing the time picking over the fruit in the bins near the front window and examining various small items for sale.

The Abes used to have small Japanese figurines and other trinkets for sale, but those items had been quickly stashed away on December 7th two years ago. In their place were small American flags on wooden dowels, along with a handwritten sign saying *Show your support for our boys, buy a flag!* Next to the flag display was a placard from the postal service encouraging women and families to send a V-mail letter to a husband or son overseas.

As they waited for Mr. Abe to collect their groceries, the two women chatted, pointing out an item here or there they felt needed some discussion. Pearl started looking at the chalkboard behind the counter indicating the points needed for various items. She took out her ration book and thumbed through it.

"Oh, I brought mine, too," Jo said, pulling her ration book from her handbag and giving it to Pearl.

"Good, I think I am getting very low on points this month."

Mr. Abe was still collecting the items on the list. He set the wooden box on the counter, indicating he needed one more box for the last items. After retrieving a second box from the back room, he set about finishing gathering the items.

"So, Josephine, have you heard from my Alfred recently?" Pearl asked, her voice forcing an inquisitive façade of someone knowing the answer. She was desperate to hear any news coming from her son halfway across the world.

"Yeah. He's doing good, but I worry."

"It's natural to worry. He's fighting a war, after all."

"I know, but it seems like I can't help worrying a bit too much. Al's the best friend I've ever had, 'cept maybe Roz."

Mr. Abe had returned with the second box full of items. Jo mentioned Roz for his benefit, but her voice resonated with truth. Roz had become her best friend, but in a different way from the way Al was her friend. Roz was the close female companion Jo never had. There were some girls at the state home with whom she had developed friendships, but it had never been very close. Getting close to someone meant risking losing them when they were adopted, *if* they were adopted. Jo knew that Roz was here to stay; perhaps a subconscious acknowledgment of that fact had allowed her to become so close to Roz.

"Okay, ladies, here you go. Do you have your ration books?"

"Right here," Pearl said as she passed over the ration books.

Mr. Abe flipped through the books, tore out the appropriate coupons, and handed the books back.

"You're a little low on your sugar coupons. You might want to keep that in mind."

"You mean no pies this month?" Jo said with a smile. "Thanks, we'll keep an eye on that."

Pearl noted the joviality Jo showed. This extroverted side of Jo had emerged over the past several weeks. Slowly, the very reserved Josephine had begun to emerge from the chrysalis in which she had spent her orphanage years. The pinholes in the shell appeared with her starting to work at Thresher. In those first few weeks of work, Pearl had seen in Jo a subtle change; she stood a little straighter, her shoulders were no longer drooping like the branches of a willow tree, and she spent more time watching people's eyes as she talked.

As the weeks passed, Pearl could see other physical changes. Jo's body grew stronger, her arms hard and shapely, her stomach taut, and her haunches firm, yet all very feminine, save her hands, which showed the calluses, scars, and wounds of daily battles with machinery and metal. Jo had always been an attractive girl, albeit one hidden behind a plain shell, but Pearl had seen Jo change into an exceptional beauty, one whom she was sure men would have been pounding down walls to be with were she not married.

It was the physical changes Pearl had noticed first, but recently—right about the time Jo had started being very friendly with Roz—other, more subtle changes began; subtle because these changes were in emotion. Jo had become not only a woman, but a woman of her own. She had developed an air of self-reliance, of boldly throwing a door open and stepping into a room with no idea of what awaited on the other side. Where *Josephine* had been reserved, pulled in on herself, *Jo* was now one to initiate interactions.

But it was more than that. Pearl could see something change in Jo's face; it at times held a slight glow. The glow came and went, sometimes being more readily apparent than other times, and it took Pearl a while to even realize its presence, but it was there. And then there was that sparkle in Jo's eyes, again not always there, but usually appearing at the same time the glow emerged.

Mr. Abe rang up the total. The two women pooled their money and paid for the groceries. They took the groceries from the boxes and stuffed them into the cotton bags they had draped over their arms. Mr. Abe helped them fill their bags. Then the two women thanked him and left the store. The smell of spices and fruit quickly faded behind them.

As Jo and Pearl walked through downtown toward the Troyers' car, they continued talking, but the conversation was more intermittent small talk instead of a continuous conversation. Then, at a lull in the talk, Jo abruptly stopped walking.

"Pearl?"

There was a hesitation in Jo's voice. Pearl sensed it, but also saw a look of trepidation on her face.

"I was talking to one of the men at the plant—this guy named Pete. Come to find out, he had a brother in the marines

who was killed in the first war, and it got me to really thinking...about Al, so far out there in the Pacific. I don't know why, but for the first time it really sank in...that Al could be killed."

"Josephine! Don't talk like that," Pearl scolded.

"I know, I hate thinking that. But, ever since then, I can't seem to get it out of my head. I just keep seeing Pete over and over, running that conversation through my head."

"Quite honestly, I think about it a lot, too. I just don't let on. I guess I feel it is one thing to think about it and another to talk about it. Plus, I'm not alone in this...you're not alone in this...there are thousands upon thousands of mothers and wives across the nation in the same situation. We shouldn't presume that our worrying is any more important than any of theirs."

"Pete told me how it hit him when his brother was killed. I just can't imagine that happening to Al and going through that. When we got married and he shipped out, I guess I thought of the war as something he was going to do, a temporary job almost, before he gets a permanent job and we start a family. Now, I understand the reality is Al may *never* come home."

"You can't start to think like that. It'll drive you crazy. You just have to pray for the best and realize that no matter what happens, you can only take care of yourself, not something you have no control over. Life usually has a way of deciding your direction for you."

"Yeah, I guess you're right. Focus on what will happen when he does come home, how we can then begin a family."

"And," Pearl abruptly shifted the topic, peering over the top of her glasses, "you shouldn't be spending time with other men. You're a married woman. What would Alfred think if he found out? What will everyone think?"

"Pearl, he's just a guy I work with. He's a friend, a coworker no different than Roz. And, I think he and Roz are kinda sweet on each other."

While she had thought that at first, she now knew it not to be true. She understood Peter and Roz were just good friends.

But telling Pearl otherwise was an easy way to deflect the conversation away from Jo's thoughts of Peter, thoughts that were both confusing and exciting.

"You may think that, but those men down there have foul minds to match their foul mouths. Those men have only one thing on their minds."

"Pearl, Pete is a lot older than me."

Jo paused and considered the situation. Yes, she knew he was many years older than her, but she never really thought of him that way. Deep inside he seemed much younger than the calendar would show, closer to Jo's own age. And Jo felt so much older herself than just a year ago. Even though Peter was in fact a few years older than she had originally guessed, she *still* had a hard time not seeing him as a peer. She chuckled inside as she recalled how when they first met she called him Mr. Messimer, and how he had been agitated by that. As the exciting and confusing of thoughts of Peter set in, Pearl's curt scolding pulled Jo back to the conversation.

"You watch yourself."

The Blooming Grove Review

VOL. XXXIV—N? 247 Saturday, September 4, 1943 Four Cents

RETRIBUTION AGAINST JAPANESE-AMERICANS
Hatred Outpaces Anti-German Feelings of Great War

WASHINGTON, D.C.—In April of this year, Elmer Davis, Director of the Office of War Information (OWI), tried to quell the fervor of calls for reprisals against Japanese-Americans. These demands came from members of Congress in response to the execution of some of the American flyers in the Doolittle raid of April last. Speaking on April 22 of this year from Corpus Christi, Texas, President Roosevelt announced the executions and declared the United States will hold "...personally and officially responsible for these diabolical crimes all of those officers of the Japanese Government who have taken part in them...". Many see the executions as a manifestation of a "...Japanese heritage of vengeance...". Will retaliation of like character indeed be seen in America?

RESTRICTIONS ON GARMENTS IN EFFECT
Conservative Groups Rail for Modesty

SPRINGFIELD, Ill.—The War Production Board (WPB) issued limitation order eighty-five (L-85) on March 8, 1942, effective August 17, 1942, to "conserve material for victory." This order freezes the silhouette of garments so no major changes can be made. Among restrictions, hems on skirts and dresses cannot exceed seventy-two inches from the collar and only one and three-fourths yards of fabric can be used in a garment. Some groups, such as the National Catholics Women's Union, urge modesty. Speaking from its annual meeting here last week, the Union asserts that "...costumes for sport and play are shamelessly brief." Instead of seeing the conservation as patriotic, the Union sees the "...moral breakdown of the people in an act of treason, not one of patriotism."

JAPANESE-AMERICANS ENDURE HATRED
Official Expresses Fear of Reprisals by Japanese

WASHINGTON, D.C.—The House Un-American Activities Committee (HUAC) was established in 1938 to investigate allegations of disloyalty and subversive actions in America. Earlier this year, HUAC, also known as the Dies Committee after its chairman Martin Dies, Jr., of Texas, released its so-called Yellow Report on the state of Japanese living in America. In July of this year, director of the War Relocation Authority Dillon S. Meyer criticized the report, expressing concern that it has "...stirred up a public hatred of Japanese...". He speculates if news of violence against those of Japanese decent in this country reaches Japan that Americans held there might receive "...further maltreatment...".

RAIDS COMING ON JAPANESE HOMELAND
Recent Raid Only 1,200 Miles From Tokyo

WASHINGTON, D.C.—American aircraft raided Marcus Island, a mere 1,200 miles from mainland Japan, in a signal of raids soon to be unleashed on Japan itself. The force consisted of one hundred and sixty aircraft from two carriers. The United States has an ever-increasing armada that will participate in a four-pronged attack this fall in Asia and the Pacific. Vice Admiral John S. McCain, deputy chief of naval operations for air, stated explicitly last night, "The attack on Marcus is only a token. Such attacks will increase in tempo, in power, and in furry...".

№ 16

Saturday morning, Jo waited for Roz to pick her up to go to the Maidens' game. This would be the last home game of the season. It had become a ritual for Jo and Roz to go to a game on those rare Saturdays they had off.

The plant had switched to running ten-hour days Monday through Friday and then a six- or eight-hour shift on Saturdays. Every three or four weeks, the company tried to give most, if not all, of the employees a full two-day weekend, but then there were other weekends when everybody had to work a full shift on Saturdays *and* a partial shift on Sundays, depending on the progress of the plant's big order.

Roz pulled into the parking lot at the ball field. She wedged the car between two others, and then she and Jo walked up to the entrance gate. After buying their tickets, they headed over to the concession stand to get a couple of beers.

"I got first round," Jo said. "You get next."

"Okay, I'll wait here."

The Ration Card

Jo got into line and waited patiently until it was her turn. She ordered two beers, paid the man behind the counter, and headed back to where Roz was waiting at the edge of the crowd. As she approached, Jo noticed Roz looked uncomfortable and then realized three men had her surrounded. As Jo got closer, she heard one of the men speaking.

"Look at *what* we have *here*." Anger reflected in his voice, and he stumbled on his words and swayed a bit.

The man was dressed in nice clothes, as were the other two. They all wore tan slacks, loafers, and button-down shirts, but he was the only one wearing a college sweater. Jo suspected the three men were either college students, came from money, or both.

"Looks like we got ourselves a little Jap here," the sweater-man continued.

Roz tried to turn away, but one of the other two men bumped into her to prevent it. Jo was struck by how the normally feisty and strong Roz seemed meek at this moment, quiet and trying to slink away. A couple of people in the crowd seemed to notice what was happening, but they just stood and watched without doing anything, one even munching on peanuts from a brown bag. Jo stepped into the middle of the three men surrounding Roz.

"Hey! What did you say?"

"I *said*, we got ourselves a little Jap here, missy. Do you have a problem?"

"Yeah, I got a problem!"

Jo was in his face yelling. The sweater-man was not big, none of the three were, but he was certainly bigger than Jo, and it wouldn't take much effort from any of the men to overpower both her and Roz. That wasn't stopping Jo. At the orphanage, she learned it was best to stay in the shadows, not to be seen, and to walk away from trouble, but seeing her friend shrinking away from the taunts made her heart pound and her ears burn. Jo quickly gave the beers to Roz, spun back around, and got in sweater-man's face again.

"Roz is my friend! You can't talk to her that way." She drew strength from deep inside her, strength Roz showed her she had.

"Listen, missy, we got all sorts of men over in the Pacific taking care of her kind for what they did. My brother was over there. He was killed a year ago...on the 'canal. Hell, might have been *her* brother who shot him."

Sweater-man raised his arm to point at Roz, but Jo grabbed it and pushed it down. He stopped just a second—his head flinched backward just briefly—before seizing Jo's arm by the wrist and pulling her close. Their faces were almost touching, so close she could feel the air rushing from his nose as he breathed. The thumping in Jo's chest felt as strong as one of the big stamping machines at the plant. A pain pierced her arm to the elbow as he wrenched her wrist. The sharp smell of grain alcohol irritated the inside of Jo's nose as he talked in a hoarse whisper.

"I have no use for Japs, and I have no use for you if you like Japs. I'll give you about two seconds to walk away from here before you end up the same way your damn Jap friend is going to end up."

Jo's heart was beating so hard and fast, she was sure not enough blood was getting to her head. Sounds were starting to echo, and everything around her began to blur. Her mind was racing, but she could not think. She wanted to snap her leg up and give sweater-man a stiff kick in the crotch. Then, as he was folded over grabbing his pride, she wanted to bring her knee up into his jaw. All of this was stampeding through her head so quickly that she couldn't get her muscles to move.

Then, Jo felt herself slowly falling away from sweater-man. It took a second, but she realized something was on her chest, forcing her backward. A muscular arm pressed against her breasts, but it wasn't sweater-man's. Her eyes flicked left and right to see if one of the other men was pulling her down. Instead, she saw Peter, pulling her backward with one arm and stepping between her and sweater-man.

Peter's eyes were locked on sweater-man's, but when either of the other two men moved, he froze for a second to assess the situation without breaking eye contact with sweater-man. When Jo was fully shielded by his body, Peter spoke, low and slow.

"It doesn't seem right that you're picking a fight with these two ladies."

"This has nothing to do with you."

Sweater-man's voice was softer and less belligerent. He fidgeted and looked away from Peter.

Something inside Jo changed in that moment. Peter was protecting her, as a person and a woman. In that single moment, she learned something about herself. She saw what she had always wanted and needed, but of which she never knew. Fear was no longer making her heart pound, but it was still pounding.

"That's where you're wrong, this has everything to do with me," Peter continued. "See, what kind of a man would I be if I let some drunk bastards like you and your boys here beat on a couple'a women?"

By this time, more of a crowd had gathered. Two men stepped out in front of the crowd. Jo recognized them as being from the foundry where Peter worked and who had been in the group that night at Tanner's when she first met Peter. That night...where, looking back, she could now see her life had taken a sharp turn. One of the foundry workers spoke, rolling up his sleeves as he did.

"Problem, chief?"

Peter still had not broken his gaze from sweater-man.

"No, I don't think we have a problem here...do we?"

The question was directed at sweater-man, who looked over at the two foundry workers. Then, he glanced at his two friends, who were both shifting back and forth, scratching their loafers in the dirt. The expectation of being in for a good beating hung on their faces. Sweater-man shook his head and took several steps back. Peter spoke louder, aiming his words not just at the three men, but also the small crowd that had gathered.

"Let's go watch some ball."

The three men disappeared into the crowd. Peter waved to his two crewmembers, who waved back and then melted into the crowd themselves. He put his arm around Jo, motioned Roz over, and put his arm around her, too. Peter's face was fixed in genuine concern for both women; Roz was still shaking from the experience. Peter held her tightly, almost holding her up so she wouldn't drop to the ground. The lighthearted exterior of Peter Messimer had disappeared; all Jo could see was the good and kind person held tightly inside. She smiled, then reached over and jokingly punched Roz in the arm.

"Hey, let's go watch some ball."

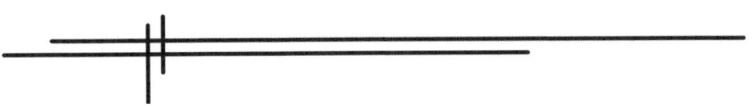

Sitting in the bleachers, Jo watched the players on the field, but her mind was not really on the game. While she was indeed looking at the field, she was not watching the action. She sat there, squirming around, starting to say something, then stopping, only to start and stop again. Finally, she spoke up.

"Those guys really burned me up! Treating you that way."

"Ya' gotta let it go," Roz said. "I be'n dealing with stuff like that my whole life, long before Pearl Harbor. Just gotten a lot worse since then."

"You mean, let them get away with it?"

"You just have to realize there are people like that out there," Peter added, "gonna act that way because somebody isn't like them. Doesn't make it okay, and you don't have to like it, but that's the reality of it. Boy, did I see it when I was playing ball down south. Just consider yourself lucky nothing came of it, and nobody got hurt."

"Jo," Roz spoke in a tone that sounded somewhat soothing to Jo, "he said he lost his brother on Guadalcanal. Don't excuse what he did, but if the tables were turned, I might not be able to act any different."

"Yeah, maybe. It just burns me up they were treating you that way. You know, Al uses…that word…in some of his letters."

"I remember when I found out my brother was killed," Peter

jumped in, steering the conversation away from the racial slur. "I was angry for a long time. At the drop of a hat, I'd try to pick a fight with anybody near me. No reason. I'd suppose it was because they looked at me the wrong way or said something I didn't like, but there never was any reason. Just 'cause I was angry. Finally, I realized I wasn't angry at everybody else, I was angry at my brother for running off to war and getting killed. Was a lot easier being around me after that."

"Yeah...I keep forgetting you lost your brother in war." A tinge of sorrow cracked in Jo's voice.

"It was a huge loss, and it forced me to change, in some ways I didn't realize I needed."

"For example?" Roz questioned.

"For example, we had always been around each other, never very far apart. Being twins and all, that was expected, I guess. Until he ran off to the war, that is. But after he was killed, I had to become independent. I didn't have a choice."

Huh, wonder if that's why I never seem to get very close to anybody? The revelation made Peter pause. He had never really thought about it before, maybe because he had never felt a need to get close to somebody, but he now realized that he had always *prevented* anybody from getting close. And then something else dawned on him; he now felt a need to be close to someone. But not just anyone, someone who was sitting next to him. He realized a weight pulling inside him, pulling him closer to Jo whether he liked it or not.

"I guess I get that independence thing. Even after Al shipped out, I was still tied to the Troyers. Don't get me wrong, I'm glad they're my family. They treat me very well. But when I started working at the plant...and when I met Roz...I started realizing a life of my own, not one tied to Al or his family."

"Part of that, Jo, is you just growin' up s'mo," Roz said.

"Maybe. I just don't feel as tied to Al now as I used to be. I mean, he's not actually here, so that's part of it, but there's more, too. I used to feel very dependent on him. Now, I feel free to do my own thing. Like I don't need him around to take care of me."

"Freedom is a nice thing. Look at Peter and me, neither of us been tied down. Don't get me wrong, I'm not knocking being married, I'm just glad I'm not married now."

"Yeah, I get that," Jo continued. "I do want kids at some point, but I like being able to take care of myself, having a job and earning my own money. When I *do* eventually have children, I hope I can keep working." She started laughing. "Maybe I'll make Al stay home and raise the kids while I work!"

"Yeah, see how well that goes over," Roz said with a snort.

"I mean, I do want a man who can protect me...stand up for me; that's important," Jo continued, as a brief flash of Peter protecting her earlier shot through her mind. "It's not that I don't care about Al, but somehow it's changed. I still feel very close to him, and God how I'm afraid that something is going to happen to him, but it seems like just that...closeness."

"You need to be close to the person you're with," Peter said.

He thought about how he wanted to be close to the woman he was with now. His heart ached for it. But he was certain Jo's interest was in his friendship. Still, he found himself lost in her, looking at every detail of her face as he talked to her—her blonde hair hanging down just covering the scar above her right eye, her eyes deep pools of dark color, her skin shimmering as the sun gently caressed her cheek the way he so longed to.

"It's all just so different now, so complicated," Jo said, bringing Peter out of his dream world. "Back when we were dating in school, it seemed so much simpler. Now, he's halfway across the world in the South Pacific. We're both worlds away from where we were then, and I don't mean that by way of geography. He's off fighting a war, and I'm punching a time clock in a factory."

Jo sat back and let her words settle in. This was the first time she had really verbalized some of the thoughts floating around in her head. She was glad Roz was there to listen, and Peter, too. One of her best friends may not be there for her, but Jo realized she now had two new best friends. Roz and Peter were there for her now when she needed best friends, and Al had run off to fight a war. Roz especially gave her a type of best

friendship she needed. Peter was always there when she needed him, it just seemed to Jo that she needed Peter in a way a bit differently than she needed Roz, even in a different way than she ever felt she needed Al. She thought it strange—and she had just realized this as she absorbed her own words—that recently when her thoughts were stressful, the first person to enter her mind was Peter; not Roz, not Al...Peter.

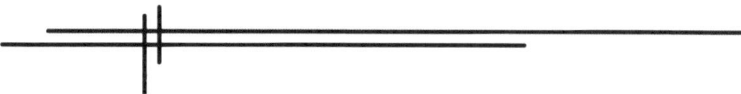

As the game entered the late innings, Jo could feel a silliness settling in over her. She knew part of it was the beers she had been drinking, but she knew a larger part was just because she was having a tremendously fun time. When the three of them were together, she always had fun. The connection she was making with Peter seemingly on a level slightly different from friendship—but she wasn't sure just how—only served to enhance whatever fun they were having. It was with this good mood that Jo laughed heartily at a joke Peter made at her expense.

She kept laughing, leaning into Roz's shoulder, waving her hand at Peter to stop. Roz shrugged Jo from her shoulder, pushing her back toward Peter. Jo let her forehead hit Peter's bicep, then slid her head up until her chin rested on his shoulder. To brace herself, she placed her hand on Peter's knee; the laughter stopped as she looked into his eyes and her face settled into a wide smile. Jo could see a burning ember in Peter's eyes, and his face looked so handsome with its rugged features. She felt like the embers were burning a heat into her soul.

Jo removed her hand from Peter's leg and pulled back from his shoulder. Still smiling, she sheepishly looked down at her feet. Then, looking up at the field, the smile not having faded, she leaned forward slightly and wrapped her hands around the edge of the wooden bleacher. Just at the same moment Peter put his hand on the bleacher in nearly the same spot. Their hands were so close—each could feel the heat from the other's hand—yet not touching. Both Jo and Peter looked straight forward, not wanting to make eye contact, and afraid to move for fear of destroying the fragile energy surging though the air between their hands. For a few minutes that seemed like an hour, they sat motionless. Jo's mind raced, trying to interpret the energy she felt from Peter; it was *something*, and she had to figure out what. She felt something stirring deep inside of her, which was exciting and frightful to her at the same time.

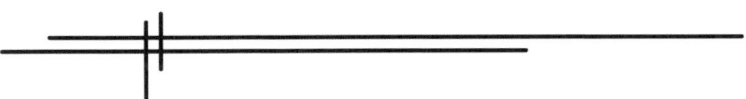

After the last out of the game—Maidens 3, Steamfitters 1—the crowd began to empty the park. Jo, Roz, and Peter joined the meandering mass of people funneling through the exit.

"So, I have to admit, this's been a lot of fun," Peter said. "I hadn't really thought too much about the game these past few years, until you got me going that one night in Tanner's."

His tone feigned a begrudging acceptance.

"Yeah, I never really paid much attention to sports before. But I'm sure glad Roz got me to start coming to these Maidens games. It *has* been a lot of fun this season. I can't believe the season is already almost over."

"Where would we be without her, huh?"

Roz reached around Jo and punched Peter in the arm. He recoiled in mock pain.

"Hey, I meant that as a compliment!"

"Uh-huh, sure you did."

"I tell you, Jo, that Roz, she don't know how to take a compliment."

"All right, you two, knock it off. I had fun today."

"Yeah," Peter scowled at Roz and she scowled back, both in mock anger. "Say, why don't the three of us head over to the bar?"

"Oh, that's a great idea," Jo bounced a bit. "C'mon Roz, let's go."

"I can't. I have to get down to my dad's store and help out for a bit."

"On a Saturday night? You sure know how to live it up."

Peter drenched his words with as much sarcasm as he could. But he quickly realized he was also hiding something with his humor, something he had not been fully aware of before then. He liked being around Roz, and Roz and Jo together, but now he understood that he wanted—needed—to be around Jo, just Jo, just he and Jo. A nervous sourness settled in the pit of his stomach, but he didn't let it show through.

"I know, wild girl, right? Dad's got a promotion starting on Monday, something with war bonds, and the whole family's gotta help out tonight and t'morrow getting ready."

"Oh..." There was genuine disappointment in Jo's voice.

"Hey, don't let that stop you two. You go have fun," Roz said, poking Jo in the shoulder in encouragement.

"What say, Jo? C'mon, I'll buy you drinks," Peter chimed in, trying not to appear overanxious to spend time alone with Jo.

"I don't know...Roz is my ride."

The hesitation was clear in her voice. Jo wasn't sure why she felt a bit of apprehension. She had never felt uncomfortable around Peter. But there it was, an uncomfortable feeling she couldn't explain.

"Hell, I can drive you."

"Well, maybe..."

Jo really didn't want the day to end. It had been so much fun with Roz. Peter being there had made everything that much more fun. Jo still hadn't been able to figure out why she had begun to expect Peter to be around.

"I guess," she looked back at Roz a bit sheepishly. "You sure you don't mind me cuttin' out on you?"

"Cuttin' out on me? Jo, I'm the one cuttin' out. Go, have fun."

"Okay," Jo said, turning and hooking her arm in Peter's. "Let's go."

Jo and Peter began walking toward his truck and Roz headed to her car. As Jo walked next to Peter, their arms locked and bodies touching, she felt a warmth passing over her, and she looked up at Peter. He saw her eyes through the curls hanging down on her forehead and smiled.

Suddenly, looking into Peter's eyes, Jo realized why she expected him to be around. The cool September breeze couldn't sweep away the warmth Jo felt; the skipped heartbeat told her this wasn't just a friendship to her anymore. She had developed a connection to Peter that pulled her soul to him. She then became very aware that they were going to be alone for the first time outside of work, and of Al—her husband.

It was a confusing thought. She had nothing to feel guilty about; she wasn't *doing* anything, just spending time with a friend. Why was she feeling guilty? Was she going to be doing something she *should* feel guilty about? Just because she found herself falling for Peter didn't mean being around him was wrong, did it? After all, he had shown no interest in her. He had never tried to touch or grab her, something that couldn't be said of the men on the city bus when she rode wearing her work slacks. Seemed like most men expected women who wore slacks to be of a certain kind, the kind to have their way with on a Friday or Saturday night, not the kind to bring to Sunday dinner with mom. But Peter had *never* treated her that way.

In fact, as Jo thought about it, it seemed to her that he had gone out of his way to treat her like a lady, but at the same time treat her as just one of the guys. She had seen the same thing in the way he acted with Roz the first night they met. Jo thought about how he'd jibe and tease her the way he did Roz, as if she were a man on his foundry crew, then moments later he'd be opening a door for her or pulling a chair out and offering her a seat. Then it struck her, on days when she was later to lunch than he, he'd even politely stand up as she neared the table and remain standing until she sat down. How had she missed that?

"Here," Peter said.

He grabbed the bill of his baseball cap, pulled it from his

head, and then pulled it down on Jo's head. Her curls mashed under the cap. She pulled the hair from her forehead to the sides. She giggled as she looked up at Peter.

"This is my old baseball cap, from back when I played in the southern league. Want you to have it. Seeing as how you've become this big baseball fan an' all."

"Thanks, Pete."

Jo tightened her arm on his to give him a little squeeze. She just couldn't bring herself to destroy the sweetness of his gesture by telling him that any lady would rather break all of her fingernails before being seen wearing a hat with a bill. Of course, Jo didn't have fingernails anymore. Factory work had seen to that. *Just wear the hat to the truck, then you can take it off and never wear it again*, she thought. It couldn't be that bad. She had gotten used to wearing slacks, after all.

Jo kept her arm locked in Peter's as they ambled toward his truck. The sun was hanging low in the western sky. The frayed edges of the bill created a shadowbox effect with the sunlight beaming onto her face. The hat had seen many miles, and she thought about Peter riding long nights in a smelly old bus to get from town to town, from game to game. She saw him there in the seat—probably alone, because, she thought, even then he preferred the solace of himself—he'd be curled up in some sort of ball, his folded glove between his head and the window. His hat, the hat he had just given her, would be pulled low over his eyes in attempt to black out any streetlights or neon signs the bus rolled past. Peter had logged a lot of miles with that hat on his head, and she realized, since he had kept it around all of these years, it was something pretty special to him.

And it hit her, as hard as if somebody had swung a baseball bat into her arm. Peter had given her something very special, very intimate—although he clearly didn't understand women, giving her a hat with a bill—and that meant he felt she was special to him. The guilt Jo felt earlier came rushing back in one giant wave overtaking her. Her smile faded, and her face took on a look of seriousness, yet her eyes were soft and held a caring energy.

"Wait," Jo stopped and pulled on Peter's arm to turn him toward her. "Pete, I don't think I can. I just…not now…I'm sorry."

Peter saw in her face genuine disappointment, but he could not press the issue, not without a clear sign from her. And, if that sign never came, then it would just mean the feelings were one sided—his side.

"No need to apologize. I'll drive you home instead."

His smile reassured her, but she also thought she saw something more in his face. It was that fleeting presence she had seen before, a thought or emotion or feeling. Whenever she caught a glimpse of it, she tried hard to bring it into focus, but it always disappeared just as quickly as she saw it. This time, as it disappeared, she let it go as she had so many times before.

"I think I can still catch Roz…Roz!"

Jo started to turn and trot after Roz. But she turned back to Peter, gave him a quick hug, and whispered in his ear.

"Thanks for understanding, Pete."

Peter tilted his head a bit until his face pressed into her curls sticking out from under the baseball cap. He thought she looked very comfortable wearing the cap. Jo pulled back and looked into his eyes for a moment, then turned and ran after Roz. Peter stood and watched her go, waiting until she was in the car before turning and walking the rest of the way to his truck.

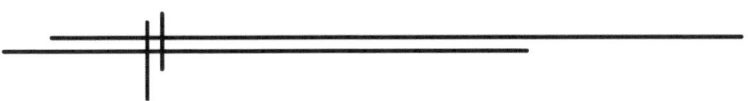

Jo slid into the Buick, leaning out of the window and waving to Peter as Roz pulled away. Settling back into the seat, she pulled the baseball cap from her head and held it in both hands in her lap, looking it over closely. She ran an index finger along the embroidery of the team name, noticing how most of the threads had become fuzzy with wear. The bill had a well-broken-in curve, forming a tight D shape. Jo ran her fingers around the outside of the cap, imaging her fingers weaving through Peter's hair.

"What 'cha got, th'air?"

Roz's voice jarred Jo from her thoughts. When she looked at Roz, the glow in Jo's face was clear. Behind the glow, though, Roz could also see turmoil.

"Pete gave me his old ball cap."

"That was nice of him, giving you that ratty old thing. Probably smells sumthin' fierce, too."

Roz's humorous sarcasm made Jo laughed. She reached over and swatted Roz's arm as laughter filled the car.

"Yeah, I couldn't bring myself to tell him that he doesn't understand what a woman will and won't wear. Still, it was very sweet."

Jo looked back down at the hat and ran her hand over it, stroking it like one would a dog's head. Her smile slowly receded and she became more serious. She looked back at Roz for a few seconds, then spoke.

"Roz…I've started to see Al differently, me and Al differently."

"How so?"

"I'm beginning to realize he's my friend."

"Hasn't he always been your friend?"

"No. Yes. No, I mean he has always been my friend, but I think that's just it…he's *just* my friend."

"Oh…"

Roz knew immediately what that meant. She knew Jo had crossed a line in her head, and most certainly in her heart. She knew Jo had started seeing her feelings toward Peter—something Roz had known for a while—and was at the point of accepting it.

"Al and I, we dated for a few months, but when it comes down to it, we got married really fast." Jo turned and looked out the window for a moment, then almost as an afterthought, added, "We were so young."

"Jo, that was only a couple of years ago."

"But he and I have grown so much since then."

"Not being around him, it can be easy to start isolating Al in a corner of your mind. I'd think you sort of have to so you don't worry yourself sick about him off fighting."

"But it shouldn't be like that. Being apart should make me think about him more, not less."

Jo paused. She let her mind drift back to thoughts of her and Al. She thought about the day he told her he had signed up for the marines, how mad she had been, and how mad he had been with her for being mad at him. Then, later that day, he had proposed. Caught up in the whirlwind of war fever, she had accepted. They were quickly married, and then Al was gone, shipped out to boot camp, and then straight to the South Pacific after that. She hadn't seen him since the day he left for boot camp.

"Roz, Al's the only man I've been with. Not that I'm a prude. I've dated other guys. I just never wanted people to think I was like my mother, a boozy slut." She turned back to the window and stared out of it for a few seconds. "And it was only the one time. Our wedding night. The very next day, I drove him to the bus depot. I stood there and watched as the bus disappeared down the street." She turned to face Roz. "He's changed. I can see it in his letters. I've changed. I don't *need* him anymore."

"What *do* you need?"

Jo was silent for a full minute, returning her gaze to the trees and streetlamps and houses floating by the passenger's window. Then, she turned to Roz and looked at her for several seconds, her face showing a solemness, yet still radiating a glow.

"I think I need Pete."

"Oh…" It was the only thing Roz could get out.

"I just don't think he feels the same way about me."

"I've known Peter several years. Seen him date women here and th'air, never anything lasted more'n a few dates, but I never seen him like I see him when he's with you. Most people'd never know it, but Peter's a real class act. He's not

gonna do anything unless he knows it's okay. You gonna have to make it clear to him."

"Yeah, I guess." There was a bit of apprehension in Jo's voice, as if she was a little annoyed it would be that hard, that she would have to take the first step.

"Jo, you're my friend and I want you to do what's best for you, what makes you happy. If this is what you want, you gonna need to be full wit'it. You can't ration out your love between two men. It ain't right. You don't got no ration card that you can mark off Al Monday through Friday, then Peter on the weekends."

"Yeah…" Jo knew Roz was right, that she had to take the full step toward Peter.

"If you ever need to talk things out, you know I'm always here for you."

Jo took the baseball cap and put it back on her head. It felt good, comforting, as if she had accepted Peter into herself. She would take to wearing it at work, she decided. Most of the women wore headscarves to keep their hair tied up, but she would wear Peter's cap. After Roz dropped her off at home, Jo drew a hot bath and soaked in it for a long time, thinking of Peter and her feelings for him, trying to sort out what to do.

Eric K. Augspurger

VOL. XXXIV—N? 298 Monday, October 25, 1943 Four Cents

FEAR STIRRED IN JAPAN BY ALLIED GAINS
Tojo, Emperor Warn Population of Threat

SYDNEY, Australia—Radio Tokyo delivered a message from Emperor Hirohito in which he urged the Imperial Diet in Japan to follow the plan of Premier General Hideki Tojo for total mobilization of the empire's resource. It is expected that this plan will involve a massive restructuring of Japan's wartime economy, and the emperor's statement seems to back up that expectation. In addressing the Diet, Tojo acknowledged what he described as a "...blind counter-offensive... lashing out..." by the forces of the United States and Britain. Tojo assessed the situation as one of the Allies trying to overwhelm Japan and, in what was likely a reference to recent Allied gains in the Pacific, said the Allies succeeded in "...overcoming many difficulties." Allied communiqués indicate the reality is much different than the Radio Tokyo broadcast stated. In just the past few days, the Empire of Japan has been dealt many significant losses. In a three-day air offensive, Allied flyers destroyed between one hundred and thirty to two hundred enemy planes. On New Britain, seventy per cent of the enemy planes were destroyed. The cumulative total of enemy aircraft destroyed in the South Pacific now exceeds eight hundred. The main enemy airfield in the Solomons on Bougainville was rendered inoperable, at least temporarily, by one hundred seventy-two tons of bombs. One Imperial Navy destroyer was put out of commission. Additionally, five Japanese coastal vessels were sunk.

INTERNMENT STILL A REALITY IN U.S.
Hero of Great War Not Excluded

WASHINGTON, D.C.—Acting attorney general Charles Fahy announced on September 12 the status of Italian-American internees is being reviewed since the armistice with Italy was signed. Many Italian-, German-, and Japanese-Americans have been interned, starting in 1942. Japanese-Americans have been relocated to internment camps in the greatest number—tens of thousands who lived on the West Coast as well as some from other areas. Tokie Slocomb was one of those Japanese-Americans, and a veteran who served in France during World War I. Slocomb stood next to the president after the war as the law granting citizenship to the Japanese-Americans who fought in the Great War was signed. The president gave Slocomb the pen he used to sign the bill into law, but this honor did not exclude him from internment.

OPPOSITION TO WAR MARRIAGES UNHEEDED
Pleas to Wait Are Usually Ignored

CHICAGO, Ill.—In her syndicated editorial yesterday, Dorothy Dix responded to a letter writer who pleaded for young men and women to wait until the war's end to be wed. Miss Dix opines these youth do not want to hear about the pitfalls—not the least of which, husbands and wives may meet as strangers after the war—nor do they want to wait for the alter. Miss Dix also states men do not want to face that a woman who has been working "...for good wages may never be willing to go back to a kitchen with no pay envelope on Saturday night." She concludes that the "...wedding bells ring merrily along and the divorce court gets ready for a rush business when the war is over."

№ 17

Standing at the front window, Jo looked at the clock on the mantle and then at her watch. Both read ten 'til eight. She stretched on her tippy toes and craned her neck to look as far down the street as she could. No sign of Roz. She was never late, let alone fifteen minutes late. Jo looked again at the clock and her watch. If she waited any longer, she would be late for work.

"Roz is late," Jo said, looking at Pearl on the couch; she nodded.

"She probably just got caught up with something, like a flat tire." Pearl turned her head toward the kitchen. "Gerald! Take Josephine to work on your way. She's got to be there by eight, you know."

"I can drive."

"Oh, don't be silly, let Gerald. Then you can ride home with Roz tonight."

"...she probably had a flat," Jo agreed, her voice quieted. "Her tires are getting pretty thin."

Jo's voice rang with hollow persuasion. She had a feeling something was wrong. It wasn't an overt feeling, just one of those gnawing sensations that appears when you think a friend is in trouble. The feeling disturbed Jo.

"Sure dear. You go on. When she shows up, I'll tell her to go on to work."

"Thank you so much." Jo raised her voice a bit and spoke to the kitchen. "I'm coming, Gerald."

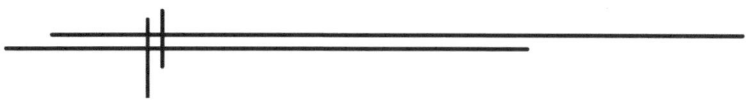

Gerald pulled the car up to the front gate of FTI, near the guardhouse. Jo barely waited for the car to stop before throwing the door open and jumping out. She slammed the door shut and hurried around the car toward the gate.

"Thanks Gerald," she turned and waved. "I'll see you tonight. Don't worry, I'll catch a ride home with Roz."

Gerald waved back and then eased the car onto the road. Jo hurriedly made her way across the yard, into the plant, and to the locker room. There she quickly kicked off her street shoes and slipped into her coveralls. Bursting from the changing room, she trotted toward the time clock, pulling on one boot followed by the other as she went. She reached the time clock as it clicked over past eight oh seven. Jamming her timecard into the slot, she then returned it to the rack and scurried across the plant floor to her mill in the machine shop.

It was only then Jo realized the atmosphere in the plant. It was different that day. Everybody was working hard, as usual, but there was not the banter to which she had become accustomed. Her first thought was she was in trouble for being late. Jo pulled down the bill of the baseball cap—the one Peter had given her—to hide her eyes a bit. Normally, she wore it bill-backward, like a catcher behind home plate, so she could lean in near the part she was machining without hitting the bill. Now she wore it bill-forward to conceal her eyes darting around the plant, nervously trying to see if Mr. Jensen or Fred Thompson

was stomping over to her station to come down hard on her for being late.

Most of the other women poked fun at her for wearing a hat with a bill. Seemed to Jo that even covered in factory grime, there were still degrees of femininity, and wearing a hat with a bill distinctly placed her on the wrong side of the arbitrary dividing line between ladylike and homely or mannish. She didn't care what they said and sharply bit back on whatever barbs were thrown her way. Jo had toughened up like that; Roz taught her very quickly to stand tall, and all Jo had to do was tap the inner defiance she had honed over years at the orphanage.

To Jo, the cap was a constant reminder of Peter. Even after many weeks, she would still catch a whiff of Peter's musk hanging over the hat, now mixed with her own scent, a blend of factory grime and conservative perfume. She had spent much time pondering her feelings for Peter, wishing he were around when he was not. Wearing his old baseball cap was a small way of ensuring he was always watching over her while she worked away the hours at her mill.

Jo continued to look around, one eye on the part she was milling and one eye scanning the plant floor, but nobody was looking at her. Then she looked over to the machinist assistant's station on the other side of the machine shop where Roz worked. It was empty and packed up just as Roz left it every night.

"Where's Roz?"

Jo shouted over the sounds of lathes and mills in the machine shop to her own machinist assistant. She only received a stare and a slow head shake in reply.

"What's going on?"

There was no reply, the assistant just looked back down at her work. Jo was starting to get frantic. She glanced around and saw Peter making his way across the plant floor toward the machine shop. After he made eye contact with her, Jo turned the baseball cap around backward and continued on the day's tasks, but she kept turning around, glancing in Peter's direction as he walked toward the machine shop.

When Peter walked up behind Jo, he softly took her arm.

"Jo…"

She flicked the switch to shut off the mill and then turned to face Peter. He was wearing his heavy gauntlets and coat from the foundry. His face was already covered by a layer of black grime, save two white circles left when he pulled off his goggles, which were now hanging around his neck. She leaned in toward him, trying as much as possible to whisper with all of the noise in the shop. His coat smelled of foundry smoke.

"Pete, what's going on? Where's Roz?"

The confusion was clear in her voice and on her face.

"Jo…" His voice was a bit louder, almost angry. Somehow, though, his voice was at the same time calming to her. "Roz was taken to one of the camps. Everybody…they took the whole damn family."

Disgust saturated his voice, drowning out the sadness he felt. Jo knew immediately what Peter meant: Roz and her family had been sent to an internment camp. Someone someplace for some reason had decided Roz and her family were a threat to national security. *Because Roz worked in a war industry?* Jo wondered.

"Gave them only an hour to pack. One suitcase each…one damn hour…one damn suitcase."

Peter was staring off into the air over Jo's shoulder as he spoke, then continued to stare in silence for a few seconds more. Jo started to tear up, but bit hard on her lip to stop the tears from breaking out. Suddenly, Peter turned and slammed his fist down on the traverse table of Jo's mill with such explosive force that she jumped.

"*Damn it!*"

She stood there nearly immobilized, in part not knowing what to do, in part wondering how Peter had not broken every bone in his hand. He saw the paralysis that had taken over Jo. He reached out and pulled her to him. She buried her face in his chest and let loose with the tears.

"Keep it together." He leaned his head over into hers. "We'll talk later, okay?"

He gave her just a slight kiss on the forehead, then held her head in both hands and looked into her eyes. It was a moment of intimacy shared right there on the factory floor, yet neither quite understood that, each awash in the sadness of a friend lost. Even in the depths of the sadness she was feeling right then, Peter's touch made her heart jump, and the caring look he gave her lifted her spirit.

Peter glanced around the machine shop. Several other workers were watching him and Jo, trying to be inconspicuous about it. But he could tell. He had heard rumors that the gossips in the plant had already been wagging their tongues, but Roz had always been a buffer. After all, she was usually there when he was around Jo. Now, with Roz gone and Jo in his arms for everybody to see, he knew the rumors would be kicked up a notch.

"Okay?" Peter asked, still cupping Jo's head in both hands.

Jo sniffed back the last of the tears and nodded.

"Get to work...it'll take your mind off it. I'll talk to you later. Yeah?"

"Yeah. Thanks, Pete."

She looked into his eyes. She could see the emotions boiling just below the surface. She saw anger and outrage, and something else, that fleeting emotion she had seen before, but this time it was not fleeting. It was there, but it was mixed in with all of the other emotions. Jo forced a little smile and reached out to gently touch Peter's chest. She had not heard any of the rumors flying around about her and Peter, but at that point the pain she was feeling over the loss of Roz gave her an impulsive need to touch him, regardless of what others may have thought. It was partly to show him affection, but also partly a need to reassure herself he was indeed real and standing in front of her.

Peter made his way back across the plant to the foundry. Jo turned back to her mill and busied herself with the day's work.

She numbly moved a part from the "in" bin to the mill table and readied it for machining. She knew the tasks she was to complete by heart, having milled the same type of part over and over for several weeks. The steps were second nature to her at that point. She could keep one section of her mind focused on the task while allowing the rest to wander. As she moved the mill cutter into place, that's exactly what she did.

The pain she was feeling at that moment took her mind back to the orphanage, to one morning when she was eight years old. It was the last morning her friend woke up in the bed next to her because it was the morning her friend's new family came to take her home. Her friend was waking up to a new life, and Jo was waking up with nothing more than a bandage on her forehead. The pain caused by the brick, and by carrying the soon-to-be scar with her the rest of her life, was much less than the pain caused by losing her friend. It was the same pain of loss Jo was feeling now, except this pain was so much worse. Roz wasn't getting a new family and a future of happy possibilities. She had been sent to live a life behind barbed wire, a life of incarceration.

Then, at the very moment she was picturing her friend in the orphanage, Jo's thoughts abruptly shifted to Peter, and a wave of calm settled in over her. This caused her to stop what she was doing for a second, even switching off the mill to contemplate it for a bit. She thought it odd that in a moment of recalled pain of loss, Peter would be there in her mind to calm her, to protect her from the pain. She pondered this a moment before switching the mill back on and continuing work.

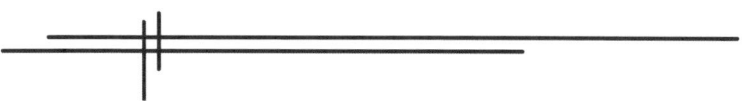

After punching out for the day, Jo headed across the plant toward the door. The normal upbeat banter of the workers heading home was muted. She herself was sullen. She thought about Roz and what she must be going through. She also selfishly thought about how much she missed Roz already. Where would she turn now? Who would be there to talk to, especially about lady stuff? Jo felt her eyes start to burn as tears welled up, and there was a slight sniffle in her nose.

"Hey!"

Peter trotted up behind her. As she turned, he saw the redness in her eyes.

"You okay? Did it just hit you?"

"Roz..." She sniffed to keep her nose from dripping. "Yeah, work kept me busy all day...I even worked through lunch; couldn't eat. Now it is really setting in."

"I know. I think it hit just about everybody hard, some more than others."

He reached out and raised her chin with one finger. As he looked into her eyes, his face spread into that reassuring, but devilish, smile of his. The wave of calm she experienced earlier when Peter had entered her thoughts again settled in over her. She smiled and forced a small laugh. While the laugh was forced, the smile was uncontrollably happy.

"I think it *just* hit me what happened, that she's not going to be here."

"Yeah. I heard they were doing that on the coast, but I really didn't think it reached here in the Midwest. Guess I was wrong..."

Peter put his arm around Jo's shoulder and started walking her to the door. He glanced around to see if anybody was staring at them. One or two people seemed to notice, but at that point he didn't care. He knew Jo needed comforting, and he was more than willing to give it to her. He just wished it could continue.

"C'mon. I'll give you a ride home."

"Yeah, okay. That'd be a pretty long walk tonight."

As the two walked across the yard, Jo leaned in a bit. Peter's arm around her felt good and safe. It numbed a little of the hurt from Roz being gone.

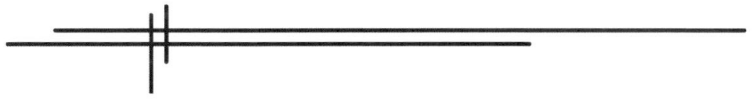

On the ride home, Jo and Peter made small talk.

"This is exactly why I never got close to anybody at the orphanage," Jo blurted through a stream of tears. "It always seemed as soon as I became close friends with somebody, they would get adopted and I'd never see them again. Same story over and over. I became friends with Al and now he's gone halfway around the world. Then I became friends with Roz and she's gone."

She folded her arms across her chest. It was an act of isolation, but in a way it was a bit of pouting. She sniffed back the tears and sighed. Her curls bounced on her forehead.

"Now, you're probably going to leave on me, too."

Peter sat silently for a couple of seconds as Jo's statement hung in the air, swinging like a great pendulum nearing his head. He wanted to tell her he would never leave her alone…he knew he couldn't. He wanted to reach over and put his arm around her…he knew she was married. He wanted to pull her in tight to his body…he knew she wasn't his to have. No matter how strongly he felt about her, no matter how fully she occupied his thoughts, she was not his to have. Finally, he settled on a consolatory statement, and to that he tagged his fallback defense—humor.

"Jo, Al and Roz aren't gone, they're just not here. And as far as me, if you think it would be that easy to get rid of me, well, you're soooorely mistaken."

Jo laughed and wiped a bit of a tear that remained in one corner of her eye.

"You always can make me laugh. That's something a girl looks for."

Peter and Jo filled the remaining drive home with talk about Roz. Jo said she would write as often as she could. Peter thought maybe her friends at the plant could pitch in and send Roz something, some bit of home. Jo called him a girl; he told her to shut up. The playful banter between them kicked up a notch. Any lingering difference in their ages was whisked away, disappearing as quickly as leaves in the wind streaming past the

truck. It was as if they were exactly the same age and had known each other since they were five.

But behind the conversation, Jo was still thinking about what Peter had made her feel, there in the parking lot walking to his truck. It was a pleasant sensation, a calming sensation, but at the same time it turned her stomach into knots. And when she thought about Peter when she wasn't around him, she found herself fidgeting and, at times, looking for her breath, only to have her chest tighten when he walked into the room.

This is it, she thought. *This is what everybody talks about.*

She looked at Peter as he kept his eyes on the road. He was saying something about how he would start a collection at work for Roz and her family, but Jo wasn't really listening. Instead, she was tracing the features of his body with her eyes, from his calloused hands up his rippling arms to his muscular shoulders, all the result of his years in the foundry. The October air blowing in through the driver's window was just warm enough that he could leave his sleeves rolled up to the elbows. She could see the ripples in his forearm as he slightly moved the steering wheel back and forth to keep the truck running straight on the road.

You have gone and done it, she thought. *You've fallen in love. Real love this time, not a high school friendship you mistook for love.*

She let herself smile at the thought, then let it fade before Peter could glance over and see. She thought about how he had stepped in to protect her when she confronted Roz's tormenter at the baseball game. She was proud of being able to stand on her own, but she found her heart jumped when she thought about how Peter could, and had, protected her. She felt a primal instinct drawing her body to his, but she also thought about how he made her laugh, how he could be very caring toward her. She pondered how he was very respectful of her independence; he never tried to force her into a mold, to get her to be somebody she was not, this new woman that had grown out of the little orphan girl she used to be.

She continued tracing his body with her eyes, from his shoulders, along his sharp jaw line—with a two-day stubble that

gave him a rugged, outdoorsman look—to his lips. She imagined those lips pressed against hers, the roughness on his face tingeing her face with a small amount of pain, in a strange way enhancing the euphoria falling over her. Would the years of tangling with metal so hot it generated its own light mean his embrace would be too strong; would she have to tell him to be gentle? Would he place his hand in the small of her back as their lips met, or would it be lower?

He'd start with it in the small of her back, she decided. Then, as she pressed her hips against him, he would let it slide down, perhaps with a soft circular motion, cupping and caressing her at the same time. No, she would not have to tell him to be softer; his arms would cradle her with just the right amount of grip and his hands would touch her skin with a kindness only certain men could show. That's the type of man he was, soft and caring, but ready to press forward when he received the signal. That's what she decided.

Jo realized the heat in her chest had settled much lower. She shifted her knees toward the truck door in an attempt at modesty, but, in doing so, the fabric of her slacks and panties rubbed against her, the sensation just serving to increase the warmth she felt between her legs.

"Right?"

"Yes…wait, what?"

Peter's question ripped her from her thoughts. She had not even heard what he had asked. She felt her face burn as the blood rushed to her cheeks. She was afraid Peter would think her an idiot, but wondered if that would be less embarrassing than if he knew what she was thinking.

"I said," Peter was now looking at her intently, barely keeping watch on the road through the corner of his eye, "does that sound like a good plan, getting some stuff together for Roz and her family."

"Yes. Yes, of course it does."

He looked at her for another long second—he always found it hard to look away from her, rather drinking in her beauty like a youthful elixir—then returned to watching the road as he drove. He continued describing in detail his plan for organizing a drive at the plant to get a care package to Roz, occasionally interjecting some tangent about how maybe he should just bust them out of the camp instead, before returning to the more sensible plan. Jo easily drifted back into her thoughts of Peter holding her close, caressing her body, their lips blistering with passion.

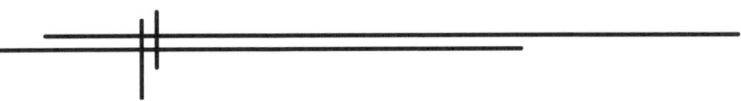

Peter nosed the truck to the curb in front of the Troyers' house.

"So, this is your house?"

Jo got out of the truck and shut the door. Then she stepped up on the running board and leaned in through the window. Peter stared at her face with an intensity that made him feel his head may explode. It was all he could do to keep himself from trying to peek down Jo's shirt, for even with the factory residue covering her clothes and skin, he still felt an intense desire to *see* her skin. Yet he didn't want to seem like just another man trying to get a cheap thrill by looking down her shirt.

"Yeah. Actually, it's Al's parents' house."

"Nice place."

He nodded as he looked across the street. He was taking in the house and neighborhood, but it was also an excuse to look away so as not to be tempted by the view offered by Jo's blouse hanging down from her chest as she leaned into the truck window. Finally, he turned back to Jo. He looked into her eyes for a long second, then she smiled.

There, just below the surface, Jo again thought she saw something. She couldn't quite bring it into focus, but this time she *knew* there was something. And then it was gone just as quickly as it appeared, flittering away like a butterfly on a breeze.

"What?" Jo asked.

The Ration Card

It was a soft, almost caring question. Jo had been caught a little off guard by the look from Peter, but partly she was caught up in thoughts of her own feelings she was realizing for him. He was a good guy; it had not gone unnoticed that he did not let his eyes drift down to her exposed chest.

"You need a ride in the morning?" Peter asked.

His voice was a little higher, slightly inquisitive, like a boy embarrassed by his own question. He cleared his throat.

"No. I'll walk, I think. Thanks for the ride. I'll see you at work."

She wanted to have Peter pick her up for work. She *wanted* Peter to be there when she got up for work. But Peter was not her husband. Her husband was fighting a war in the South Pacific. He had chosen the war over her, and he left her here alone with her heart sealed up in the covenant of a war marriage.

Peter nodded. Jo hopped off the running board and walked around the truck toward the house. She knew why she was still smiling, because her heart told her things about Peter that it had not about Al. Jo now knew—she had finally figured it out—she was experiencing true love.

Her head told her that she was indeed what ministers and newspaper editorials, even the government and military, had warned against—she was a war bride; married too young, too quickly, too impulsively with a husband shipping out too soon. She did have caring feelings for Al, and he was still important to her, but she also knew that what she felt for Al was—and always had been—a love of friendship, not a love of passion. The passion Peter stoked deep inside her told her that very clearly.

She didn't want Peter to leave; it was all she could do to stop thinking about him for just a moment. She knew how she felt; but, she couldn't figure out Peter. He clearly sought her out to spend time with, but he had always spent time with Roz, too. There were the sparks she thought she felt at the baseball games, but he had never followed through on any of them, so maybe she was just imagining things; things she *wanted* to be there. Maybe what Peter felt for her was what she now realized she had felt for Al all along. Maybe he saw her as just a friend and that was why he had never followed through on anything she thought she felt.

Almost as an afterthought, Jo turned back toward the truck as Peter started to pull away from the curb. Her voice held a tinge of girlish flirtation.

"You could give me a ride home tomorrow, though."

Peter smiled at Jo and waved in acknowledgement as he drove off. Jo walked backward a few steps as she watched the truck disappear down the street, her heart still fluttering, and a slight gnawing starting in her stomach as Peter faded from view. Then, she turned and ran up the steps to the porch and into the house.

Her life had just become very complicated. But it was time to tuck it away, time to begin leading two parallel lives, one of the dutiful war wife manning the home fires as her husband was off fighting for democracy, and a second life releasing the passion burning inside her—if only Peter would feel the same way. Was that the thing she saw flittering about in his soul, a caged passion he felt for her?

VOL. XXXIV—N⁰ 334   Tuesday, November 30, 1943   Four Cents

NEW GAS COUPONS NATIONWIDE
Intent Is to Reduce OPA Workload

CHICAGO, Ill.—The Office of Price Administration (OPA) announced today that it will begin issuing new gasoline rationing coupons starting tomorrow, Wednesday, December 1. The existing B and C coupons will be replaced with B-2 and C-2 coupons for all new and renewed applications. The new coupons are worth five gallons of gasoline nationwide; the monthly mileage limit has not changed. Issuing fewer coupons will reduce the workload for local rationing boards. Officials stress that existing coupons are still valid until their expiration dates, but will not garner the increased gasoline allotment. Drivers will be issued the new coupons when they apply for renewal of their Basic Mileage Ration books.

CAPTURED TARAWA AIRFIELD IN USE
Navy Seabees Make Ready in Four Days

WASHINTON, D.C.—Frank Knox, Secretary of the Navy, announced in a news conference today that members of the Navy construction battalion, or Seabees, had the airfield at Tarawa in the Gilbert Islands repaired and functional within four days of the start of the attack in the island. Speaking on the action in the Gilberts, the secretary said figures on American losses were not yet available. However, he reiterated earlier implications of heavy losses when he stated, "...fighting was very bitter." In an attempt to deflect criticism of the anticipated report of heavy losses at Tarawa, Knox stated that the enemy strength was not underestimated. Marines, he said, were forced to assault an enemy who had taken advantage of all natural barriers present, and that high surf and coral reefs hampered efforts of Marines getting ashore.

WOMEN LIKE WAR WORK
Vice President Speaks in Cleveland

CLEVELAND, O.—Vice President Henry Wallace speaking here last week to a group of war workers at the White Motors plant offended women war workers. In part of his speech, Wallace speculated on household amenities to come after the war, including new ice boxes and automatic diaper-changing machines, after which he stated, "these things will all be waiting for you women when you go back into the home." The overall-clad, but decidedly feminine, audience responded not with cheers, but groans. The cheers came only after Wallace hurriedly added "—if you want to go back." Given the reaction, can the vice president be faulted for doubting women war workers will ever return to the kitchen?

JAPAN ADDRESSES GILBERTS SITUATION
Announces Loss of Contact with Forces

SYDNEY, Australia—Radio broadcasts from Tokio yesterday spoke of the situation in the Gilbert Islands when it stated no updates could be offered because contact had been lost with the forces there. The report was based on a communiqué from Imperial military headquarters. In part, the report stated, "...details concerning the situation on Tarawa and Makin Islands at present are not clear due to no dispatch or communiqué from our garrison on the said islands." The report falls short of the truth: both islands have been in American hands since November 23, four days after the start of the battle.

№ 18

The factory whistle sounded, signaling the end of the first shift. In the foundry, Peter looked out at his crew, then stuck a finger in the air and circled it, in his own way saying *wrap it up*. All across the plant, the sounds of machinery began to dissipate as the workers finished up their immediate tasks and tidied up for the day. About half of the workers volunteered to pull a double shift, so they headed for the lunchroom for a quick break and bite to eat before getting back at it. Those heading home for the day made their way toward the locker rooms the same as Peter.

Tuesday...last day in November, Peter thought. *Christmas'll be here before you know it.*

Then his thoughts turned to Jo. He pictured her standing at her mill, wearing the baseball cap he had given her, flipped around backward. Just as clearly as if she were standing in front of him, he saw her slightly hunched over, looking intently through her safety glasses at the part she was machining. She had progressed in her skills as a machinist to the point where her hands and the machine were one. He smiled as he thought of the

cute way she would curl her bottom lip over her teeth, sticking her tongue out just slightly, curled to one side, and biting down a bit whenever she became transfixed on her task at hand.

Peter wondered if he should get Jo a present for Christmas. It was one of the many things he pondered as he lay awake at night, Jo ever-present in his head. She consumed his thoughts all day, and she kept him awake at night. When he finally could drift into sleep, it was while imagining her arms around him, her cheek pressed to his chest and her fingers sifting through his chest hair.

Not since he had given her a ride home from work the day after Roz and her family had been taken had Peter seen Jo outside of work. He and Jo *had* been lunching together every day the five weeks since then. At first, he thought it was mostly to help each other deal with what had happened to Roz—especially Jo; it had hit her particularly hard—but after a while, he thought he started sensing something from Jo, something he just never could quite shake. He'd always try to brush it away by telling himself they were just becoming close friends—something he never really had with a woman. So Peter convinced himself he was just seeing something that wasn't there, something he *wanted* to be there, but really wasn't. Yet no matter how strong of an argument he would make to himself, it just seemed like he was lying.

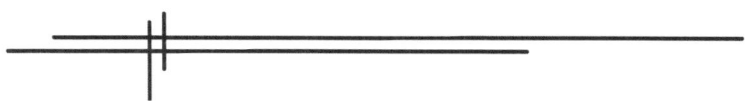

On the other side of the plant, Jo swept the last of the metal chips from her milling machine. She carefully collected them in a metal dustpan, then dumped the shavings in a bin of scrap metal near the back of her mill. Eventually, all of the chips and scraps would make their way back to the foundry to be melted down.

As she brushed the last chips from the dustpan, she thought about Peter in the foundry. She imagined him standing in front of a ladle filled with liquid metal, his face illuminated orange by the glow. Then her heart started beating faster as she thought about what she was going to do. This would be the day. Oh, there were hurdles; she *was* married, and he was older than she. But this was it; it had to be now or it would never be.

Jo pulled off her leather apron and hung it on the mill. Then she hurried to the changing room and quickly swapped her coveralls and for her street clothes. Usually, she just wore her work slacks and shirt home, but she had brought a pretty dress to wear home today, hoping it might have some sway on Peter. She pulled the small face-mirror from her locker. While the machine shop was much cleaner than the line where she had first worked, her face was still covered with metal-dirt and greasy smudges. She grunted in disapproval and tried to wipe her face as clean as possible with a towel. Then she pulled a couple of curls down across her forehead, and turned her head from side to side as she examined herself in the mirror.

She stared at the curls hanging over the divoted scar above her eye, brushed them to one side, then moved them back in place. The little orphan girl—Jo thought long gone—had crept up behind her, making the scar hurt and reminding her that boys can be mean. Defiantly, Jo pulled the curls away from the scar, sweeping away the little orphan girl as she did.

Hurrying out of the locker room and across the plant, she scanned back and forth looking for Peter. She hoped she hadn't missed him. She saw him just walking out through the door, and she hurried in that direction, only a few yards behind him. Jo got into line for the security check, impatiently craning her neck to see over those in front of her as the guard looked in everybody's lunchboxes, bags, and purses. As soon as the guard cleared her, she flung the door open and nearly jumped through it.

"Pete!" she yelled, seeing Peter about halfway across the yard walking toward the parking lot.

Peter stopped and turned to the sound of her voice. It still made him smile that she was the only one who called him Pete. He waved and waited for Jo to catch up.

"Hey Jo, what's going on?"

"I just, um..."

 The Ration Card

Jo couldn't seem to form any words; her mouth was feeling dry and stuffed full of cotton. Her heart was palpitating and she was beginning to feel a bit lightheaded. Her hands began to shake and her face felt hot and flushed, yet when she brushed away hair from her eye, her hands were stone cold.

"I just…wanted to know if you would…uh, give me a ride home."

In addition to stammering, her voice wavered and cracked slightly. She bounced a bit at the knees, trying desperately to keep Peter from seeing how nervous she was.

"Sure, Jo. You don't have to ask. C'mon."

He put his hand in the small of her back to lead her to his truck. When his hand touched her, she flinched just a bit; not enough that he could feel it, but Jo knew she had. She and Peter had touched before, but this time it was different; he wasn't guiding her through a crowd, nor was Roz around to make the context one of friendship. This time, when he placed his hand on her, it was like he had pushed a bubble of warmth into her soul, and wouldn't it be nice if his hand curled around her side and down onto her hip? She smiled and walked to the truck with Peter, the rising warmth inside her fending off the late-November chill.

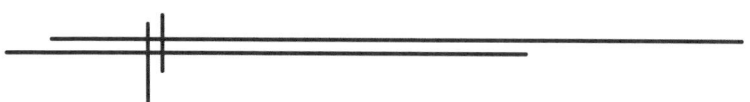

Most of the leaves had fallen from the trees, except for the oaks, which would keep their leaves all winter. The roads and lawns and sidewalks of Blooming Grove were a carpet of orange and red and yellow and brown. Every couple of houses, there was a big mound of leaves out front. After school let out, a group of kids would be playing in it, diving and splashing around just as if the leaves were water at the swimming hole, but being after dark the kids were all inside finishing up supper and listening to their favorite radio dramas.

Nearly all of the roads in Blooming Grove were still paved with brick. As such, the tires made a rhythmic da-dat-da-dat-da-dat sound as Peter guided the truck down the street. Some of the more-traveled roads, especially around the industrial areas, had been repaved in concrete over the past few years, one of the benefits of President Roosevelt's Work Projects Administration, which everybody just called the WPA. Most roads, however, were still a checkerboard of brick pavers, polished smooth in ribbons by years of tires running over them.

Peter's truck bounced and swayed across the brick roads. Being a truck, it had not been built for comfort to start with, and being an old truck meant it had more creaks and groans than others may have had. He tried as much as he could to look at Jo as he drove. Just as he did when they lunched together, he was trying to soak up as much of her with his eyes as he could, because he knew their time would be short. He made note of the dress she was wearing. She always looked good to him, even in her work slacks, but the dress reminded him just how beautiful she was. It was hard for him not to stare instead of paying attention to the road. Twice, he came close to pulling to the curb just so he could look at Jo uninterrupted for a few minutes, but he thought better of it.

"I gotta pull in here and get some gas. You don't mind, do ya'? You in a big hurry to get home?"

"No, not at all."

While that was true, Jo felt a bit of relief for the extra time with Peter. Not only was it time with him—time alone; time outside of work—it also gave her more time to get her courage up to the task at hand. She didn't think it would be easy, she just had never counted on it being this hard. She began to feel the wall she had become so accustomed to erecting at the orphanage creeping up around her, the little orphan girl placing brick on top of brick. For the first time, it occurred to her this was just like the wall she saw Peter keep around himself. She fought hard and pushed the wall back down. This *was* going to happen, she just had to make it happen.

As Peter pulled up to the gas pump, a station attendant scurried out to the truck. He glanced at the B ration sticker on the windshield as he approached the driver's window, which Peter was rolling down. Peter spoke before the attendant could greet him.

"Eight gallons, if you would."

The attendant touched two fingers to his brow and set about filling the tank. When the eight gallons were dispensed, he washed the windows and checked under the hood.

"Jo, you seem a bit on edge. Somethin' going on?"

Jo had positioned herself in the corner of the truck's bench seat, turned slightly to more-or-less face Peter and leaning back against the door. His direct question caught her off guard, and her heart skipped a beat. She felt her hands go cold again, yet her palms were sweaty. She smoothed her dress over her legs, partly to try to calm herself and partly to wipe her palms. She looked down, nervously studying how her dress folded over in her lap, almost forming pleats.

"I…uh…"

The more she stammered, the harder she looked down at her lap, brushing the folds flat.

"I like…I mean…I'm very glad…you gave me a ride home."

She immediately regretted what she said; it was an awkward turn of phrase that didn't really fit the situation by way of explanation. But getting those words out had finally given her the courage to look up at Peter, if only briefly. Once her eyes met his, she quickly looked out through the windshield and watched the attendant walking toward the driver's side of the truck.

Peter handed the attendant his mileage ration book and a two dollar bill. The attendant checked the license plate written on the coupons against Peter's truck, then removed the appropriate coupon. He handed the book back to Peter along with his change, reminding him of the adjustment in rationing when his book was renewed. The attendant then headed back to the service bay.

"A ride home, huh?" Peter's voice held a tone of skepticism.

Jo turned and looked out the passenger's window so he could not see her face, resting her elbow on the sill. She scrunched up her face and pressed two fingers into the middle of her forehead, knowing how stupid she had sounded, and now she knew Peter had picked up on it. This was getting harder by the second, but she knew she had to do it now. It had taken her a long time to admit to herself her feelings for Peter, and just as long to convince herself she could act on them, so she was doing this now; she had to. She turned from the window and again smoothed her dress, then looked at Peter.

"I'm sorry, Pete, that sounded stupid."

This time she did not look away when her eyes met Peter's, and her voice was much calmer. Peter noticed right away that something had settled in over her—something pleasant—and something was stirring in him, too. It was that same feeling he had been chasing for months, the one he had every time he was around Jo. He tried to brush it aside, then started the truck and pulled out into the street. He could see out of the corner of his eye Jo was still watching him, that infectious smile of hers beaming at him. Something was very different this time, he just had to figure out what.

"Jo, you never have to ask…it's understood."

The last sentence hung in the air in front of Jo. Was he telling her he felt more than friendship toward her? She again felt her heart skip a beat, disrupting the calm that had begun to blanket her. This was it, this was the moment, her chance. A voice was screaming in her ear, *Take it, take it, take it!*

Her mind raced, playing back all of her internal arguments, all rushing back in a wave of heat rising in her cheeks. She glanced down at her hands to see if they were visibly shaking or if she was just imagining it; they *were* shaking. Her mouth was parched, her tongue stuck in place. She opened her mouth to speak, but the dryness in her throat caused only a cracked squeak to pass her lips. She closed her eyes, tightly pressing her eyelids together, and cursing herself inside as she breathed slowly to focus. She cleared her throat and again opened her mouth, ready this time to speak those words, to tell Peter she couldn't stop thinking about him, that she was deeply and madly in love with him, that all she wanted was to be lost in his arms for hours on end, to feel his foundry-scuffed fingers running through her hair, his powerful hands gently caressing her body. But Peter broke the silence first.

"Jo...I was wonder'n if...maybe...you'd like to..."

Now it was Peter who was having trouble finding the words. But Jo wasn't listening to the words she heard. She was so focused on what she had to say, she wasn't even sure if Peter was saying anything or if it was just the sound of wind whistling through the cracks where the truck windows didn't quite seal.

"...go with me to the movies this weekend."

"Pete, I like you."

Her words were on top of his, said at the same time, with the same meaning, only slightly higher in volume. Their eyes locked; Peter and Jo sat quietly absorbing the impact of what each had just said. Their bodies bounced up and down as the truck springs squeaked and groaned with the unevenness of the brick road surface.

With his eyes locked with Jo's, Peter quickly lost track of the road and the truck jumped the curb. His head snapped forward, and he jerked the steering wheel to get the truck back on the road, then eased the truck to a stop on the curb.

"What did you say?" he asked.

Jo was still not entirely sure she had heard what she thought she had heard, either. She looked down at her lap, pressing each finger on each hand hard against her legs until knuckles popped. She responded without looking up.

"I said, I like you Pete."

She then looked back at Peter. At first, he wasn't sure what she meant—*like* can mean a lot of different things—but the look in her eyes told him she was talking about matters of the heart.

"I can't stop thinking about you. When I get up in the mornings, the first thing I think of is how long it will be until lunch, because that's when I get to be with you. And when lunch is over, I get this gnawing sensation in my tummy because I know I won't see you again until lunch the next day."

"Jo, I..."

"And I know it's wrong; I know I'm married…to a man who is overseas fighting."

All of the thoughts and emotions pent up inside her were now manifested in salty streams down her cheeks. Peter reached over and cupped her head with his hand, wiping away the tears on one cheek with his thumb. Jo pressed her head into his hand.

"I know that makes me one of those horrible women who ends up sending a 'dear John' letter, but there it is. My heart keeps telling me you are the one I am supposed to be with. You. You, Pete. Not Al. *You.*"

She sniffed and smiled through the tears. Peter lifted his hand to her forehead and brushed the hair from the scar above her eye. He gently moved his finger over the scar. She didn't move, not even a flinch. It was as if Peter was rubbing away the little orphan girl and the mean boy who threw the brick at her. Jo reached up and placed her hand over his, holding his hand over this scar.

Peter's head was racing, retracing all of the past signs he thought he had picked up on, acknowledging each one, before realizing he was losing the moment. This was not territory he was used to wandering through. It had always been very easy for him to be around women, until feelings of closeness set in.

"So…where do we stand on that movie thing?"

He smiled wide, and Jo laughed through the remaining tears. Then, she nearly jumped across the truck and wrapped her arms around him. She whispered in his ear.

"Pete, I can't be without you."

"I won't ever let that happen, Jo. I want to be with you, too. I knew from the first time we spent together—that night at Tanner's with Roz—that I wanted to be with you. I just didn't know how much, and I never thought it would happen."

She squeezed Peter tightly and held him for a second, then kissed his cheek and retreated back across the truck. She was still smiling, but it had turned into that devilish smile of hers,

the one she had stolen from Peter. She reached her leg across the truck and teasingly kicked him.

"Yes, I'll go with you to the movies this weekend."

Putting the truck in gear, he pulled out back onto the road, shaking his head with a light chuckle.

"What have I gotten myself into?"

Eric K. Augspurger

VOL. XXXIV—N° 334 Tuesday, November 30, 1943 Four Cents

NEW OFFENSIVE IN PACIFIC
Makin and Tarawa Fall on Same Day

PEARL HARBOR, H.I.—The capture of Makin atoll in the Gilbert Islands was announced last Tuesday on the fourth day of the new American offensive in the central Pacific. Secretary of the Navy Frank Knox stated the Gilbert Islands represent a "much more direct route to Japan." Tarawa atoll, south of Makin in the Gilberts chain, was also invaded in the operation that commenced on Saturday, November 20. Lieutenant Colonel Evans Carlson, of the famed Carlson's Raiders that made an attack on Makin in August of last year, said Tarawa was "one of the toughest battles ever fought in one hundred and sixty-eight years of U.S. Marine Corps history." Secretary Knox said the entire garrison of four thousand imperial Japanese marines is believed to have been wiped out.

NEW RULINGS ON TIRES
OPA Eases Restrictions to Address Continued Shortage

WASHINGTON, D.C.—The Office of Price Administration (OPA) today announced changes in the regulations governing tires. The move is intended to ease the hardship caused by the continued shortage of new tires. In one move, the OPA has reclassified tires made of principally reclaimed rubber as used (grade III), whereas they were previously declared new tires (grade I). This allows greater availability of tires to those motorists who can only qualify for used tires, holders of B and C gasoline ration stickers. These motorists have been prohibited from purchasing new tires since October 1. Beginning tomorrow, however they will be able to purchase these so-called war tires constructed of reclaimed tires. The OPA also announced the national allotment in tires for December. The allotment of grade I tires will be an increase of 37,685 passenger tires over the November allotment, but a shortfall is still expected. Synthetic tires will be available en masse in January of next year for commercial applications. While intended to ease the tire shortage, synthetic tires have provided results in early testing that leave cause for concern. Synthetic tires have been shown in these tests to be less durable under loads.

PRESIDENT'S SON TWICE ESCAPES DEATH
Gilberts Action Nearly Takes Life of Son of FDR

SYDNEY, Australia—The eldest son of President Roosevelt, Lieutenant Colonel James Roosevelt II, landed in the first wave in the invasion of Makin Island in the Gilbert Islands chain. Within the first twenty-four hours ashore, he narrowly avoided being killed not once, but twice. The first brush with death occurred in the afternoon on the first day of the assault. Roosevelt was standing within feet of regimental commander Colonel James G. Conroy when the latter was shot between the eyes by a Japanese sniper. The second brush with death occurred on the second day of battle, and was from friendly fire. One of the bombers called in for close air support of ground forces released its ordnance too early. Roosevelt was a mere fifty feet from where the bomb exploded. In both incidents, Roosevelt emerged unscathed. Roosevelt was on Makin a year ago with Carlson's Raiders. During the famed surprise raid on the Japanese-held island, Roosevelt earned the Navy Cross, an honor second only to the Medal of Honor.

№ 19

Peter turned right on Mill Road. The truck's front suspension squeaked a brief protest until the wheels were turned back and the truck was headed straight down the road. The canopy of old maples had dropped their leaves for the season, and the truck left small contrails of color in its wake.

Peter was slightly hunched over, shifting his weight onto his left elbow resting on the door, and his right hand was casually hooked over the top of the steering wheel. He would look at Jo, smile, and return to watching the road. Jo was staring at Peter, smiling widely with excitement fluttering in her stomach. After they had opened up to each other, her nervousness had quickly faded, replaced by heart-racing, exciting thoughts of being with Peter. The ride had been filled with jokes, laughter, and ribbing; not much different from any other time they were together, but it *was* different…they were *together*.

Gentle touches, knowing looks, and the occasional tracing of a finger across a hand; these were all new. With each passing house, Jo felt wave after wave of calm settle over her, waves of knowing she had been right. She couldn't stop smiling. It was as if something had pinned the corners of her mouth all the way

back to her ears. She sat there, her back leaning on the door, smiling at Peter and basking in the glow of levels of happiness she had never felt before. She just sat watching every slight move he made; the fluid motion his body made as the truck bounced, as if he was a part of the machinery; the way his hand hooked over the steering wheel would twitch to keep the truck more or less straight on the road; the way his arm seamlessly rotated the steering wheel as he guided the truck onto the street where she lived with the Troyers.

Then she noticed his finger slowly rise from the steering wheel and point down the street. Her eyes followed his finger as the smile drifted from her face.

In the middle of the block, parked in front of the Troyers' house, was a car, a '38 Chevy. As light from the truck's headlights crept onto the car, she could see it was painted olive drab with a white star on the door. Her heart jumped a beat. She could feel the bile immediately rise in her stomach. She shot a look at Peter and saw his face was like a mask of stone. Jo felt faint for a moment, as if all blood in her body had ceased to move, and then her heart raced.

Before Peter had fully eased the truck to a complete stop, Jo swung open the door and sprinted across the street. She dropped her lunch pail on the front porch, flung open the front door, and charged inside. She abruptly stopped in the foyer and stood in the entry to the front room. Sitting on the sofa, bathed in the warm firelight, were a lieutenant from the Marine Corps and Reverend Turner. Reverend Turner was leaning forward, his forearms resting on his knees, a bible held in both hands in front of him.

Across from them, Gerald sat in his chair, nervously twisting the newspaper in his hands into a tight roll. Pearl was sitting on the davenport, holding a white handkerchief to her nose. She looked up just as Jo's ears picked up the lieutenant's voice.

"...at Tarawa."

"Hon, come, sit down," Pearl said, motioning to Jo.

"Josephine..." Reverend Turner snapped to his feet, and now

had his arm around Jo's shoulder as he walked her to the sofa. "I'm afraid Alfred has been killed in action."

"Ma'am."

The lieutenant's voice again cut through the air. He was now standing straight-arrow upright, his dress uniform perfectly pressed. All of the buttons were shined to a bright polish. They glinted in the soft firelight when he moved.

"I'm very sorry for your loss," the lieutenant continued. "Your husband died in service of his country. He died a hero."

"Thank you, lieutenant," Reverend Turner said, guiding Jo to the sofa as she sat. "I think I will spend a few minutes with the family. Let me walk you to the door."

"Sir."

Reverend Turner escorted the young lieutenant to the door. They stood in the foyer for a moment and exchanged a few hushed words. Jo could hear the reverend tell the lieutenant he would be in touch regarding the details of the burial once the body was delivered. Then he opened the door for the lieutenant. The lieutenant took one step, stopped, and glanced at Pearl. He took the small, rolled-up standard he had been holding between his arm and body and gave it to the reverend. The reverend quickly unrolled it, then just as quickly rolled it back up. As he did so, Jo could see the large gold star on the standard. With her son killed in action, Pearl had become a gold-star mother...and Jo had become a young widow. The gold-star standard would replace the blue-star standard Pearl had placed in the window when Al shipped out to boot camp.

Outside, Jo could hear Peter's truck start up and pull away from the house. Jo wanted to run out and jump into his arms. She needed to be wrapped in his warmth. At the same time, the sourness in her stomach told her she couldn't do that. Though she now knew she was never *in* love with Al, she also knew she cared about him deeply in the way friends love. The pain in her chest told her that she missed Al greatly. She had to focus on Al and the Troyers. She owed Al that much, and probably more.

The Blooming Grove Review

VOL. XXXIV—N? 343   Thursday, December 9, 1943   Four Cents

TARAWA LOSSES HEAVY
Marine Dead High Price for Tarawa

SYDNEY, Australia—Tiny Tarawa atoll was won at the highest cost of human life per square yard ever paid by U.S. marines. Of the first two battalions to hit the beaches of Tarawa—two to three thousand marines—only a few hundred men were not casualties. Marine Colonel Merritt Edson, of Guadalcanal's Battle of Bloody Ridge fame, stated, "Nothing in any previous war or in this one compares with it." Admiral Chester Nimitz, visiting Tarawa on November 27, revealed that one thousand and twenty-six marines were killed in the battle and two thousand five hundred and fifty-seven were wounded. Secretary of the Navy Frank Knox said at the end of November that American losses on Tarawa were heavy, but that "enemy losses were even heavier."

ONE MILLION WOMEN STILL NEEDED
Labor Secretary Speaks at Labor Conference

KANSAS CITY, Mo.—Frances Perkins, Secretary of Labor, stated that industry still needs one million women to enter the workforce. This is in spite of the closing of certain types of war plants. The secretary was speaking at the tenth national conference on labor legislation that opened yesterday here in Kansas City. "The heavy demand for women will begin right after the next heavy selective service calls," Miss Perkins stated. She went on to say difficult tasks and jobs will be "...broken down to the point where women can handle them." The secretary indicated the needed women workers will come from the fourteen million women between eighteen and sixty years of age who are not employed and are without young children.

INCREASE IN FARM PRICES OPPOSED
Subsidies Also Opposed

CHICAGO, Ill.—Chester C. Davis, currently head of the Federal Reserve Bank of Saint Louis and formerly of the War Food Administration (WFA), stated on Tuesday before a convention of the American Farm Bureau Federation that he believes "...in the interest of longtime farm welfare, any further marked increase in the general level of farm prices is undesirable." He said only existing subsidies that resulted in expanded production should remain, and he is opposed to general subsidies.

EYE-WITNESS TO TARAWA
Marine Sergeant Tells Story of Battle

TARAWA, Gilbert Is.—Master Technical Sergeant Jim Lucas of Tulsa, Oklahoma, was the first Marine combat correspondent to hit the beaches in the battle for Tarawa. He writes Tarawa was "...the bitterest, costliest, most sustained fighting on any front." Preceding the battle was a sustained aerial and naval bombardment. Before the landings "...it was great fun. We grinned and chortled...", the expectation was no defenders would be left alive. Instead, four thousand entrenched imperial Japanese marines awaited them. "Virtually every marine on Tarawa looked death in the face." The stories from Tarawa will likely be told and retold for months to come. There will be heroes named, but "...it is impossible to single out one man...doing so we would overlook the thousands who have gone through the same thing."

N⁰ 20

The day of Al's funeral was bright and sunny, but a gray haze had hung over the town in the morning. The sun reflected brightly off of the early December dusting of snow. It was a Thursday, the 9th, just before noon. There were fewer than twenty people at Al's funeral, mostly family. His friends were either in the service or working; those who could get out of work did come.

Somehow, every once in a while, Jo caught her mind wandering to the plant. She knew by not being there—seven work days in a row now—a stack of parts was accumulating by her mill. She also knew the other machinists would try to keep up and not say one word in protest, but she still felt as though she was letting down those at the plant.

As the funeral procession wound its way from the church to the cemetery, Jo sat silently, reflecting on how she had come to this point in her life. Just two short years ago—at the same time, two long years ago—she was a completely different woman; a completely different *girl*. She was seventeen, eagerly waiting to graduate and settle down to a life with a husband and kids. Then, the cataclysm of Pearl Harbor. While she knew the

attack wasn't the cause of all changes to come, it did seem as if it was the point where her life branched from what it was to what it became. Since Pearl Harbor, she had graduated, gotten married, found a best friend, lost a best friend, found another—what exactly was Peter? she definitely loved him—and lost a husband, all in the short span of a dozen or so months.

The motorcade pulled into the cemetery and up to the top of the hill where the newest graves were. Most of the fallen were buried on the battlefield, but Al had died of his wound aboard a hospital ship, so he made the final journey back to Blooming Grove.

Jo and the Troyers had been told that Al died a hero, succumbing aboard the hospital ship to the wound he suffered in a heroic action in the battle of Tarawa. It wouldn't be until eleven years later Jo would know the sad truth—most of it, at least. Frankie Noylan, whom Jo knew only from Al's letters, contacted her out of the blue one day and asked if she could meet for coffee. He said he was finally ready to talk about the war, at least to those who deserved to hear, and he thought the family of his good buddy Alfred Troyer should hear, if they wanted to, what had really happened to him. She agreed to meet Frankie, telling herself she would decide if she would tell Pearl only after she heard what he had to say; Gerald had passed in early '52.

So over dinner one September night, 1954, in a dark and secluded booth at Tanner's bar and grill, Frankie Noylan detailed to Jo the last hours of Al's life. He and Al had embarked on the same amtrac—Jo interjected that she built amtracs during the war—and they had landed in the first wave, making it to the sea wall unscathed. He explained that Tarawa was the name of the atoll, the group of islands. The actual island where most of the battle for Tarawa happened was called Betio. He sounded it out for Jo—bee-she-oh—trying to suppress his thick Appalachian accent, then spelled it for her.

As Frankie laid out the battle for her, Jo could tell the memory was still fresh, as fresh as if the battle had happened the day before, and she wondered if it still haunted him all of those years after the war. When she asked why it took him eleven years to track her down, Frankie had willingly admitted

to having trouble overcoming everything he had seen and experienced; things he had done, too.

By the end of the night, Frankie had told her that Al had been a brave marine, but ultimately he had died because a bullet from a Japanese Nambu machine gun had found him instead of somebody else. It wasn't necessarily a well-aimed shot; the Japanese gunner was simply spraying the sand around where the squad of marines was advancing on him. Could have been any one of the dozen men in the squad that the bullet found, or none of them at all. That's just the way it was in war. One minute you're alive, the next minute you wished you were dead because you were holding your best friend's insides...well, inside...and yelling for a corpsman. At first, Frankie had thought Al was going to be okay. There wasn't a whole lot of blood—he'd certainly seen more—and Al was conscious and more or less alert when the litter bearers took him back to the aid station. When Frankie inquired at the aid station a few hours later, he was told Al was already on a ship headed home, but that he wasn't going to make it. The bullet, you see, had destroyed his pancreas. There are a few places on the human body where a wound is fatal, no matter how skilled the corpsman, or field doctor, or the surgeon aboard a hospital ship. The pancreas is one of those places.

That night, eleven years later, Jo would learn Al had simply died in combat. Not from heroic actions, but from a bullet he received while doing what marines do in war. She was glad Frankie had found her and told her, in part for herself, but in part because she was glad he didn't have to carry that pain with him in solitude any longer. She would never tell Pearl that Al died just as most men in combat died—doing what they were supposed to do, nothing more, nothing less.

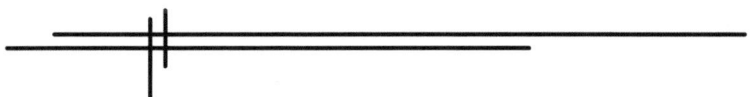

At the top of the hill in the cemetery, the funeral procession slowed and then stopped. Positioned about fifty feet away from the gravesite was the Marine Corps honor guard, presenting the nation's colors and the colors of the Marine Corps. Next to the honor guard was the seven-man rifle squad and the rifle squad

leader, standing at attention in line formation. The color guard and rifle squad were in a position where they could be seen by the family at the gravesite. As the funeral cortege stopped, the marines all came to attention.

The family and other mourners slowly gathered around the freshly dug hole in the ground. Jo noticed how neatly the corners had been cut in the earth, as if a master craftsman had lovingly carved the hole by hand with a meticulously sharpened chisel. Then it struck her as very odd she would think of that, of how a worker would go about constructing something. Two years ago, she never would have thought about how something was constructed or assembled. After starting at the plant, she had realized she began noticing machinery or equipment and wondering how the parts fit together, how the workers pushed, and pulled, and hammered, and riveted the inoperable pieces into a functioning whole.

Six marine pallbearers stood at the back of the open hearse, and, on receiving the signal, methodically removed the casket. When the casket was fully removed, they stood stone-steady as the honor guard detail leader and detail assistant unfurled an American flag and draped it over the casket, the field of blue located over where Al's left shoulder was. Every movement was choreographed and carried out with a precise meter.

With the flag draped over the casket, the pallbearers began the slow march toward the gravesite, one step, then a pause, then another step, and a pause. At the gravesite, they slid the casket onto the bier over the grave, again in choreographed, step-pause-step fashion. As they did this, the honor guard and rifle squad stood at attention, saluting the casket.

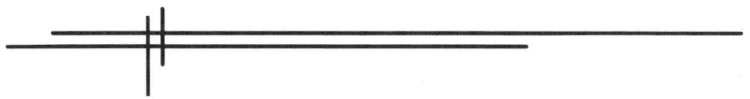

Peter had parked his truck down the block from the church, just around the corner. He sat waiting for the services to conclude. He had left work early with the intent of attending the funeral—not specifically to be with Jo, rather just to be there out of respect—but as he drove to the church, he decided even being there was probably a bad idea.

The gossips at the plant had kicked their tongue-wagging up a notch after he and Jo had shared the moment of intimacy on the plant floor the day Roz was taken, but after it became known Al had been killed, the rumors bordered on venomous. Fortunately, Jo had not been back to work since then, so she could not have known of the darker turn the rumors had taken. He wasn't even sure if she had been aware of the rumors before. He was afraid if he were seen at the funeral, the rumors would spill over outside the plant walls. The last thing he wanted was to upset Jo in any way. He needed to protect her from any pain, to keep her safe from all things bad. If that meant keeping his distance until things settled down, then that was what he would do.

Plus, the two had not spoken since that day she'd found out Al had been killed. Something had happened between them that day; they had finally acknowledged the romance between them. That had also come to a screeching halt. Peter knew Jo would need space to sort out everything.

When the funeral services ended, the mourners filed out of the church behind the marine pallbearers carrying Al's casket. He sat in silence, watching the step-by-step movement of the pallbearers. The pallbearers paused at the back of the hearse, then with the machine-like precision slid the casket into the hearse.

As the funeral procession pulled away from the church, Peter kept his eyes on the Troyers' car. He desperately wanted to catch a glimpse of Jo, just to see her face, but in the back of his mind he also knew he was hoping she would see him, too, and smile. When the procession passed the street where Peter had parked, he started his truck and pulled in at the end. He followed the procession as it snaked through town to the cemetery. When it entered the cemetery, Peter parked on the street outside.

He paused a moment, thinking about his brother, who was also buried there. He got out of the truck and walked to the bottom of the hill, below where the mourners had gathered, and stood under a hundred-year-old oak tree. Peter looked up the hill and saw the pallbearers moving Al's casket from the hearse to the gravesite. He looked at the tombstones around him. Some of

the graves dated back to the Civil War, to the beginning of Blooming Grove. He returned his gaze to the hilltop and waited in silence for the benediction and salute.

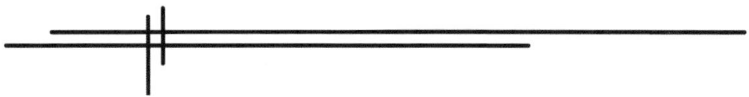

The family—Jo, Pearl, and Gerald, along with a few aunts, uncles, and cousins—were seated in wooden folding chairs in a row facing the gravesite. Two more rows of chairs behind them held the remaining mourners. They sat silently as the pallbearers moved Al's casket onto the bier. When the casket was in place, the pallbearers held the flag taut just inches above the casket.

Jo stared at the casket as Reverend Turner delivered the benediction. Her thoughts raced from images of Al in high school, to imagined images of Al on the battlefield, and—try as she did not to have them—to thoughts of being with Peter. Twice during the benediction, this stream of consciousness was broken by the slight sound of Pearl sniffing back tears. Then the cycle of thoughts would start all over again.

At the end of the benediction, Reverend Turner asked the mourners to stand.

"Please stand for the rendering of honors."

The leader of the rifle squad called the squad to attention.

"Guard, *attention!* Port, *arms!* Ready!"

Each of the seven marines, all moving in unison, faced half-left, snapped the rifle bolt back and then forward to chamber a round, and raised the rifle to his cheek, aimed in the air about fifteen degrees above the casket.

"Aim...*fire!*"

The first volley echoed across the cemetery. Each member of the squad returned his rifle to the port arms position, with the rifle held across his chest. On the next *Ready* command, which

would come after a pause of five seconds, he would chamber another round and aim over Al's casket.

"Ready...aim...*fire!*"

Jo curiously picked up on the mechanical sounds of the rifles as each member of the honor guard snapped a new round into the chamber. She imagined the inner mechanics of the rifles, seeing in her head the shapes of what she imagined the parts looked like and how she would go about machining each part.

"Ready...aim...*fire!*"

Rifle smoke from the three volleys settled in above the ground before whisping away amongst the headstones.

"Present, *arms!*"

At that command, the bugler commenced the playing of *Taps* as all of the military personnel stood at attention saluting the casket. As the solemn sounds pierced the air, Pearl reached over and squeezed Jo's arm, as if to say something. When Jo looked at her, Pearl had let go and was looking at the wreath in front of the casket.

As *Taps* played, pallbearers lifted the flag from Al's casket. In choreographed movements, they folded the flag thirteen times into a triangle with only the field of blue showing, one fold for each of America's original colonies—the triangle iconic of the tricorn hats worn by Revolutionary War soldiers. When the bugler concluded, the rifle squad leader again issued commands.

"Order, *arms!* Parade, *rest!*"

The rifle squad would remain at parade rest attention until all mourners, including the family, had left the cemetery. The honor guard detail leader took the folded flag from the detail assistant as the pallbearers stood at attention. Then, with timed steps, he walked over to Jo. As he offered the flag to her, he spoke.

"On behalf of the President of the United States, the Commandant of the Marine Corps, and a grateful nation, please accept this flag as a symbol of our appreciation for your loved one's service to country and corps. God bless you and this family, and God bless the United States of America."

Jo accepted the flag and nodded. The detail leader stood at attention and gave Jo a slow, respectful salute.

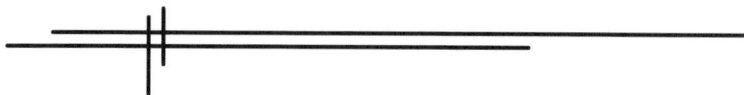

The sounds of the bugle reached Peter's ears after the last volley of rifle fire. The sound had weakened by the time it reached him, so *Taps* seemed even more solemn than he remembered from his brother's funeral so many years before. By the time the last notes reached him, he could smell the smoke from the rifle salute.

On the hilltop, he could see the mourners were filing back to their cars. The graveside service was over and everybody was returning to their lives and, whether they knew it or not, beginning the process of closing the hole left by Al's death. Peter knew it would take longer for some than others; the Troyers had lost their only son and no one expected them to stop grieving anytime soon. He knew, too, that Jo would need time to recover; she had just lost one of her best friends.

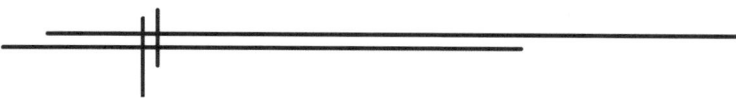

Jo stood by the casket with Pearl and Gerald, waiting for the other mourners to leave. The leader of the honor guard walked up to Jo and offered her three empty shell casings, one from each volley of the rifle squad. He explained the meaning of each casing as he placed it in her hand.

"Ma'am, these casings represent honor…duty…and country."

The honor guard stood at attention the entire time and would remain that way until the family left. When the last of the mourners' cars pulled away, Pearl again reached out and squeezed Jo's arm.

"You're our family, Josephine. Don't think otherwise."

"I know."

The three started walking to the car. For the first time that day, Jo realized how sunny it was. As they walked, Jo looked up at the sky, then around the cemetery, wondering how many other women had gone through as much as she in such a short time. She looked down the hill and noticed somebody standing under a big oak tree. It took a second to realize it was Peter standing way down at the bottom of the hill, and, when she did, she stopped. Her heart fluttered.

When Jo stopped, Pearl did, too. She looked at Jo to see if something was wrong, then followed her gaze down the hill. When she saw Peter, she squeezed Jo's arm one more time—harder—scowled a slight bit at Jo, and then continued to the car with Gerald.

Jo stood motionless, staring at Peter. She wanted to run down the hill, to have his muscular arms wrapped around her, enveloping her in comfort. She *needed* to be near him, to tell him all of the thoughts running through her head. But she knew she couldn't, not then, not there. She knew that moment was to be spent with the Troyers in her heart. Time would dictate what would happen.

Still, she had to say *something* to Peter. She slowly raised her hand in a muted wave, then smiled. After a long moment—a moment of longing—she turned and walked to the Troyers' car. Gerald and Pearl were in the car waiting for Jo. She closed the door behind her, and Gerald started the car and drove toward the cemetery entrance. As the car began to move, the honor guard saluted, holding the salute until the car disappeared from view.

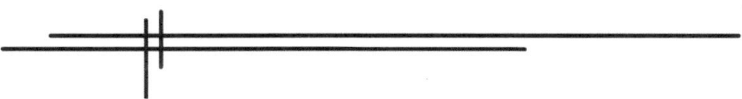

Peter watched Jo's every movement as she and the Troyers walked from the gravesite toward the car. When Jo stopped on seeing him, his mind began to race in rhythm with his heart. He wondered if he should go up the hill and talk to her, but quickly realized that would be a selfish thing to do. So he stood there, watching her watching him. Was she mad? He couldn't tell. Then she waved and smiled. That was what he needed to see,

the smile. He raised his hand in return and watched her get in the car and drive off with the Troyers.

He stood under the tree a few more minutes, watching the honor guard disassemble. The reverend oversaw the pallbearers lowering Al's casket into the ground. As they were doing this, Peter walked up the hill toward the gravesite. He nodded to the reverend, who turned and walked with the honor guard and pallbearers to the hearse. This time, their movements were not choreographed; it was just a group of men walking toward a car. Peter looked down at the casket in the ground for a second.

"Sorry, Al. Hope you really believed in what you were doing, 'cause ya' left a really great girl here."

Peter turned and walked back down the hill and to his truck.

Eric K. Augspurger

The Blooming Grove Review

VOL. XXXV—N? 32 Tuesday, February 1, 1944 Five Cents

MARSHALL ISLANDS INVADED YESTERDAY
First Attack on Territory Held Before War

PEARL HARBOR, H.I.—In a communiqué issued today by Pacific Fleet Headquarters, Admiral Chester Nimitz announced U.S. forces attacked the Marshall Islands yesterday. This is the first attempted invasion of territory held by the Empire of Japan before the attack on Pearl Harbor in December 1941. The communiqué states Japanese resistance is strong, but "...initial information indicates our casualties are moderate." Invasion of the Roi Island area of the Marshalls is being led by Major General Harry Schmidt of the Fourth Marine Division. Roi Island is the location of a first-rate airfield that is perhaps the best in the Marshalls. Invasion of the Kwajalein Island area of the Marshalls is being led by Major General Charles H. Corlett of the army's Seventh Infantry, which is the veteran invaders of Attu in the Aleutians Islands of Alaska Territory. Kwajalein Island contains an superb harbor with seaplane and submarine facilities. Capture of Kwajalein would also pose the most direct threat yet to the massive Japanese base at Truk in the Carolina Islands to the west of the Marshalls.

NEW OPA RULES FOR DISTRIBUTION OF TIRES
Use Determiner in Eligibility, Not Mileage Driven

WASHINGTON, D.C.—At a press conference yesterday by the chief of the Office of Price Administration (OPA), Colonel Brian Houston, he announced a shift in who is eligible for new tires. Effective today, the use of the vehicle will determine who receives new tires, as determined by local rationing boards, instead of mileage driven as under the previous system. Houston stated, "This means that local boards will have to decide which drivers should have priority and that others will have to go without." It is likely no holders of A gasoline ration cards will receive new tires, and only those holders of B ration cards whose driving is rated high on the OPA's list of essential drivers are expected to be eligible for new tires. Those on the list of essential drivers may apply for a ration certificate good for a grade I tire, or if no grade I tires are available, a grade III tire. Any remaining grade III tires will be allocated to those not on the essential list. There may be some variance in these expectations in different locations of the country, but in general holders of A ration cards should not expect new tires. This change in policy follows the news in the announcement that the quota of tires for February will be approximately a quarter of a million tires short of demand.

BEAUTY NEED NOT BE WAR CASUALTY
Shorter, Home Care Nails Popular

CHICAGO, Ill.—Ladies, has your favorite beauty operator heeded the call and become a war worker? Your fingernails can be saved from being a casualty of war with a home manicure. All you need is the proper equipment: an orange wood stick, Emery board, nail brush, polish, polish remover, and cotton. If you cannot maintain the polish, then go without. The long nails standard a few years ago have given way to a more graceful shorter nail. However, women war workers have quickly learned that the smarter nail is even shorter than the lady's in the typing pool. Short, polishless nails have even become popular in Hollywood, in part thanks to being sported by actress Paulette Goddard.

No 21

The noontime whistle blew and the workers started wandering toward the lunchroom. Jo picked up her lunch pail and headed for a table with several other women. Jo really missed Roz; always, but especially during lunch. Before Roz had been taken, lunch had been their daily time together, other than the few minutes in the car before they picked up the others in the morning or after they dropped them off at night. At lunch, the two would run off to some corner of the plant or outside under a tree and gab the lunch hour away, and they allowed Peter to wander in from time to time. Roz had really been the first and only girlfriend Jo had.

After Roz and her family were taken to the camps, Jo had drawn away from everybody except Peter. He and Jo would spend their lunches together, which was, looking back, time that allowed Jo to fall for Peter. When she found out Al had been killed, she started thinking that was punishment for allowing herself to fall for Peter while married to Al.

These days, Jo mostly sat quietly during lunches. Occasionally she would join in the conversation. Certainly if she was asked something directly she would answer. In general, she

kept to herself. She tried to be alone in the crowd. Many times the thought occurred to her she was becoming like Peter in that regard. He kept to himself, even when around others. When she would think about it in those terms, she realized an even greater significance to Peter admitting his feelings for her. This would briefly brighten her mood, but then the thoughts of betrayal of Al would come back around and she would retreat into her self-imposed prison once again.

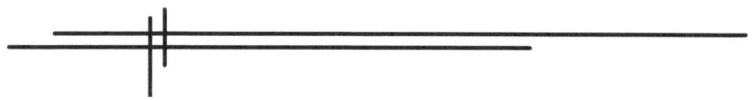

Peter walked into the lunchroom with his lunchbox in hand and scanned the room looking for Jo. He had been keeping his distance for the past few weeks, and she had made no effort to seek him out, but today he wanted—needed—to be around her. He saw Jo sitting with a group of women from the line where she used to work and made his way over there. He pulled a chair from a nearby table, spun it around backward, and sat down.

"Ladies. How we doing today?"

There was much teasing banter exchanged between Peter and the women. Jo kept quiet. She sat up straight and folded her hands on her lap, sort of pulling back from the table, if not the group. She would not look at Peter; when Peter noticed that, he cried inside through the smile on his face. Jo, straining to see Peter through the corner of her eye, saw how his face had sagged just a bit, ever so slightly and not enough for just anybody to notice, but she could see.

It made her feel bad that she had to treat Peter that way, but she could not be around him. In fact, she was just now realizing that she couldn't *stand* to be around him. Peter sitting within arm's reach of her made it impossible for her to deny what she felt, impossible to stay true to the memory of Al. As Peter continued to banter with the women, Jo felt herself becoming upset, and that turned into anger. She was so angry at Peter for thinking he could just walk up and sit down by her. He shouldn't be there; she had to get away before her mind tainted Al's memory with thoughts of being in Peter's arms.

Jo picked up the remains of her lunch and got up from the table without saying a word. She left the lunchroom and walked back to her station in the machine shop.

Peter was shaken by this, but he quickly brushed it off and restarted the playful banter with the women. This was his classic defense mechanism, and with each joke he told, another brick settled into place in the wall he surrounded himself with, the wall that Jo had been able to sneak behind. Behind that façade of humor and banter, he kept wondering what had happened, if he had done something to make Jo mad.

Finally, he convinced himself that Jo just needed more time to sort through Al's death and all that was going on. He decided he would keep his distance for a while longer, until Jo showed him some sort of sign it was okay to be around her. *She would have to be the one to make that decision,* he said to himself.

This made him very sad. It took all he could muster to keep up the jovialities with the women. Peter's heart had ached in Jo's absence; he had been so tantalizingly close to being able to cradle her in his arms, then it had all been torn away. He had managed to get through each day after so far, but when she had refused to even look at him just then—and literally walked away from him—he felt a tightness in his chest squeezing the life out of his heart.

Peter tried for a few more minutes to keep up the humor, but finally he just couldn't take it anymore, and his smile fell. He excused himself and headed back to the foundry. He would surround himself with work to not let his feelings escape into the world. Peter didn't understand that Jo was doing the exact same thing.

The Blooming Grove Review

VOL. XXXV—N° 151 Tuesday, May 30, 1944 Five Cents

MAIL DELIVERY AT SNAIL'S PACE
Delivery Especially Troublesome in Pacific

AEF PACIFIC—Reporting from somewhere in the Pacific theater with the Allied Expeditionary Force, William L. Worden describes the rampant mail delays, especially in outgoing mail. He states those with relatives in the Pacific theater generally "...have the whips and jingles about lack of mail or else have that peculiar stunned look that comes from receiving thirty or forty letters the same day." Case in point, a single shipment of over eight hundred thousand letters from the Pacific arrived in San Francisco in March of this year, which was the largest to date. The remoteness of the many outposts presents logistical problems, and many do not have the photographic equipment to process V-mail, so V-mail has never caught on for those in the Pacific.

FUTURE RATIONING TO INCREASE
New Chief Predicts More Meat Rationing

WASHINGTON, D.C.—Chester Bowles, head of the Office of Price Administration (OPA) since late last year, warns rationing will apply to more commodities in the future and will be more rigid. No details of future rationing were provided, but Bowles said, "Any hope of relaxing [rationing] would depend on the war being short and easy. If the war is tough, we'll have more and acuter shortages than we have ever seen before." The newly appointed Deputy Administrator for Rationing Charles F. Phillips adds, "Some people say rationing is about over. It is not over, or anywhere near over. We could find ourselves six, eight, or nine months from now with much tighter meat rationing." Unfortunately for consumers, this would occur right at the time of the Thanksgiving and Christmas holidays.

NEW STRIKE CLOSES WAR PLANT
Labor Crisis Eases, Continues in Michigan

DETROIT, Mich.—Workers at the main Federal Mogul Company plant went on strike yesterday, halting production at the plant. The war production facility makes bearings for engines. United Automobile Workers Local 202 representatives stated fifteen hundred men quit to protest the dismissal of two union stewards. Also in Detroit, bakery truck drivers and workers at Parke, Davis, and Co. continued their walkouts, totaling forty-four hundred men and women. Despite news of the new and continued strikes, the labor crisis in Michigan has eased this week with the ending of two other strikes in war plants, one at a Chrysler plant in Detroit and one at a General Motors plant in Saginaw.

BIAK ISLAND INVADED
MacArthur One Step Closer to Philippines

WASHINTON, D.C.—On Saturday, forces under the command of General Douglas MacArthur invaded Baik Island in the Schoutens chain, which is located two hundred miles from the north coast of New Guinea. The invasion is seen as one of the last steps before the invasion of the Philippine Islands, which MacArthur promised in 1942 when he said "...I shall return." Baik is only nine hundred miles from the Philippines. American forces met heavy Japanese resistance as they advanced on the Mokmer airdrome on Baik, including a fierce attack by enemy tanks. This is the first time the Japanese have used tanks in the Southwest Pacific.

N<u>o</u> 22

Jo nosed her car into the Troyers' driveway. Tiny slivers of light escaped around the blackout curtains hanging over the windows. The streetlamps were off, and the streets all seemed so lonely in the darkness. She still had not become accustomed to the blackout drills even two years after the town began holding them.

Driving the final rivet into an extra-hard day at work, she leaned her entire body against the car door to open it, then did the same to close it. As she walked up to the back stoop, Jo felt she was merely scraping her feet along the sidewalk even though she was, in fact, taking actual steps.

A cool, almost chilly breeze swept across the night, refreshing her only slightly as it brushed her face. The smell of fresh-cut grass dampened by an evening rain shower filled the air, fighting the scents bursting from the lavender flowers on the lilac bush by the corner of the house. The interplay of pungent aromas reminded Jo that summer was blossoming, and her thoughts wandered to ideas of planting a victory garden. Her eyes surveyed the yard for a possible site as she walked to the house.

Closing the kitchen door behind her, Jo sank into one of the chairs at the kitchen table. Pearl was cleaning up from supper.

"What can I do?" Jo asked.

"Oh, nothing, dear. I saved you a plate."

Pearl scooted over to the oven and withdrew a plate coved in foil. Placing the plate in front of Jo, she peeled off the foil. The tangy smell of barbeque sauce tickled Jo's nose as she leaned her head down over the plate to smell the chicken, baked beans, and buttermilk biscuit.

Pearl reached to the counter, picked up a balled-up mound of foil, and added the new piece to it. The ball was just about big enough to be worth taking to the scrap metal collection point, unless, of course, the neighborhood boys came through with their wagons before then.

"Thank you so much, Pearl. I feel so bad that I haven't been helping out as much as I used to."

She tore the biscuit, dipped it into the beans and then barbeque sauce before poking it into her mouth.

"You work so hard all day, the last thing you need to do is come home and work some more. You know that."

"Still, I feel like I should do more."

"You know," Pearl pulled out a chair and sat down next to Jo, "at first I really didn't like the idea of you getting a job. Not one bit. But you've shown me it was the right thing to do. You've grown into a strong woman who can take care of herself."

"Pearl, that means so much to me for you to say that."

"You and I, we share this same grief over my Alfred. I can tell he is strong in both of our hearts. I think it's good you're keeping to yourself, not straying from Alfred, and sticking it out at work will help keep your mind off things."

Almost exploding from within Jo were words about how her feelings for Al had changed—even before he had been killed—but she knew she couldn't tell Pearl. Not then, maybe not ever; she kept pushing hard on the words to keep them in. Peter had started to creep back into Jo's thoughts, along with questions if maybe the time was approaching when she could at least be around him again. At times, she wondered if the pain in her heart was truly for Al, or if it was because she longed to be with Peter. She missed him so, but she kept telling herself it wasn't right; it wasn't right before when she was married, and it wasn't right now that she was a widow.

Jo hadn't noticed that Pearl had stood up and walked over to the counter.

"Josephine...something came in the mail today."

Pulled from her thoughts, Jo looked at Pearl, whose back was still toward her. There was an awkwardness to Pearl's voice, almost quivering or breaking—something Jo had never before heard from her.

"It's...it's a letter from Alfred."

"What!"

Jo felt her heart stop, and cold sweat popped on her forehead. As Pearl turned toward her, letter in hand, a ringing started in Jo's ears. The sounds all around echoed as if the room was a cave and Pearl was speaking from outside it.

"He must have mailed it before...before...the military mail can take months sometimes, you know."

Pearl laid the letter in front of Jo and then put her hand on Jo's shoulder. Jo's heart jumped a giant thump in her chest, then started beating at what felt like a million times a minute before settling in to a slightly increased rate. She stared at the letter, then looked up at Pearl.

"Why don't you go up to your room and read it. I'll bring you up some tea in about a half hour."

The Ration Card

Jo closed her bedroom door, then leaned her back against it. She held the unopened letter in both hands, staring at it as she slowly slid down the door until she was sitting on the floor. Devoid of fingernails of any regard, she tore off the end of the envelope instead of trying to slice it open with her nubby nails. Reaching inside, she pulled out the letter. The date was six months ago...the day Al had died.

November 20, 1943

We're getting ready to load up for a big attack. I've only got a few minutes, but I wanted to write and get this to the company clerk before I have to get on my amtrac. I'm still with the _____, along with Jeb, Junior, and Frankie. I've told you about them before. Our unit is going to be in the first wave on _____. I'm sure you've read about the attack by the time this letter gets to you. There are several other units here, too, but if I told you which ones, the censors would probably just cut it out, but that's not important anyhow.

I want to let you know that I do think about you all the time. But I am not the same person I was two years ago. After all I have been through, I just can't even begin to tell you. I know you have to be different, too. Just from your letters I can tell. You have a job and a lot of responsibility. That's a far cry from the little shy girl I first met. I hope when I get home that we still have enough in common. But I want you to know that if we don't, if you have moved on, if we have both moved on to other places in life, that I understand. I care about you enough to want you to be happy, and I know you feel the same way about me.

The sergeant is calling my squad up for loading. I have to run to the company clerk to mail this and then scramble down to the amtrac.

Always

Al

As Jo was reading, tears had welled in her eyes, but now they were streaming down her cheeks. She dropped her head and rested her forehead on the back of her hand, her elbow propped on one knee. Flashing through her head were thoughts of Al and their life together. She pictured the first time Al had kissed her. He had been so nervous, as was she; two best friends taking a next step. She thought of the day Al had proposed, the same day he had joined the marines.

She thought of the day she found out Al had been killed; killed the day he wrote this letter. She could still feel that day as if it was today, seeing the olive drab car with the white star parked on the curb in front of the house. It was a numbness and a desperation. She recalled how her eyes had followed Peter's finger down the street, pointing at the car. He, too, had known just what that car meant. Peter...that was also the day she and Peter had finally admitted what they felt for each other. And then it all came crashing down. Feelings of betrayal resonated in her heart.

VOL. XXXV—N? 159   Wednesday, June 7, 1944   Five Cents

EXTRA EDITION! EUROPE INVADED!

Allied Forces Make Landings in Normandy, France

LONDON, England—Supreme Headquarters of the Allied Expeditionary Force in Europe issued this communiqué yesterday morning: "Under the command of General Eisenhower, Allied naval forces, supported by strong air forces, began landing Allied armies this morning on the northern coast of France." Berlin first announced the landings at about six-thirty a.m. Berlin time Tuesday, about twelve-thirty a.m. U.S. eastern war time. Allied command initially did not state the exact location of the invasion, but reports from Berlin were of paratroopers dropped in Normandy; Allied command has since confirmed the location. Reports today are that Allied forces have advanced as many as thirteen miles inland. Allied command states the first invasion phase is now complete.

URGE TO AVOID LABOR TROUBLE
General Comments on Work Holiday

MILWAUKEE, Wisc.—Speaking Wednesday night, Brigadier General John F. Davis told his audience of a foreman's safety school to avoid engaging in labor disruptions. Davis specifically spoke of the work holiday taken by workers at the Harley-Davidson Motor Company that morning. "Before we had peeps and jeeps, we had one hundred and sixteen motorcycles to a regiment. We have fewer now, but we still require a substantial number—we'd be paralyzed without them. ... If a worker stops on the production line, it is the same as a soldier who stops fighting, if the question is viewed on an overall war basis."

OPA PROBES TIRES
Looks at Ration Violations

WASHINGTON, D.C.—The Office of Price Administration (OPA) is looking into cases of tire ration violations. The reports accuse ration certificates are not being voided when turned in by consumers. The certificates are reportedly returned to dealers or in some cases never leave the dealers. Some of the country's biggest tire companies are mentioned in the reports.

Invasion Beaches Only Hole in Atlantic Wall

LONDON, England—Hitler's so-called and much vaunted Atlantic Wall was inadequate along the invasion beaches. The Nazis had focused preparations and fortifications around the ports in Denmark, Holland, Belgium, and France. As a result, a gap of nearly sixty miles was left from Cherbourg, Saint Malo, Brest, Lorient, Nantes, and Bordeaux on the south and, on the north, Le Harve, Dieppe, Boulogne, Calais, Dunkerque, the hook of Holland, and the Elbe and Weser estuaries. Shortages of manpower, materials, and transportation forced the Nazis to first fortify the important port areas and delayed completing the continuous line of fortifications from Denmark to Spain. Some captured enemy have said the Germans frantically tried to complete defensive fortifications in areas that were lacking, but the task proved too great. The first Nazi prisoners captured on the Allied beachheads in northern France have been moved from Normandy to England.

N⁰ 23

Wednesday morning, Jo made sure she got to work early. She wanted to look at the map in Mr. Jensen's office. She had spent the previous evening pouring over the special edition of the newspaper, as she was sure everybody in America had done. She read every last detail about the invasion in Europe that had taken place as America was asleep Monday night. All day Tuesday—June 6—Jo sensed something in the air at the factory. It wasn't just the constant buzz of conversation as everyone talked about the invasion, nor was it the radio station Mr. Jensen had piped in over the loudspeakers the entire day so they could hear the constant news updates. It was more than that. Everybody seemed to be doing just a bit more, for a bit longer, and a bit better than before, and it seemed everybody was standing just a bit taller, too.

Jo stood in front of the map in Mr. Jensen's office. He was there, as were a couple of other workers. Mr. Jensen was pointing out where Normandy was, using the point of a pencil to show what he thought would have been the course the ships had taken. Jo watched intently, hanging on his every word just as she had done with every word she read the night before.

Gradually, the other workers left. Mr. Jensen patted Jo on the shoulder and gave her a smile before leaving. She stayed for a few more minutes, looking at all of the pins in the map. Then she shifted to the left side of the map. She held up her hand and touched the red pin in Tarawa. To Jo, it seemed Tarawa was barely a dot in the middle of the Pacific Ocean. Little did she know just how small it really was, yet so many men had died there. Al had died there.

She thought about the last letter Al had sent, and how many other wives and mothers had received a last letter written the same day. She thought about Pearl and how it had to be infinitely harder on her because she lost her son. She thought of Peter's mother; she had once lost a son, too. And Peter, he had lost a brother. Did he stand in front of a map like this one, thinking about the place where his brother had been killed? Did he still think about that loss? Did he still think about her?

The moment Peter entered her head, she shook it off. She reminded herself there was work to do, and she had best stay focused on that. She left Mr. Jensen's office and headed down to the machine shop.

Eric K. Augspurger

VOL. XXXV—N⁰ 161   Friday, June 9, 1944   Five Cents

U.S. WAR CASUALTIES MOUNTING
Invasion of France Not Included in New Numbers

WASHINGTON, D.C.—The War and Navy Departments released yesterday updated numbers for U.S. war casualties, which now total 217,131. The total casualty number is an increase of over ten thousand from just two weeks ago. Of the total casualties, 48,754 are dead. This updated total does not include casualties of the invasion of France; that total is not yet known and not expected for another two or three weeks. Despite the unknown number of casualties, confident praise comes today—D-Day plus three—from Supreme Allied Commander Dwight D. Eisenhower. Ike's appraisal of the first fifty-four hours of the invasion states his faith in Allied forces was "...completely justified...". He further states the ground forces were "...performing magnificently." Ground forces are commanded by General Sir Bernard Montgomery.

OPA PENALTY MODIFIED
Senate Votes to Allow Plea

WASHINGTON, D.C.—In a 47–27 vote, the Senate on Wednesday amended the Emergency Price Control Act by allowing merchants and others to plead a violation of the price ceiling was "...neither willful nor the result of failure to take practical precautions against the occurrence of the violation." If merchants can prove price ceiling overcharges were unintentional, they will be freed from damage liabilities. Under the current rules, consumers may sue merchants for violations of price ceilings for three times the overcharge or fifty dollars, whichever is greater. The amendment is seen as a setback for the administration trying to re-enact the price ceiling change without any substantial changes. Opponents of the amendment speculated it would lead to more violations of price ceilings and argued it removed one of the main reasons for the existence of the Office of Price Administration (OPA), which is to protect consumers from overcharges.

MOKMER AERODROME FALLS
Twelve-Day Fight for Airfield

SYDNEY, Australia—For the first time since early in the Pacific war, the Allies have an airbase within bombing distance of the Philippine Islands. American forces seized the aerodrome on Baik Island in the Schouten chain north of New Guinea. Two other airfields on the island remain in Japanese hands, but American forces are driving on them. American losses are reported to be light despite twelve days of intense fighting.

FOUL WEATHER HAMPERS REINFORCEMENT
Blustery Channel Beginning to Clear, Inland As Well

LONDON, England—The foul weather in the English Channel, which delayed the Allied invasion of France by one day and almost caused disaster, began to clear today. The sea is starting to relax, allowing for easier debarkation from landing craft. The improving weather extends inland over France, which is allowing air forces to sortie in support of ground forces. More than twenty-seven thousand sorties have been flown over Europe since the start of the D-Day invasion. Allied aircraft losses are just over one per cent, a total of only two hundred and eighty-nine planes.

N⚬ 24

Early Friday morning, the mist hung in the low spot on the gently rolling field of the Blooming Grove cemetery, and the emerging scents of morning glories and honeysuckles danced across the moist air. Peter walked down the lane toward where his brother was buried. June 9 was twenty-six years to the day since his brother had been killed at Belleau Wood.

It had been at least ten years since Peter had visited his brother's grave. But the past few weeks, he had realized a loss he hadn't felt since his brother was killed—the loss of Jo—and the connection had made him start thinking about his brother more and more. If he couldn't do anything about the loss of Jo—not until she took the first step back to him, *if* she took the first step back—he could come visit his brother.

As he made his way through the cemetery, Peter looked around for things he recognized. So much had changed since his last visit. Gradually he picked up on markers, trees, and paths that he recognized. Less had changed the closer he got to his brother's grave. When he turned down the row where his brother was buried, Peter knew he was in the right place.

He stood in front of his brother's grave. The coolness of the morning drifted over his brow as he looked down at the marker.

"Hello, brother," he said aloud. "Sorry it's been so long since I've come to see you."

He continued the conversation in his head.

"Dad's still doing good. Mom's okay. Met a girl. Things are complicated. Think she really likes me, but her husband was killed in the war. Not your war. There's this other war going on now. Sort of the same stuff all over again. I really love her. Never felt this way about anybody else. You'd really like her. She's spunky. Remember how we'd both get caught up with any girl who had spunk? Wish you could meet her."

Peter looked down from the marker to the grass below it, as if he could peer through the dirt to see his brother the same as the last time he actually saw him. After a minute, he walked over to the marker, patted it, and said aloud, "Promise it won't be so long until next time." He glanced to the sky, then scanned the cemetery.

Peter thought he had been the only one there so early in the morning, but on the hill on the other side of the cemetery somebody was paying respects. He squinted and held up his hand to shield his eyes from the sun waxing on the horizon before he realized it was Jo.

He walked over to the other side of the cemetery. As he approached Jo, he tried to be respectfully quiet, yet he was conscious not to sneak up on her. Jo heard him walking up behind her and turned to see who it was.

"Oh, hi Pete."

"Hi, Jo. Hope I didn't startle you."

"No. What are you doing here?" Her tone was slightly accusatory.

"Today's the anniversary of my brother's death. Twenty-six years."

"Oh." Guilt tinged her voice having thought he might have followed her.

"Been a long time since I've come to see him."

There was a long pause. Peter stared down the hill in the direction of his brother's grave. When the silence became too much for Jo, she spoke.

"I've been thinking a lot about Al these past three days, ever since the invasion in Europe…I guess they're calling it 'D-Day'. Did you know today is six months since Al was buried?" Her tone was not accusatory, rather inquisitive.

"No, I didn't…Jo, I'm sorry."

"Don't be. I'm the one who should be sorry. I had actually stopped thinking about him. I didn't realize that until D-Day, but it's true, I had stopped thinking about him. Here I am shutting everybody out because I feel guilty about Al, and I go and stop thinking about him. Funny…I spent so much time trying to be true to his memory I forgot to leave time to remember him."

"When I first heard my brother had been killed, I did the same thing. I focused on my chores around the farm, trying to keep myself occupied. Every waking moment I thought about him. Eventually, me keeping myself occupied left little time to think about my brother."

"That never occurred to me. You never talk about him, so I don't really think about that aspect of your life."

"It was a long time ago. That's not an excuse, just a fact. Time passes, things change." Peter again paused, reflecting on how much time he had allowed to pass since visiting his brother's grave. "Doesn't mean I care for him any less, or my memory of him is any less."

"Time hasn't passed for me yet."

"It has."

"Not enough. Not enough for it to be okay that I stopped thinking about Al."

"Jo, you may have stopped thinking about him every moment of every day, but you didn't forget him, no more than I forgot my

brother even though it's been ten years since I've come here to visit him."

"Pete, I just can't stand feeling this way."

"It's hard, I know, but you can't punish yourself for something you had no control over. I did the same thing when my brother died. I talked myself into believing he had died because I didn't go to war with him. Like somehow if I had been there, that bullet wouldn't have found him. Truth be told, if I had gone over there with him, my parents probably would have buried two sons, not just one."

"Pete, that's not quite the same."

"No…and yes. Your pain and loss are real, just as they were with me and my brother. You can never forget that, but you can't ignore the future for the past, a past you can't change."

"What are you saying?"

"Jo, you have to start thinking about yourself. You can't spend so much time protecting a memory of Al's life that you have no time for your own life."

"I just need…I'm not ready yet."

Peter put his arm around Jo's shoulder. At first, she pulled back slightly, but then leaned into his chest.

"It'll take time," Peter said, "just don't let it take forever." He gave her a little squeeze, then let go and pulled back. "Take care, okay Jo?" She looked at him and nodded. "People do care about you and are here to help."

With that, Peter turned and walked away. Jo watched him for a while until he was so far away he looked to be the size of a doll. She turned back to Al's grave.

"I'm so sorry, Al. I never should have…"

She didn't finish her sentence. She couldn't bear to hear herself say the words. She looked down at where Al lay for a long minute. Then she turned and walked toward her car. She had a long day of work ahead of her.

Eric K. Augspurger

The Blooming Grove Review

VOL. XXXV—N? 176   Saturday, June 24, 1944   Five Cents

ENEMY ON SAIPAN NOW DOOMED
Japanese Fleet Abandons Garrison on Island

PEARL HARBOR, H.I.—Imperial naval forces were defeated by Allied naval forces and withdrew from Saipan, assuring American ground forces on the island of ultimate victory. A communiqué released on Thursday by Admiral Chester Nimitz, commander-in-chief of the Pacific fleet, stated, "The United States Fifth Fleet made a surprise attack on the Japanese Grand Fleet on Monday, and carrier-based planes sank four and possibly five enemy ships, including an aircraft carrier and three tankers, and damaged nine other warships." Enemy losses in the naval engagement were bested only by the actions at Midway and Guadalcanal. When American ground forces landed on the island on June 14, defenders were estimated to number twenty thousand. Marines and infantry launched a major ground attack yesterday morning before dawn. Later in the morning, the commander of the invasion and his staff transferred to shore. With its fleet no longer present, the enemy garrison is unable to receive reinforcements or resupply, while American forces steadily receive both. Saipan is located in the Marianas chain about fifteen hundred miles south of Tokio.

VICTORY GARDEN SHORTFALL
Gallup Poll Disappointment for WFA Goal

PRINCETON, N.J.—The National Garden Advisory Committee of the War Food Administration (WFA) has a stated goal that Americans maintain twenty-two million Victory gardens in 1944. George Gallup, director of the American Institute of Public Opinion, reports on May 31 of this year that Americans are falling well short of this goal. The poll claims only seventeen and a half million families have started raising their Victory gardens. Combined with those who plan to plant a garden, the total is about five hundred thousand less than the 1943 total and four and a half million short of this year's goal. Victory gardens allow commercial producers to grow, pack, and ship more food for military uses and reduce the amount of rationing that civilians must endure.

CHERBOURG FALLING
Nazis Partially Withdraw

LONDON, England—General Omar Bradley began an all-out offensive two days ago against the Cherbourg peninsula. While the port town of Cherbourg remains in enemy hands, indications are the Nazis have withdrawn from much of the peninsula to concentrate forces in the town. The belief is the Nazis will conduct a house-by-house defense of the town, and reports are Americans have already engaged in such combat. Yesterday, the Allied air forces unleashed one thousand planes on the defenses in and around the town of Cherbourg, but the enemy stands fast. By nightfall, Americans ground forces had cleared the fortified heights of Mont du Roule on the southwestern edge of the town. Only small gains have been reported around the town proper, but elsewhere on the peninsula American forces report light resistance. The town of Cherbourg is a traditional fortress, but its defenses were built to resist attacks from the sea. Fortifications on the landward sides of the town are not as formidable, and it is from there the American forces approach.

№25

Jo pulled the wire fabric and wood from her car. In doing so, she was very careful not to knock over the small wooden crate holding the four yellow chicks, each chirping like mad at being moved around. The wood she had scrounged from some broken pallets at the plant. She had purchased the wire downtown at the hardware store, along with nails, a couple of hinges, a hook latch, and some vegetable seeds and chicken feed. The chicks also came from the hardware store, sold there by S. E. Feed and Hatchery, whose operation was just outside of town.

Jo hauled the wood and wire to the side of the yard, near the back corner of the garage. Her arms were lean and taut from her work at the plant, and her back strong; she easily managed moving the materials in three trips. The corner of the yard was where she would build the chicken coop, and next to it was where she would plant a vegetable garden. Not only would this location be out of the way, it would be easy for her to feed and water the chickens on her way to the car as she left for work. The coop would be constructed so its back wall was the side wall of the garage.

Jo retrieved a hammer, hand saw, and metal snips from the garage and set about building the coop. She had made rough measurements of how much wood she had when she scrounged it, but now she took more precise measurements. Quickly, she calculated how big to make the coop based on how much wood and fabric she had. Since becoming a machinist, she had developed the ability to easily calculate dimensions in her head. She also had become quite adept at picturing the end result of taking a pile of raw material and turning it into a finished product; in this case, a chicken coop.

Bit by bit over the next couple of hours, the chicken coop took shape. Jo first assembled each wall on the ground, then rotated it up into position. She checked the squareness of the walls by measuring diagonal corners. This was another skill she had learned on the job. Once the walls were in place, she constructed a door and attached it with the hinges she had purchased. Finally, she constructed a small box in one corner where the chicks could nest. She hinged the front to swing upward so she could open it to gather the eggs and clean out the nesting boxes.

With the chicken coop constructed and the chicks at home, Jo began staking out a small plot next to the coop for the garden. She thought tending the garden would keep her distracted from other things going on, keep her distracted from Peter. She had also developed a strong sense of satisfaction from putting work into a project or task and completing it. Her job at the plant had given her that, and she hoped she would get the same satisfaction from raising a garden. She paused a moment and looked at the chicken coop she had completed. Being made of scrap wood, it may not have been worthy of any beauty awards, but it was nicely constructed, sturdy and sound. Jo wiped the back of her glove over her forehead and smiled, satisfied at the end result.

It seemed to Jo that most people she knew who had planted a victory garden did so to help keep food on the table with all of the rationing, rather than help with the war effort. Although, tending one could make gardeners feel like they were contributing to the war effort as well.

Jo's intent, too, was to ensure food was on the table, but in a slightly different way. She was bound and determined to have a

big Christmas dinner that year with the Troyers. Since Al had died, Jo began to feel like the only real family she had known was starting to die, too. The Troyers still treated her as family, but she knew it wasn't easy for them. They saw Jo every day, and it was a constant reminder Al was gone. Jo knew it was especially hard on Pearl. She had watched as Pearl had withdrawn from Jo and Gerald, spending more and more time at church functions. Jo couldn't see that she herself was doing the same thing, withdrawing from everybody, spending almost all her time either working at the plant or engaged in volunteer activities.

The Troyers could have easily asked Jo to move out—she had a job and could afford to do so—but they didn't. Perhaps instead of a continuous reminder that their son was dead, she was a continuing connection to Al.

That's what it is, she thought as she stabbed the spade into the soil. *And they are a connection to Al for me, too.*

As the sun dipped below the horizon, Jo tapped the soil over the last set of seeds. The air still turned refreshingly cool in late June as the sun set. Days were warm, but not hot like they would be in just a couple of weeks, and Jo had worked up a sweat building the coop and planting the garden. The coolness felt good on her arms and along the wet crescents under her breasts. She checked on the chicks, guided them into the overnight crib, and turned on the heat lamp. She returned the spade and hoe to the garage, then filled a watering can. She spent about fifteen minutes watering the newly planted seeds, then brushed herself to knock off some of the dirt and headed inside, where Pearl was fixing supper.

"Well, I got the garden planted and the chicks in their coop."

"What did you decide to plant?"

"There's some green beans, some potatoes, corn, and, of course, a couple of pumpkins."

"Pumpkins? Really?"

"Yeah. I want us to have everything we need for a good Christmas dinner. Who knows what rationing will allow then.

We'll have to have chicken instead of turkey, 'cause the hatchery was already all out of turkey chicks."

"A big Christmas dinner?" Pearl's inflection was halfway between a question and a statement. "That will be very nice, but this is the first you've mentioned anything about that. 'Course, I guess I wouldn't have expected you to, with Christmas still six months away."

"I know. It seems odd to think of Christmas now, but you have to grow stuff now."

"Your friend, Roz."

It was a statement, not a question, and a very abrupt change in topic, both of which caught Jo off guard. Pearl pulled out a chair and sat down with Jo at the kitchen table. There was more than a bit of apprehension in Jo's voice as she responded.

"Yeah?"

"Her family ran Abe's before...that frightful nonsense."

Pearl pronounced the family name correctly. Once Pearl had learned the correct pronunciation, she always used it, even if it meant repeating the name and explaining what she meant, and why she pronounced it as she did. Just about no one in Blooming Grove held any ill-will toward the Abes. The family had been a quiet part of the community, and Mr. Abe had been a respected member of the town's businesses. Still, since the war started Pearl—and Jo—could sense an underlying suspicion of the Abes in most people, usually more noticeable in those who had some connection to the war in the Pacific.

"Uh-huh."

Jo was completely lost now, having no idea where Pearl was heading. A bit of fear crept in, and she could feel her heart thumping in her chest. Her stomach also felt a bit sour. Had Pearl heard some bad news about Roz or her family? Had something happened to them? Jo knew Roz's brother had volunteered for the so-called *Nisei* regiment and was in Europe. Had he been wounded, or killed? Jo suddenly felt cold and shivered a bit.

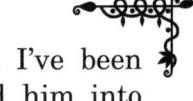

"Well, Abe's has been sitting closed since then. I've been writing back and forth with Mr. Abe, and I talked him into letting me open it up again, run it until they get back to town."

"Really! That's great!"

Warmth returned to Jo as she felt her fear melt away. She was dumbfounded and excited at the same time. She reached over and squeezed both of Pearl's hands, her own hands still slightly cold from the wave of nervousness that had just washed away.

"I didn't say anything to you. Didn't want you to get your hopes up."

"No. No, I understand."

"But I was afraid with it sitting closed people would get used to shopping at one of the other stores and then never go back when the Abes come home. Or, worse, somebody'd do something stupid, and there wouldn't be a business to come back to."

Jo was smiling and trying to fight back a small tear she felt forming in her eye. She had always wondered how Pearl felt about the Abes—and Roz—once Al had been killed. She sort of thought Pearl might be hiding some resentment, somehow holding them in part responsible for Al's death just because their ancestors were from Japan. Jo was relieved that was not the case for many reasons. She had been worrying that because of her friendship with Roz, Pearl had been by extension holding Jo in part responsible for Al's death. That, and also Peter; Jo wondered if Pearl knew anything about how she had fallen for Peter.

"I'm so happy, Pearl. I worried about the store being empty, too. Roz never mentioned in any of her letters that you were talking to her dad about reopening the store."

"I think she didn't want to get your hopes up. 'Course, she may not know, either. I don't know if her father told her. If he did, I'm sure she'll tell you about it in the next letter."

"When does the store open again?"

"Couple weeks. I've gotten the spoiled goods out now and am waiting for some new product to come in."

"I'm so happy that you would do this for them, Pearl."

And she was. Jo had always known the Troyers to be good people. They had given her more than she could have ever expected, and they had always been quick to help out others, too, but what Pearl was doing for the Abes was such a commitment to help out, it showed Jo how far their goodness extended. Her thoughts again turned to Peter; this new level of goodness she saw in Pearl heightened Jo's sense of her personal betrayal toward Al and the Troyers. She felt she had let down Al, and that if the Troyers knew what she had done, they would shame her out of their life and she would have lost every vestige of the only real family she had ever known. Jo's excitement had quickly turned to sadness as she was lost in her thoughts, but Pearl's voice drew her back to the conversation.

"It's not just for them, Josephine. It's for me, too."

"What do you mean?"

"I have to admit, I was a lot more upset about you going to work at the plant than I let on. At first. Then, I saw how happy it made you. Right before my eyes, you grew up into a woman who can fend for herself."

"Well, not entirely. I do still live here, and you take care of me quite a bit."

"That's a choice, Josephine, not a requirement. You could move out on your own. In fact, you and Roz had been talking about getting an apartment together before…everything."

"Yeah, we had talked about that."

There was a loneliness in Jo's voice that was impossible to hide. Roz and her family being taken to an internment camp had been a turning point in Jo's life, she just didn't know how much of a turning point at the time. There was the obvious aspect of her best friend being taken away, but then there were less obvious things, such as the apartment. Even though Jo could afford an apartment by herself—she was making very good

money as a machinist in a war industry—the idea just disappeared after Roz was forced into the camp.

Then, also, there was the whole thing with Peter. Roz had no longer been around to be a buffer, and the simple fact that she had been taken away also pushed Jo toward Peter. Would she have fallen for Peter had Roz been around? Looking back, Jo thought she probably had already fallen for Peter *before* Roz was gone, she just didn't realize it. Over and over, she had replayed many memories in her head. It was easy to see certain signs that Roz herself had seen Jo and Peter falling for each other long before either of them knew. Jo supposed that Roz being gone had only accelerated she and Peter falling for each other; they were already on that collision course.

"Josephine, seeing you as happy as you are working and making your own money, well...it made me jealous, to be honest."

"Really? Jealous of me? I thought you had exactly what you wanted."

"I did, too. Then, Alfred left...and then died...and with work and your new friends, you weren't really around either. I just started to feel a little empty. Don't get me wrong, I'm not unhappy. Gerald is a great husband and treats me very well, and I'm glad you are still living here, but I started thinking I should look for something more. One day I was downtown and walked past Abe's. I realized it had been sitting closed for so long and thought somebody should open it. Everything just came together at that one moment, so I went home and wrote Mr. Abe a letter."

"Pearl, I'm shocked. I'm happy, but I'm shocked. Let me know how I can help out."

"I'm trying to do this as much on my own as possible. Gerald isn't the happiest about that. He's going to help out with the books and such at first, but I made it clear to him that I want to run the show."

"That's great, Pearl. I'm so happy for you."

The Blooming Grove Review

VOL. XXXV—N? 253 Saturday, September 9, 1944 Five Cents

PALAU GROUP POUNDED
Naval Bombardment Wednesday

PEARL HARBOR, H.I.—Pacific Fleet Headquarters here announced today that a naval bombardment of the Palau group of islands in the western Carolinas chain was executed on Wednesday. Buildings and defensive fortifications were heavily damaged. Tokyo radio claimed battleships and destroyers were involved in the bombardment, but Allied sources report the vessels were cruisers and destroyers. Tokyo also made claims of five hundred Allied aircraft involved. None of the Allied vessels were damaged in the bombardment. Carrier-based planes made other attacks throughout the Carolinas.

LONE RANGER DEAD
Actor Turned Marine Killed in Action

LONG BEACH, Calif.—Marine Corps sergeant Lee Powell, who before the war played the Lone Ranger in movies, was killed in action in the South Pacific. He had been in the South Pacific since November of 1942 and had seen action on both Tarawa late last year and Saipan this summer. These have been two of the bloodiest battles of the Pacific action. Although he would survive those actions, he ultimately lost his life in service of his country. The Navy announced Powell's death on August 29. His wife Norma, now a war widow like so many other young women, said she was not informed where her husband had been killed. Powell starred in fifteen Lone Ranger serials produced by Republic Movies and released in 1938.

SCRAP METAL SHORTAGE
Steel Industry Warns of Crisis

FREDERICK, Md.—Edwin C. Barringer, of the Institute of Scrap Iron and Steel, warns the steel industry may face a crisis in maintaining output if the war continues into the winter of 1944. A shortage of high-grade scrap metal may make it impossible for the industry to maintain the current output of ninety-five to one hundred per cent of capacity. Barringer stated the steel industry used fifty-five million long tons of scrap metal in 1943. The estimated tonnage for this year is the same. It takes eighteen tons of steel to make one tank. A large naval vessel may require as much as nine hundred tons of steel in its construction.

NAZI COUNTERATTACK STOPPED
Third Army in Action Along Moselle River

LONDON, England—A large-scale counteroffensive by German forces along the Moselle River was stopped today by the American Third Army; even cooks and clerks were on the front lines. Reports are of thirty to forty enemy tanks knocked out in the action. The counterattack began yesterday from Luxembourg, moving through the enemy strongpoint of Thionville. Third Army had taken over seven hundred prisoners in the action, which at its conclusion saw dead and wounded enemy strewn throughout the woods. The size of the German counterattack is an indication the enemy is regrouped and prepared for tenacious defense. The Third Army engagement was the first full-scale battle since the breakout from Normandy on July 25. It is across the Moselle in three places. The First Army is eighteen miles from the German border in Belgium. Other forces are also closing in on Germany.

№ 26

Peter sat in his truck at the ballpark. Barney stood on the seat next to him, the dog craning his head out of the passenger's window to get his nose as close to as many smells as he could. It had been almost exactly one year since Peter, Roz, and Jo came to the last home game of the Maidens' season, and today was the last home game of this year's season. The days were still hot in early September, but Peter didn't plan on staying at the ballpark long, so Barney would be fine waiting in the truck. Still, he parked the truck under the big shade tree at the edge of the lot.

Peter sat with both hands on the steering wheel, staring down at its center. He was contemplating what he was about to do. He hadn't spoken to Jo since that day in the cemetery, just after D-Day. She told him she needed time, and he understood that, but he figured three months was enough. Today he would go to Jo, tell her it was time for them to be together, and sweep her away in his arms. He let out a deep breath, blowing it through his mouth in a silent whistle. Barney swung around and shoved his cold nose in Peter's ear.

"Ahg. All right, all right already, I'm going."

He got out of the truck and reached back in to scratch Barney's ears. He started toward the grandstand, looking for the booth for the scrap metal drive. As he got closer to the grandstand, he spotted the booth and headed over to it. His heart began to palpitate, and he was beginning to feel a bit lightheaded. His hands started to shake; the closer he got to the booth the more they trembled.

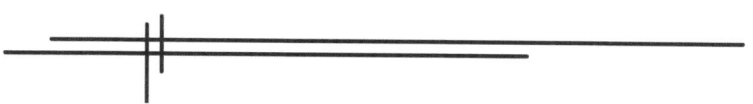

A simple banner hung across the booth thanking people for their contributions of metal to the war effort. Jo was graciously accepting any scrap metal being turned in, having cursory conversations with those dropping off the donations. A young man walked up to the booth. He was wearing an army uniform, and she thought he looked very attractive in it. His right arm was in a sling, and she could see a row of black lines running like railroad tracks up his bruised and swollen hand and disappearing behind the sling. It was the signature of the surgeon who had repaired the soldier's crushed arm.

"Hi," he said as he stepped to the booth. He was smiling, and his eyes were wandering all over Jo's face. "I'm Bill."

"Hi," she smiled back, glancing away as she felt herself blush.

It made her feel good this handsome man was looking at her in that way. She kept smiling as she looked back at him, their eyes meeting. She stammered a bit as she spoke.

"Um, do you have any metal to donate?"

"No. Well, I have about a pound of it in my arm I'd like to donate, but I can't quite get that out right now."

Jo wasn't sure if he was joking or being bitter, but when he laughed she laughed, too.

"No, I just saw you here and had to come over to meet you."

"What?"

Jo felt her cheeks flush again. She was surprised by how she was becoming shy around this man. It never occurred to her that men would look at her this way. The realization caught her off guard. Then she saw Bill staring at her left hand. She glanced down, then quickly folded her fingers in on themselves with her thumb concealing the ring.

"Widow," Jo replied to the unasked question. She glanced up at Bill through the curls on her forehead, then quickly looked down at the counter. "Last year...Tarawa."

Jo was still smiling from the attention he was paying her, but her smile had faded some as thoughts of Al surfaced. With her fingers still folded in on themselves, she unconsciously fidgeted with the ring, agitating it with her thumb.

"I'm sorry. This war has changed a lot of lives, hasn't it?"

Bill paused and looked off toward the horizon. He tried to flex his wounded hand—he could barely move his fingers—as if he were contemplating how his own life had been changed by the war, as if he were momentarily reliving the hell of action that shattered his arm. After a few seconds, he looked back at Jo. Their eyes locked for a moment before he spoke.

"Hey, listen, would you let me take you to a movie? That new Donald Duck cartoon *The Three Caballeros* is playing the matinée. We could go next weekend."

She smiled and looked down at the counter. She was completely dumfounded. Here was a man she didn't know—barely knew his name—and he was asking her on a date. Asking *her* on a date. It was very flattering that out of nowhere a man would be attracted to her. It made her feel like a desirable woman. She considered the offer for a minute.

"I, uh...don't think that would be such a good idea. I mean, I appreciate the offer, and I'm very flattered. I just don't know if I should."

"Perhaps another time, then."

He smiled and looked at Jo for a minute before turning and walking away. She watched him as he melted into the crowd heading into the stadium. Just before he disappeared into the

mass of people, he turned and looked back at Jo. It took a few minutes for her smile to fade. It wasn't until a farmer walked up to the booth with some scrap to donate that the encounter passed from her thoughts.

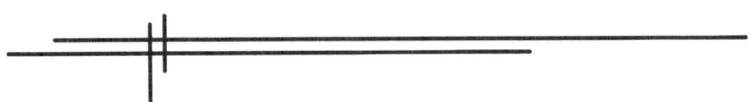

Peter's legs were shaking as he walked toward the booth; the closer he got to Jo, the more they seemed to shake. He waited for her to finish accepting some metal tubing from a farmer, then walked up to the booth. When she turned to him, her expression changed from friendly to distant. She did not say anything. She just stood there looking at Peter as she folded her arms across her chest.

Faced with this, he opened his mouth to speak, but he couldn't form any words. His mouth felt dry and stuffed full of cotton. Peter wrung his hands; they were cold as stone. He didn't realize it, but he was experiencing the same nervous affectations Jo had when she first tried to tell Peter how she felt about him. He finally forced out some words, hoping they formed a coherent sentence.

"You're working the scrap drive now, huh?" His feigned surprise was weak.

"You knew that, didn't you Pete?"

It was more of a statement than a question. She and Peter had made a connection, and it was easy for her to see he was trying to pull one over on her.

"Yeah, I guess I did."

He had also known there would be a booth set up at the baseball game and hoped Jo would be there so he could talk to her. It had been months since he had been able to spend time with her. She had effectively shut him out of her life. He understood she needed space to deal with Al's death, but he also knew he had to find a way to see her. This was an opportunity, if she was at the booth, to be in a situation where she couldn't just get up and walk away like she had in the lunchroom back in February.

"What do you want, Pete? I don't see any metal you're turning in."

There was a distinct coldness to her voice, almost how metal seems cool to the touch, which shocked Peter. He didn't know what to expect, but he hadn't expected that. However, she still called him Pete, not Peter. She was still the only one to call him Pete. Even if her coldness toward him kept him from smiling on the outside, he smiled on the inside at the recognition the intimate connection was still there.

"Jo, I had to see you…to talk to you."

"This is not a good time, Pete. I'm working."

He looked around.

"Looks like we have a few minutes. Nobody's here right now."

"You shouldn't be here."

"I miss you, Jo. You're all I think about."

"Don't say that Pete. It's confusing."

Jo started to act like she was straightening up the booth, cleaning off the counter and rearranging things, but it was just busywork so she wouldn't have to look at Peter. She felt a resentment rising in her. She didn't want Peter there; she didn't want to be around him. As she moved back and forth across the booth, Peter followed her and kept talking.

"It's true, though. And it's killing me not to be around you. That day when you told me how you feel, and me being able to tell you how I feel, was the greatest day in my life."

"Things change, Pete."

Jo's voice was still cold and distant. The resentment she felt was beginning to turn into anger. Her mind started to flash Al's

face. She stopped and looked at Peter, the rest of the world tuned out from her mind. As she stared blankly at Peter, she almost couldn't see his face, it being obscured by Al's face. She wanted Peter to leave now, to leave her alone; she wanted *both* of them to leave her alone.

"Jo, we are meant to be together. We *have* to be together. You know it was well as I."

"No, I can't."

"Jo, yes you can."

"No."

"Yes. It's been almost a year. It's time for us to be together."

"No! Don't you get it? He knew! Al knew. Somehow he knew I had grown away from him, that my heart was someplace else, with someone else. He knew you were the only thing I could think of from the time I woke up until the time I fell asleep, and for every hour while I was asleep. Somehow he *knew*...and *I* killed him."

Jo's anger burst forth in a stream of tears. Her head dropped, and the curls hanging from her forehead hid her face from Peter. She held her hand to her nose as she cried. Even in this distraught state, Peter couldn't help but think about how beautiful she was and how pretty she looked in her dress, a sight he had not seen in months and in stark contrast to the slacks and coveralls she wore at the plant.

"Jo, that can't be true," Peter responded, trying to be rational. "Just like you did, I'm sure he started to realize different feelings."

"Don't you see, he had to have felt that. Me changing. That's what I mean. He *had* to have known...somehow. How else do you explain it?"

"Jo, it's war. People get killed. My brother got killed. The fact I resented him running away to join that war didn't get him killed. It was a German bullet that killed him. Just as it was a Japanese bullet that killed Al, not anything you did."

"I just…I can't. You need to go." The little orphan girl burst forth and screamed, "It's what I want."

Jo wiped the tears from her cheeks and unconsciously dug at the divoted scar on her forehead. She stepped to the side as an elderly man and woman made their way up to the booth. They laid three slightly used steel cooking pots on the counter. She smiled and thanked them for supporting the war effort. They exchanged a few pleasantries with her, then turned and walked away.

Peter was still standing at the other end of the counter. Jo looked at him; the hurt was obvious in his face. A small pain surfaced in her stomach. Her feelings for Peter were strong, very strong, and she hated to cause him pain. But she also had very strong feelings of betrayal for having run around with Peter while Al was overseas. Anything with Peter would have to wait, if it were to happen at all.

Peter looked at Jo standing at the other end of the counter. He felt he should jump over the counter, pick her up, and sweep her away to someplace far from there where they could be together, where there was no war, where Al had grown away from Jo instead of being killed. He stood there, his eyes locked with hers, and he sensed an energy surging between them, but Jo made no move toward him.

As he stared at her, it was if some force was pulling her backward, pulling her away from him. He could almost see her getting smaller as she faded into the distance, even though she was not actually moving. A barrier was going up between them; he could feel it, and he was sure Jo could, too. It was as if a wall was sealing him off from her forever. He could feel his eyes burning, and he drew a deep breath through his nose trying to pull back the tears on the verge of overflowing from his eyes. Peter smiled slightly awkwardly, then raised his hand in a muted wave, turned, and walked away.

VOL. XXXV—N⁰ 260   Saturday, September 16, 1944   Five Cents

DISNEY ADVANCES ON BERLIN
Two Films To Be Produced in German

BURBANK, Calif.—Walt Disney is perhaps closer to Berlin than the Allies. Disney announced on August 10 that he is working on synchronization of a German-language version of the new cartoon feature Saludos Amigos for future release in Germany. After that project is completed, he stated work will begin on the masterpiece Fantasia. As everything except for the introduction of that movie is musical, the translation will be much less involved. The film already features several musical passages from German composers, including Bach and Beethoven. The move by Disney puts him far ahead of the rest of Hollywood, although several studios began work on French-language versions of films even before the D-Day invasion.

OPA ALLOWS GAS RECOVERY
Dealers Accepted Counterfeit Coupons

CLEVELAND, O.—Officials in the Office of Price Administration (OPA) announced last night that gasoline operators will be allowed to recover gallonage lost to acceptance of counterfeit ration coupons prior to April 1 of this year. The additional gasoline will be made available October 1. As explained by deputy director James C. Rodgers, Jr., under the previous system, dealer accounts were debited in an amount equal to the counterfeited coupons accepted. This system was deemed "...too harsh on the small dealer," while the new plan will allow to "...alleviate the plight of the honest and conscientious operator." Rodgers went on to say, "...we do not propose to forgive flagrant and obvious violators who take in excessive quantities of bogus coupons." The plan also allows dealers a tolerance of up to one per cent in any month to cover debits. The OPA began charging dealers for accepted counterfeit coupons shortly after rationing of gasoline began. The move was called "...great news..." by Lloyd F. Jugenheimer, secretary of the Independent Gasoline Dealers in Youngstown, Ohio. Jugenheimer added, "OPA apparently recognized that the little dealers were getting pinched hard and that something had to be done."

PELELIU INVADED
Marines Make Landing

PEARL HARBOR, H.I.—Marines made an amphibious invasion of Peleliu on Thursday, as reported in a communiqué from Commander-in-Chief of the Pacific Fleet Admiral Chester Nimitz. Marines are pushing toward the airfield, and have fought off several counterattacks by the enemy, including attacks by tanks. The airfield on Peleliu is the main airfield in the Palau group, consisting of two runways each about forty-two thousand feet in length. Light bombers and fighter planes will be able to make use of the runways as soon as they are secured. The marines in action are of the First Division, the heroes of Guadalcanal. Casualties are reported to be light, but the beachheads have been under Japanese fire, including mortar and artillery fire. Admiral Nimitz reports "...landings are continuing..." against heavy opposition. Strong support is provided to the marines by air and naval forces as they established a beachhead of about a mile and half on the southern end of the island. Air forces attacked positions immediately behind the beachhead as well as in the north.

N⁰ 27

The Castle Theater was on the south side of the square. The ornate stonework on the façade of the three-story building was capped by four menacing gargoyles. Traditionally, in old-world Europe, gargoyles were usually rain spouts, but these were purely decorations intended to enhance the name of the theater. Large block letters on the marquee announced *The Three Caballeros Starring Donald Duck*. Brightly painted trim highlighted the theater.

Jo and the soldier walked up to the ticket window. The walls to each side held large posters advertising the upcoming movies *Arsenic and Old Lace* by Frank Capra, the John Wayne feature *Tall in the Saddle*, and *Meet Me in Saint Louis* starring Judy Garland. Jo casually looked at the posters as Bill purchased tickets.

"Two, please," he said as he leaned toward the window.

"Eighty-eight cents."

He clumsily fished around in his pocket with his left hand, then withdrew a dollar bill. He handed it to the woman behind the window. She returned his change along with two tickets.

Bill walked over to Jo and placed his hand in the small of her back. He guided her through the door and inside. As they walked up to the concessions counter, Jo noticed she felt detached from his hand on her back. She felt it, but it gave her no sensation at all. It was just there. At the counter, Bill ordered a large box of popcorn.

"Ten cen'," the attendant said.

Bill gave the attendant the dime he had left over from buying the tickets. The attendant then reached into the large, glass-sided popper and shoveled two scoops into a round cardboard bucket. He moved over to the dispenser next to the popper, doused the popcorn with a liberal coating of melted butter substitute, and dashed three shakes of salt on top of that. He handed the bucket to Bill, but Jo took it instead so his one good arm would not be occupied. She had seen how he had fumbled around using his left arm; it was clear to her Bill was right handed.

"Sorry I have only a dollar," Bill said to Jo. "I haven't gotten my back pay yet."

"That's okay," she said, flashing a smile. "A cartoon and a box of popcorn are enough."

He placed his hand on her back and guided her toward the theater door. Again, it gave her no sensation. She thought about how a surge of warmth would flow over her whenever Peter touched her, guiding her through a crowd or comforting her in her sadness over Roz being taken away...or for any reason slight or significant. It was in stark contrast to the feeling of no sensation with this man's hand on her back.

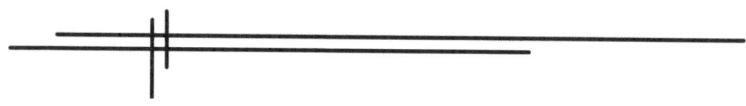

Inside the theater, Bill and Jo picked seats about halfway to the screen. Up front was a group of kids. Scattered throughout the rest of the theater were a few other people, some couples, some in groups of three or four. The theater was about two-

thirds full. As Bill and Jo sat down, the theater lights began to dim.

"I'm glad you came back to the booth after the game last Saturday," Jo said as she settled into her seat, wiggling around a bit to conform the cushions to her body.

"Not as glad as I was when you said yes."

He smiled at her for a few seconds. She returned the smile, but quickly turned away and looked at the screen. The flickering white light was just splashing onto the screen as the projector tick-tick-ticked into motion. Jo held the box of popcorn to one side on her lap so Bill could reach it.

As the sound boomed into the theater and the cartoon began to play, Jo could see out of the corner of her eye that Bill was still watching her. She glanced over, their eyes meeting just briefly before she looked back at the screen. She tried to suppress a smile as she nibbled on the popcorn. It felt good to Jo that a man was drawn to her. For some time, she had been wondering if Al and Peter would be the only men to find her attractive.

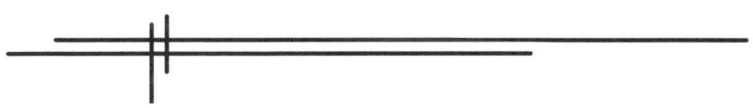

As the cartoon played, they sat watching the show and nibbling on popcorn. The cartoon was a mix of live action and animation. It was a series of vignettes connected by cut scenes of Donald opening birthday presents from his friends from Latin America. In one of the vignettes, called The Flying Gauchito, a young boy from Uruguay goes hunting for condors, but instead finds a flying donkey that he names Burrito.

As the donkey flew around the scene, repeatedly stealing the boy's hat and trying to eat it, Bill giggled at the antics. He leaned on the armrest, his good hand alternating between covering his mouth and pointing at Burrito. His giggles were very childlike. While this man may have been about Jo's age, she felt he was much more immature than she. It made her think

she didn't want to be with a man whom she had to guide to maturity. She wanted a man who was already mature…like Peter.

As the cartoon progressed, Bill's mannerisms became more boyish. Jo wasn't entirely sure if this was actually the case or if she was just becoming less and less tolerant of him. She knew for sure the whole situation was leaving her feeling empty, desolate. When she was around Peter, she was afraid their time together would end. Sitting there in the theater with this man next to her, she was afraid their time together *wouldn't* end. She wasn't upset, she just knew she wasn't where she wanted to be, or rather with whom she wanted.

About halfway through the cartoon, Bill leaned over toward Jo. He reached over the armrest and gently clasped his hand over hers. She pulled back and looked from the screen to him. She had a blank expression on her face.

"Sorry," he said, as he quickly looked away from her and at the screen.

"No. It's okay," she replied, but she did not offer her hand to him.

His hand was much softer than hers, much softer than Peter's. She thought his hand was very unmanly. His fingers were thin, not thick with muscle built up from years of labor, years of responsibility. She wondered how he could ever hope to hold a woman tightly with hands that felt devoid of power to her. She wanted a man to be able to hold her tightly, but also to move his hands around her body very gently. Could he do that? Would he know how to touch a woman in the way she needed? She figured he didn't know and it would take him time to learn. She wasn't interested in teaching him. Even if she were to take the time to teach him, Jo was sure it could never be as natural as it was between her and Peter.

With that thought, she realized she had spent almost the entire time with Bill—this man, this soldier, whom she certainly found attractive—thinking about Peter. Everything Bill did, every move he made, was compared to what Peter would do. It was in that moment, sitting in a theater on a date with a man who was not Peter, Jo fully understood her love for Peter. She understood he was right; they were meant to be together, they were right for each other, and they *had* to be together.

How would she go about getting Peter back? She felt so embarrassed about treating him the way she had, especially at the ballpark the previous weekend...the day the man sitting next to her had asked her out. An extra dose of embarrassment dripped into her heart. She leaned her elbow on the armrest and pressed two fingers in the center of her forehead. Her hand shielded her face as she winced at the embarrassment. *What am I doing?*

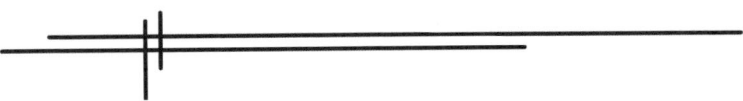

"Thank you for taking me to the show. I don't get out much anymore."

Bill and Jo paused on the sidewalk outside the theater. She held her purse in front of her with both hands. Her arms were drawn in, closing herself off from him. He started to lean toward her, clearly searching for a kiss; she shifted back just slightly and he stopped.

"Can I see you again?" he asked.

Jo looked at him for a second, glanced down, and then looked back. She was smiling as she responded, but it was a surface smile; a smile of kindness, not affection.

"I'm just in a different place right now." What she really meant was she had a different person in her heart right then. "Thanks for the afternoon, but I should go."

"Let me drive you."

"No, thanks, I'll walk."

She was still smiling. She didn't want to hurt his feelings, but she didn't want him to mistake anything she did as an invitation for a future encounter and knew it best to decline the ride. She turned and began walking down the sidewalk. With each step away from the young, handsome soldier, Peter came closer and closer in her mind and heart.

The Blooming Grove Review

VOL. XXXV—N? 295 Saturday, October 21, 1944 Five Cents

PHILIPPINE LIBERATION UNDERWAY
MacArthur Fulfills Promise of Returning

SYDNEY, Australia—Allied forces landed on Leyte yesterday in the Philippine Islands, fulfilling a promise made by General Douglas MacArthur two years ago when he stated, "...I shall return." President Roosevelt had told MacArthur, "the whole American nation today exalts at the news that the gallant men under your command have landed on Philippine soil." Indications are the entire eastern coast has been seized by American forces, and two enemy-held airfields are being threatened. The operation is being described as "...on schedule against light operation," said MacArthur in a communiqué, "The enemy's air force, partially crushed by preliminary aircraft strikes throughout Luzon and the Visayas, was able to counterattack our invading forces with but two scattered raids." There are an estimated twenty thousand Japanese forces on Leyte and two hundred and fifty thousand throughout the Philippines.

STEEL DEMAND LESSENS
Scrap Depots To Be Opened

NEW YORK, N.Y.—The industry publication Iron Age announced this week a plan by the steel industry to establish fifty scrap depots throughout the country. The purpose of the depots is to handle a "huge flood of...scrap which is expected in the next two to three months." By centralizing scrap in depots, it can be kept out of manufacturing plants, which will help keep production up. On October 6, the War Production Board (WPB) revoked five orders, lifting or easing restrictions on several metals and materials. Revoking the orders was in response to improved supplies and intended to assure civilian production continues. Production of steel ingots increased by half a point this week to ninety-six per cent of capacity.

MUNITIONS WAR PRODUCTION LAGS
May Delay V-E Day Indefinitely

WASHINGTON, D.C.—Chairman of the War Production Board (WPB), Julius A. Krug, convened a press conference on Thursday to discuss an apparent apathy by the American public toward war production. He stated in most areas, the program is successful, but went on to state that output is lagging in a "...vitally important ten per cent." Krug was specifically referring to munitions production. He warned that this lag in output could ultimately delay a victory in Europe indefinitely or at least "...by months." Krug was recalled from the Navy in August of this year to head the WPB.

AACHEN FALLS
City Inside German Border

LONDON, England—Aachen inside the German border surrendered yesterday to American forces. The city has been bombed and shelled into ruins. After days of street-to-street fighting, the last of the Nazi defenders were driven from the city. Eight hundred Nazis ignored a "fight to the end" order and surrendered to American troops. The last major strongpoint in the city was eliminated by 3:30 p.m. Aachen time. The city has been under assault since September 15. Aachen is the first large German city to be captured by the Allies. General Dwight D. Eisenhower's hard-line code for occupied Germany is being implemented in Aachen.

№ 28

The town square was decked out in red, white, and blue, from bunting hanging on every building to the small flags being waved about by little kids. Blooming Grove was having a big event to promote the war effort. Booths were set up all around the square to accept donations, war bonds were being sold, and uniformed men were wandering around encouraging young men and the occasional woman to sign up for service. A band was busy setting up in the center of the square for the rally set to start at noon. The bounty of the fall's harvest could be found all around in taffy apples, cider, gourds, and pumpkins. The sun shone brightly, warming the crispness from the October air and making only a sweater needed to stay warm.

On the corner outside Abe's grocery store, Pearl had set up a small cart with produce from the store. The controls on fresh fruit and vegetables had eased a bit recently, and she was trying to take advantage of that fact to increase sales. The store was as busy as it had been before the Abes were forced into the internment camps. Pearl was proud of that fact, and told anybody who would listen she had the store set for the Abes' return, whenever it would be.

The Ration Card

Parked on Hamilton street, on the west side of the square, was a semitruck flatbed trailer. On it was the wreckage of a Messerschmitt ME-109 German fighter plane. It had been shot down over Britain and was now touring the United States to bolster war drives. A large banner hung from the trailer stating, *Your old pots and pans helped down this Nazi bird!*

Down the street, booths were stacked one after the other. Each had a banner or placard extolling the virtue of turning in old or extra shoes, silk stockings, newspapers, animal fats, and so on. Almost every booth had a example of what "the boys" would be getting in return for the donations. Hanging from the top of the silk booth, for instance, was a parachute along with a sign saying, *Help our boys jump into Tokio with your silk stockings!*

Next to the trailer carrying the 109, Jo and another woman stood in a booth under a banner encouraging scrap metal to be dropped off. Behind the booth was an ever-growing pile of old radiators, pots, bedposts, shovels, pans, mailboxes, and various other items people had donated to the scrap drive.

A group of boys was hanging around Jo's booth. They would take whatever metal somebody turned in, make some sort of comment estimating how many bombs or bullets could be made from it, and then chuck it onto the pile. The boys were having tremendous fun helping out Jo, although they weren't actually officially part of the drive, and she was greatly amused by their antics. Whenever they saw a large item headed toward the booth, a mad dash ensued to be the one to have the honor of putting it on the pile.

All of the sudden one of the boys screamed, "Holy crap, look at that!" and pointed off to his right. Chugging down the street, straining under load, was Peter's truck. Behind it was dragging the rusted remains of an old farm tractor, the two back wheels wobbling on a bent axle. As the truck labored to make it down the street, the boys sprinted to meet Peter and lay claim to the prize. A small crowd began to follow Peter as he made his way toward the scrap metal booth.

"Right in here," one of the boys yelled, directing the truck

toward the pile of scrap. "Back 'er up in here. Our boys'll really give 'em hell with all *this* metal."

Peter wheeled the truck around and pushed the scrap tractor as far back into the pile as he could. Setting the brake, he threw open the door and stepped out of the truck. Brushing himself off, as if it had been exceptionally dusty work dragging the tractor into town, he looked at Jo in the booth. She was standing with her arms folded across her chest. She shook her head at Peter, trying to look upset, but a smile betrayed her amusement.

"Have at it, boys," he said with a grin and then walked over to Jo as the boys jumped in to remove the chains from the tractor and truck. "Looks like you've got some good helpers there," Peter said to Jo, motioning to the boys.

"Yeah, they just showed up and started throwing scrap onto the pile." Jo was now outright laughing. "Where on *Earth* did you find that, Pete?"

"Pulled it out of Talbert's back woods, down by that old still they used to run during Prohibition. That's in the back of the truck, too."

"Well, on behalf of your armed forces, we thank you for your donation."

Jo tried to hide her smile and appear professional. She looked down and smoothed her dress, waiting for Peter to say something, waiting for him to speak because she had no idea what to say. The last time the two had talked, she had really yelled at him. She had been so angry at Peter, angry and defensive, because he had showed up at the baseball game and tried to pull her back to him. She thought for sure she had lost him forever because of the way she treated him.

She had wanted to at least apologize to Peter for the way she acted, but she could never bring herself to do so. It was partly a need to remain isolated from him, but it was also partly her dumb embarrassment at how she had treated him. Now, there he was, standing in front of her with his devilish smile lighting up the entire square, any feelings of anger or resentment toward him she may have harbored completely washed away by his impish charms, and yet the words still would not come to her.

She had to be with him—when the time was right—and she needed to tell him that, but something was pulling inside her, pulling the words back down so they could not be spoken; the little orphan girl was quietly tapping bricks in place in the wall. Peter broke the silence with his usual diverting humor.

"Aw, least I could do. Talbert don't need it no more…just hope he didn't see me take it!"

"Pete!" Jo swatted his arm. "You did *not* steal that…did you?"

"Naw, 'course not, but I got you laughing."

"Yes, you did. You're always good at that."

"Listen, Jo, can you get away for a few minutes?"

She looked at Peter for a couple of seconds. Jo couldn't hide her smile, as much as she tried. She was glad to see Peter; she had missed him. At the same time, she felt guilty about spending time with him, especially alone. Still, it was clear to her how he made her feel, what he meant to her. For awhile, she was able to forget about all of the complications presented by being with him, just lost in her thoughts of being held closely—and softly. But just as they had so many times before, the complications crept back, pulling her from her imagined bliss.

She had explored other options; being on a date with the soldier she had felt nothing but an emptiness…and had spent almost the entire date thinking of Peter. That had been the point where she had proved to herself beyond a doubt Peter was the one. She just had to figure out how to make it work between them, how to overcome the obstacles—both real and imagined—and how to be together. Finally, she nodded, then turned to the other woman at the booth and jerked her head in the direction of Peter to let her know she was leaving for a bit.

As they walked toward Peter's truck, his dog stretched way out of the window, having picked up on Jo's scent. He wiggled almost uncontrollably and, as he sensed her get closer, began to whine a little bit. Jo reached out and rubbed his muzzle, then scratched behind his ears.

"He misses you," Peter said, the overtone drifting across the crisp air. "He thought you forgot about him." The dog then leaned over and stuck his nose in Peter's face, then quickly leaned back the other way for more ear scratching.

"Pete, I could never forget about him," she looked at Peter, batting the overtones back his way. "You know that."

She grabbed both of the dog's ears and shook his head from side to side. Barney happily wiggled around as he tried to bite Jo's hands. Jo knew Peter was a good man. Most people would have had the dog put down after he lost his sight, but he gave the dog a good life. Only somebody with a good heart would do that.

"I know," Peter looked down, "it just sure seems that way sometimes...most of the time these days."

Peter patted the dog's head. He and Jo turned and started slowly walking across the square. All around, people wandered the streets and square. The band was just about set up on a platform painted red, white, and blue. Several veterans of the first war meandered around in their uniforms, talking to each other and anybody else who would listen.

"I got a lot going on, Pete. I've been working double shifts. When I'm not working or helping Pearl out at Abe's, I'm helping with the scrap drive."

"I saw on the schedule you've been pullin' double duty at the plant. Everybody's real proud at how you've grown into such a skilled, dependable worker."

Jo stopped. Peter took a couple more steps, then stopped when he realized Jo was not walking. She had a look of calm satisfaction on her face. When he turned to see where she was, she quickly took two steps to catch up to him.

"Glad everybody's finally catching on," she said in a humorously sarcastic tone as she breezed by Peter. He had to walk quickly to catch up, and then they continued walking across the square.

"I know about all that stuff and...everything," Peter said. "I want to help, if you'd let me."

They had circled back toward Peter's truck. Barney yelped a greeting, his head sticking out of the passenger's window this time. Jo reached over and stroked the dog's ears as he pressed his head hard into her hand.

"Looks like your donation is already going to good use," Jo said, grinning and nodding toward the scrap pile.

The boys had finished unhooking the old tractor from the truck and were busy climbing all over it, pretending it was a Sherman tank on the prowl for Nazi panzers. Old pots became helmets, bed knobs became grenades, and shovels and rakes became rifles or Thompsons. The sounds of battle in the form of *ack-ack-ack* and *blam-blam-blam* settled in over the tractor as the boys mapped out the great Allied victory to come.

Jo looked down at her shoes. They were not the brutish man-boots she wore at work. Today she was wearing black pumps with a low heel. They went well with her dress, but then she wondered if Peter would notice, which made her realize that she *cared* if Peter noticed. With her head still bent down, she looked up at him through the curls hanging from her forehead.

"Pete, I do care for you, you have to know that, but I have to get through this on my own. I know you want to help me, but you can't. This is all me. I have to do this. The future may be different, but this is not the time for us."

Jo leaned over and gave Peter a quick kiss on the cheek. They looked into each other's eyes for a brief moment, then Jo turned and walked back to the scrap booth. As Peter watched her walk away, he drew two fingers across his cheek where she had kissed him, then held his fingers to his lips. He could just barely smell her perfume on his fingers. It made his heart ache.

Eric K. Augspurger

VOL. XXXV—№ 328   Thursday, November 23, 1944   Five Cents

MUNITIONS SHORTAGE COSTS LIVES
War Workers Quitting

WASHINGTON, D.C.—On Tuesday, President Roosevelt along with General Eisenhower pleaded for more output. The president's news conference shortly followed a statement from Eisenhower that he and his soldiers "...want more supplies than we are getting." Eisenhower earlier had told war production officials, "You tell us what you can deliver, and we'll tell you when the war will end." FDR said not enough shells are being sent to troops overseas, which has resulted in rationing of munitions that leads to lost American lives. The president went on to say that part of the problem lies in war workers leaving war production to enter civilian jobs. As the war appears to be drawing to a close, the president speculates, these individuals are hedging against unemployment after the war, but urges war workers to remain in their vital positions for the duration. FDR stated he believes reconversion to civilian production will be far quicker than most expect and anticipates pay will remain at current levels even with shorter normal hours after the war.

THANKSGIVING COSTS LESS
OPA Says Price of Feast Lower This Year

WASHINGTON, D.C.—Dr. James S. Thomas, deputy director of the Office of Price Administration (OPA), revealed the average family's cost for Thanksgiving Day dinner this year is about eleven cents lower than last year. Thomas attributes the decrease to some foods now under price controls that were not last year, and by following OPA rules, consumers and grocers have allowed the OPA to "hold the line" on other foods. The price ceiling on a fully dressed turkey—the centerpiece of all Thanksgiving Day tables—is $5.04 this year, compared to $5.12 in 1943. Some foodstuff has gone up in price this year, such as eggs, onions, celery, and lettuce; all items that can be grown or raised in a small Victory garden.

LAND-BASED PLANES REACH MANILA
Fly From Expanded Airfields on Leyte

ALLIED HEADQUARTERS, Philippine Islands—General MacArthur said yesterday that his land-based bombers are now within range of not only Manila, but the entire Philippine Islands. Previously, only carrier-based planes could reach the Philippine capital of Manila. An air raid conducted on Saturday on Manila harbor sank two enemy merchant vessels, left twelve others in flames, and damaged three additional vessels. On November 14, carrier-based planes attacked Manila harbor, leaving shipping and the waterfront in ruins. Returning the following day, pilots found the Japanese had installed barrage balloons, the first time these devices have been used by the Japanese. However, the balloons proved no impediment as the attack continued, and the enemy has since removed them.

EUROPE HUNGRY
Nazis Drained Food

LONDON, England—The liberated countries of Europe now face a new enemy: hunger. The Nazi occupiers drained the nations of food supplies to feed German soldiers and workers. Now those nations are at the brink of starvation, and, with winter nearly here, face the lowest stores ever. Civilians often protest in the streets demanding food. The depletion of food supplies extends to the still-occupied areas of Europe.

No 29

The smells of Thanksgiving dinner were starting to fade as Jo and Pearl cleared the table. The aroma of the smoked ham still lingered as the fragrance of the vegetables and pumpkin pie had already faded. Gerald helped carry the dishes to the kitchen, then returned to the living room and settled into his chair. He reached over and clicked on the radio, then snapped open the newspaper and picked up reading where he had left off before dinner.

The radio crackled to life and the notes of *Wing and a Prayer* danced across the living room, followed by the evening news reporter running down the events of the war over the past few days. As the report shifted from Europe to the Pacific, Gerald dipped the top of the newspaper and stared intently at the radio, as if his eyes could see the reporter talking directly to him. Gerald had continued to pay extra attention to details of the war in the Pacific even after Al's death, perhaps even more attention than before.

It was three years since Congress had passed legislation officially setting Thanksgiving as the second-to-last Thursday in November, following President Roosevelt's proclamation in 1939.

Before 1941, the actual day of Thanksgiving had been set by presidential proclamation. Traditionally, Thanksgiving had been the last Thursday in November. But in 1939, the way the days fell on the calendar, having Thanksgiving on the last Thursday in November meant the Christmas shopping season would be one week shorter. Roosevelt thought a shortened shopping season would hurt retailers still trying to recover from the Great Depression, so he moved Thanksgiving up by one week. For the next two years, some states followed his proclamation and some states continued to celebrate Thanksgiving on the last Thursday in November. Congress had decided to act in order to have the entire country celebrating on the same day.

None of that mattered to Jo. She didn't care if Thanksgiving was earlier or later than it always had been. She didn't care about an extra week for Christmas shopping. She didn't care about the politics involved in setting the date. To her, Thanksgiving that year was simply three days since the one-year anniversary of Al's death. From that point forward, it would always be a day falling somewhere between the anniversary of Al's death and the anniversary ten days later of when she learned a bullet ended his life. In the years to come, she would find she could push this aside enough to enjoy the festivities of Thanksgiving, of companionship with family and friends, but she would always have that fact lingering around her, like a ghost whisking around the edges of her psyche.

In the kitchen, Jo scooped up the leftover food and packed it away in jars as Pearl washed the dishes. Once all of the leftovers were in the icebox, Jo grabbed a dish towel and began drying dishes. She wiped each dish with a methodical circular motion. It was very mechanical. Pearl would hand her a clean dish, Jo would wipe it dry, and then stack it on the counter with the other dried dishes.

Pearl seemed to be washing just a bit quicker than Jo was drying, so Jo felt a half-step behind. This made her think of her first day at the plant, and how quickly the conveyor belt had seemed to be moving. She had felt that for each part she finished, one was about to pass by on the belt before she could grab it. Before half of the morning had passed that day, Jo began to wonder if she would be able to cut it, to make it through even one day, let alone survive her first week on the job. But survive she had.

Jo let her mind wander as she wiped the dishes dry. It was Roz who had gradually given Jo the confidence she needed to keep going. By noon on that first day, Jo was able to keep up with the line, and the remainder of the day Roz had showed her tricks to keeping pace with the conveyor belt, if not slightly ahead of it. Over the next few days, Roz had helped Jo focus on the quality of her work. It had been the beginnings of her close friendship with Roz.

But now, that friendship had to be conducted through letters between Roz in the internment camp and Jo living with the Troyers. She would never tell Roz, but at times she wondered if Roz would ever come home. Roz seemed so far away to her. She knew Roz was going through a very tough time, and she knew it was selfish to think of what she needed from Roz, but she *did* think about what their friendship meant, and how much it hurt for Roz to have been ripped away from her. The absence left a hole in Jo's life and heart that had not been filled, at least not fully; Peter had partially filled the void until she had stopped him from filling more of it.

When the dishes were finished and put away, Jo and Pearl got out the supplies they needed for canning the remaining vegetables from Jo's victory garden. There was the stock pot for blanching the vegetables, the dozens of Ball jars and lids, the boxes of new jar seals, and the large, two-burner water-bath pan for boiling the jars. Pearl also set out the cutting board and knife, along with several towels and potholders. Jo grabbed the colander and began washing the vegetables. They had green beans, corn, carrots, and potatoes to can that night.

"Do the green beans first," Pearl said. "That way I can snap them while you wash the other vegetables."

Jo stoppered the sink, then poured a bushel basket full of green beans into it. While the water ran filling up the sink, she shook the beans around in the water. She pulled them out one handful at a time and put them in the colander to drain. Pearl took a small handful of beans from the colander and, one bean at a time, snapped each bean into pieces about one inch in length. When all of the beans were washed, Jo dumped the colander into a bowl, put the bowl on the table in front of Pearl, and set about washing the other vegetables.

The Ration Card

Enough vegetables had been grown in Jo's victory garden that the pantry would be well-stocked through most of next summer. Jo snorted a muted laugh as the irony struck her. Working at the plant had allowed her to prove her hands were suited for something more than baking pies in the kitchen, yet there she was on her leisure time—a very precious commodity *because* of work at the plant—canning vegetables to help keep a good kitchen, just like society expected of a proper wife. The thought made her cringe. She was very proud of her work at the plant. She felt she had proved her worthiness as a skilled machinist, and she didn't want to be seen as a woman whose only role in life was to keep a good kitchen.

Then she realized how she was going about the process of canning. She was approaching it not as a housewife may, but how a machinist would. She had very methodically, and unconsciously, created a small factory in the kitchen. Every step of the process was set up in a circular line, from the pans on the stove, to the jars circling the kitchen table, to the holding area on the counter where the finished jars sat to cool. And it all started with the raw materials, which were the vegetables.

The process would start with Pearl cutting the vegetables, which would then move to the blanching station, from there to the filling station to be put into jars, to the assembly station for lids and seals, to the water bath for heating—Jo thought this might be akin to the metal-tempering station at the plant—to the holding area, and finally to storage. It was all a tidy little manufacturing operation, and Jo was serving as the plant manager. She wondered what Fred Thompson would think about that. Jo giggled a bit at the thought of seeing his face if she was promoted to take his job.

Pearl blanched the vegetables in small batches, pouring each batch when finished into a bowl that she then passed over to Jo. Jo ladled the hot vegetables and water into the sanitized jars, placed a seal on each jar, and finally threaded a lid onto each jar before moving it to the water bath.

As she filled the jars, Jo considered how the process was isolating the vegetables from the outside world. Each group of vegetables was sealed off in its own little container to be stowed away in the pantry until needed. Jo couldn't help but draw a parallel to what she had done to herself. After Al's death, she had sealed herself off from the outside world. She might as well have put herself into one of these little jars and spun the lid closed behind her.

For the first time, Jo really considered how isolated she had become. She would go to work in the morning and rarely engage in conversation throughout the day, even at lunch. After work, she would come straight home for a late dinner, then read a bit before heading to bed; depending on how late she worked, she may even go directly to bed after dinner. On the weekends—the weekends she didn't work—she would volunteer for the scrap drive, affording her only superficial socializing, which was exactly how she wanted it. Progressively over the past year, Jo had succeeded in isolating herself in a glass jar. She could see out—the little orphan girl could see out—but no one could get in. She was very good at retreating into isolation—a skill she learned early at the orphanage—but Jo surprised even herself at the realization of just how effectively the little orphan girl had cut off everybody.

Once she had a batch of vegetables sealed in jars, Jo carefully submerged the jars in the water bath. There the jars would sit in boiling water for the required amount of time, then be removed and set on the counter to cool until the seals set. Steam from the water bath and the blanching pot permeated the kitchen. It felt hotter than a humid ninety-five degree day in July. Sweat ran down the center of her chest and collected in the bottom of her brassier cups, and Jo could feel her hair matted against her forehead.

Jo thought about having to do work in conditions like this every day. She wasn't sure she could do it; she thought it'd be like stoking the fires of Hades. She imagined the guys in the foundry at the plant had to feel like this every day as they poured white-hot molten metal from giant ladles into the sand molds. And the gear they had to wear, bundled from head to toe in heavy fabric, could only make the heat worse. Yet not once had she heard Peter complain. Jo supposed if you were suited for that kind of work, you got used to the heat and learned to deal with it, just as Peter had. And with that she realized Peter had, very subtly, crept back into her thoughts. She tried to brush him away.

Pearl had finished blanching all of the vegetables and had taken over filling the jars. Jo took care of getting the jars into and out of the water bath, walking back and forth from the stove to the counter. They were just about done with processing all of the jars when there was a pop from the jars cooling on the counter. The first of the seals had set. Soon, the rest of the jars would, if Jo and Pearl had done everything right, join in with pops of their own.

For some reason, the seal popping made Jo think of the crack of the bat when a hitter gets ahold of the baseball. The sounds were only similar, not identical, but close enough that her mind made the leap. She could picture the field, the batter standing at the plate, slightly crouched, waiting for the pitcher to deliver the ball.

Jo inhaled deeply, taking in the mixing smells of cooked vegetables. She convinced herself that it was the smell of freshly roasted peanuts she was eating in the grandstand. She could see herself sitting on the wooden bleachers, the little bag of peanuts in one hand and a cold beer sitting between her feet; for a moment she could even taste the beer. She could almost hear Roz laughing to her left; Roz always sat on her left at the ballpark for some reason Jo could never figure out, nor ever bothered to ask why.

Another jar popped. This time, she saw a line drive to the shortstop—another jar popped and, in her mind, this was the ball hitting the infielder's mitt. Jo was completely lost in this intricately imagined event. It took her back to a time that seemed decades past, but was not really very long ago, when she thought her life seemed better, or more satisfying, or less complicated; what it was she wasn't exactly sure, but she knew she liked her life better then than now.

Another seal popped and Jo imagined a fly ball to left field, only to be caught just short of the wall. She could see the left fielder throwing the ball back to the infield, and the infielders throwing the ball around the horn before getting it back to the pitcher. She could also see in vivid detail a finger pointing to the scorecard she held in her hand; it was Peter's, of course, prodding her to score the play F7.

And there he was again. Peter had crept back into her thoughts. Even when she was trying not to think of Peter, some force was unconsciously pulling her thoughts toward him. It dawned on her that her heart was forcing Peter into her thoughts, yet she had to consciously force Al into her thoughts.

Trying to keep Peter at bay, Jo turned her thoughts to the approaching Christmas season. This didn't help, however, and her mood depressed a bit. She had so hoped Christmas would be very special that year, but she was suddenly worried it would be otherwise.

It's going to be a lonely Christmas this year.

VOL. XXXV—N⁰ 349   Thursday, December 14, 1944   Five Cents

FIGHT IN PHILIPPINES CONTINUES
Enemy Sustains Very High Loses, 8 To 1

ALLIED HEADQUARTERS, Philippine Islands—Japan has incurred over eighty-two thousand casualties in the first fifty-five days of operations in the liberation of the Philippine Islands, nearly all of them killed, General MacArthur announced today. This amounts to approximately fifteen hundred casualties per day. Included in the total are over thirty-three thousand dead in liberated areas, thirty thousand who drowned in the sinking of ten reinforcement convoys, and an estimate of over eighteen thousand dead behind enemy lines. By contrast, American casualties are ten and a half thousand, just over twenty-one hundred of who were killed. This means the Japanese are incurring casualties at a rate of eight to one, almost forty to one in killed.

WAR WORKERS NOT QUITTING
Figures Show Other Workers Leaving Jobs

WASHINGTON, D.C.—A special survey was published yesterday by the War Manpower Commission (WMC) that shows workers in war industries are not leaving their jobs, as was previously thought. The survey stated, "Workers are quitting nonwar jobs at a rate of sixty to seventy per one thousand a month. Workers are quitting their jobs in the munitions industries at a rate of forty to fifty-five per on thousand." The Bureau of Labor Statistics (BLS) figures show that separations—an overall term for a worker leaving a job, regardless of the reason—are down this year over last. It reports total separations in October of 1943 were seventy per one thousand, while in October of this year they were sixty-four per thousand. October showed the lowest total separations of this year. The October figures are most recent.

FOOD SHORTAGES FACED NEXT YEAR
WFA Ups Acreage Goals over This Year

WASHINGTON, D.C.— Dr. William C. Ockey, chief of the Civilian Food Requirements branch of the Office of Distribution announced yesterday the food goals for 1945 will be set as high as they have been this year. America saw its greatest output of agricultural products in history in 1944. Administrator Marvin Jones of the War Food Administration (WFA) has set the total food and fiber crop acreage goal at some four million acres more than was harvested in 1944. This goal is eight million acres below the goal of 1944, which demonstrates a shortfall of twelve million acres this year. However, due to unusually high output this year, production is expected to be lower next year even with increased acreage.

DISMAL CHRISTMAS FACED BY GERMANS
Sixth Wartime Yuletide To Be Gloomiest

STOCKHOLM, Sweden—A dispatch from Berlin reported here today by the German-controlled Scandinavian Telegram Bureau states, "The Christmas spirit cannot be found in Germany. One doesn't see any Christmas trees as in former years, nor Christmas decorations in stores. All Germans know that 1944 will be the gloomiest Christmas." Additionally, children from bombed areas will for the first time spend Christmas away from their families due to a governmental order preventing reunions, saying such reunions, permitted in previous years, would place a strain on transportation.

№ 30

Frost on the windows told Jo winter had indeed arrived in Blooming Grove, but there was still almost no snow on the ground with only about a week left before Christmas. She was a bit disappointed, but hoped there was still a chance for snow before Christmas morning. She had been looking forward to a perfect Christmas for so long, and waking up to snow on the ground that morning would certainly help, especially since other things seemed stacked against it being special.

Downstairs, Jo could hear Pearl rustling around in the kitchen. Jo quickly slipped into her work clothes, pulled and prodded her hair into some form of acceptability with three curls hanging on her forehead as she liked, and went down to join Pearl in the kitchen for a bite before heading off to work.

In the kitchen, Jo quickly made a sandwich and packed it in her lunch pail along with a pickle spear she wrapped in waxed paper. She poured herself a cup of coffee; the aroma told Jo this was a first-brew. The grounds would be used at least one more time to make the coffee ration last as long as it could. Pearl scooped up a bowl of oatmeal and handed it to Jo.

"Leave your ration book on the counter when you go to work. I'll take it with me when I head in to the store. Too bad you couldn't have raised sugar and such in your victory garden."

Since Pearl was running Abe's, it would be very easy for her to stash away the needed items without cancelling coupons in the ration books. However, she followed all of the rules to a tee. She made sure everything that came home from the store was not only paid for—she wouldn't cheat the Abes—but also accounted for in ration books as needed. She felt that circumventing the rationing rules would not only be dishonest, but somehow betray the memory of Al and all of the others who were fighting.

"Yeah, and butter. Wish we could've grown butter, too."

"Josephine, you don't grow butter."

Pearl knew Jo was joking even before Jo started laughing, but that was just her way. Pearl had a sense of humor, but she was not one to go in for silliness. On the other hand, Jo could be at her silliest when around Pearl, probably because she *knew* Pearl was not one for silliness. Jo's self-amusement lasted for a few more seconds as Pearl scowled over her glasses at her.

"Oh, too funny. Boy, I sure am looking forward to Christmas. It can't get here soon enough. They've been working us pretty hard at the plant and a couple days off will sure be nice."

The plant was once again running double shifts, but the second shift was not mandatory. Jo still volunteered for these shifts when they were offered. She liked the extra money, for one thing. Since starting work at the plant, Jo had been able to build up quite a nice savings, between her bank account and the war bonds she had purchased. The extra shifts gave her more money to save, plus she couldn't spend money if she was at work.

However, the main reason she took the extra shifts when offered was her self-imprisonment. She had devoted all of her time to either work at the plant or volunteer work for the war effort. She enjoyed working the scrap drives and hanging posters around town. It also kept her out of social situations, limiting her interaction with others to nothing more than a casual passing. Jo had, in effect, retreated inside the hard shell that she developed growing up in the orphanage. Losing Roz to the internment camps and Al dying had seen to that. At first Jo didn't realize the shell was reappearing, but after she did, she was okay with it, even holding the hand of the little orphan girl. Isolation would be her penance for allowing herself to fall in love with Peter while she was still with Al.

Jo missed Al, but she missed Roz more, and Peter even more than Roz. As the Christmas season had set in, a melancholy began to take hold of her. The closer Christmas came, the sadder she became. She wasn't just sad; a loneliness had also surfaced. She found herself thinking a lot those days—wishing, really—that she could just go back to the way things were before, before Al had been killed, before Roz had been taken. She knew that wouldn't remove the complications of being with Peter, but she would at least have Roz to talk her through it, and she thought it may have been easier to leave Al if he were still alive. With Al dead, she found it nearly impossible to leave him.

Finished with her oatmeal, Jo gave the bowl and spoon to Pearl, who was washing the dishes. Jo pulled her coat from the coat rack on the back of the kitchen door. Hanging there under the coat was Peter's baseball cap, just where it had been for the past few months. She had stopped wearing Peter's cap to work after Al died, and she had become so accustomed to seeing it on the hook under her coat that she never even noticed it anymore, almost as if it were *part* of the hook. But not today.

For some reason, she stared at Peter's hat as she pulled on her coat. She took the hat from the hook and sat down at the kitchen table. Holding the cap in front of her, she looked at the frayed edges of the bill, running her finger along it. She pulled the hat down on her head and adjusted her curls around its edges. It felt good to wear the hat again, as if she was being embraced by an invisible comfort. She missed wearing the hat. She missed a lot of things.

She sat at the table, tugging ever so slightly on the bill of the cap and thinking about Peter. She could still recall the first time she ever saw him, when she and Roz had first gone out as friends. She remembered how she had blushed after allowing her thoughts to drift to Peter's body. It had been the first time she had ever uncontrollably thought of a man in such an overt

sexual way. That night was the first for a lot of things, but it would take her the next few months to realize it.

Roz had been such a good friend to Jo, and it hurt to think of her locked up in a camp. She thought about how caring Peter had been when he told her about Roz, how he had held her in his arms and kissed her forehead—that was the first kiss they shared, even if it was just his lips touching her forehead. And she thought about personal details Peter had shared with her, details he had not, and would not, share with anybody else.

A sense of clarity settled over her. She recalled Peter describing his brother's choice to run off to war, and how his death had affected him. She could see in vivid detail his face as he told her about his brother's obsession with fighting the Germans, and she remembered how it struck her that Al had been the same way, almost completely focused on fighting the Japanese. It seemed to her their marriage was almost an afterthought to Al, something that was expected of him before he went off to fight.

Al was concerned with fighting the war, not with me, she thought, *yet I have punished myself for more than a year out of guilt over my feelings for Pete.*

She absent-mindedly knitted her fingers together as she thought about this. Feeling the roughness of her fingers, like emery boards being rubbed together, she stopped and looked at her hands. They were not the dainty hands of a teenage girl anymore, thanks to two years of work at the plant. Now her hands were tough and strong. The insides of her hands were dotted with thick yellow calluses, and red lines crisscrossed her fingers where metal had sliced them. In the past, wounds like these would have stopped her in her tracks as they occurred, but now she was apt not to even notice them until days later when the crust over the wound started to crack as she moved her fingers.

Sitting there contemplating her hands, for the first time in months she became conscious of the silver ring she wore on her left hand. It was a simple wedding ring, not the traditional engagement and wedding bands together; there had not been much time for an engagement. The small diamond caught the light as she rotated her hand, trying to make the ring glimmer. As simple as the ring was, she had always thought it a thing of beauty. It held great meaning for her. It was a connection to her life with Al. In fact, it bound her to him.

Watching the diamond sparkling in the light, and marveling at its beauty, she realized just how out of place the ring was on her hand. The beauty of the ring was in stark contrast to her rough and tough hands, with their thick calluses and metal-inflicted wounds. That was true, but it was so much more. It was a symbol of Al, and Al didn't belong with her anymore, not as her husband. She was now able to realize she had admitted that fact to herself even before Al died, and that his death had only clouded her feelings for Peter, obscuring them, but not changing them. She felt her eyes well up, but she did not cry.

She looked up at Pearl, but she was facing the counter with her back to Jo. Slowly, Jo pulled the wedding ring from her finger and held it up in front of her, mindful not to let Pearl see. She looked at the ring for a moment, then brought it to her lips in a silent kiss. Under her breath, Jo said, *Goodbye, Al,* and slipped the ring into her shirt pocket.

VOL. XXXV—N.° 357   Friday, December 22, 1944   Five Cents

TURKEY FOR TROOPS
Dinner Prepared for All Servicemen

WASHINGTON, D.C.—Two thousand tons of turkeys have been purchased to feed the troops holiday dinners. Turkey with all the trimmings are headed to all servicemen. If they are directly under fire, their dinners will be served as soon as they come off the front lines. In the fleet, the size of the celebration will depend on the size of the vessel. Some ships will even erect Christmas trees in quarters. But, no matter where they are, servicemen will receive the turkey dinners, even prisoners of war in Germany. The Quartermaster Corps has been working with the Red Cross since six months ago to prepare canned turkey to be sent to prisoners of war. For servicemen stationed on the home front, an estimated one quarter will receive furloughs to spend time with their families. Those who do not receive furloughs will receive turkey dinner from Uncle Sam.

GERMAN BREAKOUT FELT AT HOME
Places Strain on War Production

WASHINGTON, D.C.—As Allied forces struggle to stop the onslaught of the German breakout in the Ardennes forest, the need to re-equip and re-supply our forces is impacting the home front. War workers are facing increased production to meet demands, and civilians are being told they will have to do without many of the consumer items they have been missing. Samuel W. Anderson, vice-chairman of the War Production Board (WPB), said, "The purpose of the freeze is to see that rising civilian output does not interfere with urgent munitions output. I haven't any idea how long it will last, or how long we will have critical shortages in war materials."

LEYTE IN ALLIED HANDS
MacArthur Mopping Up Last of the Resistance

ALLIED HEADQUARTERS, Philippine Islands—It was announced yesterday that American forces under General MacArthur are now in the mop-up phase in the liberation of Leyte in the Philippines. Three American divisions are pursing the Japanese into the hills on the northwest corner of the island. In a communiqué, MacArthur stated, "The battle is rapidly drawing to an end." Speaking to the capability of the enemy to continue on Leyte, MacArthur says "...his cohesion is now completely broken, and he is no longer capable of an integrated defense...". It has been just two months since Allied forces began the liberation of the Philippines.

BUTTER SHORTAGE RIOT
Price to Blame, Not Farmers, Dealers

CHICAGO, Ill.—At the beginning of this month, in Watertown, N.Y., two hundred women staged a two-hour riot in the grocery store of William R. Navarra and cleaned out the store of all butter and sugar, states the proprietor. The riot started when one woman refused to abide by the half-pound allotment per customer, emerging from a storeroom with two pounds of butter. Others quickly followed suit, many leaving the store without paying for their ill-gotten baking supplies. John Brandt, president of the National Cooperative Milk Producers Federation, claimed earlier this month that farmers and butter dealers are the victims of poor planning in regard to production of butter, and they are not to blame for the current shortage of butter.

№ 31

The plant had run a single twelve-hour shift on Friday to give everyone a chance to get out and do a bit of last-minute Christmas shopping. It would run short shifts on Saturday and Sunday, then be closed on Christmas day before resuming double-shifts on Tuesday. Jo pulled her car into the Troyers' driveway and to the back. She collected her lunch pail and handbag from the seat next to her and slammed the door shut. Looking at the house, she could see light from the kitchen just barely peeking out from behind the blackout curtains.

She set her lunch pail and handbag down on the hood of her car, then checked to make sure the heat lamp was okay and the chickens had enough straw in their nests. Snow had finally come to Blooming Grove, and she needed to make sure the birds could stay warm. She poked a few more handfuls of straw around the two birds on the ends—to much consternation from the hens—then closed the front of the coop, latched the door, and headed up to the house.

As she swung the door open, the smells of cinnamon, nutmeg, and cooking pumpkin flooded her nostrils. She closed the door, set her lunch pail and handbag on the counter, and hung her

coat on the rack on the back of the door. She left Peter's baseball cap on, even though she knew Pearl hated when she wore it, especially inside.

Jo pulled up her sleeves and washed her hands and forearms. Then she reached into the icebox and pulled out a sliced tomato and some cheese. She took the loaf of bread from the breadbox and, using the slice-a-slicer, split one slice of bread in two. After assembling a light sandwich, she sank into a chair at the kitchen table.

"Mm, everything smells so good, Pearl. What can I do?"

"I'm just working on some pies and such for Christmas dinner. If I get that out of the way tonight, the only thing I'll have to cook on Monday will be the bird, what with all those vegetables we canned in the pantry. Just have to heat those up. You could be a dear and knead the oleo."

Pearl handed Jo a cellophane bag containing a white block of the butter substitute. Jo pressed her thumbs deep into the block to break the bead of yellow food coloring. Between bites of her sandwich, she kneaded the yellow bead into the white block, pressing the mass between her fingers, until the whole thing was more or less the same light yellow color, close to the color of butter.

"I don't particularly care for that stuff," Pearl said, "but real butter costs so many points these days due to the shortage."

"I agree," Jo said. "Real butter is much better, but I've kind of gotten used to oleo."

"It works just about the same in pies and such, but it sure doesn't taste like butter."

Jo finished kneading the food coloring into the block of oleo. Then she finished her sandwich and put away the fixings. Closing the icebox door, she looked longingly at the sugar canister, then turned to Pearl.

"Do you think we have enough sugar for me to make snow candy?"

"We may have to pinch a little next month, but I think it will be okay. It *is* Christmas, after all."

"Good! I'm gonna run outside and see if I can find some clean snow."

Jo quickly grabbed her coat from the back door. She surprised herself a bit by how excited the thought of making snow candy had made her. Once bundled up in her heavy coat, Jo pulled open the back door and ran out into the backyard. She spent several minutes wandering around looking for just the right snow. The snow was fresh enough—it had fallen just the previous day—but it had to be clean and the drift had to be big enough so as to be away from the ground. On finding suitable snow, she scooped it up into the pan she had brought outside, then ran back into the house.

"Okay, I found some good snow. It wasn't easy in the dark. Let's get going on the syrup."

Jo put the pan of snow in the icebox to keep it from melting. She set a small saucepan on the stove and added sugar and water to it. She stirred it constantly until the mixture had turned to a clear syrup, then mixed in a little maple flavoring and stirred some more until the syrup just began to boil.

Quickly grabbing the pan of snow from the icebox, Jo set it on the counter, then slowly drizzled the syrup into the snow. After about fifteen seconds, she pulled the now taffy-like syrup out of the snow with a fork. She pulled and twisted the candy into various shapes and laid it on a piece of waxed paper to cool, then drizzled more syrup into the snow. She continued this process until the syrup was all gone.

"Josephine, your pumpkins should be cooked down in about a half hour. Do you want to get started on some pie dough?"

The pumpkins Jo had planted in June had produced nicely, a bit too nicely. She had planted three seeds, which had turned into three sprawling vines. Jo wanted to make sure there was enough fruit for a pie on Christmas, but she had no idea that *one* good-size pumpkin would be sufficient for *two* pies, nor did she have any idea that each vine would produce a half dozen or so pumpkins.

Jo chuckled a bit as she thought about watching the vines grow and grow and grow. At one point, she was sure they were trying to capture the chickens because the vines had started to

creep through the wire fabric. By harvest time, Jo was the proud cultivator of twenty-three pumpkins, each about ten pounds.

Pearl in a very motherly fashion had simply told Jo to pick out the two best pumpkins and set them aside for pies. The rest Pearl would take down to the store and sell. One of those saved pumpkins had been used for a pie on Thanksgiving. Now, the other pumpkin had been cut into cubes and was simmering in a pot on the stove, cooking down into a thick sauce. The aroma of cinnamon, nutmeg, and ginger was carried throughout the kitchen by the steam rising from the sauce.

Jo got a mixing bowl from the cupboard and grabbed the flour canister from the counter. She measured out the flour, salt, and oleo. Then she used a pastry cutter to cut the oleo into the flour. She measured out water and added it to the flour, using a fork to mix everything until she had a ball of dough.

Spreading a pastry cloth on the kitchen table, Jo dusted it with flour, then took the rolling pin and began to roll out a circle of dough about a quarter inch thick and a foot in diameter. As she was doing this, she found her mind wandering a bit aimlessly, thinking about what Christmas would be like this year, until Pearl pulled her back to reality.

"Josephine, don't move!"

"What? What is it?"

Jo stood motionless at the table, her hands on the rolling pin. Then she saw Pearl was pointing at Jo's left hand and moving toward her. Jo looked down, and her heart skipped a beat.

"Your ring! You lost your ring!"

"Oh."

Jo's shoulders slumped, and she felt a pain in her stomach.

"Pearl...I'm not wearing my ring."

"I know. That's what I mean, we need to find it. It could be anywhere. It could be in the pie dough."

"No, Pearl, I mean I'm not wearing my wedding ring anymore."

Pearl had been frantically moving things around on the table searching for the ring, but now she stopped and looked at Jo. Her face was blank, expressionless. The two women stared at each other for a seemingly endless moment. Then, Pearl looked down and smoothed her apron.

"Oh. I see."

"I'm sorry. Don't be mad. I've been meaning to tell you, but I couldn't ever figure out how. It just seemed like I shouldn't be wearing it anymore. It didn't seem right to me to be wearing it."

"Is there…"

"No…yes…well, no. I don't know, to be completely honest."

Jo really didn't know if there was anybody. She knew how she felt about Peter and saw no point in telling Pearl that, but she also didn't know what exactly the situation was between her and Peter. She had so completely shut him out for so long that, even if she was ready to be with him, she didn't know if he would take her back. She would just have to work up the courage to find out. She had done that once before, she would just have to do it again and see if he would still have her.

"It's that man, isn't it? That Peter Messimer. I saw how you look at him, how he looks at you. I saw him at Alfred's funeral. Young lady, I *told* you to stay away from him."

Jo felt like the little orphan girl being scolded. But she imagined Pearl was feeling betrayed by her right now. Pearl was probably feeling many of the same emotions that Jo herself had been dealing with the past several months as she struggled to come to grips with her feelings toward Peter and her sense of betrayal of Al and the Troyers. Jo had already run the gamut of emotions over this and had decided what she needed to do. Pearl being upset with her wouldn't—couldn't—change that; she swatted the little orphan girl aside and tried to ease Pearl's hurt.

"Pearl, it's not what you think."

But it was. Jo had fallen in love with Peter. While she had not shared her body with him, they had shared an intense

intimacy that only true lovers can share. The fact that they had not explored the physical side of their love was immaterial. She knew they would have, given more time, probably while she was still married to Al, while he was off fighting the war.

"It's not right, you giving up on my Alfred like that. You shouldn't be running around with that man—with *any* man. Are there others? Somebody told me once they saw you in the theater with some soldier, but I just couldn't believe it, that you'd do that."

"No, no others. I didn't give up on Al, I moved on. I carry him with me wherever I go, and I always will. But Al's been dead for over a year. I kept him close to me all that time, and doing so consumed my life. You saw that, you *had* to have seen that. It's just time for me to be me again, and that me is very different from the one Al knew."

Pearl was completely unprepared to see Jo moving on from Al. If Jo moved on, it meant Pearl *had* to accept that Al would never be coming back, that he was indeed dead. She couldn't keep holding on to a nonexistent hope that a mistake had been made and her son would return home one day. She also couldn't bear to think that maybe Jo and Al would have split even if he had not died, that Jo might have been with Peter no matter what happened.

"You were with that man even before…before…*weren't* you?"

"Pearl, it's late." The conversation was being controlled by emotions, and Jo knew it would go nowhere. "I need to get cleaned up and get to bed. We can talk more tomorrow when I get home from work."

And with that, Jo left the pie for Pearl to finish and headed upstairs to her room. Closing the door behind her, she removed her work clothes and stuffed them into the hamper next to her dresser. She looked at the stack of letters on her dresser. On top of the letters from Al was her wedding ring. She picked up the ring and looked at it for a moment, then set it to the side and picked up the letter from the top of the stack. This was the letter she had received after Al had died, the one he wrote on the day he was killed. She wrapped herself in a towel and carried the letter with her to the bathroom.

After scrubbing most of the factory grime from her with a washcloth, she drew a bath. Slipping into the hot water, she leaned back and opened the letter from Al. She read the letter again, from beginning to end, just as she had so many times before. She read it a second, then a third, and finally a fourth time. Each time she reached the same conclusion, just as she had every other time she read the letter—somehow Al had sensed she had grown away from him.

And it was true, she had grown away from him. Nothing could change that. Maybe if he were to have returned from the war, the two of them could have gotten to know each other again, to fall in love again, but would it—could it—ever have been what she felt for Peter? All of that was irrelevant because Al was *not* coming home from the war. He had died on a beach on a tiny island in the middle of a big ocean ten thousand miles away from her. Whatever his reasons, nothing could change the fact that Al had left her, left her alone, left her to grow up without him. Maybe if he had never left…but then he *had* left, and he had *died*. Nothing Jo could do would ever change that. And nothing she could do would ever change the fact that she loved Peter.

She carefully folded the letter and tucked it back into the envelope. Setting the letter out of the way so it would not get wet, she got out of the tub and dried off. Returning to her room, she slipped into her nightgown. She gathered up the stack of letters from Al and tied them together with a piece of yarn, capturing her wedding ring with the yarn. She walked over to her closet and reached up to place the bundled letters on the top shelf. But, she stopped for a moment with her arm outstretched. Something lingering inside told her she just wasn't ready to pack Al away.

She turned and walked back to the dresser. She neatly laid the bundle of letters on top of it. In the middle was a stack of letters from Roz, and on the other side was Peter's baseball cap, her trinity of friendship represented there on her dresser. One friend she had lost to the war, one she had lost to the internment camps, and one she knew to be the love of her life…and she was afraid she had lost him forever.

VOL. XXXV—N° 358   Saturday, December 23, 1944   Five Cents

PRISONERS SLAUGHTERED
Nazis Murder 150 near Malmedy

LONDON, England—Nazi troops killed nearly one hundred and fifty American prisoners—some of them medics wearing the Red Cross armband—near the village of Malmedy, Belgium. Word of the massacre first broke on December 17. These reports have since been confirmed by those who miraculously survived the shootings, including Private First Class Peter Piscatelli of New York City. Piscatelli said, "We were just standing there all bunched up. It started when a German tank man fired a pistol into the crowd. He fired again, and then all the Germans—the whole gang of them—opened up. They fired their machine guns and mowed our men down." The official account from First Army Headquarters stated between one hundred and twenty and one hundred and fifty were slain, and fifteen escaped.

REDUCTION IN CIVILIAN TIRES
OPA Orders Sharp Cut in First Quarter

WASHINGTON, D.C.—The Office of Price Administration (OPA) today ordered a dramatic cut in the production of passenger tires in the first quarter of 1945. Output will be cut sharply to five million tires, a reduction of over a million and a half from current production. The announcement came yesterday from James F. Clark, director of the Rubber Bureau of the War Production Board (WPB). Under the previous production schedule, approximately eight million tires were to be produced in the first quarter of 1945, making this an effective reduction of nearly three million. Officials maintain the new output will be sufficient to cover essential needs, but Clark went on to say it is "...very apparent..." that holders of A gasoline ration cards will need to make due with their current tires "...for a good part of 1945." He said the reduction is made necessary by the increased demand by the armed forces. As a result, additional facilities must be converted from civilian to military production, as well as manpower shifted to that area. This news comes on the heels of an earnings report yesterday from Firestone Tire and Rubber Company, which stated its net sales were nineteen per cent over the previous year.

AIR BATTLES AGAINST JAPANESE
Enemy Losses in Aircraft Mount

ALLIED HEADQUARTERS, Philippine Islands—Aerial combat against the Japanese forces was conducted today over the Philippine Islands and Japan proper. The enemy lost thirty-eight aircraft, mostly over the Philippines. Radio Tokio reported the engagements over the Philippines and Japan as victories. It asserted twenty Superfortresses flying out of Saipan were shot down and twenty more damaged in an attempted strike on the large Mitsubishi aircraft factories in Nagoya, Japan. Allied reports directly contradict this by stating no Superfortresses had been lost.

WORKERS STRIKE
War Production Imperiled

DETROIT, Mich.—A strike by six hundred workers across the border in Windsor, Ontario, is threatening production of combat vehicles. The strike is at Kelsey-Hayes Company of Canada in several large auto plants that employ twenty thousand. The strike, now in its second day, is in response to the dismissal of thirty-two Kelsey-Hayes employees.

№ 32

The sky had been dark gray all Saturday, and Peter knew that meant snow was on the way. He thought the snow would make for a good Christmas morning, at least for all of the boys and girls, if it held off until the next night. The sun had just dropped below the horizon as he pulled his truck into downtown Blooming Grove. He reached forward and pulled the switch out to turn on the truck's headlights.

Peter circled the square once before finding a parking space. He pulled the truck up to the curb, rubbed Barney's ears, and got out. Walking down the street, he crossed over to the sidewalk as soon as an opening appeared in the traffic.

Downtown was busy with shoppers seeing what they could pick up for Christmas. Christmas being Monday, that evening was pretty much the last chance to buy gifts, since most stores would be closed on Sunday. All of the stores were decked out in holiday trimmings, from wreaths to green and red bunting. A speaker over the door of the department store reverberated with holiday music being broadcast by the local radio station. The department store had received a shipment of shoes, so those who had ration coupons left were scurrying around inside the store trying to get a pair before the supply ran out.

As he ambled down the sidewalk, Peter peered in the front window of each store, checking out what they had for sale. He didn't really have much to do in the way of shopping, he just enjoyed the holiday atmosphere. He was a loner by nature, but each year around this time he did start yearning for some sort of companionship. So he wandered around downtown, stopping to chat with various people. Everybody in town knew Peter, so there was no shortage of well wishes and short conversations.

Deep down, he also hoped that peering through one of the shop windows he would catch a glimpse of Jo doing a bit of last-minute shopping. The longing for companionship brought on by this particular holiday season was especially difficult for him, since Jo had shut him out of her life—isolated herself from everybody. He missed her greatly and hoped one day they could again be around each other.

Everybody inside each store was happily shopping for last-minute Christmas items, either gifts or supplies. For a moment, as he looked through the window of Bilson's Hardware, his heart jumped a beat as he thought he saw Jo, but he quickly realized it wasn't her. That really set him to thinking about how much he would like to spend the holiday with her. Instead, it would be just him and Barney.

Peter continued wandering down the sidewalk, intending to make a loop around the square. In the middle of the block, a newspaper boy was hawking the evening edition of The Blooming Grove Review. Peter stopped, flipped the kid a nickel, and snapped open the paper. He stood and leaned against the wall of the OPA storefront to read the first-page headlines.

In big, bold letters just below the masthead, the main headline simply read *Nuts!* Peter scanned the first few lines of the article and learned this was General McAuliff's response to the German general's demand for his surrender at Bastogne. The 101st Airborne was holding Bastogne in the middle of the German breakout in the Ardennes forest. History would remember the breakout as the Battle of the Bulge.

Below the fold was the headline *Halsey's Typhoon Disaster.* The article discussed the aftermath of a typhoon that hit Task Force 38 in the Philippine Sea on the 18th. Peter shook his head as he read that the destroyers USS *Hull*, USS *Spence*, and USS *Monaghan* had capsized and sank, taking almost all of their crews with them. He thought it bad enough the sailors had to be facing death from the Japanese navy, that they were killed by a storm would have to devastate the sailors' families.

In the lower, right-hand corner of the front page, the headline read *Sports in Brief.* Below that was a bulleted list of key points: *Adolf Rupp Coaches Kentucky Wildcats past Ohio State in Overtime; Blackhawks 1, Canadians 2; Blackhawks Take On Rangers Tomorrow; Complete Sports Inside.*

Peter folded the newspaper and tucked it into his armpit, stuffed his hands into his pockets, and continued down the sidewalk toward French's butcher shop. The butcher was one store in from the corner, next to Abe's grocery store. He had come downtown to get a couple of bones for Barney; good ones with a lot of fresh marrow. These would be the gifts he exchanged this year, and in return he would receive hours of fun playing with the dog. Of course, the gifts were not a requisite for the fun, but it would be Peter's Christmas. He disappeared inside the butcher for a minute, then reappeared carrying a package of bones wrapped in white butcher paper.

As the door closed behind him, the smells of the butcher shop faded and he caught a whiff of cinnamon, nutmeg, and apples. He lifted his nose and sniffed several times, trying to determine the origin of the smell. As the door to Abe's swung open, he quickly realized from where the scents were originating. He grabbed the door and held it open for a woman and her child, then went inside.

Abe's was, like every store on the square, adorned in Christmas décor. The whole store was awash in red and green and white and silver. The spicy smell that had drawn Peter into the store hung heavy in the air, only briefly interrupted by the occasional smell of pine from the many wreaths hanging around the store. The wreaths had been freshly cut just two days earlier.

Behind the counter, Pearl was ladling steaming spiced cider into mugs and offering it to anyone who wandered in. She saw Peter and cast a cold look on him until her sense of holiday spirit nudged aside her animosity.

"Cider, Peter?" She was polite, but there was a certain curtness to her voice.

"Thanks, Pearl," he said, laying the newspaper on the counter and taking the mug she offered.

"Are you heading to your family's farm tomorrow?"

"No, not this year," Peter replied. "Can't. Not with work and all. 'Sides, the farm's only 30 miles away, but I'm lucky if the ol' truck gets ten or eleven miles to the gallon. A round trip would be almost my entire gas ration for the week."

Peter lifted the mug and sipped the cider.

"I forgot you had taken over the store," Peter said, holding the mug to his chin, letting the heat warm his jaw and the aroma energize his olfactory senses.

"No, not taken over," she said sharply. "Just running it until the Abes get back."

Pearl was very particular about how people referred to her running the store. She wanted nobody to mistake that it wasn't still the Abes' store. She waved to a customer who was leaving, then smoothed her apron before continuing.

"Shame about what happened to that poor family. You hear from Roz at all?"

"No, I haven't. I think Jo is the only one at the plant who's heard from her. She took it hard, you know, Jo did. They were really close..." Peter paused just a bit, "but then you know that."

"Yes, she writes Josephine quite often. I guess there's probably not a whole lot to do in...there."

"I sure do miss her, almost as much as I miss..."

His voice trailed off as he became aware of what he was going to say and to whom. He wondered if Jo had told Pearl

anything about him—how he and she had fallen for each other, what he knew to be love in his heart and the love he was sure he saw in her heart.

"There are a lot of people missing a lot of things." A coolness in her voice touched Peter, and he wrapped his hands around the warm mug of cider. "All over this country. All over the world. Last year, Christmas was so quick after Alfred's funeral I was still numb from the shock of losing him. It never really set in with me that it was Christmastime, so I didn't connect the loss with the holiday. This year, though, I've been keenly aware that my boy is no longer here. Christmas is supposed to be a happy time. I know it's hard, certainly it is for me, but you should be happy and thankful for what you have. At least that's what I keep telling myself. Sometimes it works, but mostly it doesn't. Josephine's been a big help, keeping my mind off it. At least she tries to. But, you know, she's going through the same thing." The tone of her voice turned quite a bit colder. "It's good she's not dishonoring his memory."

Hearing Pearl say Jo's name made him uncomfortable. The look on Pearl's face—just short of a scowl—made him fairly certain she knew something of what he and Jo shared. He tried to shift the conversation away from talk of Jo.

"Can't imagine those guys over in that ar-den forest mess are happy this Christmas, or thankful for much at all."

Peter tapped the headline on the newspaper. Pearl shook her head as she responded. A bit of the coolness in her voice disappeared, too.

"And terrible business about those Malmedy killings. Hope our boys make those Nazis pay."

"We'll get 'em," Peter responded. "They've been on the run since we landed in France back in June. It's only a matter of time."

"Still, has to be even worse for the boys overseas right now because of Christmas. They should be home with their families, not alone on some battlefield. Mothers should be with their babies. The last Christmas I spent with my baby was the one right after Pearl Harbor."

"Pearl, I don't know if you know this, but I lost a brother in the first war. Don't really tell people that. Jo's 'bout the only one…fer sure the only one in a really long time."

"I know." Pearl looked Peter straight in the eye, an ever-so-slight bit of warmth crept into her voice. "Josephine told me."

"We were twins. They say twins are as close to each other as a mother to her children, closer even."

Peter stared down at the counter as he talked. Exposing his inner emotions was one of the hardest things for him to do. Over the years, a few people had poked at the mortar in the wall he built around himself, but it was only Jo who had found—no, created—the first loose brick, and once the brick was loose, she had not let go, pulling until she had created a hole and climbed inside. But Peter felt he had a point to make, a point he hoped would in some way help Pearl through her loss.

"War is a thief. It steals the world of peace. It steals boys of their youth. And it stole my brother from me."

Peter glanced up from the counter as he talked, but mainly stared distractedly at the folded newspaper on the counter. Now he paused to take a sip of the apple cider, its heat dwindling. Pearl silently absorbed his words. When Jo told her about his brother—before Al's death—she hadn't really considered how it would have affected him. Of course, she knew a loss like that would be painful, but she just didn't have a similar experience on which to base empathy. Little did she know then that in a few short months her life would be torn apart as his was. Now, she understood, standing before her was a man who had experienced the same loss she had, only twenty-odd years earlier.

"Pearl, I wish I could tell you the wound heals. It doesn't. Eventually it will look like it has, but that's only on the outside. Inside, though, it will fester…always…and sometimes it will break open again. You just can't pick at it or it will always be open."

Pearl looked away for a moment, focusing on some nonexistent spot outside the store window. Bits of snow floated by in the gentle breeze, but she didn't really see the snow. Pearl knew she had the wound Peter described. She also knew she picked at it two or three times a week. It was as if she couldn't stand to see the wound heal over, even if it were still there below the surface.

She looked back at Peter, her eyes dancing around his face. He still stared at the counter, unconsciously bending one corner of the newspaper over and back, over and back. She had known Peter for a long time, just as everybody in town knew him—from a distance, seeing him around and having the random casual conversation in passing in a store or at a social function. This was the first time, however, she had caught sight of his noble nature; she clearly read it on his face. It was a profound distance from the irascible legend that had taken hold.

Pearl could see how Jo had become close to him, perhaps without even knowing it. Her stomach soured at the thought of Jo with him—with any man other than Al. She felt hurt by what Jo had done, but immediately realized Jo was right, it had been over a year. Wasn't it okay that she was moving on, and wasn't Peter good for her? But, Jo moving on would also mean the end to her unspoken denials about what really happened to Al, that he was dead, not just gone overseas. As she wrestled with her thoughts of Jo and Peter, Pearl realized the wound Peter described was shared, not hers alone, and she knew she was not the only one picking at the wound.

"For me," Peter continued, "I couldn't stop thinking about his death, how much it hurt and how much I missed him. I kept imagining over and over what he must have gone through at the end, what he saw, what he felt. I wondered what his last thought was, the last thing he said. Was it quick or did he suffer? I pulled away from everything and everybody, just wanting to be left to myself, to drown myself in my own misery. Then some random day, I finally realized the war had taken one son from my family; I couldn't let it take another. My brother had made his choice, and I couldn't let that guide my life. It was his choice to go to war, not mine. It would be my choice to live."

As Peter talked, Pearl realized how closely she—and Jo—was playing out the same scenario over Al's death. They both pulled deep inside themselves, leaning on only each other every once in a great while.

"You still miss him?" Pearl couldn't imagine his answer to be anything but yes.

"Of course I do. The right thing would be to say I think about him every day, but that just isn't true. Do I think about him a lot? Well, yeah, more recently than I have in the past several years. I hold my memories of him dearly, but I don't allow them to rule me."

A slightly uncomfortable still settled over the conversation. Peter shuffled his feet on the floor and sipped the cider. Then he looked Pearl straight in the eye and spoke in a firm voice.

"It'd be a real shame to miss out on life 'cause 'a holdin' on to a death."

His meaning was clear to Pearl. Peter was no longer talking about himself, he was talking about her…or more likely Jo. She was dear to Pearl's heart. She had grown to love Jo like a daughter, sharing experiences only a mother and daughter can share. While she knew Jo missed Al, she also understood she missed Peter. Was she being selfish expecting Jo not to move on with her life?

"Thanks for the cider, Pearl."

Peter intentionally brought the conversation to an abrupt end, feeling Jo hovering around the edges of his conversation. He tipped the mug back and drank the last of the now tepid cider. He sat the empty mug down on the counter, returned the newspaper to under his arm, and walked out of the store. As the door closed behind him, the spicy smells were replaced by the crisp air outside. He shoved his hands into his pockets and walked back to the truck.

At the truck, Peter dropped the package of bones in the bed, then opened the door and slid in. He was met by Barney's cold nose on his cheek and a quick slooop of the dog's tongue, followed by a good once-over of sniffing. The bloodhound's nose could pick up the smell of the butcher shop on Peter, even through the spices of Pearl's cider. Peter rubbed the dog's ears, then started the truck, pulled onto the street, and headed home.

Eric K. Augspurger

VOL. XXXV—N? 359   Sunday, December 24, 1944   Five Cents

MEAT, VEGETABLES RATIONED AGAIN
OPA to Announce Returns to the List

WASHINGTON, D.C.—The Office of Price Administration (OPA) will place nearly all meats and canned vegetables currently point-free once again on the rationed list starting with the new year, sources reported yesterday. Frozen fruits and vegetables are expected to remain point-free. The official announcement from the OPA is expected next Wednesday, just five days before the new year. The affected foods have been unrationed and point-free since May. The OPA has lobbied the War Food Administration (WFA) to place point-free foods back on the rationing list for the past five months.

GIFTS IN THE BOMB BAY
Santa Delivers Yule Gifts to Troops

SAN DIEGO, Calif.— While homes around America are putting the last-minute touches on Christmas decorations, Santa Claus is making his way across the ocean. This year, the sleigh old St. Nick will be flying—at least in the South Pacific—is a B-24 Liberator. His bomber was loaded in San Diego with thousands of gifts, Christmas trees, and decorations for the fighting forces in the Pacific theater. Loading was courtesy of Convair's maintenance department, the United Service Organization (USO), the Office of Price Administration (OPA), and the Red Cross. The Convair maintenance department raised the money to purchase the items. Gifts include hard-to-get items such as sewing needles, pins, scissors, and other items.

PATTON STRIKES AGAINST GERMANS
Attacks South Flank of Breakout in Ardennes

PARIS, France—The Third Army under the command of Lieutenant General George S. Patton is slashing into the southern flank of the salient created by the German breakout in the Ardennes forest, it was reported today. The counter-offensive is an attempt to cut off the entire Nazi vanguard. It is reported tanks and armored troop carriers from Patton's army are cutting at the base of the salient near the border of Luxembourg. These reports have not been confirmed by Allied headquarters, but were broadcast in an alarm by the German DNB news agency. Yesterday, four sorties of C-47 transports were able to drop supplies to troops in the Bastogne area after the weather cleared. Adverse weather had hampered Allied air operations since the German breakout began. The defensive stand in Bastogne, a strategic town of seven crossroads, was key in preventing the two pincers of the German advance from coming together.

JAPAN FATE IS IN PHILIPPINES
Say War To Be Won There

WASHINGTON, D.C.— Propagandists in Japan are making the claim that the fate of that country rests on the battle for the Philippine Islands. Loss of the Philippines would cut off Japan from the southern and resource-rich regions of its empire. Cut off would be the Dutch East Indies, Indo China, and Malay. Resources that would be prevented from reaching Japan include oil, rubber, and tin. Japan's ability to wage war would be in doubt with the loss of these resources. The Japanese people already know the consequences of territorial losses as Superfortresses flying from Saipan regularly pound cities on the home islands.

№33

Sunday afternoon, Christmas Eve, Peter pulled his truck to the curb in front of the Troyers' house. He shut off the engine and then just sat there for a minute. Barney laid down on the seat and rested his muzzle on Peter's leg. Peter rubbed the dog's ears with his right hand as he reached for the small gift-wrapped box on the dash. He set the box on his lap and tapped it lightly in time with his rubbing of Barney's ears. Finally, he pulled one of the long, floppy ears away from the dog's head with a slow stroke, then spoke aloud.

"Well, boy, do it or don't, right?"

Barney looked up in the direction of Peter's voice, his tail thumping against the seat. Peter opened the door, and Barney stood up. Peter slid out of the truck and reached back in to tussle Barney's ears.

"I'll be right back."

Peter walked up to the porch. He paused at the stairs, took a deep breath, and stepped up onto the porch. He extended his arm, paused again, and then rapped his knuckles on the door

three slow forceful times. He turned back toward the street. Looking up and down the block, he noticed the Christmas decorations everybody had put up; much more subdued than in years past with no exterior lights, but houses were still adorned with wreaths and the occasional bunting.

Behind him, he heard steps inside the house approaching the door. He turned back to face the door as it opened. Pearl greeted him.

"Peter!" Shocked echoed in her voice. "Josephine's at the scrap drive."

"I know."

He held the gift in front of him, nervously rotating it in his hands. Peter looked down at the box as he turned it. He could not seem to bring himself to look at Pearl.

"I didn't...I wasn't...I couldn't...I haven't talked to Jo in so long—she's sort of been avoiding me—I want to give her a present, but I want you to give it to her tomorrow. Just in case she's not happy about it...me."

Pearl stood there for a moment, looking at Peter. She realized it was time to let the wound begin to heal for at least Jo. She herself may continue to pick at it for years to come, but she could not allow Jo to deny herself the good in life just because she was holding on to Al's death. She reached out and took the present from Peter. There was a warmth in her voice as she responded, which caught Peter a little of guard.

"I'll put it under the tree for her to open on Christmas. Why don't you come over for dinner? I know you can't make it to the farm this year. We eat at six."

"Oh, no, Pearl, thanks for the offer." He wanted to see Jo; it had been a long time, but the warmth in Pearl's voice was still throwing him off. "I do really appreciate it, but I just don't think I'd feel right. You got your family and all."

"Peter, family doesn't always mean blood."

"Yeah, I s'pose."

"You've been a real good friend to Josephine. With Alfred gone and Roz hauled away to that…camp…it'd be a shame if she were to lose her other best friend."

"Thanks, Pearl. I think I just need to play things by ear."

He turned and walked back to his truck. Pearl watched him drive down the block before returning inside.

VOL. XXXV—N<u>o</u> 360 Monday, December 25, 1944 Five Cents

WAR FAR FROM OVER
Casualties Mount As War Enters Fourth Year

WASHINGTON, D.C.—The War Department has released casualty numbers for the European theater for November: 57,775, including 8,259 dead. Since D-Day, the total casualty figure for American forces in Europe now stands at 258,124. Casualties in the Pacific theater remain high due to the ferocity of the enemy. The recent action on Leyte in the Philippines illustrates this; thirty-seven Japanese were killed for every one American killed. Total Japanese casualties on Leyte have been placed at 82,554 to just 10,409 American casualties. Since the beginning of the war on December 7, 1941, total casualties for all American armed forces has reached 536,950. The number missing in action since the beginning of the war is up to 57,514.

WAR A SHADOW OVER CHRISTMAS
May Be White, but Not Peaceful

PARIS, France—The first Americans to celebrate Christmas this year will be those servicemen in the Gilbert Islands. When Christmas arrives on the other side of the international dateline, it will be 8 a.m. Sunday Eastern War Time. Those servicemen will not have a white Christmas, unlike servicemen in Europe. A heavy snowfall blankets the Western Front. While the European Christmas may be white, it certainly will not be peaceful. The German breakout in the Ardennes forest continues to be resisted by Allied forces, and many troops are actively engaged in combat. British Field Marshal Sir Bernard Montgomery shared a Christmas message with his troops: "Together, you and I, we have achieved much, and together we will see the thing to the end."

BUTTER RATION POINTS JUMP
Expanded Ration List Starts Tuesday

WASHINGTON, D.C.—The number of ration points needed for butter jumps from twenty to twenty-four per pound tomorrow morning, the day after Christmas. This was among the changes announced today by administrator Chester Bowles of the Office of Price Administration (OPA). Other changes include cancellation of all red and blue points active prior to December 1, all sugar stamps, and all canning certificates. Stamp number 34 will be still valid. Bowles states, "Civilian supplies of sugar, butter, and commercially canned fruits and vegetables are at the lowest point since the war began and meat supplies are declining." The announcement was made earlier than originally intended "...to protect existing supplies on store shelves from buying runs."

GI HIJACKERS ARRESTED
Sit in French Jails for Black Market

PARIS, France—Over one thousand American servicemen have been arrested in hijacking schemes and now sit in French jails. It is reported that thousands of gallons of gasoline are stolen daily and fed into the French black market. The GIs are also accused of selling stolen cigarettes and other items. The French government is cracking down on black-market operations. In November, two American servicemen were sentenced to life imprisonment for selling governmental property to black market agents. Over eight hundred servicemen are arrested in Paris each week.

N⁰ 34

Jo could smell the bacon frying downstairs. Pearl was already up and fixing breakfast that Christmas morning. Jo pulled back the curtains and looked outside her bedroom window. A thin blanket of new snow had fallen overnight. The sun was now just starting to crest over the eastern horizon. The pale blue glow of the snow was slowly starting to change to orange as the sun rose. Soon, it would be pure, blinding white.

Jo thought about how the boys and girls on the East Coast were probably already playing with their new toys, while in the Midwest kids were wondering if it was too early to get up and poke around the tree. Thinking back to the orphanage, she remembered that the excitement they felt began in the evening with the sounds of snow crunching under tires as the staff returned to celebrate with the children. Then, just for a brief moment, she could swear she heard that same sound. Her heart skipped a beat—which surprised her—but she quickly convinced herself she was a grown woman just hearing things.

Jo removed a pretty dress from the closet. She had purchased it one day when she went shopping with Roz, before Roz had been taken away, but had never worn it. Today would be a good

day to wear it, she decided, and slipped it on. Dressing up nicely would be the first step in making that Christmas day special. She walked over to the mirror and began brushing her hair, paying special attention to get the curls just right.

Satisfied with the way she looked, Jo slipped on a pair of leather flats she had bought over the summer. She hadn't worn them but once or twice and then only around her room. New shoes were so hard to come by with the rationing that it was rare when the department store had them, let alone by the time Jo could get there after work. So she had told herself only to wear them on a special occasion. Christmas day would be that special occasion.

Jo headed downstairs, following the scent of bacon. It was not often Pearl cooked bacon, for breakfast or otherwise. Meat was among the many food items rationed, so Jo knew this was a treat specially for Christmas breakfast. It would be a welcome change from oatmeal. Jo walked into the kitchen and greeted the Troyers.

"Morning. Merry Christmas!"

"Merry Christmas to you, too," Pearl replied. "My, you look very nice today."

"Thank you."

Jo spread her dress and turned like a model showing her wares. Gerald peered over the top of the newspaper and nodded approvingly. His eyes bulged slightly through his reading glasses. Jo wasn't entirely sure if the lenses were distorting his eyes or if they were indeed bulging because he hadn't seen her in anything but slacks for months. He snapped the newspaper taut and returned to reading. Jo read the headline on the front page as it faced her: *Air Drops Relieve Bastogne; Patton Swings North*.

"I was just getting ready to call you to see if you were up. Breakfast is ready," Pearl said.

Pearl removed the crispy strips of bacon from the pan. Then she took a tin from the icebox and poured the grease into the can. Once the can was full, she would take the grease to the

recycling center, and from there the grease would be sent off for use in munitions manufacturing. After draining the grease into the tin, Pearl filled three plates with bacon, eggs, and hash browns and set them on the table.

"'Cept for the bacon, breakfast from your victory garden, Josephine."

"The bacon is going to be so good. We don't have it much anymore."

Jo leaned down and took a big whiff of the smells coming from her plate. She smiled and then they all dug into the hearty breakfast.

After breakfast the three shared two full pots of first-brew coffee, another rare treat. The grounds from both pots were saved for the rest of the week, to be brewed a second and a third time until the last of the essential oils were completely drawn from the grounds and the coffee could be best described as only slightly stained water.

As the smell of bacon began to subside, Pearl set about getting the turkey into the oven for its long, slow roasting. It was by chance they had turkey instead of one of the chickens Jo had been raising. Pearl had accepted it at Abe's as payment from a local farmer for an overdue tab. With his three sons overseas, he had not had enough manpower to bring in all of his crops that fall, so he and his wife were really struggling to make ends meet. Pearl graciously thanked him for the bird, trying in her way to make him feel as though he had done her a favor. She knew how proud families who worked the land were to be indebted to no one. And, after taking the bird as payment, she dutifully and immediately sat down to write a letter to Mr. Abe explaining the situation, assuring him she would pay for the turkey in an exact amount equal to the debt it cleared for the farmer.

A couple of weeks later, Mr. Abe had written back telling her it was an honorable thing she had done and that her honor had been enough payment for the store. He assured her any money of hers she intended to add to the store coffer for the bird would be unnecessary. Pearl, of course, had indeed slipped the money in. For ten straight days the store register was forty-three cents over, then it returned to her nearly impeccable plus or minus two cents.

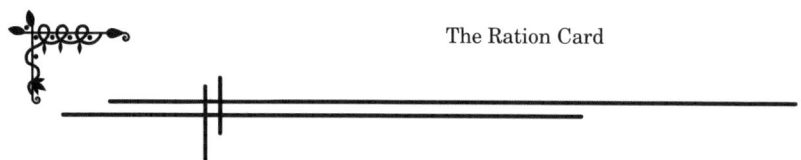

Jo pulled up the collar on her wool coat to protect her neck a bit from the wind. The noon church service was over, and everybody was off to their homes to enjoy the rest of Christmas. Jo and the Troyers, however, would be making a stop on the way home. Jo stood at the bottom of the church steps waiting for Gerald to pull the car around, then she and Pearl climbed into the car.

As Gerald guided the car through the streets, Jo stared aimlessly out the window. She watched kids playing in the fresh snow, mothers scolding them not to get their church clothes dirty.

Gerald turned the car into the cemetery. They were the only ones there. Jo was glad they would be alone. She was a bit ashamed that she actually had to think when was the last time she had come to visit. She had been so focused on keeping Al's memory alive that she had lost track of visiting his grave. As she thought about it, the last time had been over the summer. Then it hit her; the last time she was at the cemetery Peter had been there, too. She had been very short with him, to the point of being mean. He had a good heart and was trying to help her, but she knew how they felt about each other, and that had upset her—especially at Al's grave.

Strangely—to Jo, at least—thinking about Peter now while at the cemetery didn't cause her the same torment as it had before. She pondered this for a moment, wondering why that was the case. She knew Al was still dear to her heart, and always would be, but her unexpected thought of Peter also brought back a certain realization of the nature of her feelings. There was the man she had married, whom she loved as a very dear friend, then there was the man she loved very dearly, and they were not the same man. She knew this to be true.

Suddenly, Jo was afraid something on her face was revealing her thoughts. She quickly glanced to the front seat, but neither

Pearl nor Gerald was paying any attention to her. Jo shifted uncomfortably in the backseat, picking up the bouquet of flowers from the seat and resting it on her lap as Gerald eased the car to a stop near Al's gravesite.

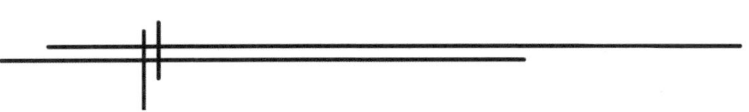

Gerald said a brief prayer, then walked to the headstone and patted it. Pearl followed him to the headstone, but rubbed her hand across the top as if smoothing her son's messy hair. Then, the two returned to the foot of the grave where Jo was standing. She stepped forward and laid the bouquet at the base of the headstone.

Pearl watched Jo as she kneeled. She saw how Jo mechanically drew her fingernails—such that they were—across her left ring finger, where her wedding band used to be, as she spoke softly to the grave. Gone were the days of fidgeting with the scar on her forehead. Taking the place of that foible was provoking the ghost of Al. It was suddenly very clear to Pearl: Jo would never stop picking at the wound, keeping it open forever, unless someone helped her move on. The wound would always be open, scratched open again just as soon as it began to heal. Jo would ruin her life unless she moved on, but Pearl now knew Jo would not move on by herself.

"C'mon, dear, it's time to go." Pearl reached down and softly grasped Jo's arm, pulling up just slightly. "It's time to get on with things."

Jo cocked her head upward and looked Pearl in the eye. Jo stood and hooked her arm into Pearl's. Halfway to the car, Jo drew the back of her thumb across the corner of her eye, wiping away the slight tear that had formed. Inside, Jo felt an emptiness. She thought of Al and, as they walked from his grave, she could feel the emptiness growing greater.

Jo turned her head to get one last glimpse at Al's grave before she ducked into the car. It seemed to her there was some underlying sense of finality, but she couldn't quite put her finger on what she felt. It was not unlike how, at first, she couldn't quite nail down that fleeting emotion she saw just behind the wall Peter had surrounded himself with...Peter, there it was again, she was at Al's grave and a thought of Peter crept into her mind, as if it was unstoppable, burrowing into her head. Or, was it that the thoughts had always been there, she just no longer had suppressive control over them and couldn't keep them hidden any longer?

Eric K. Augspurger

The Blooming Grove Review

VOL. XXXV—N? 360   Monday, December 25, 1944   Five Cents

VICTORY PRAYER OFFERED YESTERDAY
FDR Radio Broadcast to Armed Forces Worldwide

WASHINGTON, D.C.—"We cannot say when our victory will come. Our enemies…themselves know that they and their evil works are doomed." So was part of the president's pray offered yesterday in conjunction with the annual lighting of the Christmas tree on the White House lawn. The president also said victory will bring "…a new day of peace on earth in which all the nations of the earth will join together for all time." He went on to speak directly of the servicemen and women when he said, "The Christmas spirit lives tonight in the bitter cold of the front lines in Europe and in the heat of the jungles and swamps of Burma and the Pacific islands. Even the roar of our bombers and fighters in the air and the guns of our ships at sea will not drown out the messages of Christmas…". A crowd of approximately twenty-five hundred gathered on the lawn, while more were lined up outside the grounds. The United States Marine Band and a Navy chorus provided music for the hour preceding the president's address.

GROUP WANTS SHOE HOLIDAY
Claims New Ration Stamps Being Saved

WASHINGTON, D.C.—The National Association of Popular Price Shoe Retailers, Inc., on December 21 proposed a rationing holiday on shoes. It asked that the temporary holiday be initiated immediately for fifteen million leather shoes. This is the number of shoes the retail group states is frozen on store shelves, all in the four-dollar class. The group claims the public is refusing to use ration stamps, instead saving the new stamps to purchase higher-priced shoes. The group also claims the temporary holiday would offset inflation of shoe prices and allow the currently short supply to be extended. The group states the current system "…has operated like a glacier, freezing one price line after another in its path…" opens up.

HARD FIGHT STILL AHEAD IN PACIFIC
Nimitz Warns of Worst to Come

NAVAL HEADQUARTERS, Guam—Commander-in-chief of the Pacific Ocean Admiral Chester W. Nimitz, yesterday warned "…until we have bases close to the Japanese homeland, the tough part of the war will still be ahead of us." Nimitz, who was recently promoted to five-star admiral, was in Guam on a surprise Christmastime visit to his sailors in this forward area. Cautioning against over optimism, he said, "I don't want to give the impression the Japanese navy has been completely defeated. It has not, but it has not been able to stop our advance. We hope and expect that our advance will continue." The admiral addressed the growing length of Allied supply lines in the Pacific. "As the war progresses, the supply problem grows and the need for shipping increases. This all combines to make it a very major effort—to defeat the Japanese." Nimitz declined to predict the immediate future of action against the enemy. He says Japan's ability to defend itself has not been diminished. "We may expect the bitterest kind of opposition from the air as we advance toward the homeland and come within range of shore-based aircraft. They still have the capacity to deal damage with surface units, but we expect to be on hand always with superior naval forces to meet that kind of threat."

№ 35

In the evening, with the smell of Christmas turkey still hanging in the air along with the scent of pie made from homegrown pumpkins, Jo, Pearl, and Gerald gathered around the Christmas tree in the living room. The tree shimmered with silvery tinsel catching the lights strung around it. The tinsel danced as anybody walked near the tree, throwing glinty sparks of red and green and yellow and blue light into the room. Gerald said a brief prayer of thanks, and of remembrance, then handed out the presents.

Jo eagerly ripped open her presents with the glee of a little girl. She gasped as she pulled a beautiful dress from one present, jumping up to hug Pearl in thanks. Pearl squeezed her and gave her a quick kiss on the cheek. Then Jo handed Pearl a gift from her, a leather-bound accounting ledger with *Abe's* embossed in gold leaf on the front cover. Pearl tried to deflect a growing tear in her eye by half-heartedly scolding Jo for the unneeded expense.

Jo held the dress in front of her as she briefly twirled around the room. Then she dropped to the floor and ripped open another present, this one from Gerald. Inside was a pair of old work

boots with fresh new soles. She again jumped up, this time hugging Gerald, who shifted uncomfortably in his chair. Jo then handed Gerald her gift to him. He pulled off the wrapping paper to reveal a wooden magazine rack with finials Jo had machined herself. He immediately set the rack next to his chair and began filling it with the stack of magazines he had accumulated.

Jo felt very content, glad that Christmas had turned out to be so happy for all of them. She felt surrounded by comfort, from Pearl and Gerald to the house itself, like a soft, snuggly blanket was wrapped around her.

Jo was actually more pleased with the work boots than the dress, but she would never say so to avoid hurting Pearl's feelings. The soles on Jo's work boots had worn through months ago, and every other day when she got home from work she had to cut out a new piece of cardboard to fit inside in an attempt to make the boots last longer.

Jo knew how much trouble Gerald had gone to in getting her even used boots with new soles. She clearly saw why Al had developed such a good heart, and she tried to picture Al in her mind, but she couldn't quite bring him into focus.

It was at that moment, the very moment while thinking of Al, Jo felt a familiar sensation. It was a shade of the feelings she had when around Peter. It seemed to her as if he was standing across the room, watching her with smoldering eyes, his lips forming silent words that she would strain to make out. It had been weeks since she had talked to Peter, and she missed him dearly. She had come to think she may have lost two men on the day Al died, but if she *had* lost Peter it was all her fault, and she knew that. Maybe that was why she felt his essence right then, because her heart was telling her not to be too happy this day for she had pushed Peter away despite her feelings for him.

Jo kept her head down, hiding her face from Pearl and Gerald, but the feeling continued to gradually build, almost like a pressure in her chest, and she resisted until her body felt like it was going to shatter into a million little pieces right there on the living room floor. She slowly turned her head, still hanging down, and looked toward the front door. There, below the garland and sprig of mistletoe, the door stood closed, tightly sealing the rest of the world from the warmth of the Christmas evening inside. Peter was not there, and Jo thought herself a fool for allowing herself even a sliver of a belief that he may have been standing in the foyer, waiting for her to run and jump into his arms. Still, she couldn't shake the feeling of a presence, an essence of Peter.

Across the room, the fire popped and crackled. Gerald got up from his chair and poked at the logs with the fire iron, sending specks of orange up the chimney to be carried off into the night sky by the December wind. He settled back down into his chair, reached over, and clicked on the radio, twisting the dial until Christmas music drifted from the speaker. He leaned back, pulled the day's paper from the magazine rack Jo had made, and picked up reading where he left off, fighting a losing battle against the turkey to keep his eyes open.

Pearl had been scurrying around the living room, picking up the discarded wrapping paper and neatly pressing each sheet flat. She stacked the paper in a cardboard box, then carefully collected the bows and placed them on top. The box would go into the attic until next year, when it would again be time to wrap presents. Wrapping paper and bows would serve their purpose for years to come.

With the wrappings all cleaned up, Pearl stood in the doorway between the kitchen and living room. She adjusted her sweater on her shoulders, then placed her hands on her hips and looked at Jo. Sitting on the floor with her legs crossed ruminating over her gifts, she looked to Pearl like a giddy child. But at the same time, Pearl saw a strong young woman. A woman who had grown right before her eyes the past two years, taking the responsibility of a job, becoming independent, and developing from an orphaned child into a desirable woman. Pearl could see much happiness in Jo, though she had no way of knowing most of the happiness at that precise moment was from the unexpected thoughts of Peter.

Pearl decided it was time. She walked across the room to the fireplace. Reaching behind the clock on the mantle, Pearl pulled down the box Peter had dropped off the day before. She paused for a moment, realizing she had not even been conscious of the fact the clock was right next to the triangular display case that

held the flag from Al's funeral. Pearl could feel herself picking at the wound inside her as she looked at the neatly folded flag. *This is why Josephine has to move on, so she doesn't spend the rest of her life feeling this way.* Pearl swallowed hard to force back the welling in her eyes, then took a deep breath and calmed herself. She gave one last look at the flag, turned around, and held up the present from Peter.

"There's one more here, Josephine."

Pearl walked over to Jo and handed her a small box wrapped in plain green paper. A length of thick red yarn was wound around the box in place of a ribbon and tied in a knot. Jo, still seated on the floor with her legs crossed, took the box from Pearl and rested it on her lap.

"Goodie!"

Jo was so excited. This day had been almost as perfect as she had hoped for. She flipped the nametag over so she could read it.

"Okay, so this one is from…" Jo stared at the tag for a few long seconds, then looked up at Pearl. "…Pete?"

"He dropped it off yesterday evening when you were working the scrap drive."

Should she open it? Jo looked back up at Pearl, hoping to see something in her face telling Jo what to do.

"Well, go on, silly, open it."

Jo picked up the box from her lap and held it with both hands. She shook it slightly, just as a kid would trying to figure out what was inside. She only heard a little shifting around from inside of the box. She placed the box in one hand and pulled on the yarn to undo the knot. She slide one finger under the edge of the paper and pulled it back. Finally, she cracked opened the lid to the box so she could see what gift awaited her. Her heart skipped a beat when she saw. Suddenly, everything flooded through her head and heart, and she burst out in tears.

"What's wrong, Josephine? What is it?" Confusion resounded in Pearl's voice.

"It's a baseball scorecard," Jo said through the sniffles and tears.

Jo carefully picked up the card and tried hard to focus through the tears. It had been filled out all the way through the top of the seventh inning. From the bottom of the seventh inning onward was blank. Jo recalled the first time she had gone to a baseball game, the one Roz had dragged her to.

"I don't understand. Why would he give you a scorecard?"

"Not too long after I first met Pete, Roz and I went to a Maidens game with him. He used to play ball, you know. He explained the game to me, showed me how to keep score."

"Oh, I see," but confusion still tinged Pearl's voice.

"He explained the seventh inning stretch, and how he felt it was after the stretch that the game really started to get interesting. He said he thought that was true about relationships, too. That they really started getting interesting after they had matured."

Jo held up the scorecard so Pearl could see. She dragged her finger down the card to the seventh inning boxes.

"See, he filled in the box scores all the way through the top of the seventh inning. He's saying we're at the seventh inning stretch. He means it's time for things to get interesting."

"Ohhhh," this time, the inflection in Pearl's voice made it clear she understood; this card was his way of telling Jo she was the one he wanted to play out the end of the game with. "You should thank Peter for that gift."

"Yeah, I'll have to see if I can find him at work tomorrow."

Tears were still streaming down Jo's cheeks, but she was smiling. Her nose was running as well, and she kept wiping the back of her hand across her nose. She laid the score card on her lap and looked at it, trying to assimilate all of her thoughts and feelings. Jo looked up at Pearl when she spoke.

"Josephine, I meant you should thank him now." She gave Jo a motherly smile, one of having inside information. "It would be the polite thing to do."

"Yeah?" She glanced at the clock on the mantle. "Is it too late to call?"

"I meant you should *go* and thank him."

"Yeah?"

"Yeah."

Jo looked at Pearl, then smiled, and stood up, trying to brush her dress smooth in the process. There was a softness in Pearl's eyes.

"Okay."

Jo rubbed the tears from the corners of her eyes with the backs of her thumbs and fanned her eyes with her hands. She took the handkerchief Pearl offered her and wiped her nose. She walked to the entryway, took her coat from the hook, and slide into it. She pulled on a knit hat and looked back at Pearl.

"It's not that I'm better off without Al, you know. Al was a great guy and he was great to me. It's just that *I'm* better with Pete; *we're* better together."

"I know, dear," Pearl said and, after a pause, waved with her hands in a shooing motion. Jo then opened front door and stepped out onto the porch.

Eric K. Augspurger

The Blooming Grove Review

VOL. XXXV—N° 360   Monday, December 25, 1944   Five Cents

FOURTH WARTIME CHRISTMAS
President's Gift Reflects Hope of Victory

WASHINGTON, D.C.—The fourth wartime Christmas is here, and President Roosevelt gave White House employees a special gift: a scroll of his D-Day prayer for victory over the "unholy forces of our enemy." Each scroll measured twenty-one by fourteen inches and is engraved in black, gold, red, and blue letters. The first lady visited a Salvation Army party, where she was given a gift of roses and listened to carolers. She gave a special Christmas message to mothers with sons in the war. Later, the president and first lady enjoyed a quiet yuletide with their daughter and some grandchildren. Their four sons in the armed forces were not present.

FRENCH FESTIVAL OF RÉVELION
France Celebrates Liberated Yuletide

PARIS, France—The French celebrated their first Christmas of liberation beginning last night with révelion. This traditional French yuletide begins with midnight mass on Christmas Eve, followed by a huge dinner at 1 or 2 a.m. and dancing until dawn. In Paris, the dancing lasts until the Metro resumes service at 6 a.m. American GI's pitched in by throwing parties for French children, many of whom have known no Christmas without occupation. Many GI's will themselves be treated to feasts by French citizens, who are opening their houses to share preciously guarded meager larders of meat, vegetables, and spirits.

EUROPEAN BATTLE THREATENS PACIFIC
Need for Supplies Tightens Shipping Crisis

WASHINGTON, D.C.—Navy officials are concerned regarding efforts to divert shipping from the Pacific to the Atlantic for the purpose of transporting civilian supplies to Europe. It contends a shipping crisis exists in the Pacific, and that the full potential of the American forces in the Pacific cannot be brought to bear against Japan due to the shipping crisis. The German breakout in Europe and seizure of vital supplies there has necessitated shipment of more war matériel there, thus delaying or preventing the transfer of some ships to the Pacific. This has further tightened the shipping crisis.

WRAPPINGS SHOULD BE SAVED
WPB Urges Waste Paper Be Salvaged

WASHINGTON, D.C.—Today, after the presents are opened and the toys are in use, gather up the wrapping paper and send it to the salvage station. The War Production Board (WPB) says the need for such heavy paper and paper board is so great, it would be unpatriotic not to do so. The paper, cardboard boxes, corrugated wrappings, tissue, and Christmas cards are all a goldmine for war purposes. Some of the military uses for products created from salvaged paper include: waterproof paper wrappings for shipment of military clothing, three and one-half pounds of paper for each propelling charge of a 155-millimeter shell, and the twenty-five tons of blueprint paper needed to design and construct one battleship. America's paper mills face an ongoing fight to keep up with output demand, in part due to a shortage of manpower in the forestry industry that supplies wood pulp for making paper. Waste paper can directly replace wood pulp in the process, but mills face an ongoing shortage of wastepaper as well.

№ 36

Jo pulled the front door closed behind her and turned toward the street. She immediately stopped as her heart skipped a beat. There, parked on the curb opposite the Troyers' house, was Peter in his truck. The driver's window was rolled down and he had his elbow resting on the top of the window, the fabric of his heavy coat pressed down over the window frame. When he knew she had seen him, he lifted his arm in a wave.

The sound of the door closing and Peter moving his arm made Barney stand up on the seat, lean across Peter, and stick his nose out of the window. As he drew in deep breaths of the crisp air, he began to wiggle, recognizing Jo from her scent all the way across the road. The sight of the nearly blind dog wiggling in recognition of her made Jo smile. Then the smile faded as the surprise had returned along with another skipped heartbeat.

As she started slowly walking toward Peter's truck, he got out and started walking toward her. Barney jumped from the truck and ran in the direction of Jo's scent, weaving back and forth in a triangular fashion as he honed in on her. When he got to her, she kneeled down and rubbed his ears.

"Hi ya', boy. Sorry I haven't been around to see you."

The moon reflected brightly on the fresh snow. The blackout curtains on each house up and down the street kept most of the light sealed inside, and the streetlights were off this night, too. Just a few flakes of new snow were dancing in the air as Peter made his way across the street to Jo. Barney licked her face a couple of times and then ran off to chase some other scent hanging on the snow. Jo stood up, pulled the lapels of her coat closed tighter, and waited for Peter.

Her heart was pounding. She was happy. She was nervous. She was afraid. The months since they had shared anything beyond casual greetings was all on her. *Will he yell at me?* But he wasn't that kind of a person; she knew it, too. As Peter stopped in front of her, Barney trotted up behind him, bumped into his leg, then leaned into Jo until she reached down to rub his ears before he was off again chasing scents across the snow.

"He missed you," Peter said, breaking the silence.

"Yeah. I missed him, too." She paused just a bit. "A lot."

"I know. He's not the only one."

Suddenly, the awkwardness rushed away from Jo, and she almost jumped forward a bit as she blurted out.

"Pete, I never should have pushed you away like I did."

Peter held up his hand in a stopping motion.

"It's the bottom of the seventh now, Jo, and you're on the mound. What'er ya' gonna do?"

Jo looked deep into Peter's eyes. For the very first time, she could clearly see the thing that had always been just behind the surface, that fleeting thought or emotion. But it wasn't below the surface this time. It was right there before her. The softness of his eyes, every slight crease in his face—he had just shaved for this—the way he had shoved his hands into his pants pockets not just to stay warm, but the last vestige of a wall that had crumbled from around him—a wall she had torn down—all told her this was it. This was the moment. She would either acknowledge her heart and be with Peter or push him away forever. She stared into his eyes and the thoughts flooded through her head and the emotions flooded through her heart. Her face lit up with a wide smile, and she answered.

"I'm coming inside with the high heat, so get ready."

Then, she jumped into his body and wrapped her arms tightly around him. He responded in kind and squeezed. Out of the corner of her eye, she saw the sliver of light coming from the front room window disappear behind the blackout curtain. Jo could feel Pearl's smile on her shoulders. She raised her head from Peter's chest, lifted up on her toes, and kissed him on the lips. As she pulled back to see his eyes, she was bathed in his smile—a contented smile of joy she had not quite ever seen from him. She took his hand.

"Come inside, Pete."

Tin Whiskers Publisher
www.TinWhiskersBooks.com

Tin Whiskers Publisher was born in the American heartland from over twenty years of experience in the publishing world. We are an independent publisher of historical fiction. We have a passion for history intertwined with a good story, or a good story intertwined with history. What sets us apart from other publishers is we publish only historical fiction. We publish all epochs with a special interest in the twentieth century.

Visit our website with online store, join our blog, and follow us on Twitter!

www.TinWhiskersBooks. com

TinWhiskersBooks.blogspot.com

www.twitter.com/TinWhiskersPub

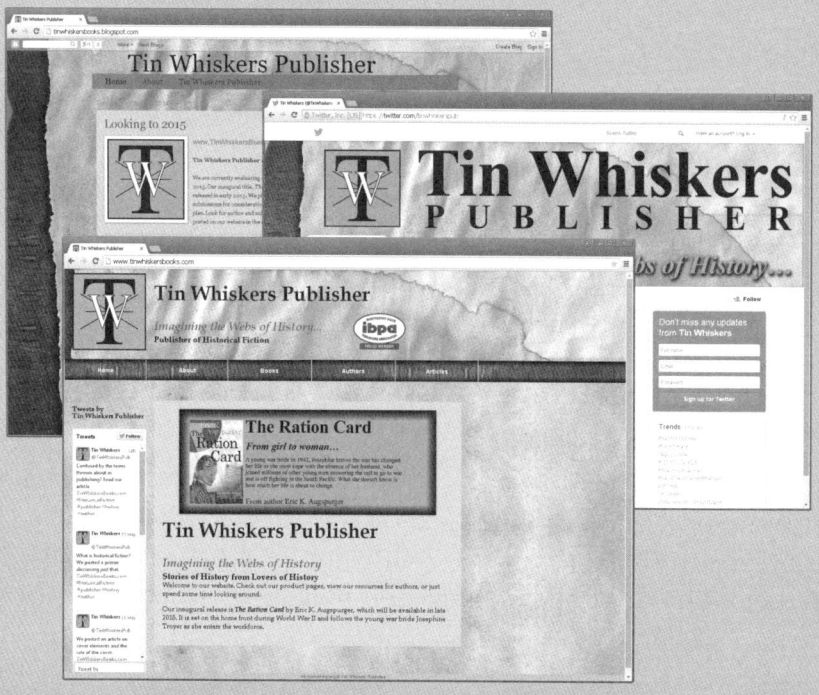